THE
EDITORS'
CHOICE

VOLUME III

THE EDITORS' CHOICE

VOLUME III

COMPILED BY
GEORGE E. MURPHY, JR.

A BANTAM/WAMPETER PRESS BOOK

BANTAM BOOKS
TORONTO · NEW YORK · LONDON · SYDNEY · AUCKLAND

THE EDITORS' CHOICE, VOLUME III
A Bantam Book / January 1987

*Windstone and accompanying logo of a stylized W are trademarks
of Bantam Books, Inc.*

This book was published simultaneously in hardcover and trade paperback.

"Ice" by Marian Thurm. First published in *MS*. Copyright © 1985 by Marian Thurm. Reprinted by permission of the author.

"Safe" by Ellen Wilbur. First published in *Redbook*. Copyright © 1985 by Ellen Wilbur. Reprinted by permission of the author.

"Health" by Joy Williams. First published in *Tendril*. Copyright © 1985 by Joy Williams. Reprinted by permission of the author.

"Soldier's Joy" by Tobias Wolff. First published in *Esquire*. Copyright © 1985 by Tobias Wolff. Reprinted by permission of the author.

Library of Congress Cataloging-in-Publication Data
(Revised for vol. 3)

The Editors' Choice.

"A Bantam/Wampeter Press book."
 1. Short stories, American.   2. American fiction—
20th century.   I. Murphy, George E.   (George Edward),
1948–
PS648.S5E34   1985   813'.01'08   84-24157
ISBN 0-553-34176-6 (U.S. : pbk. : v. 1)
ISBN 0-553-05179-2 (U.S. : hard : v. 3)
ISBN 0-553-34333-5 (U.S. : pbk. : v. 3)

Published simultaneously in the United States and Canada

Bantam Books are published by Bantam Books, Inc. Its trademark, consisting
of the words "Bantam Books" and the portrayal of a rooster, is Registered
in U.S. Patent and Trademark Office and in other countries. Marca Registrada.
Bantam Books, Inc., 666 Fifth Avenue, New York, New York 10103.

PRINTED IN THE UNITED STATES OF AMERICA

FG   0 9 8 7 6 5 4 3 2 1

NOMINATING MAGAZINES

Antaeus, 18 West 30th Street, New York, New York 10001

The Atlantic, 8 Arlington Street, Boston, Massachusetts 02116

Cosmopolitan, 224 West 57th Street, New York, New York 10019

Esquire, 2 Park Avenue, New York, New York 10016

The Georgia Review, University of Georgia, Athens, Georgia 30602

Harper's, 2 Park Avenue, New York, New York 10016

Mademoiselle, 350 Madison Avenue, New York, New York 10017

The Missouri Review, Department of English, 231 A & S, University of Missouri, Columbia, Missouri 65211

Ms., 119 West 40th Street, New York, New York 10018

The North American Review, 1222 West 27th Street, Cedar Falls, Iowa 50614

The Paris Review, 45–39 171 Place, Flushing, New York 11358

Playboy, 919 North Michigan Avenue, Chicago, Illinois 60611

Ploughshares, Box 529, Cambridge, Massachusetts 02139

Redbook, 959 Eighth Avenue, New York, New York 10019

Seventeen, 850 Third Avenue, New York, New York 10022

Tendril, P.O. Box 512, Green Harbor, Massachusetts 02041

TriQuarterly, 1735 Benson Avenue, Evanston, Illinois 60201

Vanity Fair, 350 Madison Avenue, New York, New York 10017

CONTENTS

INTRODUCTION

It is with great pleasure that I introduce *Volume III* of *The Editors' Choice: New American Stories.* Since this series was launched three years ago, the talk of the eighties as a "Silver Age" for short stories continues (the 1930's was the "Golden Age"). There is still a notable trend in the increasing number of story collections being published. Happily, even a commercial market for books of short stories has reemerged, making publishing houses more willing to acquire collections. Only a few years ago, most houses were reluctant to take on what seemed to be a rather risky commercial proposition. The change is perhaps best illustrated by the fact that, over the past few years, *four* story collections have made it onto the best-seller list. That's news.

After years of efforts in what is known as the small-press world of publishing, I have noted two prevailing facts. First, the number of stories being published in the best-known national magazines is fairly limited. *Esquire,* for example, well known for its fiction, actually publishes fewer than twenty stories each year. Second, because of this, many well-known authors saw a literate and growing readership in university and independent magazines. Often, their stories ended up being published alongside the work of younger, lesser-known, but often extraordinarily talented writers, writers who had yet to break into those larger-circulation publications or whose work was less "commercial" than it was "literary."

The quality of much of the work being published in those independent and university journals was receiving wider recognition in other circles as well. The annual short story anthologies have, over the past four years, contained *twice* as many stories from these "small" magazines as from the better-known nationally distributed magazines.

And so, *The Editors' Choice* comes from two simple ideas:

One, the *fiction* editors of America's commercial magazines— that hardy breed of seemingly tireless readers who labor daily behind the scenes to find and publish the very best fiction available to them—were in an opportune and unique position to select stories that were among the most noteworthy of those published each year.

Two, any new collection of American fiction should also represent the numerous literary journals which, for years, have offered a forum for both new and talented writers and our best and more commercially successful authors. (Though the magazines included here are representative of the best of such journals, these magazines are so diverse and numerous that my great regret is that I could not have included more of them.)

For this series, we asked editors to select the stories that they, for any reason, were particularly pleased to have had come across their desks, the stories they took the most pleasure in having published. In some cases, the editors have selected stories they thought represented the best of their publishing efforts; in other cases, the nominations represented the work of particularly talented "newcomers." In all cases, the stories were of exceptional quality.

Once again, I am impressed both by that high quality and by the variety of the nominations. Once again, as well, I am pleased to note the inclusion of a first-published author, Paul Leslie, an undergraduate at the University of Wisconsin, as well as such established writers as T. C. Boyle, Bob Shacochis, Tobias Wolff, Ellen Wilbur, Tess Gallagher, Ellen Gilchrist, and Joy Williams. And there are those recently recognized on the literary scene: Deborah Eisenberg, Marian Thurm, Madison Smartt Bell, and Lee K. Abbott.

All jobs should be as pleasurable as mine: reading the various editors' nominations and making final selections for this anthology. I hope now that it becomes your reading pleasure. Enjoy.

George E. Murphy, Jr.
April 1986

THE EDITORS' CHOICE

VOLUME III

LEE K. ABBOTT

TIME AND FEAR AND SOMEHOW LOVE

FROM THE GEORGIA REVIEW

∽

SINCE, AS SHE CONCEIVED IT, the letter was to be the final word on the subject, she endeavored to start slowly, then lead up to, as fine drama does, those moments of lamentation, those periods—always potent and manifold—of ruin and dismay which are like, her daddy had said once, mangy wildcats with wings. She would begin with how it was in those olden days, when the man who would be the Colonel, her husband, used to drive straight to her home in Portland from his father's hotel in Old Orchard Beach; he would take her dancing on the pier where Count Basie, Ella Fitzgerald, and the Dorsey Brothers played, and where he had a circle of pals with names like Digger and Fuzzy, and from where it was impossible to imagine that now, forty years later, she had neither him nor any of it, and that one day she would be sitting at her typewriter, writing to her son, and saying, as if speaking of another, "Elaine was a drinking woman."

1

Which was, really, not the way to begin at all, for despite the bad stuff—being divorced, for example, and having come scarcely an hour from death—this letter was to have its share of happy times, times which made you think of laughter, of swimming parties at the country club, of driving home backwards from the Moderns' house. Yes, she would mention the lovely house in Panama, three stories with a maid on each floor, and those trips by boat to Havana—which is pronounced Ha-*ban*-a by the way, and calls to mind Major and Mrs. Geist, and night-clubs and people gay as Ricky Ricardo—as well as the phone call from Harlingen, Texas, with the electricity which shot through her when he said *come on down and let's be married*; and the trip by train with those other WW II soldiers, each a gentleman, who watched over her and played bridge with her and protected her privacy as she slept through Ohio.

Yes, she conceived of a letter to her son which began, "Kit, you are ignorant and unfeeling as stone, and thirty-four years of being alive haven't taught you the least about me or my life." She imagined a letter, alive with all the truth she had, which wouldn't go away or sink harmlessly into memory or get mistaken for the confession it was not. She meant to show that living remained a difficult enterprise, moilsome with hoopla and hurly-burly, the whole of it insensible as chaos yet dear as love; and she wanted her letter to possess the authority of that elephant gun the Colonel had forced her to fire when they were stationed in Peoria, Illinois, a weapon which went *Bang* like the word of God Himself, shook her insides like dominoes, and seemed to ring even now like the first note of doom. It was to be a letter about love and suffering, which would leave him standing alone in his kitchen, as she had stood alone when she learned the Colonel was dead, saying, "Shit" and "My God" and "What now?" It was to start with this line: "Here, Mister, here is the hurt and how it lasts forever."

At first, she tried to put everything in—how, for example, she was only a Virginia girl, taught well how to comport herself as a lady, who had been brought North by a daddy who sold Hartford insurance and played a gentleman's billiards; and by a mother, Elaine had now to admit, she did not remember too clearly because of alcohol's effect on memory and Mother's being finally a figure of shadow and secret, always elsewhere, never here. On those early pages, she recalled her favorite songs—"Tonight We Love" by Bobby Worth and "Angel with the Laughing Eyes"—and where the Colonel had gone to college (Dartmouth), and her fondness for the Episcopal litany— particularly the verse which said "we have left undone those things which we ought to have done" so the Lord was to have mercy on us, miserable offenders. She made a list of bric-a-brac she retained from her marriage: a vase for bachelor's buttons (the Colonel's favorite flower), his porringer, his silver baby cup, a card tray, an embroidered hanky he'd bought in Korea, and a charcoal iron she now used as a doorstop. She quoted Mister Henry Van Dyke on Time, which was "too slow for those who wait, too swift for those who fear." And then, because she could avoid it no longer, she recalled again that place—a crossroads of time and character—where, even without drink itself, drunkenness had begun.

"I dwell on it now," she wrote, "because it is full of despair." In 1942, this man who was to be her husband was in Harlingen, Texas, over a thousand miles away, at gunnery school. "My beautiful wedding gown hung in the closet, the invitations had been mailed, the reception planned, and I had been busy writing thank-you notes for our gifts as well as working at the law firm daily." She was happy, life no more fragile than rock or steel from Pennsylvania. So it was here— when she was most deceived, she said—that the phone rang one night and her mother called upstairs that she should hurry, it was Lyman. "Remember," Mother said, "it's long distance." A big deal then, when all distances seemed novel and fraught with peril. Breathless, Elaine flew down two flights of stairs, taking several steps at a time, and squatted near the phone. Mother was in the kitchen doing dishes, and Daddy was in his library working on his new accounts. And she remembered clearly, as if hearing anew Lyman's scratchy New England voice, how the bottom fell out of her when he said he couldn't get home for the ceremony; instead, he was wiring money for plane fare and arrangements had been made with the base chaplain. A Lieu-

tenant Borders, he said, would be his best man and somebody
named Joyce who worked at the PX would be her bridesmaid.
What is happening in me, she thought. I should know that
thing sinking down.

"Elaine," he said, "did you hear me? It's all fixed here."
She said yes, she heard, her voice choked and suddenly older
than the twenty-one she was; and then Mother—"for such a
tiny woman, she had the dignity of a queen!"—was beside her,
holding the receiver, saying, "Yes, we understand" and "Please,
don't worry" and "Oh, she'll get over this." Yet now, decades
removed from the event but again in that house she had enjoyed so much as a girl, she still had not gotten over anything.
After all, there were plans to change, apologies to offer—to
dear Mrs. Sweem, the organist, to Dr. Butler, the priest, and to
Wendy Smythe, who was traveling all the way from Vassar.
And there was Texas itself, out there as a horror of outlaws,
whiskered galoots, and their tarts. The state had endless vistas,
Lyman had told her, big and strange as color movies. Plus
storms, with winds that could heave aside houses—not to mention ignorance, and squatty towns without paved roadways or
dependable telephones. It was a place of guns and drought and
public figures named Cooter or Joe Bob—not the place at all
for one who had dined with Mr. Cole Porter and the president
of the Boston Shoe Company.

"I can't do this," Elaine said; but her daddy said this was
wartime, allowances had to be made. Sacrifice was the hallmark
of her ilk, she heard him say. "So I bucked up," she wrote. "I
got myself up like Mrs. Astor, with a Bonwit Teller suit and
my sister Dolly's hat with the veil and feathers and a proper
lady's gloves, and put three weeks of apparel in an eighty-
dollar Gladstone bag that had buckles and straps enough for
Harry Houdini himself." There were no planes for civilians in
Portland at the time, nor in Boston; and it was by a mix of
fortune and force of will—like an episode from *The Unforgotten
Prisoner* by R. C. Hutchinson, or *One Light Burning*—that
she found herself aboard a troop train, a girl among hundreds
of men, terrified of their poker, their Mister Kelly comic books,
and their songs ("What the Wolf Did at the Ca-Ca-Castle"),

but most of all frightened of their sprawl, their violent laughter, the smell of an army rattling in a single direction toward death.

"Then a most curious thing happened," she wrote. "They treated me like a movie star." They said, "Hey lady, sit over here," and "Don't get off, ma'am, we'll get you something." It was like one of those Mickey Rooney musicals where everybody, from yokel to snotty scion, is composed of good nature and sense, talented enough to dance the Cleveland Chicken or repeat a memorable joke. A boy who said he was from Tufts University—but actually looked sly enough to be an artful liar—juggled oranges; and another, this one imitating a Tidewater bumpkin, did a trick with the ace of spades, which was so much more than sleight of hand it appeared sinister. They treated her as a kid sister, fetching USO goodies at every stop and telling her their life stories, all of which involved the infuriate and featured folks—like herself, she would admit—foolish, bewildered, and astray, folks with an outstanding defect like a withered limb or romantic habit of mind. In Missouri, above the rumble and squeal of the train, one private claimed to be a poet and read several stanzas titled "Bolts of Melody," which had, as its hero, a devious personage named Mu Mon Kwan; in Arkansas, another said his favorite from history was Batygh the Tartar, a villain renowned for murder and such savagery as blasphemy. "Best of all," Elaine wrote, "they gave me advice." One who seemed too stunted for even Uncle Sam said, "Don't never trust someone who smiles overmuch. They're backstabbers and what my old teacher calls minions." And another, this one standing in the cluttered aisle, erect and sincere as virtue, declared, "Lady, what do you think of jazz? I think it's money, almost, for those of us without." Whereupon there was such good-natured hooting and brotherly punching of the thick parts as you now see at sport when the home squad triumphs.

"I slept, too," she wrote, "hours and hours in those five days. I had dreams in which there were noises like dogs make coughing up a bone, and dreams full of pictures I suspect you find in Chicago police stations, and dreams in which I was a moll named Judy French or Marjorie from Downtown and spoke like a heroine invented by Frank Slaughter—all of which you must not make too much of, there being in this world already too many excuses for the evil we do."

Then she was there—in a place of dizzying sunlight, heat, and apparently mutinous activity, a train depot so full of coming and going and hubbub that, in the banging and clatter, it took several minutes to find him, Lyman, standing by a jeep, waving. He was dressed in spotless suntans, his silver lieutenant's bar gleaming, a wilted gardenia in one hand, his garrison cap in the other; and though he did seem like a prince to her, she knew now that this was merely another charade of memory, for he was already, even as he hugged and kissed and grinned like Little Jack Horner, the Colonel he would become—full of temper and rage, knobby-kneed, given to intolerance, with a bad heart and a dark slice of lung that would have to come out, and a Chinaman's belief in unnatural powers, a man made mournful by sentiment.

"Hurry," he was saying now, flopping her suitcase into the jeep. "I got the Chaplain waiting."

She was shocked. Her dress was shabby with wrinkles, her gloves were as filthy as a hobo's, and her hat—which over a thousand miles ago had been, well, jaunty—drooped like a sock, its feather greasy and wilted.

"Lyman, you take me somewhere to clean up," she said. "Don't they have a hotel here? I need a bath."

He looked befuddled. He said, "You look gorgeous. They won't care." *They*—this Fergus who was chaplain, and the sweethearts Frank Borders and Joyce—they'd understand.

"Nobody understands me but me," she said. "These people don't even know me."

It was not here, she wrote, that the despair she was thinking of overtook her. Nor was it on the ride which she remembered as bumpy and windblown, through a town which looked like what the carnival leaves behind. Lyman was talking like crazy—not closemouthed as he would become—but chattering. War talk. What that far-off cannon might do and what a lummox the DI was and how orders were cut. He'd heard from his father, who was going blind, and his brother who was already in England, working Top Secret for the Signal Corps. "You know how he's getting around in the blackouts?" Lyman said. "Holding hands, that's how." There was nothing funnier, according to Lyman, than the idea of his brother, the biggest of the big track stars at Hebron, holding hands in the dark with a bunch of men.

"No, I suppose not," she said, noting how in the heat—which had the density of a fat man—the buildings seemed flatter and weaker, as if the chief materials of construction in this corner of the world were straw and mud, the whole of it held fast by hope.

Nor did the despair she was addressing grip her when they reached the base chapel, the jeep skidding to a stop. A border of whitewashed rocks marked the road and the chapel—itself white and covered with silly gingerbread—looked like a structure thrown up by Las Vegas hoodlums.

"C'mon," he said, "let's get a move on."

It was here, then, that she began to feel it—the quake in the underhalf of her heart, the bitterness, the numbing shiver like a lance through an organ she imagined as thick and heavily veined—as he hustled her inside a building that was not St. Paul's with its spires and shiny woodwork. He introduced her to Lieutenant Borders (who, in another life, certainly had been a felon preying on the feeble-witted) and his girlfriend Joyce (who wore a red Elvis Presley hairdo long before the advent of the so-called King of Rock and Roll). And then, in an instant which seemed to be the penultimate stroke of an epoch, they were walking her forward, with a dour figure—Major Fergus, Chaplain, USA—waiting on them.

He had, she wrote, that face you expect to see the day after Mardi Gras, dark with turmoil and excess, and she knew, well before he said *hello, how are you*, that his was the God of the Baptists, fugitive and slack-minded, that parlous shade which gave us talking fish and centuries of carnage.

"I had my heart set on Dr. Butler's God," she wrote to her son, "that one I still advise you to believe in—that one of books and manners and reasoned faiths."

But then, in these merry olden times she was concerned with, she said, "Lyman, could I have some water, please?"

She was scared. She felt nerve and fiber giving way inside her, swelling or shrinking or stiffening to stone.

"Here you go, honey." It was Joyce, bosomy and smelling virtually fertile. "You learn to drink a lot down here. The dust and all."

After many deep breaths, each of which seemed the first following years of paralysis, Elaine said, "All right, I'm ready."

Whereupon they stood—for an hour, she swore—while Major Fergus, florid and smiling wide as a pumpkin, read a hodgepodge of *do*'s and *do not*'s; and Joyce, misty-eyed as a schoolgirl, breathed with her mouth open; and Frank Borders puffed himself up like a William Makepeace Thackeray roué; and Lyman held on to her elbow as if he expected to topple over and disappear.

Then it was over, except for that noise.

"Who's crying?" she wondered. "That person does need some help."

And then she realized it was she herself crying—a remote, sad wail which involved time and fear and somehow love.

The next four pages she filled with random events, parties foremost. She was approaching one soiree in particular—that one of consequence in which she got a hard glimpse of her future—but she would come to it, she said, as she had come to these other truths about herself: by indirection and by surprise, its method its point. "It's as my daddy says," she wrote, "I am going in that back door of insight, that one approached through bramble and dense thicket, along a disordered, overgrown path."

Lord, there were parties—for occasions slight and grand. In the fifteen years she meant to ignore, there were parties everywhere: in De Funiak Springs, Florida, and in San Diego (where the Colonel bought the bungalow on Pacific Beach), in Illinois and again in Old Orchard Beach when he went to Korea. The parties had booze, of course, rivers of it, which were aids for those with horselike behinds to do the cha-cha-cha. Booze made the befuddled eloquent; the loutish, lovely.

There were parties for George Washington and Black Jack Per-shing, as well as for St. Valentine, Army–Navy football, and Armistice Day. One party mourned Adlai Stevenson, another condemned the bearded bumbler Fidel Castro. "In those days," she wrote, "parties were as common as dollar bills; be it birthday, anniversary, promotion, or national holiday, they were a chance for us to do mischief, to come near catalepsy."

Oh, life was as fine as grade-school arithmetic. "I was meeting folks from the larger world—generals and their wives who read more than recipes; and I was seeing life as it was meant to be led; and though I was drinking Bacardi and real Russian vodka, I could, at any time, say that rhyme about seashells at the seashore or hold up my end of the conversation about, say, Mr. Dulles's unseemly connection with the United Fruit Company, or what to do about Bishop Sheen." Which, to be true, should have alerted her to what she knew now was the principal certainty of her age: Life is rampant with folly and misdeed, and no number of Japanese lanterns or ice sculptures or paper hats can make up for the fact that man is a jackass; and belief in higher powers which reward sense and privilege is no more attractive than hair on a woman's lip.

"I am referring," she wrote to her son, "to New Mexico, where you were born and where, I do imagine it now, every-thing comes to an end." She remembered all the details of the Colonel's letter from Seoul—its tissue-like texture, his cramped boarding-school penmanship, those Kodak snapshots of him looking as overwhelmed as a child in front of a dozen jack-in-the-box temples. She remembered, too, reading over and over that line which said he'd been transferred to White Sands Proving Ground, in the desert, but they could live in a little town called Las Cruces in a civilian house, and that she wasn't to upset herself because Frank Hollar—did she remember him from Camp Crowder?—was already there and said the place, though small, had its virtues. Neighborliness among them. She imagined that if this had been a movie or the product of the slumped brain of one like Ed Sullivan, there should have been a thundering upswell of background music—notes the hero never hears when doom portends, a boom-boom-boom on the drums which say, in effect, *don't go in that room, please, just stay out here where all is light and sweet air.* "I don't have to do this," she said, realizing immediately that she did; and she remembered, at last, opening the *Rand-McNally* atlas and seeing a place as empty as map space itself, a place of 6,000 people with a college of agriculture and mechanical arts, where there was no spring and no fall, neither snow in winter nor rain in summer. She could hear, as she stared at the negligible black dot which she feared would be her home forever, a voice, mirthful and deranged, crying, "Here, you won't need that leg, nor that eye, nor that beating foolish heart."

They squabbled when Lyman arrived home and on the trip down, their belongings stacked atop and stuffed into his Chevrolet. And once—was it in Oklahoma?—when what sat at the horizon looked as vast and featureless as melancholy, the Colonel (who was a captain then) jerked the car to the shoulder and jumped out, grabbing her door, his lips narrow and bloodless, his eyes furious with fatigue. "I could slug you," he said. He was shaking her by the shoulders, whispering as if beyond, in the shade of a scrawny tree or in the lee of a no-account hill, huddled thousands of upright, fearsome sodbusters each of whom would be offended by his angry, endless talk. "Why are you doing this?" he said. "I could hurt you. Just shut up." To which she, stiff-necked as a schoolmarm, said, "No, you couldn't. Not you and millions like you." Which is how, this son of hers was to understand, drunks speak when they feel courageous, mighty, and righteous to their soaked souls.

There was a party when they arrived. Another when they bought the house on West Gallagher. And more when they joined the country club, when the son was born, when Lyman made major, and when he won the club championship by beating Billy Newell 3 and 2 with a putt that was part miracle, part guts. They met the Bissels, the Georges, and Dalrymples; the E. J. Akers and Mrs. Sally Brickman; Alice and Johnny Ostriker; Nelson Popp and his first wife Vivian; Professor Beeker and Ivy Martin, the club pro; the Blairs, Joan and Harvey, plus his cousin from Fort Worth—168 folks ("Honest," she wrote, "I counted them once!"), all of whom, from time to time, did like to throw off their current selves and, charmed by liquors, sport about in the truth. A terrible and inward tribe, these were folks who dressed up like slatterns or Dracula or mayors of desert towns to indulge in hijinks; made honest by booze, they would sashay right up to you and say your eyes were mismatched or that your gown from the White House in El Paso was a most unbecoming shade of aquamarine or that Republicans knew how to run this universe, which they would do wonderfully, your backbiting and carping notwithstanding. They were citizens who hollered when they ought not and made scenes few forgot and bruised feelings which grew sorer over time; folks—"I am thinking of myself now," she wrote—who one evening, despite Fourth of July merriment, the marvelous notes from Mister Albert Grady's clarinet, and the toothsome chitchat from Betty Turner, said to themselves, "I will not have this any more; I am going home."

Elaine couldn't find the Colonel immediately—not in the ballroom, which was dark and smoky, nor in the pro shop, where the stuffed shirts went to prattle about life and its meanings, nor in the men's locker, which she searched like a sneak thief. Ed Keating, who fetched her a Bloody Mary, thought he'd seen Lyman at the bar; Peyton Miller, with whom Elaine drank rum and grapefruit juice, said she'd seen him and Frank Papen banging practice balls into the tennis court from the first tee. And then she saw him, by the pool, with the Clute brothers, Mickey and M.L., and what's-his-name, the Bulldog coach who always looked sweaty and unstable—all of them in swim trunks which looked as silly as boxer shorts.

"Give me the keys to the car," she said, "I'm bored."

He heard it, she knew—the note in her voice which hinted she might, as she had done before, stomp her feet and curse and throw her purse at him.

"Where is your hair?" she wondered when he came to the fence. "You used to have hair on your chest, and now you don't."

She should stay, he said, it was early. The Clutes were planning a pancake breakfast at their place.

"You are so collapsed," she said, looking at his stomach. "I mean fallen down. I like men with—what?—pectorals!"

"I'll get dressed," he offered. "I'll go with you."

So she said to him, quietly, to protect his vanity, "If you try, I'll throw this glass at you and you'll be embarrassed. Now, stand up straight."

"Why are you doing this?"

She took a drink. "Why am I doing what?"

Which led her to tell a joke to those men while the Colonel went for his pants—a joke they couldn't appreciate because they were such poops, clodhoppers like the Colonel himself, who had the big mitts of an ape and big feet and smoked like a coal house and swore at Gary Moore on the TV.

"Don't you worry about me," she said, snatching the keys. "Daddy said I was a big girl, and I believe him."

So we are brought, she wrote, to the thing we goddamn Anglo-Saxons know rapture is not: mishap, when the world's music is clamor and din.

She remembered marching across the squishy practice green, first throwing away those shoes with heels too high to drive with, and coming to the parking lot, weakly illuminated by one bulb above the members' entrance to the pool snack shop. The cars had been parked, it seemed, by the same spirit which controls Ouija boards and water witching. "This is what I'm looking for," she said, "a brand-new Ford Fairlane 500." She imagined it took her twenty minutes of wandering through the aisles to find it wedged between an Oldsmobile and a boat of a Dodge which—"If objects and possessions in this world do imitate their owners, as I believe"—belonged to Dottie Hightower, herself windy laughter, ponderous as the tides.

"I had to climb through the window," she wrote, adding that the car still smelled new. She thought of fear, which had a head and a he-man's arms; and briefly she felt the word wobble then tilt, light itself going cockeyed and runny. "Calm down," she told herself. "Say those old-timey things you know: *Mary, Mary, how does your garden grow?*" Trying to start the car, she felt clumsy and sore-hearted, feckless as an orphan. A song came to mind: "Who Does It to You, Me?" There were, surely, one thousand keys to fumble among: for the steamer trunks in the utility room, the garage, the house, the glove box, the back door, and one, from the Arrow Lock Corporation, which appeared to belong to a hole infernal and crooked as this life itself. There was a screech, too, metal on metal, when she hit the accelerator and jerked the steering wheel, and then there was no sound at all except a lonesome lady's voice from the parking lot, hollering, "Jesus H. Christ."

Rocking back and forth, she swung the wheel wildly, at last ending up facing the wrong way, the front of the car aiming toward a cyclone fence; behind her, she could see the entrance now as dark and distant as sleep. "Okay," she said, "I'll do it this way," and jammed the shift lever into reverse.

"Imagine now," she wrote, "that you, highball in hand, are standing at a second-floor ballroom window and you see what I describe. You are likely to say, 'What the hell is going on?' for there is obvious chaos at ground level, a car going hither and yon at breakneck speeds, some squealing of tires, and such horn-honking as is found every day in New York. It is a fascinating display, and maybe you are inclined for a second to think, 'My, this is comedy.' But if you are the kind I imagine, then you are apt, given a peek at the stricken, baffled face behind the wheel, to declare, 'This ain't funny at all.' For what you see is that newish machine, its lights off, swerving too swiftly toward a so-called Immovable Object."

She believed she hit the solid brick posts at thirty-five miles per hour—fast enough that the noise, calamitous and loud as mayhem, took an hour to reach her. She recalled flying backwards, the stuff of the world liquid or air. Somewhere she saw a face and a dozen shapes sweep past, tall with the stemlike grace of jonquils. She could hear her heart, heavy with fear. And then, in an instant composed more of surprise than dread, the gate loomed upward, and every joint—from ankle to hip to neck—seemed to lock; and the noise began to reach her, *crunch* and *whang* and *thump* so profound there could have been giants outside pounding on the roof, plus a tempest of glass and something metal—chrome, perhaps—which went *whip, whip, whip,* until the radio, glowing weakly, said, "*No more, no more,*" and the harps, the brass *oompah-pah-pah,* and the squeaky woodwinds poured over her like a flood.

Too drunk to be sore, she didn't know how long she lay on the front seat, the motor clanking. She saw herself explaining to the Colonel how this had happened: the late hour, the unwise mixing of spirits, the inconsiderate way the cars were parked, the downright stinginess of muckamucks whose responsibility it was to provide enough light so a person—most especially a person unfamiliar with the layout, and ragged of thought—could find her way home. She saw, too, the Colonel standing over her, his face like a martyr's. "I have had an accident," she would say, "and I know why."

And here it opened—that spook-house back door of insight Daddy has spoken of—and she could see herself, a generation older, shrunken as a corpse, and whey-faced, curled on a couch as she was drawn up on this front seat: the hour was noon, the curtains closed, this person she was to become no more fetching than misrule itself.

"It was an unadorned vision," she wrote. "I was swollen at the belly, glassy-eyed, wearing a nightgown not fit for the Wicked Witch of the West, with skin as waxy as paper."

Elaine was thinking—each thought impossible with wings and scales.

And then she was hearing the whisper that eternity, beastly and common, had begun.

"So I became a homebody," she wrote, "either a slugabed or industrious as a coolie." Her hair wild with exhaustion, she developed the habit of shaking her fingers near her eyes. Early and late, she drank, and took shorthand from the TV, once hurling at the Colonel a dozen scribbled pages which, she claimed, were *Gunsmoke*, the tragic events especially bold with energy. One night she pitched chicken bones at the living room clock above the desk. She wound up like Feller or Mister Don Drysdale, saying "Strike goddamn one!" Hour after long hour, while the Colonel was out playing golf, she listened to Paul Whiteman and Platters records. Woozy with sentiment, she sat cross-legged on the floor, smoking L&M's. She saw herself jeweled, heavily powdered, and smelling of Je Reviens. "Life is better," she sang, "in France, Persia, or Heaven." She wrote letters, too—hundreds of them: to Senator Montoya, complaining of injustice and blight in this orb; to her daddy, saying, "I am truly sorry that you are ill, but I can do little here and can see where you are as a mist or shade, nothing more"; to Mister John O'Hara, asking for more of that menace which passed for lust; to Lyman's parents, saying, "Your boy has made colonel now and looks most splendid when he yells"; and once to Dr. Butler, at St. Paul's: "Maybe you are dead and, if so, how goes it up yonder among the winged many?"

In the summers, wearing a kimono and the overlarge straw hat of a woman named Ida or Fitz, she sat in a chaise in the backyard, drinking. "Oh, I was some gardener in those days," she wrote. She had a trowel and garden rake and pruning shears; and she wielded them with the fury of defeat itself, snipping at rose and willow, studying seed catalogues, and ordering ferns which withered immediately. She watered, and drank Cuba libres and screwdrivers, uprooting one bush a dozen times before it looked okay near the patio. Dry as dust, the heat came down hard and thick; and she drank old-fashioneds, trying to read about princes, rakehells described as "devilishly handsome" and who embraced breathless, short-sighted females; and when the Colonel came home, she'd say, "Look up the word *bilious* for me. And *thrall*. My vocabulary needs broadening." Then one afternoon, as she leaned against the back gate, staring into the yard, she said, "I want a swimming pool," falling in love as quickly as thought with words like *glistening* and *ripples*.

"This is how it was," she wrote. "I called up Frank Papen at the bank and said *gimme my money*, and he said *what money?* And I said *from the mutual funds and have one of your people bring it to me,* and he said *how much?* And I told him *fifteen thousand dollars, please.*" Which caused some fluster and white-collar sputtering, but there it was by midafternoon, a certified cashier's check, nubby as braille—which, she told a contractor named Dupard Epps, was all his if he and his equipment could begin within the hour.

"I want it shaped like a piano," she said, "a grand piano, black and white tile with no diving board."

When they arrived—several burly sorts with two trucks and a digging instrument she now knew was a backhoe—they found her at the already disassembled gate, pounding happily on the cinder block with the Colonel's hammer. The wall was gouged and deeply hacked. She was a sight, she knew, addled and jittery as if she'd emerged from a century of sleep. "Pull this old thing down," she ordered. "Which one of you is Mr. Epps?" A short fellow stepped forward; he resembled the kind who counted on his fingers or believed in UFO's. "Well," she began, "you fellows get started, then we'll drink some." Which was when—"As it was meant to happen," she wrote—the Colonel pulled into the drive in his staff car, an ugly olive-colored heap, and told weak-minded Mr. Epps to go on home, there'd been a mistake. "Wait," Elaine said, "what about my money?" She had the check out, waving it, wondering what it took, if not money, to move men and machine to build something as simple as an itty-bitty swimming pool with stairs and rope and, now that she was thinking of it, a cabana so guests could change clothes without having to walk dripping into the kitchen to make a sandwich.

"What're you doing here?" she said. "It's only afternoon, so you're supposed to be someplace else."

He had a miser's face, such as you used to find on walking sticks or umbrella handles.

"Go on," she said, "scoot on out of here."

She could hear roaring from somewhere near, and a crack which sounded like thunder. "Don't mumble," she said. "I was taught to speak up. What'd you say?"

Again he told her: her father had died. A stroke.

And now, as she sat typing this whole story out, she thought, *how convenient, how tidy,* noting how fortune and circumstance had converged at this point to produce tragedy in the faraway place of her youth. Instantly, she became as clearminded as a judge. She had these thoughts: This is 1967, I am almost forty-six, take me home now. She saw the Colonel standing in the brilliant sunlight. He expected something—hysterics or the rage of a Joan Crawford heroine.

"How do you know?" she said.

"Your sister," he said. "Nobody was answering the phone here."

She felt weightless and numb, fixed at the fierce center of a hundred ragged, freezing winds. Near the fence, on her knees, she began sweeping brick chips into a pile. It was amazing what a hammer could do in the hands of a wounded woman.

"I believe I am meant to do something in this life," she said. "Just what, I don't know."

The next morning, he drove her to El Paso. At the airport, he told her he'd be along in a few days: he was directing an exercise—was it Operation Climate?—he couldn't leave, and someone, maybe the Zants, would have to be found to look after this son she was now addressing. She said *yes* for the millionth time and tried to ignore the nerve twitching in her neck; and then, while she stood at the gate, waiting to board, it occurred to her—the way, she believed, insight occurred to such genius as she had read about in history: swift as terror and with the same chill—that maybe she wouldn't be coming back to this place. "You know where I see myself now?" she asked. "Aloft and beautiful, that's where."

Which, this son of hers was to know, was the little ding-dong bell saying that the thing she knew as climax was beginning. It was the part, she wrote, where knowledge was revealed and you felt better facing it. "In the mysteries I read and wonder about, it's the part of shoot-'em-up's and fistfights, and you know it's serious because everyone weeps; and what's left is hope or resignation or gobbledygook only Harvard eggheads fret about. There is time, which is long, and it is filled with hugger-mugger, escapades which aim to delight. Plus, you have a creature to root for, who finds himself in jeopardy, as well as pauses for rumination—all of it unhappy as Christmas in Russia. Imagine. So organized and well said. You get angry words, folks tugging at each other's hair, then the treachery is over, and you can go to sleep now—which convinces me that it does require drink to appreciate such neatness." She had figured out drink—which was not woe or pity or such. Drink was charm and magic and everlasting weal. "I know booze," she wrote. "Booze is love—cheap as death and meant for all."

Elaine didn't tell the Colonel she was through when he flew in the following week. She had Mother to worry about, as well as a myriad of details to discuss with the estate lawyer. Condolence cards had to be answered, calls made. Lyman tried to be helpful; he went to her daddy's office and carted home boxes of papers, most of which she threw out. One night he visited his own parents, reading to his father who was virtually blind now. The Colonel was as polite as a bankrupt pasha, she remembered, begging her pardon and wearing a tie to dinner. He drove her to the pier one day, but the dance house was gone; and he took her on the road to Biddeford. She couldn't get over the trees, towering and plentiful and ancient. One day she went to the beach alone, sitting in the sand for hours, watching the waves. It was cold. The water was always cold.

So she told him then.

"I dressed up as I had for that train ride to Texas," she wrote. "I wore my finest hat and gloves with seed pearls, plus a dress Jackie Kennedy herself couldn't afford now, and I presented myself as Daddy said I ought. Which means that I went to my sister's room, which Lyman was using, and knocked before entering."

He was not sleeping, as she had expected, but reading. Except for the table lamp, there was little light in the room; for a second she believed she was speaking to a ghost.

"I have known you a long time, Lyman," she began. "And you are, mostly, a good person." She felt as she had years before, when she was making thirty-five dollars a week in Mr. Gray's law firm and there were stars she knew the names of.

"Lyman," she said, "go on home now, please." She had had a whole speech, at least five minutes of talking (not counting the hems and haws which would appear in the natural course of things), but it was gone now—as these times themselves, careless and omen-filled, were gone.

"In the morning he left," she wrote. "And a couple weeks later, my trunks began arriving from New Mexico, and in the time since then I have not been more than five miles from this desk I sit at now."

She was still a drunk, she wanted her son to know: "Indeed, I am drunk now." She was coming to the end of it now. "I shall be drunk tomorrow, too, and drunk always until I die, for it is by booze that I know myself best." It was booze—the charm and wiles of it—which had sprung her free of the times he was reading about; and it was booze which had given shape to her life, made it an enterprise of the elements he could look forward to in his own—namely, passion and want, and the darkness which imperils it all. "Mister," she wrote, "I want you to drink—and be content in its tender, adult arms."

LINSEY ABRAMS

SECRETS MEN KEEP

FROM MADEMOISELLE

ॐ

SITTING FORWARD ON HER TOWEL and squinting in the direction of the ocean, Ellen lowers her sunglasses to cross the bridge of her nose. The nearly opaque lenses, framed in black, cut the noon glare as she scans the beach between where she sits and the water, a good twenty yards away. Some other sense notes Jeffrey's whereabouts just before her eyes locate his small torso, wrapped in a terry-cloth Union Jack, which matches her own towel, at the furthest boundary of dry sand. He is her brother's child, and because of that she feels a fierce, irrational love for him that has to do also with having loved Warren, his father, as a boy. The six-year-old, his legs collapsed under him, is filling a red plastic pail.

As she lies down again, the sound of the surf catches Ellen's attention. A white noise, it underpins the shouts of children and the AM radio band that issues from the blanket of a nearby couple, both men. Public sexuality, music, this now-crowded beach on Cape Cod where their family has vacationed for more than three decades—many things about the world have changed since she and Warren were children. Their own father died shortly after Jeffrey was born—life in that year defied understanding, such a composite of hopes fulfilled and unbearable sadness—and everyone joked that the boy was his grandfather come back to life. But nothing bears this out. As Jeffrey has grown up, there are no indications of common personality traits or even of physical resemblance.

It is she, Ellen reflects, who is most like their father. They shared the same wiry build and straight dark hair, in sharp contrast to the fleshier good looks of the rest of the family, her nephew included. Now that Ellen is older and her personality, both for good and for bad, has crystallized, she recognizes in her own actions her father's resolve, his impatience.

Glancing over at the two prone bodies of the men with the radio, Ellen feels pale and scrawny in their presence. Today is her first day all summer at the beach, reason enough to experience herself in this way, but she realizes that the feeling, which oddly persists as she lies on her back with her eyes closed in the hot sun, is connected to something else, too: Maleness seems alien now in a way it did not while she was living with Ted.

Jeffrey is suddenly at her side, announced even in his silent approach—his most recent fantasy is of being an American Indian—by a spray of sand against her ear. Having opened her eyes, Ellen finds her nephew's beaded-moccasin toes, soggy from the water, level with her gaze.

"You shouldn't wear moccasins in the surf," she says, cocking her chin to stare up at his face.

Even in summer, his skin looks translucent, making the two chubby cheeks seem almost delicate. Jeffrey is inclined to burn and now wears a stripe of white down his nose, which causes his eyes to appear even lighter than usual, though within the family no one can agree on exactly what color they are: amber, violet, gold. Reflective of any nearby hue, today they're tawny like the sand.

"These are water moccasins," Jeffrey says, deadpan.

Above her, his hair rises straight up from his forehead, resembling a hat, the salt from the ocean having stiffened his brown curls like lamb's wool. Out of this mass sticks a single white feather.

"You gave them to me," Jeffrey reminds her, pointing first one leather-wrapped foot and then the other. She reaches up as if to pull off his bathing suit. Her nephew's voice ascends into a giggle as he holds on to the drawstring of the plaid trunks, "They're my property." The boy resembles his mother Joanne in his full mouth and square chin, but in his being, in the way he moves, Ellen sees only Warren. Not as her brother is now, but as he was.

"You'll wear them out before you even get back to D.C.," Ellen replies, with effort pulling herself to sitting. Her muscles have gone slack since she left the more rigorous life of the New Hampshire countryside. The new apartment in Allston, an affordable suburb west of Boston and a fifteen-minute drive from her mother's home, is equipped with central heating and air conditioning; no more rising at six to fill and then stoke the wood stove, a task more usually hers than Ted's. It could take her an hour or more in winter to drive to Hanover, where she worked in the public library. Ted had a cabinet-making shop in their basement.

On his last visit to New Hampshire, the previous Thanksgiving, Jeffrey explained why he wanted to be an Indian. He said that when he was in the woods, he tried to move so as to make no sound as he passed among the trees and through underbrush, leaving every twig whole, each leaf unturned. Others could tell that an Indian had passed by only if, on purpose, a trail were left. It occurs to Ellen now that in between their conversation in November and just yesterday buying Jeffrey the moccasins, which the boy said he needed to perfect his method, nearly every particular of her own life had changed— home, job, lover—as if she, too, wished to leave no trail.

"The point is," she says, reaching to poke one of her nephew's deerskin slippers, "these are lined. It was the only kind I could get. Aren't they hot?"

"Not when they're wet," answers Jeffrey, who, dropping to his knees, starts to dig again in the sand. His child's logic is faultless.

The most surprising thing about adult life is the way logic

has lost its simplicity. Now either too many things have to be taken into consideration or one is trying to reason out matters that seem never to have a precedent. Ellen thinks of the immense mental effort she had to summon to make sense of leaving Ted last March. Something in her, which even now she can't name, made it nearly impossible to break the tie, at the same time that, on a conscious level, she knew their being together was no longer fruitful: during the false intimacy of sex, at Saturday night parties with friends, or awaiting the snowplow in the early morning. Just a week before she left, Ted had come close to convincing her that it was not their relationship but winter that had so disheartened her over the last months.

Ellen wonders if Warren and Joanne ever have come to such a crossroads or if living with a child simply shifts areas of concern. They were married twelve years ago this summer, when both were twenty-five, soon after Warren returned from Vietnam. Ellen was going to college then. At the end of that summer, with two years left to graduate, she simply never went back. Her father first tried to persuade, then to bully, her into finishing. But she was as stubborn as he was, and again, there was a different kind of necessity operating so that it seemed impossible, in 1972, to remain in school, to go on living as one had while the war was still on. Later, she moved to New Hampshire with Ted, who was nine years older than she was, and a veteran.

"Hello?" says Jeffrey, standing next to her, his arm raised to knock in greeting on her forehead. This is their private joke. She feels his knuckles lightly brush her skull.

"Come in," she replies, and moves over to make room for him. Her nephew flops down beside her on the towel, having discarded his own, which is wet, on the white Styrofoam cooler a few feet away.

"They're getting hot now," he says, pushing both heels against the red-white-and-blue terry cloth until his knees lock. Sitting side by side, the two of them study the new moccasins. "But I won't take them off," Jeffrey adds, glancing in her direction. At six, he's becoming expert in using language like an adult. Stating facts and conveying information is no longer his sole intention. Recently, he's been trying on attitudes, donning and then discarding them as if they were a matter of fashion, like hats.

"It's your feet's funeral," Ellen tells him, shaking her head in mock grief. Jeffrey laughs. His chunky torso stretches the waistband of his suit as he kicks off the moccasins and abruptly rolls onto the sand. Bending over to dig two shallow pits, her nephew then sticks his feet in these and begins to cover them. He reminds her of a little bulldog.

"I'm burying my dead feet," he explains, his tone suddenly serious. He turns away, and she hears the rhythm of his breath shift and accelerate. He turns back and looks up into her eyes. Aware of the quivering of the feather in his hair, Ellen watches him study her face, searching it for something. "My dad's legs are dead," he ventures.

This is the territory of adult logic, Ellen thinks: no simple reasons anymore, no simple answers to things. Warren knew this better than any of them.

"Is he ever going to walk again in his whole life?" Jeffrey asks next, though he knows the answer to this question. Joanne and Warren tell him the truth in everything.

"No," says Ellen. "Your father's legs are paralyzed."

"Paralyzed," Jeffrey repeats, his face setting in concentration as if he's reached some familiar boundary of thought.

There was fear, for a time, that Warren would be impotent, too. She remembers the terrible whiteness of his face during that year—how odd to remember skin color above everything—and the unnatural thinness of the once stocky 25-year-old. But they had gotten him out of the VA hospital, and a specialist in Pittsburgh worked with both him and Joanne. Ellen will always love her sister-in-law, no matter what happens in the future, for the way she behaved during those six months. Before anyone could know how things would turn out, she had set a wedding date.

It was easier after their sexual life had started again for Warren to live with the dead legs. Of his friends who lived— his was an infantry unit—two that he knew of were sterile from the Agent Orange. Jeffrey's conception and his birth as a healthy baby seemed to the family a miraculous event. And by the time their son was born, both Warren and Joanne had found jobs in Washington, he working for a veterans' group and she for a private lobbying concern.

One of the two men on the blanket nearby pushes himself to standing. A short, prematurely gray-haired man, his build is muscular, oversize chest and arms glistening with oil in the sun. Surveying the territory around him, he waves in their direction. Ellen smiles and raises her hand to return his greeting.

"Hey sport!" he calls to Jeffrey, who rises jerkily from the sand and, turning his back, sits on the cooler that serves as a boundary between their two sections of beach. The boy will not speak to men who can walk. Her nephew has been seeing a psychologist since he was four.

"When's lunch?" Jeffrey asks, that same perplexed expression rising like a blush to his face. Behind him, the man tugs at his salt-and-pepper mustache, then sits down again, turning up the volume of the radio.

Ellen turns away and fishes for her Timex in the straw bag, big as a suitcase, that Joanne gave her to carry Jeffrey's toys to the beach. The Big Bird doll, a tape deck shaped like a guitar, assorted and multicolored rubber balls, a set of alphabet blocks— the innocence of these playthings belies her nephew's more complicated childhood.

Locating the watch by feel against the thatched bottom, Ellen lifts it up to her face to read on the little oval the digital figures: 12:50. This morning Warren and Joanne had planned to arrive at the beach by noon.

"Get up," she says, swatting her nephew's behind. "You're sitting on the peanut butter and jelly."

Ellen often behaves gruffly with him, like this, to hide the immense tenderness she feels in his presence. Everything he does touches her—the way now he invents a little dance, the kind that later will be referred to as effeminate if he persists, circling the Styrofoam chest as if he were some primitive being and the white cube a gift from the gods. After the requisite number of times around it, he lifts the lid and puts it down beside the chest.

"Let's see just what we have in here," Jeffrey says, the words artificially stressed. It's obvious that the boy is trying out a sentence he heard someone else say. That's what we're all doing now, Ellen thinks. We're trying out a life that we've heard other people live.

It still seems impossible to believe that it happened to their family—to Warren and not someone else. Suddenly, Jeffrey's hand flies past his shoulder, pointing in the direction of the parking lot. She turns and sees Joanne quite some distance away at the top of a ridge of dunes which obscures the acre of cars beyond. Joanne waves in a way that reminds Ellen of how people's mothers wave. Ellen doesn't know if this impression is due to the fact that Joanne is now a mother or if this simply is a part of who her sister-in-law has always been. The truth is, Ellen realizes, everyone has grown older and the generations have each traded in familiar definitions for newer, yet-to-be-understood roles, both outside of and within the family. In the face of her father's death, Warren's disability, her mother's consequent emotional frailty, and now the loss of Ted, she is comforted by the solidity of Joanne's character. One had the feeling Joanne could endure anything.

"Where's Daddy?" Jeffrey asks, abruptly plucking the white lid from the sand and hugging it to his chest. Ellen watches the energy leave his body, as if traveling the full length of his height and through both feet into the ground, having been conducted, in the manner of a lightning rod, by the feather in his curls above.

"He must have stayed home," she says, finding her brother nowhere in sight. And because it's the first day of her only week at the cottage, Ellen feels disappointed he hasn't come. Immediately, she reprimands herself: Warren forgot to call ahead in April, and this season they had to settle for a saltbox much farther from the beach than usual. Sheer physical distance was an obstacle to a man who couldn't walk; using the car posed its own difficulties.

Each time, even in imagination, her mind still balks upon finding Warren in the wheelchair. It is as if, for a second, she knew better; that something about what she sees isn't quite right. And then she remembers. Once, right after she'd quit smoking, she saw a picture of herself holding a cigarette. Some knowledge of the body—it felt like a slight electric shock—rejected the image as being incompatible with what Ellen knew about herself, before she remembered that the picture had been taken months earlier. This is the same feeling she experiences in the presence of her brother; something inside her rejects what she sees, before, a moment later, she is able logically to reconcile what has happened to him.

"I'm going to meet Mom," Jeffrey says, taking a manic skip around Ellen and the towel. He weaves in and out of clusters of sunbathers until he reaches the deep sand where the sea grass grows. Along this strip, empty of people, he makes awkward progress toward his mother, who has descended from the rise and, not seeing him, now heads for the water. Ellen watches the boy cut a diagonal back through the more populated section of beach. She sees them meet at the shifting edge of the ocean, two stick figures against a backdrop of mirrors, the sun's glare reflected, in patches, off the whitecaps. Hand in hand, they walk toward her, closing the distance.

If Warren had come, Ellen thinks, the trip from the parking lot would have taken twice as long. Even in sand, he never let Joanne push him; he insisted on doing everything himself. This was a part of his character that had hardened into an awful pride. People would turn around and watch him, as if they thought he was not only crippled but blind too, as he maneuvered the big front wheels through the shifting, granular terrain. Because of his exertions in the wheelchair, his upper arms and torso were unusually developed for a man of thirty-seven. He was as muscular as the much younger man with the mustache on the blanket just a few yards away. Turning her head to look again, Ellen verifies this before lying back down and closing her eyes. *Hard-nosed,* their father had called Warren's attitude. A different life, Ellen considers, might have brought out a different side of who her brother had been as a young man, a teenager, a boy.

The image of this boy triggers a memory, vivid as the heat of the sun now baking her black suit, of the day their father took them on the swan boats in Boston Common. It was early fall, just before the boats closed down for the season, the afternoon that the three of them had walked, passing by their own reflections, in the tall windows of the Ritz-Carlton Hotel and then across the leaf-scattered pavements that divided the

grass into territories, toward the body of water that was the
home of the two passenger boats in the shaped of swans.
Warren must have been ten then, so she herself five.

Ellen remembers riding in her father's arms, higher above
the ground, as if atop a tower, than she could have been.
Coming over a rise, she glimpsed an enormous swan and did
not really understand at first that it was one of the boats. Or
rather did and didn't all at the same time, fantasy being as real
to her then as what she knew to be factual: the department
store through whose revolving doors she had watched her
mother swing just an hour earlier, the cloudless Indian-summer
sky, the wood floor of the boat as then they stepped inside the
shoulders of the swan and sat down, all three together, on a
bench.

In memory, there are no other people in the vessel, as
there must have been, just a man at its stern, controlling their
progress across the surface of what seemed like glass below.
Looking over the side, they had been surprised by a family of
real swans, bright white bundles marking the water. *I wish we
were those swans,* she remembers her brother saying, his husky
chest against the railing, leaning over it, and her father grabbing
him by the belt so he shouldn't fall.

She opens her eyes to find Joanne and Jeffrey standing above
her, her sister-in-law facing away toward the ocean and the boy
extending a handful of tiny, ear-shaped shells. The white feather
in his hair takes her breath away, as she reaches up to touch the
snails in her nephew's palm.

Ellen lifts her sunglasses and, rising to her knees, turns to
the cooler. With two hands, she removes a stack of sandwiches
and the ribbed aluminum thermos, whose cups, in descending
size, rest inside one another beneath its cap.

"Warren decided to stay home?" she asks.

"He hasn't come to the beach once since we got here,"
Joanne replies. She shrugs off her beach coat and, after spreading it on the sand beside Ellen, drops down on top. The two
exchange a look that Jeffrey, arranging his shells in a pattern
between the V of his outstretched legs, doesn't see.

Warren's not coming to the beach is the most recent example of the lesson that is adult life. Each year, everyone Ellen

knows seems to be able to do a little bit less, to stretch a little less far. Things happened; they undermined people. Possibilities became closed, simply. Who could have known that the aging of the body was mirrored by another process, as profound, in the mind?

Ellen hands Jeffrey a sandwich wrapped in wax paper, a family custom left over, like the silver thermos, from when her father was alive. He had always been the one to see to the arrangements for the vacation and had considered it tradition that in those two weeks he take over his wife's twin jobs of housekeeping and cooking. In no way up-to-date, except in his own profession, which was electronics, in August he bought the products his mother had used: wax paper, Bon Ami, wood clothespins.

"Eat the crusts. That's where all the vitamins are," Joanne tells Jeffrey, holding up the last half of her own sandwich and taking a bite out of the edge. Jeffrey dangles the thin brown strips of crust above his open mouth and then dutifully lowers them inside.

Growing older, you receive more and you lose more. You learn more and you forget more, her father used to say. Ellen has understood this information differently at different stages in her own life. Today she wishes that her father were still alive—not because, even with this kind of wisdom, he could be expected to do anything about what has befallen the family, but because his death marked the beginning of a series of losses that ensued after Warren was wounded. The wish is not really sentimental, but utterly practical.

"Has Warren said anything about not coming to the beach?" Ellen asks Joanne, now that Jeffrey, who is busy transporting snails across the sand on the pieces of wax paper, has moved out of earshot.

"Not really," Joanne answers, reaching to apply lotion to her shoulders, already deep pink from the week just past. Encased in a gathered strapless suit, a diminutive check cocoon, her sister-in-law's body has a compelling fullness. It is she and Warren who look like siblings. "It's hard to know what he's thinking," says Joanne. "But you know your brother . . . he keeps everything to himself."

This is one of the truths of living with men, Ellen can see that now. Having spent the last six months on her own, she's come to experience a different momentum to her daily life. There isn't the enormous expenditure of energy, trying to make another person reveal himself. She realizes just now that she never actually discussed with Warren what the damaged legs had meant to him, though all any of them had talked about for months was the legs.

"Men don't talk that way, do they?" Ellen muses aloud. She follows Joanne's gaze across the sand. Jeffrey has dragged the empty Styrofoam cooler up to the ragged edge of the surf. Bent double, he's lifting handfuls of sand into the receptacle.

"Have you been in touch with Ted recently?" her sister-in-law asks. She lifts her fingers to stroke the white lotion across her cheeks and nose.

"No," Ellen answers, always a little amazed at the ease with which Joanne assumes intimacy. "It's funny, but I feel as if that's a part of my life that's definitely over." She pauses to think, sipping from the iced tea in her cup. "I mean, I don't regret it . . . it's just that everything from that time seems way behind me."

"My God," says Joanne. "Already?"

"I know." Ellen lowers herself onto her elbows and stretches out again. "It *is* sort of spooky, feeling this way." She stares up into the sky.

Oddly, the years with Ted now seem to her a kind of random occurrence, one that could just as easily not have happened, like a potential storm that will brew or not according to weather conditions. Some of her friends described the beginnings of their own love affairs as being somehow irrevocable, a question of fate. The truth was that at the time she met Ted, as for a long time thereafter, all irrevocability in her life seemed somehow to be connected to Warren's legs. Living with Ted was a choice she had made.

"We call him up every now and then," Joanne tells her, dropping the capped tube of lotion into the beach bag between them. "Warren misses seeing Ted. They went through so many of the same things."

"I miss him, too," Ellen says, closing her eyes against the

brightness. It doesn't seem incongruous to her to feel this way at the same time that she feels all the other things. "I wonder what they talk about," she thinks out loud. "I wonder what men talk about with each other."

"Maybe they talk about the things they won't talk about with us," Joanne suggests. Ellen rolls her head to the left to see that her sister-in-law is now stretched out beside her.

"I doubt it," she answers.

"Me, too," admits Joanne. "Besides"—she points a finger in Ellen's face—"all those articles in my monthly magazines insist that men need women because women help them express their emotions."

"No kidding," Ellen says. "I thought they needed us to get laid." They both start laughing. "The thing is," she continues, "what do we need men for?"

"Same reason," says Joanne.

"Not really, though . . ." Closing her eyes, Ellen faces back into the sun.

"I know," Joanne agrees. "I guess we need someone to save," she adds, the pitch of her voice oddly high, and Ellen knows immediately that this is true, or at least has been for her and Joanne. As she hears a gull's cry, an idea rises in her mind that takes her completely by surprise at the same time that she realizes how obvious and simple a conclusion it is: Her relationship with Ted had to do all along with Warren.

Every event for some years, it occurs to her now—her own choice of a lover, Jeffrey's inability to speak to men, her father's early death—was secretly motivated by her brother's legs even where something else masqueraded as a cause. As if the dead legs, a reality Warren had never talked about, except to reiterate the blunt and irreducible facts, possessed a life all their own that would regenerate itself within the family, when least expected, like a virus or a parasite. A terrible emotional energy—the result of feelings none of them knew how to put to rest—had been running their lives for years now. It was a hidden logic, unbeknownst to any of them, but to which they all nevertheless subscribed.

Suddenly, there is a commotion around them, voices lifting like a ground swell. Hearing a guttural moan emitted from somewhere deep inside her sister-in-law's body, so deep that it sounds almost distant, Ellen knows, even before a second later she opens her eyes and thrusts herself to sitting to find Joanne already on her feet, that it is Jeffrey. There is another shout from down by the water, and pitching herself along the sand churned by Joanne's feet running just ahead of her, she feels her legs go weak, a chemical panic running down into the ankles. *Like Warren,* Ellen says to herself, while remaining aware, really, only of the knot of torsos several feet out into the water. But she can't get to them, as if the beach were growing, a living thing, yards lengthening, the sky rearing back like a horse. It is then that Ellen notices the bobbing white cooler, blown partway out to sea.

Unaware that she is holding her breath until suddenly her lungs ache, Ellen releases it as she sees the boy. In the arms of a man up to his waist in the waves, she sees Jeffrey move. Then his head is obscured by Joanne's hands, her shoulders, and according to a chronology of moments of which, afterward, Ellen will never be sure, she meets up with a small party of rescuers just inside of the reach of the tide.

Jeffrey is crying, and so is Joanne, hovering awkwardly above his limp body so that she slows the progress of the man against whose muscular chest her son is being held. Another, taller man forms the third side of the triumvirate bearing the boy toward dry sand. Ellen realizes now that these are the two men with the radio. The taller one spreads a towel at her feet, as the mustached man drops to his knees and lays Jeffrey on top of it. His mother kneels beside him, while, straightening up, the two men turn to wave away the dozen or so people starting to crowd around. Sensing these onlookers by means of their shadows and voices only, all peripheral vision gone as she crouches down, Ellen inspects her nephew's alabaster face, then body. His suit is twisted up into his groin, as if he had wrestled the sea.

"I was in the cooler," Jeffrey tells his mother between sobs. "It was . . . supposed to be a boat." He hiccups. As Joanne leans closer to him, her shadow, in the declining afternoon, darkens his face and shoulders. Ellen watches her run two fingers across the boy's forehead.

"It's all right now," Joanne says. "You're all right."

Suddenly Jeffrey's eyes sweep upward, to the few people left standing above them, but he doesn't seem to see anything and lowers his gaze to rest on Ellen.

"The moccasins," he says, and it is only then that she notices his bare feet, the pale amphibious-looking toes.

"You lost them in the water," she confirms.

"I needed them," the boy says, his face distorted by what seems to Ellen a much larger grief than even that of the loss of a treasured childhood gift.

"Why?" she asks him.

"I needed them," he starts to answer in a whisper, and Ellen has to lean closer to hear him, "because I don't want to get caught like Daddy was." She glances at Joanne, her sister-in-law's brow creasing in momentary lack of comprehension.

"Sweetheart," Joanne says presently, her voice choking, "no one's going to hurt you. What happened to Daddy happened in a foreign country. He was in a war. There's no war now."

"You can't make a sound and you can't leave a trail," Jeffrey replies, his voice insistent. Last Thanksgiving Ellen wondered at the particularity of his imaginings, at the intensity of the then five-year-old's interest; now she knows. His is the same necessity that has motivated them all. He wants to prevent what has already happened.

Ellen watches her sister-in-law's hands travel over the boy's body, as if she could tell by touch where something might be wrong. "Do you feel well enough to walk back to the car?" Joanne asks Jeffrey. He nods. One taking each hand, the women lift him to his feet.

Ellen bends to pick up the towel. Turning around, she sees the tall, fair-haired man to whom it belongs, standing a few yards away in conversation with his friend.

"Thank you doesn't seem enough to say," Joanne begins, approaching them first. She can't stop shaking her head.

"Just as long as he's all right," answers the tall, midwestern-looking one. Readjusting one of his long bare legs, he peers down at Jeffrey. Ellen extends the towel.

The gray-haired man reaches out for it and, taking the

towel, smiles. Despite his build, up close he looks older, nearer Ellen's own age, early thirties; she can see tiny crow's-feet at his eyes. His other hand rests for a moment on top of Jeffrey's bushy hairdo, before the boy pulls away, twisting into his mother's thighs.

"That was quite a boat ride you took out there," says the tall one, bending at the waist to speak to Jeffrey. "It's lucky George saw you." He gestures at his friend. "I'm Brian," he adds.

Her nephew claps his hands over his ears and closes his eyes.

"He's shy," says Brian good-naturedly. "Just like George." He pats the shorter man on the back. George smiles, pulling at his mustache.

"He thinks you're going to hurt him," Joanne answers, starting to cry. At the end, Ellen should have known before, of any endurance. "You have such hopes for your kids," she sobs, trying to explain, the tears spilling down her face. Jeffrey is now sitting on the sand, his knees to his chin, in a little ball.

The truth of people's lives comes out in their children, Ellen thinks. The gains or the losses of each generation are reflected in the childhood of the one that comes after. She pictures the gentleness of her father in his apron, bent over the stove to fry codfish. Or outdoors, pinning their clothes to the line strung from one of the evergreens to a hook above the kitchen door. And hearing the clothesline squeak as it's pulled, she sees that boy who wanted to be a swan—before he went to Vietnam, from which, she admits now, he will never recover. She sees his arms, thick as lambs' legs, resting against the metal of the wheelchair. He was a boy transformed by violence, into a man whose own son now wanted to be as silent as an Indian, so no one would be able to hurt him.

"Say thank you to George," Ellen projects her voice in Jeffrey's direction. She reaches for his arm and pulls him, struggling, to his feet.

"El . . ." Joanne takes a step toward them.

"This thing has got to stop somewhere," Ellen tells her. "Say thank you," she repeats, lowering herself to her knees in order to look directly into her nephew's face. A defiant child readjusts his weight to plant his two bare feet.

"Never mind," says Brian.

"It's okay. Really," George says, touching his friend's elbow, as if to go.

"No, wait. Please . . . Say it," Ellen pleads, taking Jeffrey into her arms, wrapping them tight around his body. He's shivering in the wet trunks.

"See what happens. Be brave," she whispers into the boy's ear, reaching to rub his cheeks with her thumb, smoothing out the white gel still covering his nose.

He shakes his head.

"Say it!" she shouts, suddenly furious with the boy for everything he embodies.

Ellen sees her brother, separated from his unit. She tries to imagine his being ambushed by the two Vietcong in the jungle, as Warren explained matter-of-factly he had been, how they had damaged his spine with his own hand grenade, attempting to set it off between his legs. She cannot, she doesn't have the words or the understanding, not a metaphor, to describe it to herself. No wonder men seldom spoke in intimacy; the things they needed to air were unspeakable.

"Thank you," Jeffrey utters, a hoarse, terrifying moan. He dives onto the sand, reaching for George's ankles, and hugging them, will not let go.

MADISON SMARTT BELL
ZERO DB

FROM HARPER'S

⟡

A GOOD SOUND MAN is someone who drives to work at twenty miles an hour.

Well, that's what they say. I am a sound man, though not necessarily and not always a good one. But I work. Correction. Until approximately seven o'clock this evening, I *did* work.

Twenty miles an hour. We may assume that that implies meticulousness, a close attention to detail, and great patience, near absolute.

Though some people say it merely means that a good sound man has his trunk full of expensive tape recorders.

Now I am sitting in a bar on Fourteenth Street. I am here and come here often because of the bartender, who remembers what I drink (shot of bourbon and a beer chaser) and pours it for me without my having to ask. Ever. What you might call a high-fidelity memory.

Ordinarily I sit at the bar, where the service is faster. But tonight I am sitting in a booth in the back of the place. The seats in the booth are dark red vinyl, stained near black with smoke and spillage and age. Between them is a brown Formica table. There is very little light.

On the table is a shot glass and a beer glass, each half empty. A couple of cigarette filters I have stood on end because there seems to be no ashtray for me to put them out in. And at the very edge of the table, a Nagra III tape recorder, my pride and joy.

The Nagra is sealed up in its black leather case. This is so no one will realize that I have several thousand dollars' worth of tape recorder here, because if they did, they might try to take it away from me. Now the tape recorder is running, and I am recording the sound of my own voice. I am using a lavalier microphone, about the size of a button on your shirt. Too small for anyone to notice, and besides, I have it cupped in my hand, practically inside my mouth. The lavalier is plugged into the line input on the side of the Nagra, and the headphones are plugged into the front. If anyone is watching, they may think I am listening to the radio.

Not so. The tape is running at 7.5 i.p.s., hi-fi not being a great issue here. Between one reel and the other the tape crosses three heads: record, sync (not now in use), and playback. Thus I hear my own words a half-second after I say them. This situation can cause problems for novices, making it near impossible for them to talk, but I am accustomed to it.

I am whispering so softly that without the Nagra I could hardly hear myself. But with the Nagra, I can boost the signal. The needle on the VU meter is flicking just short of zero db, the point it must always approach but never reach. If the needle rises above that mark and stays there, the tape will be saturated. The tape will have received more information than it can absorb, and my words will degenerate into noise.

As it is, my whispering is loud and clear, what I imagine the wind might sound like if it could shape words.

I am hunched over the table, holding up the case flap with my thumb, peeping in at the front panel of the Nagra, where the VU meter and the level controls are. Above these instruments I can also see the three tape heads under clear plastic, with the tape running so reliably across them. The heads are, quite simply, beautiful. The face of each one resembles a little Mondrian painting. And the whole of the Nagra is beautiful as well. It is an apotheosis of form following function, the best tape recorder made. The Nagra will not fail.

Except, of course, in case of operator error.

It occurs to me that my greatest hope and ambition might be to emulate this beautiful machine. Or that I need no other reason for being other than to contemplate it. Though in fact, I do have another reason for being. Soon I will make a telephone call. But first I will finish this drink.

When I set my glasses back down on the table, it sounds like an explosion. Operator error. I will buy another. Always with one eye on the booth where the Nagra is waiting to see what more I have to say.

By any ordinary judgment, today has been a very bad day for me. Listen, and I will tell you what happened.

A week ago I finished a documentary shoot for Harold Brinks. Harold usually makes commercials. He is well suited to commercial shoots, where all the conditions are under his control and he can bully the cast and crew to his heart's content. But he is eminently unsuited to documentary work, where the conditions cannot be controlled and bullying is inappropriate. Especially a documentary shoot in a mental hospital.

I don't know why he decided to do it. Harold is a connoisseur of Good Things. Good Food, Good Wine, Good Music, Good Art selected by a Good Decorator on the walls of his Good Location in midtown. Maybe he thought it was time to go in for Good Works. I don't know and I don't care. I hate Harold, a stupid, venal man whose bad temper is his most valuable stock in trade. Harold is rather fat, balding, his skin taut and swollen like a pig's. His nose comes out in a big sweeping hook, then chops off at the end as though maybe it has suffered some sort of accident. Harold's nose makes him look like a tapir. I work for him because he pays. But there's a limit to everything.

This morning Harold calls me up and displays his bad temper and says that the sound from the shoot is a mess.

Which I already know, because Harold had a cameraman who wouldn't take direction, so there was no direction, so I had to run tape hour after hour while the cameraman shot when he felt like it. Now Harold has discovered that there is a ten-to-one sound/picture ratio and no slates, and his intern can't sync up the rushes; in short, he wants me to come up and do it. Well, I would call that about a week of work, and I could use the money.

Sure enough, it is a mess when I get on Harold's flatbed. An hour of tape to five minutes of picture. Times fifteen. But I'm patient, meticulous, attentive to detail. I sit there watching picture for three hours, looking for a clue.

Then I find it. On the screen is a woman's face. Her mouth opens and closes; her throat throbs. Although I cannot hear it, I know that she is screaming.

It takes another hour to find the scream on all that tape. But when I find it, I enjoy it. The scream is pure, almost melodious. I am pleased to find that because I twiddled the knobs correctly when I taped it, it did not overload.

Now I know where to begin. After the scream there is a cut to a man talking. I watch his mouth until his lips shut firm.

The speech on the tape goes like this: "Listen. Listen. Listen. Anybody here that's got something to say . . ."

Anybody. Body. *B.* A letter where the mouth must close. I sync up, play back—it works. Not much, but it's a start.

By six-thirty I've synced up about twenty minutes' worth and put it on cores for coding. I pack up and get ready to leave. Harold comes boiling out of his office.

"Where you think you're going? Is it finished already?"

"Of course it's not finished," I say. "But I'm an hour into overtime."

"What overtime," Harold says. "This situation is your responsibility. It comes under your fee for the shoot."

"Oh no," I say, and I sit down. "Oh no, Harold, I don't know how to tell you this."

"Tell me what?" he says.

"Your nose, Harold," I say. "What happened to your nose? Did it get caught in a door somewhere?"

Harold begins to turn purple.

"Or did somebody maybe bite off the end of it one time? Could that have been what happened?"

Harold is beginning to sputter. I worry he may have a heart attack.

"You look a good deal like a tapir with that nose," I say. Harold is still inarticulate.

"A tapir is a South American pig," I explain. "It has a nose sort of like a little trunk. In case you didn't know. That's what I'm talking about. That's what your nose looks like, a tapir's nose."

That was the end of my employment with Harold, and probably with all of Harold's friends, who unfortunately are numerous and have given me a lot of work. That was an example of what Rosemary, to whom I will place a telephone call quite soon, would call self-destructive behavior.

Operator error, perhaps. I'll have another drink.

Getting back to the table, I see that two strange men have taken the booth behind mine. They are huddled so close together that I think they must be telling secrets. Very carefully, without turning around, I work the lavalier into the crack between the padding of my seat and the wall. There is noise in the headphones when I do this, like the microphone is being stamped on. But once I have it in place I can hear what the two men are saying.

"So why don't you use your Chink? The one that makes like Bruce Lee, I forget his name."

"Si Mung. Didn't you hear? He's no good anymore. Been out of the picture for four, five weeks."

"Didn't hear that. He get hurt?"

"He went mental. I thought you would have heard about it. Whole town must be laughing."

"No."

"Okay. Remember that guy, Greg Tate? Lives out Flatbush Avenue. Biker. Kept a dog, a monster Doberman. Would kill you. Like a wolf, that dog."

"Haven't seen him around, recent."

"You probably won't. See, Greg had been owing us money. For months. Since even before we had Si Mung. He was hard to get to because of the goddamn dog. Which was attack trained. A dog a cop should have. Greg sits out on Flatbush Avenue, he laughs when we call up.

"Si Mung, he works for us a month, six weeks. Used him on people four or five times—we didn't hardly have to use him anymore. People knew. They would just pay up, no problem."

"That, I did hear."

"But, Si Mung . . . a very cold guy. I never much liked to watch him work. Like a machine ripping into somebody. It was weird."

"Self-control."

"Self-control like that, it makes me nervous. But he was sitting around, not much to do. So I talk to him about Greg Tate. Just, you know, see what he thought about it. And he goes into this heavy Chinese silence of his. Then gets up and says, Okay.

"Okay what, I say. I mean, what about the dog? How are you gonna handle it? I mean, I don't want the dog to eat you or something.

"Si Mung says, I don't wanna hurt the dog. That's all he says. Goes out, stands next to the car and waits, like maybe he was a dog himself.

"So I think, Okay, I'm a gambler, right, I get in the car, drive Si Mung out Flatbush Avenue. Greg Tate is sitting right out there on the stoop. Got the dog on a leash, spiked collar on the dog. Greg got on a collar too, looks about the same. Si Mung gets out the car. Me, I stay in. Motor running, too.

"Si Mung stands out on the sidewalk. Does his little Chinese breathing thing. Greg shakes the leash and the dog pulls out to the end of it and hangs there snapping at the air. More teeth than a shark, that dog.

"Si Mung looks up, says, I don't wanna hurt the dog.

"Greg laughs. Si Mung takes a step up the stairs. Dog comes off the leash, teeth everywhere, and Si Mung, I see this, puts his hands *into the dog's mouth*, like he's making his hands into a sandwich for the dog, and *rip*, the dog is running back up the steps. Howling. Si Mung broke his jaws, see. Had his hands cut up a little and that was all. Greg starts in the house after the dog, going for a piece we found inside later, and good thing he never got to it, a sawed-off shotgun. Si Mung caught him in the doorway. Kicked in a knee, broke his right arm, broke his left arm. Laid his head into the doorpost and slammed the door on it till Greg Tate got no face left anymore. I mean, it was *flat*, where his face used to be."

"That's too much."

"Don't tell me. I get out the car, try to stop it, say, Si Mung, money's all we want, not dead people. But he didn't stop till, I don't know, he got tired or something. He turns around and says, I didn't wanna hurt the dog."

"Crazy. Like you said."

"Don't tell me. We got out of there clean, at least. Greg's in the hospital, never gonna pay anybody anything, maybe he's gonna die. But what the hell, it's an example for people. But Si Mung. He sits around the club a week, won't do anything, won't even say anything except, I didn't wanna hurt the dog. Si Mung, I say to him, you wanna eat, you wanna drink, you wanna shoot up, you wanna go out and beat somebody to death maybe? He says, I didn't wanna hurt the dog. Like that.

"Week of this, I say, Okay, let's go see about the god-damn dog. Back out Tate's place we find the dog lying down cellar, about half starved to death. Si Mung picks him up like he was a baby, carries him back to his place. Splints up the jaws, starts making the dog soup. And ever since that's the way it's been. Si Mung's good for nothing but making the dog soup. Even the *dog* is good for nothing anymore. All he can do is eat soup. It's a mess is what I'm saying. How should I know what to do?"

How should anybody? I pull the lavalier back through the crack and cup it to my mouth so I can hear myself whispering again. What a funny story. It is so funny that I am starting to cry. Big blubbering sobs come back to me through the head-phones with a half-second delay. Doesn't sound good. It's overloading, and I reach out my thumb and turn the level down. I stop and listen and I forget to cry.

There are certain sounds that don't seem very loud at all, but somehow they can push the level up and up. Well past the machine's greatest tolerance, above and beyond all the headroom there is. These situations can be difficult to anticipate and control, and the possibility for operator error increases.

When I call Rosemary, which I will certainly do as soon as I stop sniffling, I will tell her that I absolutely cannot tolerate my life without her any longer. Nor should she be able to tolerate her own life without me. I will convince her that I still love her and that she must love me too.

We will not discuss the lawyer whom she plans to marry in the spring.

I may perhaps even promise certain things that I may not be able to deliver. To stop smoking, to stop drinking. To stop throwing away good jobs because of my bad temper. To make a serious and concerted effort to get into the union. To spend no more nights in this bar on Fourteenth Street, whispering into the Nagra. To engage in self-destructive behavior no longer. So long as we both shall live.

At the phone booth, something new occurs to me. I take my telephone tapper from the side pocket of the Nagra's case and plug it into the line. I press the suction cup down over the earpiece of the phone and set the level to the dial tone. Now I will be able to record this important call. And listen to it at half-second delay.

I hear the coins fall, then the tones that represent the numbers. And now the phone is ringing. Three times.

"Hello," Rosemary says.

I listen. I can hear her breathe.

"Hello?"

I wait, expectant.

"Whoever you are," Rosemary says, "don't call again."

Dial tone.

Back in the booth it seems better to think about the dog with its broken jaws, to wonder if it will recover and hope by all means that it will. Water is lipping up to the lower rim of my eyelids and running down my face. I look around the bar, but no one notices; what I especially like about this place is that no one notices anything unless you hit someone. Through the headphones I can hear myself saying words like "Why will no one help me?" and "I've failed, I've failed." These words come back to me at half-second delay, fixed already on the tape and in the past, and they sound ugly and fatal. And the tape is overloading, distorting into noise.

Operator error. I turn the level down.

Over and over, I repeat new words:

I didn't want to hurt the dog.

I didn't want to hurt the dog.

And I feel much better. Twenty miles an hour. Perhaps I have only been going too fast.

I stop talking, turn the level up. The background sounds of the bar fill up the instrument: hiss of voices, clink of glasses, slow shuffling of feet. Room tone. On the lids of my closed eyes I see images.

I see the woman screaming in the film with all the force and power she can summon, without making the least sound.

I see the dog lying on the basement floor, breathing painfully, inaudibly, through his ruined jaws.

I see that Rosemary and I are walking arm in arm along a brick waterfront pier. The sun is low on the water, its reflections too painful to regard. Fat gulls swoop shrieking all around us. I see how the water meets the edge of the pier so precisely, no hint of drop or gap between them, the land dovetailed so smoothly into the sea.

I open my eyes, adjust the level. When I speak, the needle flicks toward zero and trembles exactly there, its perfect limit. I have just one thing more to say.

Listen. Listen. Listen. We can never be too attentive to our world.

T. CORAGHESSAN BOYLE
THE HAT

FROM ANTAEUS

∽

THEY SENT A HIT SQUAD after the bear. Three guys in white parkas with National Forestry Service patches on the shoulders. It was late Friday afternoon, about a week before Christmas, the snow was coming down so fast it seemed as if the sky and earth were glued together, and Jill had just opened up the lodge for drinks and dinner when they stamped in through the door. The tall one—he ordered shots of Jim Beam and beers for all of them—could have been a bear himself, hunched under the weight of his shoulders in the big quilted parka, his face lost in a bristle of black beard, something feral and challenging in the flash of his blue eyes. "Hello, pretty lady," he said, looking Jill full in the face as he swung a leg over the barstool and pressed his forearms to the gleaming copper rail, "I hear you got a bear problem."

I was sitting in the shadows at the end of the bar, nursing a beer and watching the snow. Jill hadn't turned up the lights yet

45

and I was glad—the place had a soothing underwater look to it, snow like a sheet stretched tight over the window, the fire in the corner gentle as a backrub. I was alive and moving—lighting a cigarette, lifting the glass to my lips—but I felt so peaceful I could have been dozing.

"That's right," Jill said, still flushing from the "pretty lady" remark. Two weeks earlier, in bed, she'd told me she hadn't felt pretty in years. What are you talking about? I'd said. She dropped her lower lip and looked away. I gained twenty pounds, she said. I reached out to touch her, smiling, as if to say twenty pounds—what's twenty pounds? Little Ball of Suet, I said, referring to one of the Maupassant stories in the book she'd given me. It's not funny, she said, but then she'd rolled over and touched me back.

"Name's Boo," the big man said, pausing to throw back his bourbon and take a sip of beer. "This is Scott," nodding at the guy on his left, also in beard and watchcap, "and Josh." Josh, who couldn't have been more than nineteen, appeared on his right like a jack-in-the-box. Boo unzipped the parka to expose a thermal shirt the color of dried blood.

"Is this all together?" Jill asked.

Boo nodded, and I noticed the scar cut along the ridge of his cheekbone, thinking of churchkey openers, paring knives, the long hooked ivory claws of bears. Then he turned to me. "What you drinking, friend?"

I'd begun to hear sounds from the kitchen—the faint kiss of cup and saucer, the rattle of cutlery—and my stomach suddenly dropped like an elevator out of control. I hadn't eaten all day. It was the middle of the month, I'd read all the paperbacks in the house, listened to all the records, and I was waiting for my check to come. There was no mail service up here of course—the road was closed half the time in winter anyway—but Marshall, the lodge owner and unofficial kingpin of the community, had gone down the mountain to lay in provisions against the holiday onslaught of tourists, skimobilers and the like, and he'd promised to pick it up for me. If it was there. If it was, and he made it back through the storm, I was going to have three or four shots of Wild Turkey, then check

out the family dinner and sip coffee and Kahlua till Jill got off
work. "Beer," I said.

"Would you get this man a beer, pretty lady?" said Boo in
his backwoods basso, and when she'd opened me one and come
back for his money, he started in on the bear. Had she seen him?
How much damage had he done? What about his tracks—
anything unusual? His scat? He was reddish in color, right?
Almost cinnamon? And with one folded ear?

She'd seen him. But not when he'd battered his way into
the back storeroom, punctured a case of twelve-and-a-half-
ounce cans of tuna, lapped up a couple of gallons of mountain
red burgundy and shards of glass and left a bloody trail that
wound off through the ponderosa pines like a pink ribbon. Not
then. No, she'd seen him under more intimate circumstances—in
her own bedroom, in fact. She'd been asleep in the rear bedroom with her eight-year-old son Adrian (they slept in the
same room to conserve heat, shutting down the thermostat and
tossing a handful of coal into the stove in the corner) when
suddenly the back window went to pieces. The air came in at
them like a spear thrust, there was the dull booming thump of
the bear's big body against the outer wall, and an explosion of
bottles, cans, and whatnot as he tore into the garbage on the
back porch. She and Adrian had jolted awake in time to see
the bear's puzzled shaggy face appear in the empty window
frame, and then they were up like Goldilocks and out the front
door, where they locked themselves in the car. They came to
me in their pajamas, trembling like refugees. By the time I got
there with my Weatherby, the bear was gone.

"I've seen him," Jill said. "He broke the damn window
out of my back bedroom and now I've got it all boarded up."
Josh, the younger guy, seemed to find this funny, and he began
a low snickering suck and blow of air like an old dog with
something caught in his throat.

"Hell," Jill said, lighting up, center stage, "I was in my
nightie and barefoot too and I didn't hesitate a second—zoom,
I grabbed my son by the hand and out the door we went."

"Your nightie, huh?" Boo said, a big appreciative grin
transforming his face so that for a minute, in the dim light, he

could have been a leering, hairy-hocked satyr come in from the cold.

"Maybe it wasn't just the leftovers he wanted," I offered, and everyone cracked up. Just then Marshall stepped through the door, arms laden, stamping the snow from his boots. I got up to help him, and when he began fumbling in his breast pocket, I felt a surge of relief; he'd remembered my check. I was on my way out the door to help with the supplies when I heard Boo's rumbling bass like distant thunder: "Don't you worry, pretty lady," he was saying, "we'll get him."

Regina showed up three days later. For the past few years she'd rented a room up here over the holidays, ostensibly for her health, the cross-country skiing and the change of scene, but actually so she could display her back end in stretch pants to the sex-crazed hermits who lived year-round amidst the big pines and sequoias. She was from Los Angeles, where she worked as a dental hygienist. Her teeth were perfect, she smiled nonstop and with the serenity of the Mona Lisa, and she wore the kind of bra that was popular in the fifties—the kind that thrust the breasts out of her ski sweater like nuclear warheads. She'd been known to give the tumble to the occasional tourist or one of the lucky locals when the mood took her, but she really had it for Marshall. For two weeks every Christmas and another week at Easter, she became a fixture at the bar, as much a part of the decor as the moose head or the stuffed bear, perched on a barstool in Norwegian sweater, red ski pants and mukluks, sipping a champagne cocktail and waiting for him to get off work. Sometimes she couldn't hold out and someone else would walk off with her while Marshall scowled from behind the grill, but usually she just waited there for him like a flower about to drop its petals.

She came into the white world that afternoon like a foretaste of the good times to come—city women, weekend cowboys, grandmas, children, dogs, and lawyers were on their way, trees and decorations going up, the big festival of the goose-eating Christians about to commence—rolling into the snowbound parking lot in her Honda with the neat little chain-wrapped tires that always remind me of Tonka Toys. It was

about four P.M., the sky was a sorrowful gray, and a loose
flurry was dusting the huge logs piled up on the veranda. In she
came, stamping and shaking, the knit cap pulled down to her
eyebrows, already on the lookout for Marshall.

I was sitting in my usual place, working on my fifth beer,
a third of the way through the check Marshall had brought me
three days previous and calculating gloomily that I'd be out of
money by Christmas at this rate. Scooter was bartending, and
his daughter-in-law Mae-Mae, who happened to be a widow,
was hunched morosely over a Tom Collins three stools up
from me. Mae-Mae had lost her husband to the mountain two
years earlier (or rather to the tortuous road that connected us
to civilization and snaked up 7,300 feet from the floor of the
San Joaquin Valley in a mere twenty-six miles, treacherous as a
goat trail in the Himalayas) and hadn't spoken or smiled since.
She was a Thai. Scooter's son, a Vietnam hero, had brought
her back from Southeast Asia with him. When Jill was off, or
the holiday crowd bearing down on the place, Scooter would
drive up the mountain from his cabin at Little Creek, elevation
5,500 feet, hanging his ski parka on a hook in back, and shake,
stir, and blend cocktails. He brought Mae-Mae with him to get
her out of the house.

Scooter and I had been discussing some of the finer points
of the prevent defense with respect to the coming pro football
playoffs when Regina's Honda had rolled into the lot, and now
we gave it up to gape at her as she shook herself like a go-go
dancer, opened her jacket to expose the jutting armaments of
her breasts, and slid onto a barstool. Scooter slicked back his
white hair and gave her a big grin. "Well," he said, fumbling
for her name, "um, uh, good to see you again."

She flashed him her fluoridated smile, glanced past the
absorbed Mae-Mae to where I sat grinning like an overworked
dog, then turned back to him. "Marshall around?"

Scooter informed her that Marshall had gone down the
mountain on a supply run and should be back by dinnertime.
And what would she like?

She sighed, crossed her legs, lit a cigarette. The hat she was
wearing was part of a set—hand-knit, imported from Scandina-
via, woven from rams' whiskers by the trolls themselves, two

hundred bucks at I. Magnin. Or something like that. It was
gray, like her eyes. She swept it from her head with a flourish,
fluffed out her short black hair, and ordered a champagne
cocktail. I looked at my watch.

I'd read somewhere that nine out of ten adults in Alaska
had a drinking problem. I could believe it. Snow, ice, sleet,
wind, the dark night of the soul: what else were you supposed
to do? It was the same way up on the mountain. Big Timber
was a collection of maybe a hundred widely scattered cabins
atop a broad-beamed peak in the western Sierras. The cabins
belonged to summer people from L.A. and San Diego, to
cross-country skiers, gynecologists, talent agents, ad men,
drunks, and nature lovers, for the most part, and to twenty-
seven hard-core antisocial types who called the place home
year-round. I was one of this latter group. So was Jill. Of the
remaining twenty-five xenophobes and rustics, three were
women, and two of them were married and postmenopausal to
boot. The sole remaining female was an alcoholic poet with a
walleye who lived in her parents' cabin on the outer verge of
the development and hated men. TV reception was spotty,
radio nonexistent, and the nearest library a one-room affair at
the base of the mountain that boasted three copies of *The
Thorn Birds* and the complete works of Irving Wallace.

And so we drank.

Social life, such as it was, revolved around Marshall's
lodge, which dispensed all the amenities in a single huge room,
from burgers and chili omelets to antacid pills, cold remedies,
cans of pickled beets, and toilet paper, as well as spirits, human
fraternity, and a chance to fight off alien invaders at the controls of the video game in the corner. Marshall organized his
Friday-night family dinners, did a turkey thing on Thanksgiving and Christmas, threw a New Year's party, and kept the bar
open on weekends through the long solitary winter, thinking
not so much of profit, but of our sanity. The lodge also
boasted eight woodsy hotel rooms, usually empty, but now—
with the arrival of Boo and his fellow hit men, Regina, and a
couple other tourists—beginning to fill up.

On the day Regina rolled in, Jill had taken advantage of

the break in the weather to schuss down the mountain in her station wagon and do some Christmas shopping. I was supposed to have gone with her, but we'd had a fight. Over Boo. I'd come in the night before from my late-afternoon stroll to see Jill half spread across the bar with a blank bovine look on her face while Boo mumbled his baritone blandishments into her eyes about six inches away. I saw that, and then I saw that she'd locked fingers with him, as if they'd been arm wrestling or something. Marshall was out in the kitchen, Josh was sticking it to the video game, and Scott must have been up in his room. "Hey," Boo said, casually turning his head, "what's happening?" Jill gave me a defiant look before extricating herself and turning her back to fool around with the cash register. I stood there in the doorway, saying nothing. *Bishzz, bishzz*, went the video game, *zoot-zoot-zoot*. Marshall dropped something out in the kitchen. "Buy this man a drink, honey," Boo said. I turned and walked out the door.

"Christ, I can't believe you," Jill had said when I came round to pick her up after work. "It's my job, you know? What am I supposed to do, hang a sign around my neck that says 'Property of M. Koerner?' "

I told her I thought that was a pretty good idea.

"Forget the ride," she said. "I'm walking."

"And what about the bear?" I said, knowing how the specter of it terrified her, knowing that she dreaded walking those dark snowlit roads for fear of chancing across him—knowing it and wanting for her to admit it, to tell me she needed me.

But all she said was "Screw the bear," and then she was gone.

Now I ordered another beer, sauntered along the bar and sat down one stool up from Regina. "Hi," I said, "remember me? Michael Koerner? I live up back of Malloy's place?"

She narrowed her eyes and gave me a smile I could feel all the way down in the remotest nodes of my reproductive tract. She no more knew me than she would have known a Chinese peasant plucked at random from the faceless hordes. "Sure," she said.

We made small talk. How slippery the roads were—worse than last year. A renegade bear? Really? Marshall grew a beard?

I'd bought her two champagne cocktails and was working on yet another beer when Jill catapulted through the door, arms festooned with foil-wrapped packages and eyes ablaze with goodwill and holiday cheer; Adrian tagged along at her side, looking as if he'd just sprung down from the back of a flying reindeer. If Jill felt put out by the spectacle of Regina—or more particularly by my proximity to and involvement in that spectacle—she didn't miss a beat. The packages hit the bar with a thump, Scooter and Mae-Mae were treated to joyous salutatory squeals, Regina was embraced, and I was ignored. Adrian went straight for the video game, pausing only to scoop up the six quarters I held out to him like an offering. Jill ordered herself a cocktail and started in on Regina, bantering away about hairstyles, nails, shoes, blouses, and the like as if she were glad to see her. "I just love that hat!" she shouted at one point, reaching out to finger the material. I swung round on my stool and stared out the window.

It was then that Boo came into sight. Distant, snow-softened, trudging across the barren white expanse of the lot as if in a dream. He was wearing his white parka, hood up, a rifle was slung over his shoulder, and he was dragging something behind him. Something heavy and dark, a long low-slung form that raveled out from his heels like a shadow. When he paused to straighten up and catch his streaming breath, I saw with a shock that the carcass of an animal lay at his feet, red and raw like a gash in the snow. "Hey!" I shouted, "Boo got the bear!" and the next minute we were all out in the wind-blown parking lot, hemmed in by the forbidding ranks of the trees and the belly of the gray deflated sky, as Boo looked up puzzled from the carcass of a gutted deer. "What happened, the bar catch fire?" he said, his sharp blue eyes parrying briefly with mine, swooping past Scooter, Adrian, and Mae-Mae to pause a moment over Jill and finally lock on Regina's wide-eyed stare. He was grinning.

The deer's black lip was pulled back from ratty yellowed teeth, its eyes were opaque in death. Boo had slit it from chest to crotch, and a half-frozen bulb of grayish intestine poked from the lower end of the ragged incision. I felt foolish.

"Bait," Boo said in explanation, his eyes roving over us again. "I'm leaving a blood smear you could follow with your eyes closed and your nose stopped up. Then I'm going to hang the meat up a tree and wait for Mr. Bear."

Jill turned away, a bit theatrically I thought, and made small noises of protest and disgust on the order of "the poor animal," then took Adrian by the hand and pulled him back in the direction of the lodge. Mae-Mae stared through us all, this carnage like that other that had claimed her husband's life, end-over-end in the bubble of their car, blood on the slope. Regina looked at Boo. He stood over the fallen buck, grinning like a troglodyte with his prey, then bent to catch the thing by its antlers and drag it off across the lot as if it were an old rug for the church rummage sale.

That night the lodge was hopping. Tourists had begun to trickle in and there were ten or twelve fresh faces at the bar. I ate a chicken potpie and a can of cold beets in the solitude of my cabin, wrapped a tacky black and gold scarf round my neck and ambled through the dark featureless forest to the lodge. As I stepped through the door I smelled perfume, sweet drinks, body heat, and caught the sensuous click of the poolballs as they punctuated the swell of riotous voices churning up around me. Holiday cheer, oh yes indeed.

Jill was tending bar. Everyone in the development was there, including the old wives and the walleyed poetess. An array of roaring strangers and those I recognized vaguely from previous seasons stood, slouched, and stamped round the bar or huddled over steaks in the booths to the rear. Marshall was behind the grill. I eased up to the bar between a bearded stranger in a gray felt cowboy hat and a familiar-looking character who shot me a glance of mortal dislike and then turned away. I was absently wondering what I could possibly have done to offend this guy (winter people—I could hardly remember what I'd said and done last week, let alone last year) when I spotted Regina. And Boo. They were sitting at a booth, the table before them littered with empty glasses and beer bottles.

Good, I thought to myself, an insidious little smile of satisfaction creeping across my lips, and I glanced toward Jill.

I could see that she was watching them out of the corner of her eye, though an impartial observer might have guessed she was giving her full attention to Alf Cornwall, the old gasbag who sat across the bar from her and toyed with a glass of peppermint schnapps while he went on *ad nauseam* about the only subject dear to him—i.e., the lamentable state of his health. "Jill," I barked with malicious joy, "how about some service down here?"

She gave me a look that would have corroded metal, then heaved back from the bar as if she had a piano strapped to her back and poured me a long slow shot of Wild Turkey and an even slower glass of beer. I winked at her as she set the drinks down and scraped my money from the bar. "Not tonight, Michael," she said, "I don't feel up to it," and her tone was so dragged down and lugubrious she could have been a professional mourner. It was then that I began to realize just how much Boo had affected her (and by extension, how little I had), and I glanced over my shoulder to focus a quick look of jealous hatred on him. When Jill set down my change I grabbed her wrist. "What the hell do you mean 'not tonight,' " I hissed. "Now I can't even talk to you, or what?"

She looked at me like a martyr, like a twenty-eight-year-old woman deserted by her husband in the back end of nowhere and saddled with an unhappy kid and a deadbeat sometime beau to whom the prospect of marriage was about as appealing as a lobotomy, she looked at me like a woman who's given up on romance. Then she jerked her arm away and slouched off to hear all the fascinating circumstances attending Alf Cornwall's most recent bowel movement.

The crowd began to thin out about eleven, and Marshall came out from behind the grill to saunter up to the bar for a Remy Martin. He too seemed preternaturally interested in Alf Cornwall's digestive tract, and sniffed meditatively at his cognac for five minutes or so before he picked up the glass and strolled over to join Boo and Regina. He slid in next to Regina, nodding and smiling, but he didn't look too pleased.

Like Boo, Marshall was big. Big-headed, big-bellied, with

grizzled hair and a beard flecked with white. He was in his mid
forties, twice-divorced, and he had a casual folksy way about
him that women found appealing, or unique—or whatever.
Women who came up the mountain, that is. Jill had had a thing
with him the year before I moved in, he was one of the chief
reasons the walleyed poetess hated men, and any number of
cross-country ski bunnies, doctors' wives, and day trippers
had taken some extracurricular exercise in the oak-framed water bed that dominated his room in the back of the lodge. Boo
didn't stand a chance. Ten minutes after Marshall had sat down
Boo was back up at the bar, a little unsteady from all he'd had
to drink, and looking Jill up and down like he had one thing on
his mind.

I was on my third shot and fifth beer, the lights were low,
the fire going strong, and the twenty-foot Christmas tree lit up
like a satellite. Alf Cornwall had taken his bullshit home with him,
the poetess, the wives, and two thirds of the new people had
cleared out. I was discussing beach erosion with the guy in the
cowboy hat, who as it turned out was from San Diego, and
keeping an eye on Boo and Jill at the far end of the bar. "Well,
Christ," San Diego roared as if I was half a mile away, "you
put up them godforsaken useless damn seawalls and what have
you got, I ask you? Huh?"

I wasn't listening. Boo was stroking Jill's hand like a glove
salesman, Marshall and Regina were grappling in the booth,
and I was feeling sore and hurt and left out. A log burned
through and tumbled into the coals with a thud, Marshall got
up to poke it, and all of a sudden I was seething. Turning my
back on San Diego, I pushed off of my stool and strode to the
end of the bar.

Jill saw the look on my face and drew back. I put my hand
on Boo's shoulder and watched him turn to me in slow motion,
his face huge, the scar glistening over his eyebrow. "You can't
do that," I said.

He just looked at me.

"Michael," Jill said.

"Huh?" he said. "Do what?" Then he turned his head to
look at Jill, and when he swung back round he knew.

I shoved him, hard, as he was coming up off the barstool,

and he went down on one knee before he caught himself and lunged at me. He would have destroyed me if Marshall hadn't caught hold of him, but I didn't care. As it was, he gave me one terrific shot to the breastbone that flattened me against the bar and sent a couple of glasses flying. Bang, bang, they shattered on the flagstone floor like lightbulbs dropped from a ladder.

"Goddamit," Marshall was roaring, "that's about enough." His face was red to the roots of his whiskers. "Michael," he said—or blared, I should say—and then he waved his hand in disgust. Boo stood behind him, giving me a bad look. "I think you've had enough, Michael," Marshall said. "Go on home."

I wanted to throw it right back in his face, wanted to shout obscenities, take them both on, break up the furniture and set the tree afire, but I didn't. I wasn't sixteen: I was thirty-one and I was reasonable. The lodge was the only bar in twenty-six miles and I'd be mighty thirsty and mighty lonely both if I was banished for good. "All right," I said. "All right." And then, as I shrugged into my jacket: "Sorry."

Boo was grinning, Jill looked like she had the night the bear broke in, Regina was studying me with either interest or amusement—I couldn't tell which—Scooter looked like he had to go to the bathroom, and San Diego just stepped aside. I pulled the door closed behind me. Softly.

Outside, it was snowing. Big, warm, healing flakes. It was the kind of snow my father used to hold his hands out to, murmuring *God must be up there plucking chickens*. I wrapped the scarf round my throat and was about to start off across the lot when I saw something moving through the blur of falling flakes. The first thing I thought of was some late arrival from down below, some part-timer come to claim his cabin. The second thing I thought of was the bear.

I was wrong on both counts. The snow drove down against the dark branchless pillars of the tree trunks, chalk strokes on a blackboard, I counted off three breaths, and then Mae-Mae emerged from the gloom. "Michael?" she said, coming up to me.

I could see her face in the yellow light that seeped through the windows of the lodge and lay like a fungus on the surface of the snow. She gave me a rare smile, and then her face changed as she touched a finger to the corner of my mouth. "What happen you?" she said, and her finger glistened with blood.

I licked my lip. "Nothing. Bit my lip, I guess." The snow caught like confetti in the feathery puff of her hair and her eyes tugged at me from the darkness. "Hey," I said, surprised by inspiration, "you want to maybe come up to my place for a drink?"

Next day, at dusk, I was out in the woods with my axe. The temperature was about ten degrees above zero, I had a pint of Presidente to keep me warm, and I was looking for a nice round-bottomed silver fir about five feet tall. I listened to the snow groan under my boots, watched my breath hang in the air; I looked around me and saw ten thousand little green trees beneath the canopy of the giants, none of them right. By the time I found what I was looking for, the snow had drunk up the light and the trees had become shadows.

As I bent to clear the snow from the base of the tree I'd selected, something made me glance over my shoulder. Failing light, logs under the snow, branches, hummocks. At first I couldn't make him out, but I knew he was there. Sixth sense. But then, before the shaggy silhouette separated itself from the gloom, a more prosaic sense took over: I could smell him. Shit, piss, sweat and hair, dead meat, bad breath, the primal stink. There he was, a shadow among shadows, big around as a fallen tree, the bear, watching me.

Nothing happened. I didn't grin him down, fling the axe at him, or climb a tree, and he didn't lumber off in a panic, throw himself on me with a bloody roar, or climb a tree either. Frozen like an ice sculpture, not even daring to come out of my crouch for fear of shattering the moment, I watched the bear. Communed with him. He was a renegade, a solitary, airlifted in a groggy stupor from Yellowstone, where he'd become too familiar with people. Now he was familiar with me. I wondered if he'd studied my tracks as I'd studied his, wondered what he was doing out in the harsh snowbound woods instead of curled cozily in his den. Ten minutes passed. Fifteen. The woods went dark. I stood up. He was gone.

Christmas was a pretty sad affair. Talk of postholiday depression, I had it before, during, and after. I was broke, Jill and I were on the outs, I'd begun to loathe the sight of three-hundred-foot trees and snow-capped mountains, and I liked the rest of humanity about as much as Gulliver liked the Yahoos. I did stop by Jill's place around six to share a miserable, tight-lipped meal with her and Adrian and exchange presents. I gave Adrian a two-foot-high neon-orange plastic dragon from Taiwan that spewed up puddles of reddish stuff that looked like vomit, and I gave Jill a cheap knit hat with a pink pompon on top. She gave me a pair of gloves. I didn't stay for coffee.

New Year's was different.

I gave a party for one thing. For another, I'd passed from simple misanthropy to nihilism, death of the spirit, and beyond. It was two A.M., everybody in the lodge was wearing party hats, I'd kissed half the women in the place—including a reluctant Jill, pliant Regina, and sour-breathed poetess—and I felt empty and full, giddy, expansive, hopeful, despondent, drunk. "Party at my place," I shouted as Marshall announced last call and turned up the lights. "Everybody's invited."

Thirty bon vivants tramped through the snowy streets, blowing party horns and flicking paper ticklers at one another, fired up snowmobiles, Jeeps, and pickups, carried open bottles out of the bar, and hooted at the stars. They filled my little place like fish in a net, squirming against one another, grinning and shouting, making out in the loft, vomiting in the toilet, sniggering around the fireplace. Boo was there, water under the bridge. Jill too. Marshall, Regina, Scooter, Mae-Mae, Josh and Scott, the poetess, San Diego, and anybody else who happened to be standing under the moose head in a glossy dunce cap when I made my announcement. Somebody put on a reggae album that sent seismic shudders through the floor, and people began to dance.

I was out in the kitchen fumbling with the ice cube tray when Regina banged through the door with a bar glass in her hand. She gave me a crooked smile and held it out to me. "What're you drinking?" she asked.

"Pink Boys," I said. "Vodka, crushed ice, and pink lemonade, slushed in the blender."

"Pink Boys," Regina said, or tried to say. She was wearing her knit hat and matching sweater, the hat pulled down to her eyebrows, the sweater unbuttoned halfway to her navel. I took the glass from her and she moved into me, caught hold of my biceps and stuck her tongue in my mouth. A minute later I had her pinned up against the stove, exploring her exemplary dentition with the tip of my own tongue and dipping my hands into that fabulous sweater as if into the mother lode itself.

I had no problems with any of this. I gave no thought to motives, mores, fidelity, or tomorrow: I was a creature of nature, responding to natural needs. Besides which, Jill was locked in an embrace with Marshall in the front room, the old satyr and king of the mountain reestablishing a prior claim, Boo was hunched over the fire with Mae-Mae, giving her the full flash of his eyes and murmuring about bear scat in a voice so deep it would have made Johnny Cash turn pale, and Josh and the poetess were joyfully deflating Edna St. Vincent Millay while swaying their bodies awkwardly to Bob Marley's voodoo backbeat. New Year's Eve. It was like something out of *La Ronde*.

By three-thirty, I'd been rejected by Regina, who'd obviously been using me as a decoy, Marshall and Jill had disappeared and rematerialized twice, Regina had tried unsuccessfully to lure Boo away from Mae-Mae (who was now secreted with him in the bedroom), San Diego had fallen and smashed my coffee table to splinters, one half-gallon of vodka was gone and we were well into the second, and Josh and the poetess had exchanged addresses. Auld lang syne, I thought, surveying the wreckage and moodily crunching taco chips while a drunken San Diego raved in my ear about dune buggies, outboard engines, and tuna rigs. Marshall and Jill were holding hands. Regina sat across the room, looking dangerous. She'd had four or five Pink Boys, on top of what she'd consumed at the lodge, but who was counting? Suddenly she stood—or rather jumped to her feet like a marine assaulting a beachhead—and began to gather her things.

What happened next still isn't clear. Somehow her hat had disappeared—that was the start of it. At first she just bustled round the place, overturning piles of scarves and down jackets, poking under the furniture, scooting people from the couch and easy chair, but then she turned frantic. The hat was a keepsake, an heirloom. Brought over from Flekkefjord by her great-grandmother, who'd knitted it as a memento of Olaf the Third's coronation, or something like that. Anyway, it as irreplaceable. More precious than the Magna Carta, the Shroud of Turin, and the Hope Diamond combined. She grew shrill.

Someone cut the stereo. People began to shuffle their feet. One clown—a total stranger—made a show of looking behind the framed photograph of Dry Gulch, Wyoming, that hangs beside the fireplace. "It'll turn up," I said.

Regina had scattered a heap of newspapers over the floor and was frantically riffling through the box of kindling in the corner. She turned on me with a savage look. "The hell it will," she snarled. "Somebody stole it."

"Stole it?" I echoed.

"That's right," she said, the words coming fast now. She was looking at Jill. "Some bitch. Some fat-assed jealous bitch that just can't stand the idea of somebody showing her up. Some, some—"

She didn't get a chance to finish. Jill was up off the couch like something coming out of the gate at Pamplona and suddenly the two of them were locked in combat, pulling hair and raking at one another like harpies. Regina was cursing and screeching at the same time; Jill went for the vitals. I didn't know what to do. San Diego made the mistake of trying to separate them and got his cheek raked for the effort. Finally, when they careened into the pole lamp and sent it crashing to the floor with a climactic shriek of broken glass, Marshall took hold of Regina from behind and wrestled her out the door, while I did my best to restrain Jill.

The door slammed. Jill shrugged loose, heaving for breath, and turned her back on me. There were twenty pale astonished faces strung round the room like Japanese lanterns. A few of

the men looked sheepish, as if they'd stolen a glimpse of
something they shouldn't have. No one said a word. Just then
Boo emerged from the bedroom, Mae-Mae in tow. "What's all
the commotion?" he said.

I glanced round the room. All of a sudden I felt indescrib-
ably weary. "Party's over," I said.

I woke at noon with a hangover. I drank from the tap,
threw some water in my face, and shambled down to the lodge
for breakfast. Marshall was there, behind the grill, looking as if
he was made of mashed potatoes. He barely noticed as I
shuffled in and took a window seat among a throng of chipper,
alert, and well-fed tourists.

I was leafing through the *Chronicle* and puffing away at
my third cup of coffee when I saw Regina's car sail past the
window, negotiate the turn at the end of the lot, and swing onto
the road that led down the mountain. I couldn't be sure—it was a
gloomy day, the sky like smoke—but as near as I could tell she
was hatless. No more queen of the mountain for her, I thought.
No more champagne cocktails and the tight thrilling clasp of
spandex across the bottom—from here on out it was stinking
mouths and receding gums. I turned back to the newspaper.

When I looked up again, Boo, Josh, and Scott were stepping out of a Jeep Cherokee, a knot of gawkers and Sunday
skiers gathered round them. Draped over the hood, still red at
the edges with raw meat and blood, was a bearskin, head
intact. The fur was reddish, almost cinnamon-colored, and one
ear was folded down. I watched as Boo ambled up to the door,
stepped aside for a pair of sixteen-year-old ski bunnies with
layered hair, and then pushed his way into the lodge.

He took off his shades and stood there a moment in the
doorway, carefully wiping them on his parka before slipping
them into his breast pocket. Then he started toward the cash
register, already easing back to reach for his wallet. "Hey," he
said when he saw me, and he stopped to lean over the table for
a moment. "We got him," he said, scraping bottom with his
baritone and indicating the truck beyond the window with a
jerk of his head. There was a discoloration across the breast of
his white parka, a brownish spatter. I swiveled my head to

glance out the window, then turned back to him, feeling as if I'd had the wind punched out of me. "Yeah," I said.

There was a silence. He looked at me, I looked at him. "Well," he said after a moment, "you take care," and then he strode up to the cash register to pay his bill and check out.

Jill came in about one. She was wearing shades too, and when she slipped behind the bar and removed them, I saw the black-and-blue crescent under her right eye. As for Marshall, she didn't even give him a glance. Later, after I'd been through the paper twice and figured it was time for a Bloody Mary or two and some Bowl games, I took a seat at the bar. "Hi, Michael," she said, "what'll you have?" and her tone was so soft, so contrite, so sweet and friendly and conciliatory, that I could actually feel the great big heaving plates of the world shifting back into alignment beneath my feet.

Oh yes, the hat. A week later, when the soot and dust and woodchips around the cabin got too much for me, I dragged out the vacuum cleaner for my semiannual sweep around the place. I scooted over the rug, raked the drapes, and got the cobwebs in the corners. When I turned over the cushions on the couch, the wand still probing, I found the hat. There was a label inside. *J. C. Penney*, it read, *$7.95*. For a long moment I just stood there, turning the hat over in my hand. Then I tossed it in the fire.

RON CARLSON
AT THE HOP

FROM THE MISSOURI REVIEW

᠎

I'M TRYING TO SING the most popular song of the year, "The Hop," by Danny and the Juniors as I whip the towel around my arms and legs. I'm not much at grooming. It's hard to sing it for more than a minute without stopping and thinking you're silly. *At the ha-ha-ha-hop! At the ha-ha-ha-hop! At the hop! You can rock it! You can roll it! You can really start to stroll it at the hop! hop! hop! hop!* But on the radio it's a pretty strong song and has me hooked. I never even listened to the radio before, except for the goof songs which my brother Bobby likes, such as "Please Mr. Custer, I Don't Wanno Go!" Now, I listen to the radio all the time. My dad framed it in the wall when he built our basement. After I switch it on I fall back on the bed and do a backward somersault naked to dry my back.

Hopping up to grab some underwear, I find something different on my bureau. Oh I've been finding these clippings out of *Ladies Home Journal* for a while now. My mother cuts them out and puts them on my bureau. They're about things like "Surviving the Troublesome Teens" and "The Six Teenage Dangers." I try not to touch them. I don't move them or go near my bureau top while they're up there. After four or five days they disappear. My mother and I have never talked about them, nor have I ever seen her place them or take them away. The last one was titled: "What Teenagers Want to Know About SEX." The word "SEX" was stenciled in red block letters on a picture of a big wooden crate, the kind they must keep dynamite in. It scares the shit out of me that they print things like that in magazines; what are they trying to do, embarrass everybody in the whole world? For that week, I gave my bureau plenty of room. I didn't change my underwear for three days and when the article disappeared, I finally felt free to sleep late the next day.

Standing there with one leg in my shorts I see something new on the old bureau. A pamphlet. Picking it up, I read: *Understanding Puberty.* Oh my God. I drop it like a firecracker. What a word: *puberty.* It should be in the pledge of allegiance: "with puberty and justice for all." The truth is: I don't even know exactly what it is. They showed a film last year to all the girls while the boys were kept in Mr. Donaldson's class. Mr. Donaldson wouldn't tell us what the film was about, and I remember walking home with Fenn that I felt hurt and kind of sad that we'd been dealt with unfairly. Something was going on and no one would tell us what it was. Mrs. Talbot had been our teacher all year and then they show a film; and without a word to us, she and all the girls go into the auditorium leaving us with Mr. D., the fool.

And now, my mother is leaving pamphlets on my bureau. Next, I can already see it: she'll start leaving whole books and stacks of books. It's all not quite working.

Well, I've touched the pamphlet, moved it, and I snap on my undershorts and go back to it. *Understanding Puberty.* It could be a travel brochure. Inside I see the diagram of the male reproductive organs. It all looks a lot like Florida, the capital of which is Tallahassee. Two pages later are the female reproductive organs, the side view, internal. It looks like nothing, like lines. I try to imagine Linda Aikens or Carol Wilkes with one of these. And the truth is: My imagination won't work. If I saw some girl naked and she looked like this I would scream and tear my eyes out. No wonder sex is such a big secret: it's brutal. And this is just the puberty part. A couple of pages later there is the bold print phrase: "adolescents are torn by the violent distractions of puberty. . . ." As I'm looking at it, my mother yells down the stairs to me: "Larry, don't be late!" I drop the pamphlet again as my heart explodes and my face heats up. She knows I'm down here reading this dirty pamphlet!

"I won't be! I'm coming!" I call back, but my voice is changed, all throaty, so now she knows for sure.

I spend the next five or ten minutes trying to remember exactly how the little book was originally sitting on the bureau. I adjust it around an eighth of an inch at a time trying to get it just right. Then I picked it up again and wipe my fingerprints off the glossy cover, but the towel is wet and leaves a little smear, so I toss it back up on the dresser and try again to turn it around and around so it looks untouched. Then I take it down and check out the female reproductive organs again. I can see the buttocks, but the rest is a terrible puzzle. This time, when I replace it, I see that the cover is bent, so I leave it there all wrong and sit on my bed, sick right through the heart. By this time I don't even want to go to the party.

The song on the radio now is, *Who put the bop in the bop-she-bop, she-bop? Who put the ram in the ram-lama-ding-dong?* I sit on my bed and pull on the first pair of long pants I've worn all summer, not counting my baseball uniform. They are one of the strangest pairs of pants I've ever worn: my first pair of corduroys. My mother bought them for me as part of my school clothes. The pants are chocolate brown, and when I stand up in them and brush my hand on the leg, they feel wonderful. I run my new belt with the modest brass C-shaped buckle through the loops. Tucking in my white shirt, rolling up the sleeves, and buckling the belt, I feel better. I actually feel mature. Maybe that was puberty I just passed through. In the mirror, I look like any twelve-year-old lawyer. My hair is too short to comb, but I comb it anyway, just to see if I look right doing it.

Who was that man? the song cries. *I'd like to shake his ha-a-and; He made my baby fall in love with me!*

I slip right out of my room and head up the stairs and then go back to my room and then go back again to the stairs and finally stop and look at my new shoes. They are slip-ons and have little tassels instead of laces. I return to my room. The pamphlet glows in the dark. Finally I take it up and fold it right in half and stuff it in the back pocket of my new trousers. I button the pocket.

Upstairs in the kitchen, my mother looks at me and says "Well!"

"Yeah," I say. "Fenn and I are going to walk over to the class party."

"Vic, come in here," my mother calls.

My father comes in the kitchen. He is carrying my baby brother, Regan. "Say, you look pretty good, Larry. What is this, a party?"

"Yeah, Fenn and I are going to walk over to the class party."

"Isn't Butch going?"

"Naw. He doesn't go to many things like this."

"Butch is dropping out of school," my little brother Bobby says. He's sneaked up behind me and rubs the leg of my corduroys.

"He is?"

"No, he's not!" I say to my mother. "Bobby doesn't know anything."

"Roto said so!"

"Roto's a dope."

"Is Butch dropping out of school?"

"I don't know anything about Butch. He's confused me all summer," Fenn says. Fenn is wearing his glasses again. They're not his old glasses but new ones he bought for school. The frames are little chrome girders and they make Fenn look ready for the new age. I don't know if he ever found out that the cardboard baseball goggles we gave him were made using his old lenses; I doubt it. The goggles now dangle from the nose of the B-52 suspended from the ceiling in his room. And I don't actually know what made him decide on wearing glasses again after this wild summer of banging his head against things.

It might have been when we went downtown on Butch's birthday to see *Sink the Bismarck!* which wasn't as good as the song, and then Fenn talked us into going across the street to the Gem to see *Love Me Tender* again. We actually saw it twice in a row that afternoon, and the second time through, when Elvis gets shot and his face is superimposed over the scene of the little house, Fenn rose before the song was even over and said, "Well, that's enough of that." The next day he put on his new glasses.

"Don't you want to look like Elvis anymore?" we had asked him.

"It's all over. Rock and roll has six months to live. I'm going to save my money so that when I'm fifteen and a half, I can buy a car."

"A car?" It was the first time anyone had mentioned a car that way to me. Ever.

Later, Butch had said to me quietly: "Fenn's a goner."

And he may be. Now, as we walk toward the class party, he seems a lot different from the blind kid I swindled all summer. He's wearing a red shirt, short sleeves, and chinos. I haven't seen him in a button shirt in my whole life.

Linda Aikens lives just across the river from our new school: the junior high. It's a good walk because most of the way you can stay by the river and throw rocks at the passing debris. It's just getting dark when we step down the flagstone steps into the junior high school yard. The asphalt yard is criss-crossed by a complicated series of lines painted in yellow paint which has swollen from seventy coats and the weather. The track and the dash marks and the baseball diamond and the basketball courts are all printed on top of each other on the old blacktop. There are several gigantic intersecting circles. I hate not knowing what those circles are for. The entire yard is, in fact, just a scary diagram of our futures, and it makes my stomach feel the same way that the diagram of the female reproductive organs did. I feel my pocket and take the pamphlet out and hand it to Fenn.

"Check this out."

He takes it and turns a few pages, still walking. It's funny to see him read without holding the paper against his nose. He hands it back.

"Wonderfully informative."

"My mother left it for me."

"Your mother! What for?"

"I don't know." We walk by the huge brick siding of the gymnasium. Someone has thrown a bottle of ink against it and a blue stain flashes dead center. The whole school scares me. In four days I'll come here as a student.

"You ever jack off?" Fenn asks.

"Yeahnn," I say automatically.

"What? Do you?"

"Not exactly." I try to say it as if I know what I am saying *exactly*. Jacking off is something I've heard about. Lannie and Cling are always telling the little kids to jack off. They take the kids' nickels and then say, "Now, why don't you go soap it up in the tub and jack off." Then Cling makes an ape stance and grasps his crotch and laughs.

I have soaped it up in the tub, but I know that I have not jacked off. I still have two toy boats that I keep by the tub. That's a fact. Well, one's a submarine. I bought it at Woolworth's the day we saw *Sink the Bismarck!* I don't know. I look around at the trees, swelling in the late summer dusk, and I think that: I don't know.

"You haven't have you? Have you? Do you know about it?"

It's becoming a long day for me. I try to keep walking.

"Hey. It's okay. I just learned."

"You went over to Lannie's club."

"Yeah, I went over to Lannie's club. They go up there and jack off. He's got some magazines."

"I know all about it." And I kind of do. I gave Lannie the magazines over a year ago. I found them in the vacant lot. Somebody had thrown them out of a car and they were blown into Roto's fort, which was nothing but a hole with a car battery sitting on a dirt shelf. In war, that was the radio. I remember one picture from all three magazines. It showed a woman sitting at a glass table as if she was about to eat a bowl of peaches. She had huge, featureless breasts that fell over onto the table in two piles. At that time it had seemed the most hilarious photograph I had ever seen. And, even in retrospect, it seemed that someone had been out to make fun of the woman. I could hear the photographer pleading, "Come on, now lean forward and flop your tits up on the table and take a rest."

"They showed me how to do it. They did it for me the first time. It's great; it makes you feel all lit up."

"I'll bet."

"And then you can go back whenever you want and see the magazines."

"If you join."

"Yeah, you have to join, but it's great."

We're about to step off the asphalt playground and go down the grassy slope to the walkbridge across the river, when there's a friction noise and a bicycle slips by in front of us. There is no rider. It runs in a slowing curl and finally clatters to the pavement. I already know that it's Butch's bike because the front wheel is smaller than the other, but Fenn calls, "What the hell?" Then I see Butch clear back across the painted asphalt, hanging by his hands on the chinning bar where he dismounted like a cowboy on a branch, sending his bike after us. I can barely see him; he looks like a brown flag.

"Hey, Butch!" I call.

"Better get on to the party, boys!" he cries back. Then I see that he's not coming over as he lifts a knee through his hanging arms, and swings himself up onto the bar.

"The kid's got a problem," Fenn says. He's walked on ahead. "Butch is beyond help."

I look at Fenn in his new glasses and that red shirt and I hardly know him. This kid used to be a friend of mine, I think. And now I spot another difference: This Fenn is two inches taller than I am. That wasn't true at the beginning of the summer. His face is different too in a way I can't describe except to say it seems to have more separate parts. And his eyebrows have grown together over his nose.

On the walkbridge, we stop and lean on the rail and look upstream. Cling and some of his punky pals from the junior high are upriver swinging on a rope. We can see the orange stars of their cigarettes in the dark, and the ape-form Cling is outlined clearly against the river as he swings back and forth on the rope. Each time he swings back, his pals won't let him land, and eventually, he ends up, slower and slower, hanging there straight over the river.

"You dirty bastards!" he says the twenty feet across to the group, and he drops into the water.

We hear the splash, and I lean over the rail and fold "Understanding Puberty" in half again and again and then twist it into a fat cigar and release it over the river. It hits the water right alongside a white quart bottle which glints once coming out from under the bridge, and we hurry and ramble after it along the ruined river trail, throwing rocks as fast as we can find them. Fenn finally swamps the bottle by heaving a boulder the size of a skull right next to it. It's not as satisfying as hearing the muffled crash and watching a bottle really go down, but we stand there in the thicket, breathing, and for a moment, it's just like old times; we're just dressed differently.

"Hey," Fenn says, pointing: "Check that!" There across the river, high in a tree, which is dead from the waist up like so many of the giant trees in the river vines, hangs a bra, a brassiere. Fenn laughs. The bra is outlined perfectly against the last yellow tinge in the purple sky. "Think of that," he says. "Think of what went in that."

"I can imagine." I lie. I can't imagine. I can't imagine how it ever got up there. I've never seen anything so wrong, so out of place.

On the way back to the bridge, Fenn asks, "Are you going to dance?"

"I don't know. Are you?"

"You kidding? Name one girl in our class who isn't a skagg."

Linda's house is a long, low brick house, much nicer than anything in our neighborhood. I've seen pictures of houses like this in magazines and they are called "Ranch Houses" for some reason. The brick walkway up to her front door is curved, and they have a miniature street lamp in the front yard. It's a stupid idea because it ruins what could have been a decent Sockball field. The front door has an "A" in it, and Mrs. Aikens opens the door and welcomes us in.

There are a bunch of kids in the kitchen who spill out a large sliding glass door onto a patio. The kids in the kitchen are mainly girls and the kids on the patio are mainly boys. Lannie is out there nodding at Mr. Aikens over the barbecue grill. Lannie can con anybody. Standing there with his black hair combed out of his face and his hands in his pockets, nodding at Mr. Aikens, he looks as if he's never punched little kids in the throat for a nickel. Cling won't be here; he dropped out of school "in first grade!" he says. Behind Lannie, I see Keith Gurber talking to the Starkey twins. They're all drinking orange soda pop. Max has one hand in the air, flattened as a plane, turning real slow figure eights. Keith is transfixed. Before I can get out of the kitchen, Carol Wilkes turns from where she's been filling bowls with potato chips and says, "Larry! What have you been doing all summer?"

I look at her face, and it is a beautiful face, my favorite face in the whole grade school. Her eyes are taller than they are wide and her upper lip flips up a little. It makes her look like she's always about to flirt. "Not much, Carol," I say. I remember everything I've ever said to her. "Playing baseball." A strange impulse rises in me to say to her, "Carol, you know you're one of my favorite people," or some such silly thing, but I will never be able to. Girls are always older than you; you can never catch up enough to know them well. Before I can embarrass myself, Mrs. Aikens takes my arm and says she wants to show me where the soft drinks are. She takes me in the bright yellow utility room right across from the kitchen.

"Well?" Mrs. Aikens says.

"It's a nice room."

"No, Larry, do you know where the soft drinks are?"

"In the fridge?"

"No!" she laughs and laughs as if I'd said "in the hedge." I kind of smile while she has a good time laughing. She recovers and says, "No, no, no. Here they are!" She opens the washing machine lid and I see that it's full of ice. "What would you like?"

"Is there any creme soda?" I'm just going along with her all the way.

She reaches into the washing machine and extracts a tall bottle of Nehi Creme Soda. "And here's the opener." It's dangling on a string above the washer. "I read about this party trick in 'Party Hints' in the paper. Of course, you have to unplug the washer to be safe!" She bends and shows me the three-prong washer plug as proof that we're safe.

"That's a great party idea, Mrs. Aikens," I say, hoping she'll just hand me the soda and let me go. "I certainly wouldn't have thought of that."

"Yes, well, a good party starts with good planning!" Finally, she awards me the creme soda and we step back into the kitchen, and I'm able to fade out into the backyard. Linda Aikens is in the corner of the patio, fiddling with her hi-fi. She has a wire rack full of 45's, and she's arranging and rearranging them.

"Hi, Linda."

"Larry!" She turns to smile at me. There's a record on every one of her fingers. "Oh, I'm glad you came." And you know, the way she says it is right: she means it. She's parted her dark hair in a new way, right down the middle, real tight and shiny, and the rest of her hair is pinned up in two braids. She kind of looks like Heidi in the movie.

I hold up my soda. "In the washer. You want one?"

"No, I want to get the records ready. Will you dance with me later?"

The backyard is hard to figure out. There is another lamp post on one side gathering bugs in a busy halo, above four wrought iron chairs, and instead of a fence a tall hedge surrounds the whole thing. The lawn is great; it just makes you want to practice a few slides. They're not storing anything out here, any lumber, a wheelbarrow or even an old boat, and it doesn't look like anything is *played* out here. The yard is filling up with kids from Edison, but it still seems like such a waste, all that thick lawn. It's a hard yard to figure. I say hello to Mr. Aikens, who looks pretty young to be somebody's father. He's got freckles on his forehead. "You guys all know each other?" he says to us and I say yes, we do. Lannie gives me a sly look.

I'm mainly trying to do the three things my mother told me: stand straight up; not drink my soda in four gulps; not hang around the potato chips. Fenn is hanging around the potato chips. Evidently, his mother didn't talk to him.

Then for a while, Mr. Aikens is serving hot dogs and Mrs. Aikens is showing everybody the washing machine. Then Linda puts on a record, "Stagger Lee," a song I never could understand, and kids start dancing on the cement patio. It's mainly the bigger kids, Howell and Kidder, kids who aren't afraid of having girlfriends.

I watch the group dance for a while and then between "Twenty-Six Miles" and "Who Wrote the Book of Love" I stand up and take my paper plate back into the kitchen. Though I made my soda last longer than any in the history of my life, it has been empty for half an hour. The bottle's warm. No one is in the kitchen except two girls who are leaning over the sink to look out the window at the dancers. Turning into the utility room, I bump into Mrs. Aikens. I show her the empty bottle and make a friendly gesture toward the washer, saying, "Unplugged, right?" But she's taking another bag of chips outside, and so I am spared a second tour, and simply help myself to another cold bottle of creme soda.

When they play "At the Hop" about a dozen kids do the hop, a dance I can't master, and it looks pretty neat the way they raise one heel over the other toe and then slip into the opposite position by just lifting their shoulder. Something like that. Now, Keith Gurber is handling all the records. He runs the projector at school sometimes and he's good at those technical things, only occasionally snagging his dangling belt in the mechanism.

"I haven't seen you dance yet." Linda has come up behind me on the lawn. "Are you ready?"

"Sure, I'm ready." The party has continued easily through the evening. I've mainly been experimenting with new ways to hold my soda so as not to warm it up so much with my hand. I've watched Fenn move to three stations, each beside a recently filled potato chip bowl, and stuff his face. Tomorrow there's going to be a triangular trail in the lawn from his feeding pattern. For a few minutes Grant and Max and some guys started having chicken fights, riding piggyback all over the yard, but Mrs. Aikens stopped that. She rushed out and asked Max, who was riding on Grant's shoulders, if he was all right. It took the spirit out of it for them, I guess, because they all settled down and headed for the washing machine.

But mostly it has been couples dancing, doing the Twist and the Hop and a little of the Pony and once Linda and Carol led four other girls in the Stroll, which looked real smooth and ancient, like a dance they'd known forever. I thought: How do they know how to do these things? And now, I stand with Linda Aikens, one arm on her hip, the other in her hand, as the next record drops. I look over at Keith and he smiles at me. He's a kid just happy to be playing records. He hasn't had to drop any pamphlets in the river or have his friends ask if he jacks off. The song is "Earth Angel" and as it starts, I commence the two-step as taught by Mr. Donaldson, but instead of it becoming the stepping and steering activity I'd known last year, this dance changes. First, Linda's head collapses against my chin. For a minute I think I might have to carry her to a chair. But no, she's moving, she's all right, she's just moving slowly in microscopic shuffle steps. I can do this. I can do this. I think: I can do this. For a while I concentrate hard on not kicking her over as I stare out on the lawn where my half bottle of creme soda stands alone. Then, without trying, I've got it. Linda's forehead, the very start of her part, is against the corner of my mouth, and though I try to stand up straight, I soon find my head against her head that way as we dance. It is the easiest thing I have ever done.

As the song ends, I peel my face from Linda's forehead; sweat has stuck us together. Linda says. "Just a minute," to me and goes over to give Keith some help. While I'm standing on the edge of the patio, Fenn calls my name and I watch him walk over and gently toe my soda over onto its side. He smiles at me as if he's just done a classic party stunt. At this distance, I look at his new chrome glasses and red shirt and I swear I don't know him anymore. I don't really even know where I am or what I'm doing, but Linda is back at my hand, pulling me through the dancers, off the patio, around the redwood trellis, into the darkness of the side yard. We can hear the music start:

"Poetry in Motion." When Linda stops, I almost run into her. The sweat in the fringe of her hair is reflected in the starlight.

"Did you get my note?"

"Yeah," I say. She is still holding my hand. "I did." She doesn't say anything, just looks up at me, so I add: "I found it in my book."

I hear the part of the song I like: that neat rhyme: "motion" and "ocean." Linda looks up at me with a look I've never seen anybody make, not even in movies, and she lifts her arms around my neck and pulls herself up as I reach down and we kiss. I don't know if it is a long or a short kiss, just that she is against me, her lips against mine, and when I place my arms around her back one of my hands flattens on her bra and I move that hand. I look once and see her eyes are closed.

Then she stands back down on her heels and smiles at me, looks at the ground, lets go of my hand, and walks back around to the party. The first thing I do when she leaves is look around to see if anybody saw us; then I realize I am not going back to the party. I can do everything there is to do, dance, find soda in the washing machine, stand up straight, not gobble the potato chips, but I cannot walk back around that trellis and have Fenn smile at me again with his big fake face. What I do is look at my shoes, those little tassels.

I find the redwood side gate which is six feet tall, but I can't work the old latch, so I pull and scramble up and finally place a foot on top of it to climb over. But, with one of my legs still hanging and kicking, the gate starts to swing open. I can't do anything but ride it around until it stops against the house, and I find myself looking in the bathroom window. Carol Wilkes is sitting in there knee to knee with Linda, who is sitting on the tub, and they are talking like two maniacs planning an escape. Linda has her hands over both of her ears as if to hold her head together, I guess, and, though I can't hear a word they say, it is the one time in my life when I am sure that somebody is talking about me.

DEBORAH EISENBERG

A LESSON IN TRAVELING LIGHT

FROM VANITY FAIR

∽

DURING THE BEST TIME, when it was still warm in the afternoons and the sky was especially blue and the smell of spoiling apples rose up from the ground, Lee and I drove down from the high meadows with our stuff in the van, looking for someplace to live.

The night before we left we went down the road to say good-bye to Tom and Johanna. Johanna looked like glass, but Tom was flushed and in a violent good humor. He passed the bottle of Jack Daniel's back and forth to Lee and slapped him on the back and talked a mile a minute about different places he had lived and people he had met and bets he had won and whatnot, so I figured he and Johanna had been fighting before we got there.

"Done a lot of traveling?" Tom asked me.

"No," I said. He knew I hadn't.

"Well, you'll enjoy it," he said. "You'll enjoy it."

Tom was making an effort, I suppose, because I was leaving.

"Hey," he said to Lee, having finished his effort, "are you going to see Miles?"

"I guess we might," Lee said. "Yeah, actually, we could."

"Who's Miles?" I said.

"Is he still with that girl?" Tom said. "The one who—"

"No," Lee interrupted, laughing. "He's back with Natalie."

"Really?" said Johanna. "Listen, if you do see him, tell him I still wear the parka he left at our place that day." Tom stared at her, but she smiled.

"Who's Miles?" I said.

"Someone who used to live around here. Before I brought you back up the mountain with me," Lee said, turning full around to me. His eyes when he's been thinking about something else are like a blaze in an empty warehouse, and I caught my breath.

After dinner Lee and I walked back to our place, and as the house came into view I tried to fix it in my memory. It already looked skeletal, though, like something dead on a beach.

"That's what it is," Lee said. "Old bones. A carapace. You're creating pain for yourself by trying to make it something more."

I looked again, letting it be bones, and felt light. I wanted to leave behind with the house the old bones of my needs and opinions. I wanted to be unencumbered, a warrior like Lee. When we'd met, Lee had said to me, "I feel like I have to take care of you."

"That's good," I had said.

"No it isn't," he had said.

I wondered if he ever thought about places he had lived, other faces, old girlfriends. Once in a while he seemed bowed down with a weight of shelved memories. But having freight in storage is what you trade to travel light, I sometimes thought, and at those moments it was as much for him as for me that I wanted Lee so badly to stay with me.

The first night of driving we stopped in Pennsylvania.

"We're very close to Miles and Natalie's," Lee said. "It would be logical to stop by there tomorrow."

"Where do they live?" I said.

Lee took out a big US road map. "They're over here, in Baltimore."

"That's so far," I said, following his finger.

"In a sense," he said. "But on the other hand, look at, say, Pittsburgh." His finger alighted inches from where we were. "Or Columbus."

"Or Louisville!" I said. "Look how far that is—to Louisville!"

"You think that's far?" Lee said. "Well, listen to this— ready? Poplar Bluff!"

"Tulsa!" I said. "Wait—Oklahoma City!"

We both started to shout.

"Cheyenne!"

"Flagstaff!"

"Needles, Barstow, Bishop!"

"Eureka!" we both yelled at once.

We sat back and eyed the map. "That was some trip," Lee said.

"Are we going to do that?" I said.

Lee shrugged. "We'll go as far as we want," he said.

After all that, it looked on the map like practically no distance to Baltimore, but by the time we reached it I was sick of sitting in the van, and I hoped Natalie and Miles were the sort of people who would think of making us something to eat.

"What if they don't like me?" I said when we parked.

"Why wouldn't they like you?" Lee said.

I didn't know. I didn't know them.

"They'll like you," Lee said. "They're friends of mine."

Their place turned out to be a whole floor of a building divided up by curves of glass bricks. Darkness eddied around us and compressed the light near its sources, and the sounds our shoes made on the wood floor came back to us from a distance.

Natalie must have been just about my age, but there might be an infinite number of ways to be twenty, I saw, shocked. She sat us down on leather sofas the size of whales and brought us things to drink on a little tray, and she wore a single huge red earring. It was clear that she and Miles and Lee had talked together a lot before. There were dense, equidistant silences, and when one of them said something, it was like a stone landing in a still pond. I watched Natalie's earring while a comma of her black hair sliced it into changing shapes. After a while Miles and Lee stood up. They were going to see some building in another part of the city. "Anything we need, babe?" Miles asked Natalie.

"Pick up a couple of bottles of wine," she said. "Oh, yeah, and some glue for this." She opened her fist to disclose a second red earring in pieces in her palm.

"What's the matter?" I heard Lee say from far away, and it was to me.

Natalie and I moved over to the kitchen to make dinner, and she asked me how long Lee and I had been together.

"He's so fabulous," she said. "Are you thinking of getting married?"

"Not really," I said. We'd discussed it once when we'd gotten together. "It seems fairly pointless. Is there anything I can do?"

"Here," she said, handing me a knife and an onion. "Miles and I got married. His parents made us. They said they'd cut Miles off if we didn't."

"Is it different?" I said.

"Sort of," she said. "It's turned out to be an okay thing, actually. We used to, when we had a problem or something, just talk about it to the point where we didn't have to deal with it anymore. But now I guess we try to fix it. Does Lee still hate watercress?"

"No," I said. Watercress? I thought.

"It's very good," Natalie said, "but I still wouldn't be surprised if it ended tomorrow."

"Natalie," I said, "would you pierce my ears?"

"Sure," she said. "Just let me finish this stuff first." She took back from me the knife and the onion, which was still whole because I hadn't known what to do with it.

When Lee and Miles got back, I put the ice cube I was holding against my earlobe into the sink, and we all sat down for dinner.

"Nice," Lee said, holding his glass. Lee and I drank wine out of the same glasses we drank everything else out of, and it was not the sort of wine you'd have anything to say about, so Lee raising his graceful glass was an odd sight—a sight that seemed to lift the table slightly, causing it to hover in the vibrating dimness.

"It is odd, isn't it," I said, feeling oddness billow, "that this is the way we make our bodies live."

Miles lifted his eyebrows.

"I mean," I said, forgetting what I did mean as I noticed that Lee had picked the watercress out of his salad, "I mean that it's odd to sit like this, in body holders around a disk, and move little heaps of matter from smaller disks to our mouths on little metal shovels. It seems like an odd way to keep our bodies alive."

I looked around at the others.

"Seems odd to me," Miles said. "I usually lie on the floor. With my chin in a trough. Sucking rocks."

"*Miles,*" Natalie said, and giggled.

That night the clean, clean sheets wouldn't get warm, so I climbed out of bed and put on Lee's jacket and sat down to watch Lee sleep. He shifted pleasurably, and in the moonlight he looked as comfortable and dangerous as a lion. I watched him and waited for day, when he would get up and I would give him back his jacket and we could leave this place where he drank wine from a wineglass and strangers knew him so well.

The next day Natalie and Miles asked if we wanted to stay, but Lee said we couldn't. We had planned to start out by the end of summer, he told them, and we were late.

Outside we saw how the light was already thin and banded across the highway, and we drove fast into sunset and winter. We were quiet mostly, and when we spoke, it was softly, like TV cowboys expecting an ambush.

That evening we got medicine at a drugstore because my ear had swollen way up and I had a fever. I laid my head back into sliding dreams and woke into free-fall.

"Hey," Lee said, smoothing my hair back from my face, "you're asleep. You know that?" He scooped me over into his lap, and I nuzzled into his foggy-gray T-shirt. "So look, killer," he said, "you want to stay here or you want to come in back with me?"

The next day my fever was gone and my ear was better.

For a while we were still where the expressways are thick coils and headlights and brake lights interweave at night in splendor. In the dark we would pull off to sleep in the corner of a truck stop or a lot by a small highway, and in the morning, heat or cold, intensified by our metal shell, would wake us tangled in our blankets, and we would make love while fuel trucks roared past, rattling the van. Then we would look out of the window to see where we were and drive off to find a diner or a Howard Johnson's.

We were spending more money than we had expected to, and Lee said that his friend Carlos, who lived in St. Louis, might be able to find him a few days' work. Lee looked through some scraps of paper and found Carlos's address, but when we got there a group of people standing on the front steps told us that Carlos had moved. The group looked like a legation, with representatives of the different sizes and ages of humans, that was waiting to impart some terrible piece of information to a certain traveler. One of them gave us a new address for Carlos which was near Nashville. Lee had never mentioned Carlos, so I assumed they weren't very close friends, but expectation had whetted Lee's appetite to see him, it seemed, because we left the group waiting on the steps and turned south.

Lee and Carlos were all smiles to see each other.

"What kind of money are you looking to make?" Carlos asked when we had settled ourselves in the living room.

"Nothing much," Lee said. "Just a little contingency fund. I'm clean these days."

"Well, listen," Carlos said, "why don't you take the store for a week or two. I had to fire the guy I had managing it, and I've been dealing with it myself, but this would be an opportunity for me to look into some other stuff I've had my eye on." Carlos opened beers for himself and Lee. "Could I get you something?" he asked me, frowning.

"I'd like some beer, too," I said.

"Here," he said. "Wait. I'll get you a glass."

"Get back to Miami much?" Lee said.

"Too crowded these days, if you know what I mean,"

Carlos said. "Besides, I've pretty much stopped doing anything I can't handle locally. This is just where I live now, for whatever reason. And I've got my business. I don't know. It's a basis, you know? Something to continue from." He looked away from Lee and sighed.

During the days, when Lee and Carlos were out, I sat in back watching the sooty light travel from one side of the yard to the other. Sometimes a little boy played in an adjoining yard, jabbing with a stick at the clumps of grass there, which were stiff and gray with dirt. He was gray with dirt himself, and gray under the dirt. His nose ran, and the blue appliquéd bear on the front of his overalls looked stunned.

I wondered what that boy had in mind for himself—whether his attack on the grass was some sort of self-devised preparation for an adulthood of authority and usefulness, or whether he pictured himself forever on that bit of dirt, heading toward death in bear overalls of graduated size. I took to going in, when I saw him, and watching TV.

The night before we left Carlos's, Lee and I were awake late. We didn't have much to say, and after a while I noticed I was hungry.

"What? After that meal I made?" Lee said. "All right, let's go out."

Carlos was still awake, too, sitting in the living room with headphones on.

"Great," he said. "There's an all-night diner with sensational burgers."

"Burgers," Lee said. "You still eat that shit?"

Going into the diner, Lee and Carlos were a phalanx in themselves with their jackets and jeans and boots and belts, and I was proud to have been hungry. I ordered warrior food, and soon the waitress rendered up to me a plate of lacy-edged eggs with a hummock of potatoes and butter-stained toast, and to Lee and Carlos huge, aromatic burgers.

"Are you going to see Kathryn?" Carlos asked.

"I don't know," Lee said. "It depends."

"I'd like to see her myself, come to think of it. She's a fantastic woman," Carlos said, balancing a french fry beam on a french fry house he was making. "I really love that woman.

You know, it's been great having you guys stay, but it makes me realize how much I miss other people around here. Maybe I should go out to the Coast or something. Or at least establish some sort of nonridiculous romance."

"What about Sarah?" Lee said.

"Sarah," Carlos said. "Jesus." He turned to me. "Has Lee told you all about this marvel of technology?"

"No," I said.

"Well, I mean, listen, man," Carlos said, shaking his head. "She's a hot-looking lady, no question about it, but when I said nonridiculous I had in mind someone you wouldn't be afraid to run into in the living room." He shook his head again and started drumming his knife on the table. "She sure is one hot-looking lady, though. Well, you know her."

"We have to get up really early," I said.

"That's okay," Lee said, but Carlos stood up. He looked exhausted.

"Yeah, sorry," he said. "Let's pull the plug on it."

Over the next few days I thought of Carlos often. His face had been shadowed when we said good-bye, so I couldn't recall it, and I thought how if I had been his girlfriend instead of Lee's I would have stayed there with him in that living room that seemed to just suck up light and would have heard from the inside the door slam and the van's motor start.

Lee and I drove back east a bit, to have a look at the Smokies. We parked the van in a campground under a bruise-colored sunset and set off on foot to pick up some food to cook outside on a fire. But there were bugs, even though it was chilly, and the rutted clay road slipped and smacked underfoot, so we stopped at a Bar-B-Q place, where doughy families shouted at each other under throbbing flourescent lights.

I had a headache. "It's incredible," I said, "how fast every place you go gets to be home. We've only just parked at that campground, but it's already home. And yesterday Carlos's place seemed like home. Now that feels like years ago."

"That's why it's good to travel," Lee said. "It reminds you what life really is. Finished?' he said. "Let's go."

"Let's," I said. "Let's go home." I inserted my finger under the canopy of his T-shirt sleeve, but he didn't notice particularly.

In time we came to a part of the country where mounds of what Lee said were uranium tailings winked in the sunlight, and moonlight made grand the barbed-wire lace around testing sites, Lee said they were, and subterranean missiles. It was quite flat, but I felt that we were crossing it vertically instead of horizontally. I felt I was on ropes behind Lee, struggling up a sheer rock face, my footing too unsure to allow me to look anywhere except at the cliff I clung to.

"What is it you're afraid of?" Lee said.

I told him I didn't know.

"Think about it," he said. "There's nothing in your mind that isn't yours."

I wondered if I should go back. I could call Tom and Johanna, I thought, but at the same instant I realized that they weren't really friends of mine. I didn't know Johanna very well, actually, and Tom and I, in fact, disliked each other. I had gone to bed with him one day months earlier when I went over to borrow a vise grip. He had seemed to want to, and I suppose I thought I would be less uncomfortable around him if I did. That was a mistake, as it turned out. I stayed at least as uncomfortable as before, and the only thing he said afterward was that I had a better body than he'd expected. It was a long time before I realized that what he'd wanted was to have slept with Lee's girlfriend.

When I got back home that afternoon carrying the vise grip that Tom remembered to hand to me when I left, I felt as if it were Lee who had spent the afternoon rolling around with Johanna, not me with Tom, and I was splitting apart with jealousy. I couldn't keep my hands off Lee, which annoyed him—he was trying to do something to an old motorcycle that had been sitting around in the yard.

"Lee," I said, "are you attracted to Johanna?"

"What kind of question is that?" he said, sorting through the parts spread out on the dirt.

"A question question," I said.

"Everyone's attracted to everyone else," he said.

I wasn't. I wasn't attracted to Tom, for instance.

"Why do you think she stays with Tom?" I said.

"He's all right," Lee said.

"He's horrible, Lee," I said. "And he's mean. He's vain."

"You're too hard on people," Lee said. "Tom's all tied up, that's all. He's frightened."

"It's usual to be frightened," I said.

"Well, Tom can't handle it," Lee said. "He's afraid he has no resources to fall back on."

"Poor guy," I said. "He can fall back on mine. So are you attracted to Johanna?"

"Don't" Lee said, standing up and wiping his hands on an oily cloth. "Okay? Don't get shabby, please."

He had gone inside then, without looking at me.

Now home was wherever Lee and I were, and I had to control my fear by climbing toward that moment when Lee would haul me up to level ground and we would slip off our ropes and stare around us at whatever was the terrain on which we found ourselves.

We started to have trouble with the van and decided to stop because Lee knew someone we could stay with near Denver while he fixed it. We pulled up outside a small apartment building and rang a bell marked "Dr. Peel Prayerwheel."

"What's his real name?" I asked Lee.

"That is," Lee said.

"Parents had some strong opinions, huh," I said.

"He found it for himself," Lee said.

Peel had a nervous voice that rushed in a fluty stream from his large body. His hair was long except on the top of his head, where there was none, and elaborate shaded tattoos covered his arms and neck and probably everything under his T-shirt.

We stood in the middle of the kitchen. "We'll put your things in the other room," Peel said, "and I'll bring my cot in here. That's best, that's best."

"We don't want to inconvenience you, Peel," Lee said.

"No, no," he said. "I'm only too happy to see you and your old lady in my house. All the times I came to you. When I was in the hospital. Anything I can do for you. I really mean it. You know that, buddy.

"He took me in," Peel said, turning to me. "He was like family." Peel kept standing there blinking at the floor, but he couldn't seem to decide what else to say.

While Lee looked around town for parts and worked on the van, Peel and I mostly sat at the kitchen table and drank huge amounts of tea.

"Maybe you'd like a beer," he said one afternoon.

"Sure," I said.

"Right away. Right away," he said, pulling on his jacket.

"Oh—not if we have to go out," I said.

"You're sure?" he said. "Really? Because we can, if you want."

"Not unless you want one," I said.

"No, no," he said. "Never drink alcohol. Uncontrolled substance. Jumps right out of the bottle, whoomp! . . . Well, no real harm done, just an ugly moment . . ." He blushed then for some reason, very dark.

When Lee came home, Peel and I would open up cans of soup and packages of saltines. "Used to cook like a bastard," Peel said. "But that's behind me now. Behind me."

One morning when we got up, Peel was standing in the middle of the kitchen.

"Good morning, Peel," I said.

"Good morning," he said. "Good morning." He stood there, looking at the floor.

"Do you want some tea?" I said.

"No thank you," he said. Then he looked at Lee.

"Well, buddy," he said. "I got a check from my mother this morning."

"Was that good or bad?" I asked Lee later. Lee shrugged. "How does he usually live?" I said.

"Disability," Lee said. "He was in the army."

At night I felt so lonely I woke Lee up, but when we made love I kept thinking of Peel standing in the kitchen looking at the floor.

One morning I had a final cup of tea with Peel while Lee went to get gas.

"Thank you, Peel," I said. "You've been very kind."

"Not kind," Peel said. "It doesn't bear scrutiny. I had some problems, see, and your old man looked out for me. He and Annie, they used to take me in. He's a fine man. And he's lucky to have you. I can see that, little buddy. He's very lucky in that."

I reached over and touched one of Peel's tattoos, a naked girl with devil horns and huge angel wings.

"That's my lady," Peel said. "Do you like her? That's the lady that flies on my arm."

A day or two later Lee and I parked and sat in back eating sandwiches. Then Lee studied maps while I experimented along his spine making my mouth into a shape that could be placed over each vertebra in turn.

"Cut that out," Lee said. "Unless you want to lose an hour or two."

"I don't mind," I said.

"Oh, there," Lee said. "We're just outside of Cedar City."

I looked over Lee's shoulder. "Hey, Las Vegas," I said. "I had a friend in school who got married and moved there."

"Do you want to visit her?" Lee said.

"Not really," I said.

"It isn't too far," he said. "And we can always use a shower and a bit of floor space."

"No," I said.

"Why not?" Lee said. "If she was your friend."

I didn't say anything.

Lee sighed. "What's the matter?" He turned and put his arms around me. "Speak to me."

"We'll never be alone," I said into his T-shirt.

"We're alone right now," Lee said.

"No," I said. "We're always going to stay with your friends."

"It's just temporary," Lee said. "Until we find a place we want to be for ourselves. Anyhow, she isn't my friend—she's your friend."

"Used to be," I said. Then I said, "Besides, if we stayed with her she'd be your friend."

"Sure," Lee said. "My friend and your friend. The people we've stayed with are your friends now too."

"Not," I said, letting slow tears soak into his T-shirt.

"Well, they would be if you wanted to think of them as

friends," Lee said. His voice was tense with the effort of patience. "You're the one who's shutting them out."

"Someone isn't your friend just because they happen to be standing next to you," I said.

Lee lifted his arms from around me. He sighed and leaned his head back, putting his hands against his eyes.

"I'm sorry you're so unhappy," he said.

"You're sorry I'm a problem," I said.

"You're not a problem," he said.

"Well, then I should be," I said. "You don't even care enough about me for me to be a problem."

"You know," Lee said, "sometimes I think I care about you more than you care about me."

"Sure," I said. "If caring about someone means you don't want anything from them. In fact, you know what?" I said, but I had no idea myself what I was going to say next, so it was whatever came out with the torrent of sobs I'd unstoppered. "We've called all your friends because you don't want to be with me, and you even want people I know to help you not be with me, but we won't call my parents and they're only less than a day away anyhow because you don't want to know anything about my life because I might turn out to be real and then you'd have to figure out what to do with me instead of waiting for me to evaporate because you're tired of me and we're going to keep going from one friend of yours to another and making other people into friends of yours and then if I don't just happen to fall off a cliff they'll all help you think of some way to leave me so you can go back to Annie whoever she is or grind me into a paste just like come to think of it you probably did to Annie anyhow and send me back in a jar for Tom to bury."

"Oh, Jesus," Lee said. "What is going on."

I leaned my head against his arm, and let myself cry loudly and wetly.

"All right," Lee said, folding his arms around me again. "Okay."

"Come on," Lee said after a while. "We'll find a phone and call your parents."

I was still blinking tears when we pulled into an immense

parking lot, at the horizon of which was a supermarket, also immense, that served no visible town. It had become evening, and the supermarket and the smaller stores attached to it were all closed, even though there were lights inside them.

"There—" Lee said. "There's a phone, way over there." He reached for the shift, but I jumped out.

"I'll walk," I said.

There was a shallow ring of mountains all around, dark against the greenish sky, and night was filling up the basin we were in. The glass phone booth, so solitary in the parking lot, looked like a tiny, primitive spaceship.

I rarely spoke to my parents, and I had never seen the mobile home where they'd now lived for years. It couldn't be possible, I thought, that I had only to dial this phone to speak to them. Why would the people who were my parents be living at the other end of that phone call?

When I sat down inside the phone booth and closed the door, a light went on. Perhaps when I lifted the receiver instructions would issue from it. How surprised Lee would be to see the little glass compartment tremble, then lift from the ground and arc above the mountains. I picked up the receiver, unleashing only the dial tone, and dialed my parents' number.

My mother was out playing cards, my father told me. "Why aren't you with her?" I said. "I thought you liked to play, too."

"You thought wrong," my father said. "And anyway," he said, "I can't stand the scum she's scooped up in this place."

"Well," I said. "I guess you've probably found friends of your own there."

"Friends," my father said. "Poor SOBs could only make it as far as a trailer park—you'd think they were living in Rolls-Royces."

"Well," I said.

"They're nosy, too," my father said. "These people are so nosy it isn't funny."

"Sorry to hear it," I said.

"It's nothing to me," my father said. "I don't go out, anyhow. My leg's too bad."

A tide shrank in my chest.

"Hear anything from Mike and Philly?" I said.

"Yeah—Philly's doing quite well, as a matter of fact," my father said. "Quite well. Spoke to him just the other week. He's managing some kind of club, apparently."

"Probably a whorehouse," I said, not into the phone.

"What?" my father said.

I didn't say anything.

"What?" he said again.

"That's great," I said. "What about Mike?"

"Mike," my father said. "He left Sharon again. That clown. Sharon called and said would we take the kids for a while. Of course we would have if we could. I don't think she's too great for those kids, anyhow."

A Greyhound bus had appeared in the parking lot, and a man carrying a small suitcase climbed out. I wondered where he could possibly be going. He walked into the darkness, and then the bus was gone in darkness, too.

"What about you?" my father said. "What're you up to? Still got that boyfriend?"

"Yes," I said. I glanced over at the van. It looked miniature in front of the vast supermarket window, itself miniature against the line of mountains in the sky. "In fact," I said, "we were thinking of coming to visit you."

"Jesus," said my father. "Don't tell me this one's going to marry you. Hey," he said suspiciously, "where're you calling from?"

It was almost totally dark, and cold lights were scattered in the hills. People probably lived up there, I thought, in little ranch-style houses where tricycles, wheels in the air, and broken toys lay on frail patches of lawn like weapons on a deserted battlefield.

"I said, where are you calling from?" my father said again.

"Home," I said. "I have to get off now, though."

As soon as I hung up, the phone started to ring. It would be the operator asking for more money. It was still ringing when I climbed into the van, but I could hardly hear it from there.

Lee and I sat side by side for a moment. "It's peaceful here," I said.

"Yeah," Lee said.

"No one was home," I said.

"All right," Lee said—there were different reasons he might have let me say that, I thought—"let's go on."

That night I apologized.

"It's all right," Lee said.

"No," I said. "And I really do like your friends. I liked staying with them."

"We won't do it anymore," Lee said.

"We can't stay at motels," I said. "And it's nice to get out of the van."

Lee didn't say anything.

"Besides," I said, "we don't even know where we're going."

I wondered if Lee had fallen asleep. "What about your friend Kathryn"—I said it softly, in case he had—"that Carlos mentioned? Would you like to see her?"

"Well," Lee said finally, "she doesn't live that far from here."

As soon as we climbed out of the van in Kathryn's driveway a girl flew out of the door, landing in Lee's arms. They laughed and kissed each other and laughed again.

"Maggie," Lee said, "what are you doing here?"

"Fact is, Lee," she said, "Buzzy's partner got sent up, so I'm staying here awhile case anybody's looking for anybody."

"Yeah?" Lee said. "Is Buzzy here?"

"He's up in Portland," she said. "He said it would be better if we went in different directions, just till this cools off. I guess he's got a honey up there."

Lee shook his head, looking at her.

"Never mind, baby," she said. "I'll win, you know that. I always win." Lee laughed again.

Inside, Kathryn put out her hands and Lee held them. Then she looked at me. "You're cold," she said. "Stand by the fire, and I'll get you something to put on."

"I'm okay," I said. "Anyhow, I've got things in the van." But she took a huge, flossy blanket from the back of the sofa and wound it slowly around and around me.

"You look like a princess!" Maggie said. "Doesn't she? Look, Lee. She looks like a princess that's—what are those stories?—under a dark enchantment." Kathryn stood back and looked.

We drank big hot glasses of applejack and cinnamon, and the fire splashed shadows across us. Kathryn and Maggie and Lee talked, their words scattering and shifting with the fire.

Numbness inched into my body, and my mind struggled to make sense of what my ears heard. Maggie had left the room—I grasped that—and Lee and Kathryn were talking about Carlos.

"I miss him. You know that, Lee?" Kathryn was saying. "I think about a lot of people, but I miss Carlos."

"You should call him," I tried to say, but my sleeping voice couldn't.

"Well," Lee said.

"Wait—" I wanted my voice to say. I knew I wouldn't be able to listen much longer. "He talked about you—"

"I don't know," Lee said. "I found myself feeling sorry for him. It was pretty bad. I hated to feel that way, but it seems like he hasn't grown. He just hasn't grown, and the thing is, he's lost his nerve."

"Kathryn—" I wanted to say, and couldn't, and couldn't, "Carlos wants to see you."

I slid helplessly into sleep, and it must have taken me some time to struggle back to the surface, because when I'd managed to, Lee was saying, "Yeah, she is. She's very nice. We're having some problems now, though. And I don't know if I can help her anymore."

I heard it as a large globe floating near me, just out of reach. I tried to hold it, to turn it this way and that, but it bobbed away on the surface as I slipped under again.

I woke in bed in another room, bound and sweating in the blanket, and I could hear Lee's and Kathryn's voices as a murmur. I flung the blanket away and pushed myself out of my clothes as sleep swallowed me once more.

In the morning I awoke puffed and gluey from unshed tears. I wrapped the blanket around myself and followed voices and coffee smell into the kitchen, where Maggie and Kathryn and Lee were eating pancakes.

"That's one sensational blanket," Maggie said. "This morning it makes you look like Cinderella."

I dropped the blanket. "Now it makes me look like Lady Godiva," I said, not smiling. Kathryn's laugh flashed in the room like jewelry.

When I came back to the kitchen, dressed, the others were having seconds. "Oh, God," Maggie said. "Remember those apple pancakes you used to make, Lee? Those were the best."

"I haven't made those in a long time," Lee said. "Maybe I'll do that one of these mornings."

"If we're going to be staying for a while I want to go get some things from town," I said, standing back up.

"Relax," Lee said. "We'll drive in later."

Kathryn and Maggie gave us a list of stuff they needed, and we set out.

"Kathryn's very beautiful," I said. "Maggie is too."

"Yeah," Lee said.

"You and Kathryn seem like good friends," I said.

"We're old friends," Lee said. "Your feelings never change about old friends."

"Like Carlos," I said. "Hey, why is Maggie's boyfriend giving her a hard time?"

"He's an asshole," Lee said.

"Kathryn doesn't have a boyfriend," I said.

"No," Lee said.

"She must get lonely up there," I said.

"I don't think so," Lee said. "Besides, people come to her a lot."

"Yes," I said.

"Like Maggie," he said. "People who need something."

We parked in the shopping-center lot and went to the supermarket and the hardware store and the drugstore, and Lee climbed back into the van.

"You go on ahead," I said. "There's some other stuff I need to do."

"It's a long walk back," Lee said.

"I know," I said.

"You're sure you know the way?" he said.

"Yes," I said.

"It's cold," he said.

"I know," I said.

"All right," he said, "if that's what you want."

I felt a lot better. I felt pretty good. I looked around the parking lot and saw people whose arms were full of packages or who held children by the hand. I watched the van glide out onto the road, and I saw it accelerate up along the curve of the days ahead. Soon, I saw, Lee would pull up in front of Kathryn's house, soon he would step through the door and she would turn, and soon, not that afternoon, of course, but soon enough, I would be standing again in this parking lot, ticket in hand, waiting to board the bus that would appear so startlingly in front of me, as if from nowhere.

TESS GALLAGHER
THE LEPER

FROM THE PARIS REVIEW

᎐

WHEN A PLACE IS TOO BEAUTIFUL, there will be repercussions.
Such places attract disruptions, encroachments, noxious pollut-
ants of sound and deed. Things of the daily sort that would
pass unnoticed in an ugly suburb, or even on some normal
residential street, work a vengeance here. It is a burden, I'm
saying, to live where I live.

Below the house is the beach. The bay is bright with water
and light, and there is the wistful cry of gulls. But even now
this is spoiled by the pounding of hammers against wood. It is
my neighbor's porch steps being rebuilt. The pounding should
stay attached to this. But in this place of relative tranquillity
my mind flings itself into gruesome possibilities—one moment
there is the idea that a guillotine is being constructed, the next
that a man-sized cross is being readied, or that someone is
assembling a coffin board by board outside my window. But all
the while, it is only the domestic carpentry of my neighbor's
workmen.

Nonetheless, there is a privacy to be had here like no other. I can settle myself nicely into a sun-warmed chair and put my feet up on the railing and dream. But just then someone might come to knock at the door—the same neighbor who is building his steps, for instance, insisting, as he did once, that black ants have made a nest under the property and are threatening to carry away the entire hillside.

But not all disruptions to the beauty of this place are entirely unpleasant. Some fall into the range of what one might call "spectacle."

Our house overlooks other well-kept houses in this development, which is situated outside a small seaport. One morning not long ago we looked down and saw a naked woman bicycling toward the tennis courts. It was raining. Not heavily, but enough so that those who would have been going for their morning walks had stayed inside. I put the binoculars on the woman and watched as she entered the fenced and forbidden tennis court of our neighbor. She pedaled round and round the court in wide, opulent circles.

"What does she think she's doing?" my husband said, drying his hands on his darkroom apron. He had already been at work printing the latest photographs he'd taken of the mountains of our area. "She's got to be nuts," he said and reached for the binoculars. "Give me a break!" he said, and shoved the binoculars back into my hands. I lifted them to my eyes again and saw that the woman had a message smeared on her back: COWARDS! it said in what I thought was lipstick.

"She probably knows everybody in this place just picked up their binoculars," I said, handing the glasses back to him.

"Not bad looking," my husband said, pressing the lenses to his face. "But old Rosenthal won't like it a bit, her ruining the surface on his tennis court."

But no one came out of his house and no one interfered with the woman's methodical desecration of the tennis court. The rain kept falling. We ate our toast in the breakfast nook and went about our daily tasks. We had learned by now that it was best not to devote too much time to such occurrences.

Sometimes the assault on our tranquillity persists and becomes an unwelcome, permanent part of our days, as when one of our neighbors, against all regulations, erected a bell tower into which he installed a carillon. At precisely noon and at six o'clock in the evening, it played notes approximating "Amazing Grace." There were complaints, of course. A vote was taken, as it is for any adjustment in our community. But unaccountably, there were more consenting households than not, so the carillon became a fixture in our days beside the beautiful light-shattered bay.

But when all seems *too* calm from without, my husband and I become uneasy. It is then that a rupture is most likely to come from within. Thus, with a certain false confidence, we noted that during the past several days of hammering, nothing untoward had happened—no arguments had broken out between us, no malfunctioning of appliances, no lost items that needed searching for. The snarl of saws, the thudding of hammer blows, seemed to have absolved our days of a beauty too open to decay or of the wearied bliss of resort havens, which our area most resembles.

But today, just as we began to settle into the relative comfort of this routine, the phone rang. It was my friend Jerome, a sculptor. He is a man who treads an uneasy path between fear and despair, and someone who could ill afford to be calling me at two o'clock in the afternoon on a weekday when telephone rates are at their peak.

"Jerome," I said, "this is costing an arm and a leg."

"I know. I can't help it," he said grimly. "I'm furious and I can't stop myself. Catlin was supposed to call me two hours ago. I'm about to be evicted. I've got to get payment on those pieces he sold. Why didn't he call when he said he would? Why does he torture me like this?"

Catlin is the gallery manager who handles Jerome's work. He is a conscientious fellow but recently had taken a lover and fallen into domestic problems.

"I'm sure there's a reasonable explanation for why he hasn't called," I said, trying to wipe flour off my hands. I'd begun to roll out pie dough when the phone had rung. I cradled the receiver on my shoulder and continued to shape the oval of dough into a circle with the rolling pin as I listened. Jerome was always working himself into a frenzy over things normal people would have shrugged off. But Jerome would take nothing for granted. There was no such thing as an unwilled act. If someone failed to answer his call or letter, it could mean one thing and one thing only—malicious, intentional neglect. He was forever bludgeoning himself with imagined betrayals—so much so that his anguished phone calls brought ridicule from our mutual friends, including one who even bragged that he kept crossword puzzles near the phone to amuse himself during calls from Jerome. My husband was similarly unsympathetic to Jerome's panics and turmoils.

"Tell him everyone hates him. Who'd want to call him anyway?" my husband shouted, then slammed the door to his darkroom. As I say, we live in a beautiful place and this puts an unnecessary strain on our lives.

"Jerome," I said. "Something must have come up. Catlin's a fair man. He means only the best. Remember he's just been through a hard time and it still isn't easy. Maybe he isn't attending to business as well as he should."

"You can say that again!" Jerome said. "It's no excuse. I'm tired of their breakups, their influenzas and visiting in-laws. They won't get away with it!" I thought I heard him bang his fist down on something. But just then there was an awful rash of pounding close by that I mistakenly took for the sounds of the carpenters. I placed my free hand over my ear and pressed the receiver against my head with the other. Jerome's plaintive voice continued to enter my head despite the noise.

"Why? Why should I waste my forgiveness on such people?" he was saying.

"Jerome, dear, why don't you hang up and write me a letter. This is costing a fortune," I said. Yet the moment I suggested it, a fear rose up in me that this might lead to disaster. Jerome had once tried to gas himself but had been discovered by his landlady. Another time he'd thrown himself in front of a passing car. Luckily the driver had slammed on the brakes in time. Jerome had actually been committed to an institution for the mentally disturbed for a brief period during our college days—a time during which he got hold of a packet of matches and inflicted burn wounds on 15 percent of his body. He joked about these scars now as "outbreaks of insanity." I was terrified of his silence, yet this too was an expected ritual of these conversations. As I listened for his reply, my front door opened.

A man in a green delivery uniform walked cautiously into my living room and placed a large pot of lilies on the dining room table. Then he gave a respectful nod and backed out of the room, easing the door shut behind him.

I stared at the lilies as Jerome spoke and tried to work my way over to them so I could read the little white card that was attached. But the phone cord was too short.

"I can't hang up," Jerome said. "Someone's got to witness this cruelty. I'm sorry it has to be you. But I don't have that many friends left."

I caught a glimpse of myself in the hallway mirror as I moved back toward the kitchen. There were daubs of flour on my neck and chin. My left ear was white and there were pale blotches on my arms as well. God, I thought, I look like a leper. I remembered photographs of lepers in a *National Geographic* I'd seen as a child. The lepers looked doomed—participants in a ritual which left them no choice but to stumble from one rude hut to the next in search of shelter and companionship. As children we'd even played a game called Lepers. It was a game where one person was the leper and tried to touch the others who ran away. The article had described how the lepers had to eat apart from the healthy members of the tribe. They were often removed to remote areas where they were photographed with their bony arms extended—whether to display their ulcerated skin or toward some longed-for embrace, I never understood.

"Are you going to hang up on me?" Jerome asked. "What do you know about having to borrow money and to beg for the things you need? Go ahead, hang up. Live there in comfort and peace and forget about your friend."

"Jerome, I always listen. I do what I can," I said. I was used to these attempts to get me to abandon him. When that failed he would try to make me feel guilty because my fortunate circumstances separated me from the uncertainty he suffered daily. "Try to be a little more normal, Jerome," I pleaded.

"Try to understand that the world is a busy place, that the world—" But before I could finish he was shouting into my ear.

"I'm not normal! This is Jerome and I'm not normal. I'll never be normal!" he cried.

I held the receiver away from my ear and felt the scald of his words ripple over me. He was right, and no amount of pacifying and reassuring could cover up that truth—indeed the very truth I loved him for.

"Hurry up! Get off the phone, will you?" my husband called from inside the darkroom. Sometimes when I was talking to Jerome he would come out and turn the radio on full blast. This time he contented himself with turning on the faucets and rattling things in his sink.

As I worked out the pie dough and listened to Jerome's distraught voice, I remembered the Jerome I'd met fifteen years ago, the Jerome who'd taken me to a deserted warehouse one night to show me his latest creation. He'd flicked a switch that ignited a row of light bulbs suspended down the center of the high-ceilinged space. There, miraculously floating in midair, dozens of feathers clung as if to the air itself. On closer inspection I saw that the feathers were attached to nylon fishing line strung from the ceiling. At the center of each feather-cluster was a metal nub.

"Magnets," Jerome said proudly. "Watch this." Then he switched on a fan and all the feathers began to blow in exactly the same direction, holding their course as if by some strong unseen force that synchronized their motions.

"They're set to magnetic north," Jerome explained. He moved the fan around in the room but the feathers inevitably stabilized toward the same direction—magnetic north. I understood then that Jerome, like these feathers holding formation in an otherwise empty warehouse, took his marching orders from somewhere as far off and crucially situated as magnetic north itself. Yet only after I'd gone to the dictionary and looked up these words did I perceive their full import as regards my friend—that magnetic north was in fact nearly impossible to locate if another magnetic field were to come into proximity of the compass needle. So it was for Jerome—a man

easily pulled off course, sent twirling and plummeting earth-
ward at the smallest gust of wind.

"Stop arguing against yourself and listen," I said sternly
into the receiver. "Suppose Catlin *is* mistreating you. Suppose
he wants you hanging there by your thumbs as you suspect, sick
at heart, humiliated, waiting for him to call you."

"Okay," Jerome said in a small voice, satisfied that at last
I was going to hear him out.

"Supposing," I said. "Supposing all that's true. What should
I *do*?"

Jerome seemed to consider a moment as if *doing* were the
last thing on his mind. "Just tell me Catlin doesn't mean it," he
said at last. "Tell me he's had an emergency. His dog died. His
teeth fell out. Anything. But don't let me believe he's treating
me this way on purpose."

Someone began to pound on the door again. My husband
cursed and thumped about in the small space of the darkroom,
but did not venture out. I was afraid, for Jerome's sake, to put
the phone down to go see what was happening. Then the door
opened and two men in coveralls entered the living room. One
was carrying a small pine tree and the other had a spray of
gladioli and a pot of lavender mums. A white satin ribbon hung
down from the mums across the man's arm. BELOVED
MOTHER it read in gold lettering. The men placed the flowers
and the tree near the lilies and turned to leave, but at the front
door one of the men paused, then gave a quick tug at the bill
on his cap. They didn't even have a chance to close the door
when a heavyset woman moved tentatively into the living room.
She saw that I was on the telephone and placed an index finger
over her lips as she tiptoed into the kitchen. She was carrying a
covered casserole dish.

"You must be Treena's daughter," she said and gave me a
little peck on the cheek. She set the dish on the counter, patted
me on the shoulder, and then broke into muffled sobs. "I can't
stay. Harold's in the car. God bless you," the woman said,
wiping her eyes on her sleeve. Then she retraced her steps
toward the door.

"There must be some mistake," I said.

"I'm tired of mistakes," Jerome said. "Nobody takes life

seriously anymore. Look at all the injury it does. Excuse-me-
excuse-me! It's a litany from morning till night."

"I'm in the middle of somebody's funeral," I said aloud.

"Don't toy with me," Jerome said. "Don't mock me."

"I'm not mocking you. I'm your friend. I don't know
why I am, but I am," I said.

"Some friend!" came my husband's muffled voice from the
darkroom.

The sweet odor of flowers had begun to fill the living
room. Now it drifted into the kitchen where I was about to
move the piecrust into the pan. I maneuvered the dough with
both hands, holding the telephone receiver to my shoulder with
my ear. Jerome wasn't talking, but I knew he was still there. I
felt him there. As I looked up from the pie, I saw that a light
fog was beginning to drift in from the bay along the shore. The
pounding next door had stopped altogether now, but the memory of it was there like an undercurrent as I gazed out toward
the bay.

"Jerome?" I said. But he didn't answer. "Jerome?" I
repeated. I held the receiver and listened. As I waited I rested
my gaze on the shoreline. The fog was lifting. Then, through
the light-filled haze I saw horses, a small band of them. They
were riderless, yet intent, as if someone or something was
guiding them, urging them forward. The lead horse plunged
without hesitation into the surf and began to swim toward a
small island a few miles away. The other horses followed and I
could only press the receiver against my neck in amazement
and watch. There on a beach where neither dog nor child ran
free, a band of horses had clattered over stones, over sand, and
into the waves. I put the receiver down on the counter and
moved into the dining room to where the binoculars lay on the
table near the lilies. I raised the glasses to my eyes. Striving
above the waves I saw the heads of the horses. I could not take
my eyes from them.

"What's this? What's going on here?" my husband demanded. "Is this some kind of bad joke?" he asked. I knew he
was talking about the flowers. He went into the kitchen, and I
heard him lift the lid on the casserole.

Through a break in the fog I could still see the horses. For a moment I imagined I could feel the steady pull of their legs in the current. Waves broke across my chest. I could see land in the distance like a thin silver streamer on the water.

I heard a click as my husband dropped the receiver into its cradle. Jerome, I thought with a leap of regret. But then I stood and listened as if our hold on each other had nothing to do with telephones, as if his silence still questioned me, implored me to hold a course for him in the tumult and battering of the waves. My husband opened a drawer and I heard the clink of silverware.

"At least that damned pounding has stopped," he said. "It was driving me nuts. What a day!"

I held my gaze on the horses. I felt possessed of a surety, a strength that surprised me. Even my long hair seemed infused with an energy of its own as it flowed down my back. I was sure that if I were to take a boat to the island tomorrow I would find hoofprints along the beach. They would have arrived, obedient to whatever instinct or necessity had drawn them there. And my friend Jerome, he too had an uncanny fidelity for destinations of which I was often the baffled lodestar.

I lowered the binoculars and turned toward my husband. He was at the table helping himself to the casserole. His spoon scraped against the sides of the dish. The overpowering sweet scent of the flowers made an invisible current in the room, and although they seemed to indicate a sadness for which I could do nothing, I leaned over and took in my breath from their fragrance.

My husband lifted food to his mouth. As I sat down at the far end of the table, he looked up in such a way that I remembered the flour on my brow and neck. But he said nothing and looked down at his plate again, as if thinking. Then he looked up and smiled with the fondness of one who endures much for the sake of a few moments' peace.

I saw that the fog had begun to move in around the house. We could be anywhere, I thought. Anywhere. But we were here. I held out my hand as he offered me my plate.

ELLEN GILCHRIST
THE PERFECT STONE

FROM COSMOPOLITAN

～

RHODA WOKE UP DREAMING. In the dream she was crushing the skulls of Jody's sheepdogs. Or else she was crushing the skulls of Jody's sisters. Or else she was crushing Jody's skull. Jody was the husband she was leaving. Crunch, crunch, crunch went the skulls between her hands, beneath her heels.

As the dream ended her father was taking her to the police station to turn herself in. The family was all over the place weeping and wringing their hands. Her mother's face was small and broken, peering down from the stairwell.

She woke from the dream feeling wonderful, feeling purged of evil. She pulled on Jody's old velour bathrobe and sat down at the table to go over her lists. Getting a divorce was easy as pie. There was nothing to it. All you needed was money. All you needed for anything was money. Well, it was true. She went back to her lists.

Today the real estate agent was coming to see the house.

Then she would sell it. Then she would get a cute little shotgun in the Faubourg Marigny. Then she would get a job. Then she would get a new boyfriend. Everything would fall into place. Jody would hang himself and the will would still be made out in her name and she would quit her job and go live in New York. In the meantime she might have to be poorer than she was accustomed to being.

That's okay, she told herself. She took off her robe and went into the dressing room and stood in front of the mirror. Dolphins don't have anything, she told herself. A hawk possesses nothing. Albert Einstein wore tennis shoes. I am a dolphin, she decided. I am a hawk high in the Cascade Mountains. I am not a checkbook. I am not a table. I am not a chair.

She got into the bathtub and ran the water all the way to the top, pretending she was a dolphin in the summer seas somewhere off the coast of Martinique or Aruba. The morning sun was coming in the window, making long slanting lines on the walls and shutters and the water in the tub . . . now what about those tablecloths, she began thinking, imagining the contents of a closet she hadn't opened in years. What am I going to do about all those tablecloths? She saw them stacked in rows, tied with small blue ribbons, monogrammed with her initials and her mother's initials and her grandmother's initials. Oh, God, she thought, what will I do with all those goddamn tablecloths. There won't be room for them in a tiny house in the Faubourg Marigny. She sat up in the tub and began cleaning the tile between the cracks with a fingernail brush.

She had worked her way up to the hot water faucet when the phone rang. "Oh, my God," she said. She jumped out of the bathtub and padded into the bedroom and answered it. She grabbed the receiver and threw herself down on the unmade bed, letting the sheets dry her body.

"Mrs. Wells," the soft black voice said. "I hope I didn't wake you. I've been trying to get hold of you for days."

"Who is it?" she said. But she knew who it was. It was the insurance adjuster who was in charge of her claim for the diamond ring she had sold last month.

"It's Earl," he said. "Earl Treadway. Remember we talked last week."

"Oh, Earl. I'm so glad you called. I talked to Father Ryan about getting your son into the summer arts program. He said he was sure it could be arranged. Are you still interested in that?" Five thousand dollars, she thought. She shivered, a wonderful shiver that went all the way from her scalp to her groin. Five thousand dollars. Easy as pie.

"I told my son about talking to you," the black voice said. "He was excited about it. But listen, before we start talking about that, I need to see you about your claim. I think we have it straightened out now."

"Oh, God," she said. "I'd almost forgotten about it. It's all so embarrassing. I can't believe I left that ring lying out when there were workmen in the house. I guess I've just always been too trusting. I just couldn't believe it would happen to me."

"It happens to everyone sooner or later," he said. "That's what I'm for. Look, would it be possible for me to come by on my way to work? I have the check. I'd like to go on and deliver it."

"A check?"

"For four thousand six hundred and forty-three dollars. Will that settle it?"

"Oh, well, yes. I mean, a check. I didn't know they did those things that fast. But, sure, come on by. I mean, I'm up and dressed. How long will it take you to get here. I mean, sure, that'll be fine. Then this afternoon I can go out and start shopping for a new diamond, can't I?"

"I'll be by in about thirty minutes," he said. "I'm glad you were there. I'm glad it's all working out. I'm looking forward to meeting you after all these nice talks we've had." Earl hung up the phone and leaned back against the refrigerator. The baby's bottle was spilled on the counter. He reached for a rag to wipe up the milk, then changed his mind and left it there. He straightened his tie and took his coat off the back of the highchair and put it on. It was too hot for the corduroy suit but he was wearing it anyway. All those nice talks, he was thinking. All those nice long talks.

*   *   *

Rhoda rolled off the bed and started trying on clothes. She settled on a tennis skirt and a red sweater. They love red, she told herself. They love bright colors. Besides, what had she read about red? Wear red, red keeps you safe.

Well, I don't need anything to keep me safe, she thought. All I'm doing is cheating an insurance company. It's the first time I ever stole anything in my life except that one time in the fifth grade. Everybody gets to steal something sooner or later. I mean, that little Jew stole my ring, didn't he? And Jody stole five years of my life. And this black man's going to bring that check and I'm going to take it and I don't give a damn whether it's honest or not.

She sat down on a chair and pulled on her tennis shoes and tied the strings in double knots.

Cheating an insurance company hadn't been Rhoda's idea. All she had started out to do was sell her engagement ring. All she had done was get up one morning and take her engagement ring down to the French Quarter to sell it. A perfect stone, a two carat baguette. A perfect stone for a perfect girl, Gabe Adler had said when he sold it to Jody. It was insured for five thousand dollars. Rhoda had thought all she had to do was go downtown and turn it in and collect the money.

She drove to the Quarter, parked the car in the Royal Orleans parking lot, and proceeded to carry the ring from antique store to antique store. One after the other the owners held the diamond up to the light, admired it, and handed it back. "There's a place down on the Avenue that's buying stones," the last dealer told her. "Near Melpomene, on the Avenue. A new place. I heard they were giving good prices. You might try there."

"Oh, I don't think I really want to sell it," she said, slipping it back on her finger. "I just wanted to see what it was worth. I'm a reporter, did you know that? It would be a real pity if all those people out there buying diamonds found out what it's like to try to sell one, wouldn't it? If they found out what a racket you guys have going? This ring's insured for seven thousand dollars. But no one will give me half of that. I ought to write an article about it. I ought to let the public in on this."

"There's no need to talk like that," the man said. He was a big, sad-looking man in baggy pants. He took the glass out of his eye, his droopy face the shape of one of his chandeliers. "There's no need for that." A group of tourists lifted their eyes from the cases and turned to watch.

"You antique dealers are just a bunch of robbers," Rhoda said as loudly as she could. "Selling all this goddamn junk to people. And the jewelry stores are worse. How can my ring be worth seven thousand dollars if no one will buy it when I want to sell it? You want to tell me that? You want to explain that to me?"

"Leave the store," the man said, coming around the counter. "You just go on now and leave the store." He was moving toward her, his stomach marching before him like a drum. Rhoda retreated.

"Thanks for everything," she said. "Thanks for the diamond lessons."

The place at Melpomene and St. Charles was a modern showroom in an old frame house. There were gardens in front and a shiny red enamel door. This looks more like it, Rhoda thought. She opened the door and went inside, pretending to be interested in the watches in a case. "Can I help you," the myopic face of the boy behind the counter said. He was a very young boy dressed like an old man. "I don't know," she said. "I have some jewelry I'm thinking of selling. Some people I know said this was a good place. I'm thinking of selling some things I don't wear anymore and getting a Rolex instead. I see you sell them."

"What was it you wanted to sell? Did you bring it with you?"

"I might sell this," she said, taking off the ring and handing it to him. "If I could get a good enough price. I'm tired of it. I'm bored with wearing rings anyway. See what you think it's worth."

He took the ring between his chubby fingers and held it up above him. He looked at it a moment, then put a glass into his eye. "It's flawed," he said. "No one is buying diamonds now. The prime was 20 percent this morning."

"It is not flawed," she said. "It came from Adler's. It's a perfect stone. It's insured for six thousand dollars."

"I'll give you nine hundred," he said. "Take it or leave it."

"How old are you?" she said. "You don't look like you're old enough to be buying diamonds."

"I'm twenty-five," he said. "I run this place for my father. I've been running it since it opened. Do you want to sell this ring or not? That's my only offer."

"I don't know," she said. "I don't know what to say. It's insured for six thousand dollars. I only meant to sell it for a lark."

"Well, I guess it depends on how badly you need the money," he said. "Of course if you don't like the ring, there's not much sense in keeping it."

"Oh, I don't need the money." She had drawn herself up so she could look at him on a slant. "My husband's a physician. I don't need money for a thing. I just wanted to get rid of some junk." She squared her shoulders. "On the other hand, I might sell it just so I wouldn't have to bother with keeping it insured. There's a painting I want to buy, at the Bienville. I could sell the ring and buy that painting. It's all irrelevant anyway. I mean, it's all just junk. It's all just possessions."

"Well, make up your mind," he said. He held the ring out to her on a polishing cloth. "It's up to you."

"I'll just keep it," she said. "I wouldn't dream of selling a ring that valuable for nine hundred dollars."

It was almost a week before she went back to sell the ring. "Seven hundred and fifty," he said. "That's the best I can do."

"But you said nine hundred. You definitely said nine hundred."

"That was last week. You should have sold it then." Rhoda looked into his little, fat, myopic piggy eyes, hating him with all her clean white Anglo-Teutonic heart. "I'll take it," she said, and handed him the ring.

He left the room. She sat down on a chair beside his desk, feeling powerless and used. He came back into the room. She

was trying not to look at his hands, which were holding a stack
of bills.

"Here you are," he said. "We don't keep records of these
things, you know. We don't give receipts."

"What do you mean?" she said.

"There isn't any record. In case you want to file a claim."

She took the money from him and stuffed it into her handbag without counting it. "My God," she said. Her power was
returning. She felt it coursing through her veins. Her veins
were charged with power. A thousand white horses of pure
moral power pouring up and down her neck and face and legs
and arms and hands. "I've never filed an insurance claim in my
life," she said. "I probably wouldn't bother to file one if I
actually lost something." She had stood up. "You are really
just the epitome of too goddamn much, are you aware of
that?" Then she left, going out into the sweltering heat of the
summer day, out onto St. Charles Avenue, where a streetcar
was chugging merrily by.

I'm going to turn them in, she thought. As soon as I get
home I'll call the mayor's office and then I'll call the Better
Business Bureau and then I'll write a letter to *Figaro* and the
Times-Picayune. I'll get that little fat Jewish bastard. My God,
it must be terrible to be a nice Jew and have to be responsible
for people like that. No wonder they all want to move to
Israel. Oh, well. She got into the car and opened her bag and
counted the money. Seven hundred and fifty dollars. Well, it
would pay the bills.

It was several days before she called the insurance company and filed the claim. "It was right there in the jewelry box
on the dresser where I always leave it," she told the police
when they came to make a report. "I can't imagine who would
take it. The housekeeper is the most honest person in this city.
My friends come in and out but none of them would touch it. I
just don't know . . ."

"Have you had any work done on the house?" The police
officer was young. He was standing in the door to her bedroom getting a hard-on, but he was trying to ignore it. She was
very pretty. With a big ass. He liked that in a woman. It

reminded him of his mother. He shifted his revolver to the front and looked up into her face.

"Oh," she was saying. "I forgot all about that. I had the bedrooms painted last month. I had a whole crew of painters here for three days. You don't think. I mean, they all work for Mr. Saunders. He's as honest as the day is long. He paints for everyone. Still the ring is gone. It isn't here. It was here and now it isn't."

"I'd bet on the painters," the policeman said. "There's been a lot of that going on lately. This is the third claim like this I've had in a week. In this same neighborhood."

"But why would he only take the ring?" Rhoda said. "Why didn't he take anything else? There's other jewelry here. Expensive things."

"They're after diamonds. And flat silver. They don't mess with smaller things. No, I think we've got a pretty professional job here. Looks like he knew what he was looking for."

"I only want my ring back," she told Earl the first time he called. "Or one just like it to replace it. I'm so embarrassed about this. I've never filed an insurance claim of any kind. But everyone said I had to go on and report it. I didn't want to."

"There's a lot of unemployment right now," he said. "It makes things happen."

"I know," she said. "That's why I hate to report this. I don't want to get anyone in trouble, any poor person or someone that had to steal to eat or something like that."

"You sure sound like a nice lady. I'd sure like to meet you sometime."

"Well, sure," she had said. "Before this is over we'll have to see about that."

That had been the beginning. He had called her several times, asking for details of the robbery, checking facts. The conversations had drifted into discussions of movies, city politics, civil rights, athletics, her divorce, his divorce, his little boy, her connections that could get his little boy into a summer painting program. Somewhere along the way she told him the rest of the story and he filed the claim and the money had been sent on its way from the home office of the insurance company.

Then he was there, standing on her doorstep, all dressed up in a corduroy suit with an oxford cloth shirt and a striped tie, six feet three inches tall, big enough to spar with Ali, soft brown eyes, kinky black hair.

"Come on in the kitchen," she said. "Come have a cup of coffee." She led him through a dining room filled with plants. Rhoda's whole house was filled with plants. There were plants of every kind in every room. Lush, cool, thick, every color of green, overflowing their terra cotta pots, spilling out onto the floor. It took the maid all day Tuesday just to water them. Earl followed her into the kitchen and sat down on a maple captain's chair. It looked like a doll's chair with his body in it. He put his briefcase beside him and folded his hands on the breakfast-room table. He smiled at her. She was trying not to look at the briefcase but her eyes kept going in that direction.

"Where are you from, Earl Treadway?" she said. "What Delta town did you escape from with that accent? Or was it Georgia?"

"I escaped from Rosedale," he said. He was laughing. He wasn't backing off an inch. "My daddy was a sharecropper. How about you?"

"I escaped from Issaquena County," she said. "Sixty miles away. Well, not really. I only lived there in the summers. In the winter I lived in Indiana. I lived up North a lot when I was young."

"Are you married? Oh, no, that's right. You told me you were getting a divorce. We talked so much I forgot half the things we said." He picked up a place mat from a stack of them at the end of the table. It was a blue and yellow laminated map of the British Virgin Islands—bright blue water, yellow islands. The names of the islands were in large block letters: Tortola, Beef Island, Virgin Gorda, Peter Island, Salt Island, the Indians. All the places Rhoda had been with her husband, summer after boring summer, arguing and being miserable on the big expensive sailboat, mornings with whiskey bottles and ashtrays and cigarettes and cracker crumbs all over the deck. Anchored in some hot civilized little harbor. While on shore, oh, there Rhoda imagined real life was going on, a dark, musky, musical real life, loud jump-ups she heard at night, hot black wildness going on and on into the night while she sat on the boat with her husband and people they had brought along from New Orleans, talking about people they knew, gossiping, planning their careful little diving trips for the morning, checking the equipment over and over, laughing good-naturedly over their escapades in the water, wild adventures thirty feet below the dinghy with a native guide.

Earl picked up one of the place mats and held it in his hand. "What is this?" he said again. He was looking right at her. His face was so big, his mouth so red and full, his voice so deep and kind and rich. It was cool in the room. So early in the morning. I wonder what he smells like, she thought. I wonder what it would be like to touch his hair.

"My husband bought those," she said. "They're maps of the British Virgin Islands, where I have a sailboat. I used to go there every summer. I know that place like the back of my hand. I've been bored to death on every island in the Sir Francis Drake Channel. I guess I still own part of that sailboat. I forgot to ask. Well, anyway, that's what that is. On the other hand, it's a place mat."

"I like maps," he said. "I remember the first one I ever saw, a map of the world. I used to stay after school to look at it. I was trying to find the way out of Rosedale." She smiled and he went on. "Later, I had a job at a filling station and I could get all the maps I wanted. I was getting one of every state. I wanted to put them on a wall and make the whole United States."

"How old are you?" she said.

"I'm thirty-four. How old are you?"

"I'm thirty-four. Think of that. Our mothers could have passed each other on the street with us in their stomachs."

"You say the funniest things of anyone I ever talked to. I was thinking that when I talked to you on the phone. You think real deep, don't you?"

"Oh, I don't know. I read all the time. I read Albert Einstein. Oh, not the part about the physics. I read his letters and about political systems and things like that. Yeah, I guess that's true. I guess I do think deep."

"You really own a sailboat in this place?" he said. He was still holding the place mat.

"I guess I do. I forgot to put it in the divorce." She laughed. His hand had let the place mat drop. His hand was very near to hers. "It isn't nearly as much fun as it looks in pictures," she said. "It's really pretty boring. There are boats all over the place there now, big power boats from Puerto Rico. It's all terribly middle-class really. A lot of people pretending to have adventures." She was looking at the briefcase out of the corner of her eye. It was still there. Why don't you go on and give me the check, she wanted to say, and then I'll give you a piece of ass and we'll be square. She sighed. "What did you want to talk to me about? About settling the robbery I mean."

"Just to finalize everything. To give you the check they cut this morning."

"All right," she said. "Then go on and give it to me. Just think, Earl, in my whole life I never collected any insurance. It makes me feel like a criminal. Well, you're an insurance salesman. Make me believe in insurance."

He put down the place mat and picked up the briefcase and set it down in front of him on the table. "Will this hurt the finish on your table? It's such a pretty table. I wouldn't want to scratch it up."

"Oh, no," she said. "It's all right. It's an old table. It's got scratches all over it."

He opened the briefcase and moved some papers and took out the check. He held it out very formally to her. "I'm sorry about your ring," he said. "I hope this will help you get another one."

She took it from him. Then she carelessly laid it down behind her on a counter. She laid it down a few inches away from a puddle of water that had condensed around a green watering can. Once she had laid it there she would not touch it again while he was watching. "Thanks for bringing it by. You could have mailed it."

"I wanted to meet you. I wanted to get to know you."

"So did I," she said. Her eyes dug into his skin, thick black skin, real black skin. Something she had never had. It was cool in the room. Three thousand dollars' worth of brand new air conditioning was purring away outside the window. Inside everything was white and green. White woodwork, green plants, baskets of plants in every window, ferns and philodendrons and bromeliads, gloxinias and tillandsias. Leaves and shadows of leaves and wallpaper that looked like leaves. "What are you doing tonight?" she said. "What are you doing for dinner?"

"I'll be putting napkins in your lap and cutting up your steak if you'll go out with me," he said. "We'll go someplace nice. Anywhere you want."

"What time?"

"I have to go to a meeting first. A community meeting where I live. I'm chairman of my neighborhood association. It might be eight or nine before I can get away. Is that too late?" He had closed his briefcase and was standing up.

"I'll be waiting," she said. He locked the briefcase and came out from beside the table. "Don't lose that check," he said. It was still sitting on the edge of the counter. The circle of water was closing in. "Don't get it wet. It would be a lot of trouble to get them to make another one."

When he was gone Rhoda straightened up the house and made the bed. She put all the dishes in the dishwasher and watered the plants. She cleaned off the counters one by one. She moved the watering can and wiped up the ring of water. Then she picked up the check and read the amount. Four thousand six hundred and forty-three dollars. Eight months of freedom at five hundred dollars a month. And forty-three dollars to waste. I'll waste it today, she decided. She picked up the phone and called the beauty parlor.

At six o'clock she started getting dressed. Six o'clock is the time of day in New Orleans when the light cools down, coming in at angles around the tombs in the cemeteries, between the branches of the live oak trees along the avenues, casting shadows across the yards, penetrating the glass of a million windows.

Rhoda always left the drapes open in the afternoons so she could watch the light travel around the house. She would turn on *The World of Jazz* and dress for dinner while the light moved around the rooms. Two hours, she thought, dropping her clothes on the floor of her bedroom. Two hours to make myself into a goddess. She shaved her legs and gave herself a manicure and rubbed perfumed lotion all over her body and started trying on clothes. Rhoda had five closets full of clothes. She had thousands of dollars' worth of skirts and sweaters and blouses and dresses and shoes and handbags.

She opened a closet in the hall. She took out a white lace dress she had worn one night to have dinner with a senator. She put the soft silk-lined dress on top of her skin. Then, one by one, she buttoned up every one of the thirty-six tiny pearl buttons of the bodice and sleeves. The dress had a blue silk belt. Rhoda dropped it on the closet floor and opened a drawer and found a red scarf and tied it around the waist of the dress. She looked in the mirror. It was almost right. But not quite right. She took one of Jody's old ties off a tie rack and tied it around the waist. There, that was better. That was perfect. "A Brooks Brothers' tie," she said out loud. "The one true tie of power."

She went into the kitchen and took a bottle of wine out of the refrigerator and poured herself a glass and began to walk around the house. She stopped in the den and put a Scott Joplin record on the stereo and then she began to dance, waving the wine glass in the air, waiting for Earl to come. She danced into the bedroom and took the check out of a drawer where she had hidden it and held it up and kissed it lavishly all over. Jesus loves the little children, she was singing. All the children of the world. Red and yellow, black and white, all are precious, precious, precious in his sight. Four thousand six hundred and forty-three dollars and thirty-seven cents. A day's work. At last, a real day's work.

The doorbell was ringing. She set the wine glass down on a table and walked wildly down the hall to the door. "I'm coming," she called out. "I'll be right there."

"Now what I'd really like to do with you," Earl was saying, "is go fishing." They were at Dante's on the River, a restaurant down at the end of Carrollton Avenue. They had stuffed themselves on crab Thibodeaux and shrimp mousse and softshell crabs Richard and were starting in on the roasted quail. It was a recipe with a secret sauce perfected in Drew, Mississippi, where Earl's grandfather had been horsewhipped on the street for smarting off to a white man. But that was long ago and the sauce tasted wonderful to Rhoda and Earl.

"I'm stuffed," she said. "How can I eat all this? I won't be able to move, much less make love to you. I am going to make love to you, you know that, don't you?"

"If you say so," he said. "Now, listen, Miss Rhoda, did you hear what I said about going fishing."

"What about it?"

"I want to take you fishing. I'm famous for my fishing. I won a fishing rodeo one time."

"We don't have to do it tonight, do we? I mean, I have other plans for tonight as I just told you."

"We'll pretend we're fishing," he said. "How about that?" He was laughing at her but she didn't care. Black people had laughed at Rhoda all her life. All her life she had been making black people laugh.

"What are you thinking of?" he said.

"I was thinking about when I was little and my mother would take me to Mississippi for the summer, and if I wanted attention I would take my underpants off and the black people would all die laughing, and the white people would grab me up and make me put them back on. Well, I guess that's a racist thing to say, isn't it?"

"You want to see if it makes me laugh?"

"Yeah, I do. So hurry up and finish eating. When I think of something I like to go right on and do it. In case they blow the world up while I'm waiting." Earl took a piece of French bread and buttered it and laid it on her plate. "Are you sure you aren't married, Earl? I made a vow not to mess around with married men. I've had enough of that stuff. That's why I'm getting a divorce. Because I kept having these affairs and I'd have to go home and eat dinner, and there the other person would be. With no one to eat dinner with. That doesn't seem right, does it? After they'd made love to me all afternoon? So I'm getting a divorce. Now I'll have to be poor for a while but

I don't care. It's better than being an adulteress, don't you think so?" She picked up the bread and put it back on his plate.

"Why don't you stop talking and finish your quail?"

"I can't stop talking when I'm nervous. It's how I protect myself." She pulled her hand back into her lap. Rhoda hated to be reminded that she talked too much.

"I'm not married," he said. "I told you that on the phone. I've got a little boy and I keep him part of the time. Remember, we talked about that before. It's all right. There isn't anything to be afraid of." He felt like he did when he coached his Little League baseball team. That's the way she made him feel. One minute she reminded him of a movie star. The next minute she reminded him of a little boy on his team who sucked his glove all the time. "We've got plenty of time to get to know each other. We don't have to hurry to do anything."

"Tell me about yourself," she said. "Tell me all the good parts first. You can work in the bad parts later."

"Well, I'm the oldest one of thirteen children. I worked my way through Mississippi Southern playing football. Then I spent three years in the Marines and now I'm in insurance. Last year I ran for office. I ran for councilman in my district and I lost, but I'm going to run again. This time I'll win." He squared his shoulders. "What else? I love my family. I helped put my brothers and sisters through school. I'm proud of that." He stopped a moment and looked at her. "I've never known anyone like you. I changed shirts three times trying to get ready to come and get you."

"That's enough," she said. "Pay for this food and let's get out of here."

"My grandmother was a free woman from Natchez," he continued. They were in the car driving along the Avenue. "A light-skinned woman, what you'd call an octoroon. She lived until last year. She was so old she lost count of the years. Her father was a man who fought with Morrell's army. I have pictures of many of my ancestors. They were never slaves . . . you sure you want to hear all this?"

"Yeah, I want to know who I'm going to bed with."

"You talk some. You have a turn."

"I have two sons. They go to school in Virginia. They're real wild. Everyone in my family's wild. It's a huge family, a network over five states. I love them but they don't have any power over me anymore. Not that they ever did. I think I'm the first person in my family to ever really escape from it. It's taken me a long time to do it. Now I'm free. I might learn to fly. I might teach in a grade school. I might be a waitress. I might move to Europe. I might learn to sew and take up hems. I don't know what I'm going to do next. But right now I'm going to go home and fuck you. I'm tired of waiting to do it. I've been waiting all day."

"So have I," he said and pulled her closer to him.

"Another thing," she said. "I stole that money from you. I sold that diamond ring you paid me for. I sold it to this fat piggy little Jewish boy on Melpomene. He paid me in cash and told me I could file a claim. I'm thinking of reporting him to the Jewish temple. Well, he thought it up. But I'm the one that did it."

"Did you see that mule?" Earl said. "That mule flying by. That's the damnedest thing. A gray mule with black ears."

"I stole the money from you," she said. "The money for the diamond. Don't you care? Don't you even care?" She moved his hand from around her waist and put it between her legs.

"That's the damnedest thing about those mules when they get to town," he said, turning down the street to her house. "You can't keep them on the ground. They'll take off every time. Also, I am married. I guess we might as well go on and get that on the table."

"What mule?" Rhoda said. "I don't see any mules. There aren't any mules on St. Charles Avenue."

ERNST HAVEMANN

DEATH OF THE NATION

FROM THE ATLANTIC

ꝏ

IN MY BOYHOOD every small white boy on a farm in Natal had a
black companion, an "umfaan." The umfaan was usually three
or four years older than the white boy, so that he could take
care of his charge and carry him piggyback when necessary.
My umfaan was called Fakwes. His real name was Ukufakwezwe,
"The Death of the Nation," because he was born at the time of
an epidemic that killed a great many people, including his
father.

He was ten or eleven when he came to work on my
family's farm, which meant that he had had five or six years as
a herdboy, spending all day every day in the veld with the
other boys of his family. He knew the name of every bird,
every little animal, even every insect we came across, and he
knew what one should do about each of them—which bees
sting and which merely buzz, how to salute the praying man-
tis, and what to cry out to the nightjar when it suddenly flies

up and then flops down invisible in deep shadow. (You say, "*Savolo, savolo,* milk for my people.")

We collected quails' eggs, flying ants, and small white tubers and roasted them on the lid of a cast-iron pot. We hunted cane rats and lizards and helped herd the cattle. Sometimes we went with one of Fakwes's relatives to visit the native reserve adjoining the farm. We took salt, tobacco, and matches as gifts, and perhaps a beer bottle of lard, liquid in the heat. We were received ceremoniously, like adults, and when Fakwes's grandfather took the tobacco, he invited us into his hut, which was very special because of his spears and his big oxhide shield.

An exciting thing happened on one of those visits. On our way home we heard a shout from very far away, then a louder one close by from a man high in a tall tree. He was shouting, "The goats are in the field!" In a moment we saw a boy scramble up the rocks to the top of a little hill and heard him scream, "The goats are in the field!" Fakwes ran to a big tree, climbed up, and shouted the same words. Someone picked up the message, and we could hear it repeated from the next hilltop and then the next, far away.

"Where are the goats?" I demanded: "Shouldn't we run and chase them?"

"You will see the goats in a little while," he said. "They will be riding horses and carrying revolvers."

Some time afterward—I think we had ridden more than a mile—the "goats" appeared. They were two policemen on horseback. Fakwes said that by the time they reached the kraals all the men who did not have passes or poll-tax receipts would be hiding in deep bush, together with all the unlicensed dogs.

"You have seen a secret thing," he said. "You must never speak of it." He knew that if he said it was secret I would not tell, just as I did not tell when we killed the prize rooster with our catapults. I never did tell, though I felt guilty and anxious whenever a policeman looked directly at me, in case he knew.

My first few school years were in a one-roomer a few miles from our place. I rode a pony to school; Fakwes walked or trotted alongside. Out of sight of adults we both rode, or Fakwes rode and I tried to keep up. When we reached the school, I went into the playground while Fakwes joined the other umfaans and the ponies in the school's field. The umfaans played games of guessing how many pebbles there were under which condensed-milk tin, breaking off to listen to our singing lessons. When we emerged, they would break into "John Peel" or "Land of Hope and Glory," rendering it loudly and perfectly but with a distinctive African flavor.

On the way home I regaled Fakwes with what I had learned that day. After lunch we usually went down to the reservoir to draw in the soft mud left by the receding water. (There must also have been times when the water was rising, but I don't remember them.) There were long, flat, absolutely smooth stretches of yellow ooze. Whatever one scratched on it stayed put while the mud dried and finally cracked into big flat pieces like gigantic slabs of chocolate. Fakwes drew bulls with enormous horns and genitals and cows with long teats. I drew faces and wrote letters. He laughed when I wrote FAKWES and said it was his name. In response he scratched zigzag lines and said they were my name, but after a while he took writing seriously and began to copy letters from my books. He was quicker and neater than I was. He wanted to write his whole, long, real name, but I could not cope with long words and we had to abandon it. He drew one of his fearsome bulls and said, "Let that be the writing for my name."

We had trouble with other Zulu words, because I did not know how to write the click sounds. The teacher said that Zulu was not made for writing, it was for savages, but by the time I left the one-roomer to go to Big School in the village, twenty miles away, Fakwes and I could both read the Zulu on the packets of baby formula at the trading store. It said that baby formula was better than milk.

Once I was at Big School, I saw Fakwes only when I came home on weekends. Though only fifteen or sixteen, he received a full man's wages, because he could read and write figures and work out piecework tasks and things like that. I brought him a Zulu New Testament, which was the only Zulu book I could find. He was ecstatic. "I shall be as clever as a preacher! I shall know all that he knows, from this Believers' book. But I will not be a Believer." He wrote me a careful letter of thanks in Zulu and signed it with one of his drawings of a bull.

The New Testament was full of place names—Nazareth, Bethlehem, Rome, Ephesus. But where were they? We went through my school atlas. What really gripped him in the atlas was England. He scoffed at the idea that such a small red patch could be the England that had defeated the Zulus, the Boers, and the Germans. His grandfather liked to tell how *his* father had fought at Isandhlwana, where the Zulus wiped out Lord Chelmsford's column, and at Ulundi, where the British broke the Zulus. The withered old man had a deep respect for British soldiers. "They were all heroes," he recounted. "They died without flinching. And they killed without flinching. Like Zulus." He enjoyed the little red-coated lead soldier I brought him, and attached it to the end of a spear.

Fakwes shared his grandfather's admiration for British soldiers but deeply resented settlers. "One day we will take back all this land," he declared. "We will burn the sugarcane and take the horses and cattle and sheep. The farmers will load their trucks and go, go to the south, away from us. I will be a great man in the council of chiefs, because I can read and I know where England is, and Bethlehem. I will write letters for the council of chiefs, and I will live in Armstrong's house." Armstrong, the storekeeper, had a place in the East Indian–colonial style, with little turrets and fretwork lattices, painted what we called coolie pink. "On letters to friends I will draw a bull. And you, my brother"—he put his arm around me—"you will be our adviser. The great chiefs always had a white man to tell them the thoughts and deceits of the English. We will give you many wives and red Boer cattle with their horns swept back, and a little band of warriors to guard you and greet you with praises. Which house would you like?"

One weekend when I came home, Fakwes was not there. No one knew where he was, and the police were looking for him. A youth with whom he had quarreled at a beerdrink had been found unconscious by the roadside, with a head wound. If he died, the police would probably charge Fakwes with murder. My father let it be known that we would arrange a lawyer if Fakwes turned himself in, but that proviso was unnecessary. The wounded youth recovered and refused to make a complaint—it was a fair fight, he said—and so no charge was recorded against Fakwes. Fakwes nevertheless stayed away. We heard rumors that he had been seen in Durban, and then in Cape Town. About a year after Fakwes disappeared, I received a card with a London postmark. It had a picture of a red-coated soldier. There was no message, only a drawing of a bull with big horns and genitals.

About five years ago I had a visit from Benny Miller. He was, and is, an undistinguished lawyer with a drinking problem. Most of his clients appeared to be shopkeepers charged with minor breaches of municipal bylaws, but he had also, surprisingly, appeared in two or three African political trials.

He phoned me one evening at my house. "I didn't want to be seen coming to your office," he said. "Your friends might think you were involved with one of my clients, and that wouldn't do, eh?"

"What do you want?" I snapped.

"I'm representing an old friend of yours. You may be able to help."

I agreed to see him, and within twenty minutes he arrived through the backyard servants' entrance. He was a plump, sallow man with curly gray hair and a practiced, self-deprecating smile. He accepted a drink, looked around the room, and remarked, "Nice place you have here."

I waited, not concealing my dislike.

"Do you know a man called Mkize? Big fellow, around forty."

I could not recall a black acquaintance by that name.

"He says to tell you the goats are in the field."

"Oh, Fakwes!" I exclaimed. I had forgotten that his clan name was Mkize. "Fakwes. Sure. We grew up together, but I haven't seen him for years. Where is he?"

"In jail. Forged papers and possession of an offensive weapon. But that's just to hold him until they get to the red meat. I think the prosecution is after conspiracy or sabotage or worse. He was abroad a long time and he speaks fluent Portuguese and French."

"French! Fakwes speaks French?"

"Quite educated French, as far as I can judge. He seems to have got around."

"Portuguese and French, eh?" I could not believe it. "Well, how can I help?"

"Perhaps you can't help at all. But if there's no concrete evidence against him, just suspicion, then they might go for detention without trial. In that case character evidence may ease his lot. Someone like you—upright, prosperous, right-wing—could carry weight, perhaps pull a string or two. I understand you have friends in government circles. Well, we all have our weaknesses. I should warn you, though, a dossier is bound to be opened for anyone who's connected with him."

"I'll think it over," I said.

He took it as a refusal. "I don't blame you. Things are never quite the same once you've been mixed up in one of these affairs."

"I'm not mixed up in anything," I protested.

"No? Consider this: You're a friend of a subversive character. He sent you a code message through me, which you obviously understood. Perhaps on your trips abroad you stopped over in Nairobi or Lourenço Marques or Marseilles, where he also happened, just happened, to be at the same time. Adds up. So you're probably wise to turn your back. Boyhood pals across the color line is one thing—touching, in fact—but in adults it's suspicious."

He rose to go, putting his glass down noisily. I held it up and looked inquiringly.

"I thought you'd never ask," he said, sitting down.

"Can I see Fakwes?"

"How naive can you get!" He threw up his hands. "The man doesn't say 'Can I see the accused?'—or Mkize, or anything like that. No! He uses some kind of pet nickname! How do you suppose you would sound in court? What does it mean, anyway?"

"Fakwes is short for Ukufakwezwe."

"I see. Does Uku-whatever mean anything?"

"It means 'The Death of the Nation.'"

"Christ!" he exclaimed. "Imagine what a prosecutor could make of that in a subversion case! Imagine, The Death of the bloody Nation! 'And which nation were you planning the death of, Mr. Mkize?' "

"Can I see him?" I repeated impatiently.

"I wouldn't advise it," he said seriously. "It would tar you a bit. In case you change your mind, I'd prefer you to stay remote. It would be better for you, too."

"Can I do anything else? Clothes, cigarettes, money? Your fees?"

"Since you ask, since you ask, I'll tell you. I earn my living helping small businessmen who make mistakes. Clients like your friend usually don't have a penny. I handle them *pro deo*. Naturally, I try to avoid incurring expenses. But even so, there's stationery and postage and official fees. And tobacco for the poor bastards. I try to look after things like that, and perhaps get a wife in from the country to see her husband for the last time. It costs. Of course, it's a mitzvah." He assumed a mock Yiddish manner and spread his palms. "You know vot is a mitzvah? A credit up there." He jerked a thumb at the ceiling. "Mitzvahs I got like Job had boils. But can you mit a mitzvah buy a bottle visky?" He reverted to normal. "You stock an excellent spirit, by the way. Not like some cheap-skates, who put away the Black Label and bring out the Japanese when they see me coming."

I refilled his glass and took out my wallet. I like to carry a reasonable amount of cash, and that afternoon I had drawn an extra sum because my wife and I were going to the races the next day. There were always races in Durban on Wednesday afternoons. I took all there was in the wallet and gave it to Benny Miller without counting it.

He weighed it in his palm. "I wish I had a boyhood chum like you," he said. "It's understood that this is an uncondi-tional gift? I use it as I choose, and I don't account for it?"

"I don't know what happened to the money," I replied. "It must have slipped out of my hip pocket in the street when I was tying my shoelace."

He put the money in his pocket. "Okay. But remember what I've said. Once you've done something like this, things are never quite the same. As the rabbi says, one mitzvah leads to another." He drained his glass and left.

My wife was horrified when I told her what had occurred.

"You've always told me of your wonderful Zulu friend, the David to your Jonathan," she jeered. "And now, when he might be in jail for the rest of his life and you might get a chance to speak for him, you'll think it over. Think it over! I'm ashamed."

"You'd be more than ashamed if the police came and turned the house inside out, looking for God knows what," I retorted.

I kept telling myself that I didn't owe Fakwes that much. I would have owed him if he had been just an ordinary, or even a rather special, black man, like those I met on the Bantu Welfare Committee. With his brains and a bit of help he could have got more education and perhaps become a teacher, or my head clerk, which would pay better. We would have remained friends. He would come to dinner from time to time. My European friends would recognize that they were being given a special treat if they were invited when he and his wife came. But as it was . . . He had nearly killed that youth years ago, and now it seemed he might be a terrorist. Perhaps he was. When he was a boy, he wanted to take the land back from the settlers. Fancy his learning French! I wondered what he looked like. Was he the same person that I had known twenty-five years ago? I was guiltily certain that if I were a fugitive, he would risk his life for me. Or would he? Several kids with whom I had been friendly at school were now only distant acquaintances, whom I might see at Rotary but not otherwise.

At the races the next day my wife ostentatiously put all her money on Bosom Friend at fifty to one and won. Someone assured us that Beesknees was a certainty for the main race. I backed him without excitement. Fakwes and I used to rob wild bees' nests. We got up early, because in the cold dawn bees huddle together, more or less inactive. We collected twigs and leaves, made a smoky fire, and blew smoke deep into the nest, which was usually a hole in the ground or in a hollow tree. The smoke stupefied the bees. Fakwes always made me stand some distance away while he chopped and dug to get at the honeycombs. He was often stung. I was occasionally stung too, but I learned not to cry out: one of Fakwes's rules was that one was never allowed to cry for pain. I was always the one who carried the honey home, like a conquering hero, while Fakwes stood by, waving an insect-repellent herb and describing how we had located the nest by following the flight of bees from a flowering tree or by listening to the bee-eater. The bee-eater has a very pronounced swallowtail and . . .

"Wake up, dreamy Daniel!" My wife shook my elbow. "When you come to the races, you're supposed to care which horse wins." She pointed to the board flashing BEESKNEES 12–1. He had won by three lengths.

The next day I phoned Benny Miller. As soon as he heard my voice he said, "I'll ring back" and put down the receiver. Ten minutes later he called from a pay phone.

"My office phone is tapped," he explained. "What's on your mind?"

"I've decided I will be available as a character witness, or do whatever else you think may help."

"Congratulations. Or perhaps you're psychic. Your friend escaped from custody last night. There is the usual loose talk about venal guards. Anyway, I don't suppose you'll see your pal again unless you rendezvous abroad. Well, so long."

About a month afterward I received a postcard from Spain. It showed a black bull, its shoulder bristling with lances, kneeling on a bullfighter. That was all. No message, just the wounded black bull triumphing over its adversary. I burned the card. It is not the sort of thing one wants to keep around.

Benny Miller was in the news a couple of times during the next year. A technicality saved him from conviction on a charge of corrupting a customs officer, and he was knocked down the courthouse steps by women protesting against his defense of a black girl who had organized a union of nursemaids.

He called me soon after my return from a visit to Europe. He spoke from a phone booth. "Did you have a good trip? See all the old friends you wanted to see? Look, a fund you know of has developed a deficit like the national debt. Would you care to perpetrate a mitzvah?"

We met in a bar. We did not drink together or greet each other, but he picked up an envelope that I left on the counter.

Eight or nine months later he phoned again, soon after the

African bus riots. "Miller here. I'm sure you know why I'm calling."

I hesitated, and he said urgently, "Look, man, the bloody goats are in the field, man."

"Okay," I said. "The Four Seasons bar. Tomorrow at six."

"Bless you," he responded. "Thank God for boyhood chums, eh?"

He phones once or twice every year. He now announces himself as "Benjamin" (that is what his friends call him, he explains) and always asks what news I have from abroad. I always answer "Nothing," but he enjoys teasing me with the suggestion that I am connected with an underground movement. I inquire after his health and may refer to a trial in which he is appearing. Then I mention goats, and he makes a little joke about my accumulation of credits "up there." A good act qualifies as a credit even if it is not entirely voluntary, he says.

NORMAN LAVERS
BIG DOG

FROM THE NORTH AMERICAN REVIEW

ဢ

SHE OF COURSE wanted the old villa about five miles out of
town, surrounded by lantana and bougainvillea, with its quaint
patio and tile roof through which, in places, you could see the
metallic blue Mediterranean sky. He looked at the plumbing,
the improvised electric wiring, the inconvenient distance from
the shops—"We'll have our bikes," she said. "Winter, wet and
rainy, is coming even here," he said—and gave a decisive
negative. He wanted the brand new apartment on the fourth
floor in the middle of town, everything working, right in the
center of things. She saw the sterile functionalism, the cool
anonymous neighbors, the lack of anything alive and growing,
and in her own passive way dug in her heels. She apologeti-
cally asked, he abruptly demanded, that the real estate agent
show them something else, and they compromised on an older,
more lived-in apartment on the edge of town with fields and a
lagoon to look at off their balcony, which was only one floor

up from the ground. Also, they were childless, and she had noticed a frail elderly couple in the little house next door. Her curiously inverted maternal instinct always needed old people to protect and preserve.

He for his part—well—he didn't know what he was going to do, only that, when he found it, he would rush at it head first, and it would not long resist him. Some people in this world are dreamers, sleeping light and dreaming through the night, half awake by day, their dreams rushing in at every odd moment. For such people—she was a bit like this—the place is only partly important, because so much of their life goes on independently from place. He was the other way, constantly fully alert, taking in everything, obsessively seeing and learning every process around him at the top of his speed, putting all of himself into it. But it had to be the *it* that was objectively out there, and when it was not there for him, and his interest flagged, he was deeply asleep in a moment, his face sagging, his mouth drooped open. In this way he was like those sharks who must swim constantly their whole life, because if they pause, the oxygen is no longer carried past their breathing apparatus, and they die.

But the doctor had ordered him to rest, and he had taken the long overdue sabbatical. He meant to rest, however, 100 percent. He laid out the campaign in his head. He had first of all quit smoking cold turkey, and after reading every book, had set up a balanced diet for himself that would work off his extra sixty pounds. He would go down to the beach and do distance swimming in the morning as long as the weather stayed warm—it was already the end of September—and he had bought a knife-thin racing bike for distance biking in the afternoon till he had lost his extra weight, at which time the doctor told him he could begin running. Right now the weight would be too much strain on his knees.

On the day they looked at their apartment, clouds covered the distant view. But on the day they moved into it from their hotel it was clear. They did their grocery shopping, haltingly in the unfamiliar language—and she made them their first pot of tea, and they sat out on their balcony, and at that point for the first time realized that it was the mountain that would dominate their view. It was Puig Mayor, rising six thousand feet straight up out of the sea. In the local island dialect *Puig* was pronounced like *pooch*, so he dubbed the mountain Big Dog. It was a bare pinnacle of rock. She decided it was a volcanic spewing, magma pressing up from the dark middle of the world. He saw in it another—to him even more dramatic— orogenetic force, the great African plate pressing north into the Eurasian plate, pushing and squeezing up the land between this wrinkle which went from the Atlas Mountains in Morocco the length of the western Mediterranean at last curving northward and culminating in the Alps.

"What are you going to do?" he said.

"For the rest of my life?" she said. "For this year? Or just this morning?"

"Those three in that order."

"I'm just going to go on puttering for my life. For this year I want to do some different kind of painting, but I don't know what yet. And for this morning I'm going to lie on the beach with my new bikini. I'll be the one you don't notice because I'll still have my top on. And you're coming too. This is vacation, rest, change. You're going to lie on the beach and take it easy on your heart."

"My heart is okay."

"Now. But you're in the number one risk category."

"Yeah, well there's another side to that equation. More and more evidence is coming in that there is also a number one risk cancer personality, and that's marked by people who are too passive."

"I'm not too passive."

"Only because I keep agitating you."

"Well, if I keep pulling you back, it's for your own good."

"Hey, stop pushing me around," he said, smiling and she smiled too, both because it was so unusual for her to be assertive in anything, and because on the face of it the idea was so ludicrous. She had never weighed over ninety pounds. He wasn't tall, but he was broad as a door, and had gone to university on football scholarships till he got a head injury and began passing out. Then to the amazement of his jock friends,

he went on and made it through academically, even through
the Ph.D., and taught in a university with surprising brilliance.
He took his first chance to move to a department chairman-
ship, and then to a Dean of Arts and Sciences position. No
matter where he was, he systematically set about learning his
and everyone else's job, then began working on ways to im-
prove them, and by the time he had made himself indispensable
was beginning to get bored.

They were funny to see together on the beach. She was
like his child with her tiny perfect body. When he put suntan
lotion on her, one of his hands could cover her whole back.
His stomach was big, but his chest was massive.

"I'm going for a swim."

"I'm going to lie here and soak up the sun."

He marched out into the sea up to his knees. At the
farthest end of the harbor, two or three miles away, was the last
out ship channel marker. He dove in with an immense splash
and struck out toward it. He was so buoyant he seemed to
wallow at the surface, rolling from side to side with his form-
less but powerful crawl stroke. He did not let up his pace till
he reached the marker. There, he held on for a few minutes,
breathing hard, and waited, but nothing struck his heart. He
swam back at a somewhat more leisurely pace, and walked out
onto the beach, water streaming off his shaggy body, his
muscles pumped up to even more herculean proportions.

He lay down next to her and watched the topless bathers
for a while, then watched all the people on the beach one after
the other, trying to guess about their lives from what they
looked like. He watched the windsurfers for a while, but that
didn't seem very challenging.

"I can't stand lying here doing nothing," he said.

They went back to the apartment and had lunch and she
went on sunbathing on the balcony, this time with no bikini.
He liked that and watched her for a while, and then they made
love. Once when they were staying with friends they had been
making love in the guest bedroom when they realized there was
a long mirror beside the bed. They looked over and saw the
huge hairy monster with the tiny fragile child engulfed under
him, and they both laughed so hard they had to stop what they

were doing. But luckily for the most part they made love with their eyes closed, and it was the one thing he did gently, and she did fiercely.

When he stood up, the mountain was there in his view. He rode his bike up as high as the road went, chained it to a tree, and climbed to the top of the mountain. He looked around and saw water on all sides. "So much for that," he said, and was back at the flat in time to fix a drink before dinner.

"This island might start getting a bit small," he said. And while she watched him, his attention lapsed, and his eyes lost focus, and his face sagged in the direction of gravity. It was the end of their first day in the apartment.

However, he threw himself into his study of the language. He was fascinated to see how logical it was, how efficient. How by merely changing a to e in the verb paradigms they could be made to reflect action from a different perspective. He would study a particular point of grammar all morning, wandering around the house muttering, then in the afternoon he would walk downtown and try to talk to a newsagent, to a shopkeeper, working everything they said around so that he could use that particular point of grammar. He bought a tiny tape recorder which he kept in his pocket where it couldn't be seen, and recorded conversations, then played them over and over again when he got back to the apartment, analyzing them. He saw the ad, taped to a shop window, for a group of language tutors, and hired one to come by every morning for an hour class.

She in the meantime in her very quiet way slowly put her stamp on their living space. She filled the balcony and every empty spot with pots of growing plants. The rather standardized furnishings in their furnished apartment seemed as if they would resist personalization, but with the tiniest shifts—the equivalent of changing a to e—she turned each area into something recognizably her own. Each meal she fixed was individual and beautiful to look at, the local food and dishes given a slightly oriental quality. She had gone to Japan one summer to study painting and was delighted to find a whole country just her size, and designed and organized the way she designed and

organized a meal or a room. She had studied Japanese for
several months before going over, and he told her it was the
perfect language for her, as it seemed to consist of dozens of
ways of apologizing for your presence.

He was not by any means blind to the small and perfect
beauty always surrounding her, and that he himself sat in
somewhat jarringly, but no longer uneasily. He liked it. Maybe
she could extend her subtle power to him, and make him,
within her magic circle, somewhat less gross and incongruous.
She seemed to think it was no problem.

"You mean strength matters too, not just beauty."

"Not exactly," she said. "I mean they're not different. My
painting master showed me a very old painting. There were
three figures. Quite intentionally, I'm sure, there was no at-
tempt to make the composition interesting. It was just three
forms, all the same size, placed equidistant across the board
they were painted on. One was a peony, traditionally epito-
mizing beauty, but that only lasts for a day. The next was a
lion, incredible strength and fearlessness and vitality. The third
was a rock, perdurable, resistless, eternal."

"And they all belonged in the same painting."

"More than that. They were all the same shape. If you
squinted your eyes slightly—"

"So you would see them as an Oriental would."

"Yes, I hadn't thought of that—you would see that the
stone really looked very much like the peony, the peony like the
lion, and so on. That what was perfect in the flower was
enduring, that what was beautiful in the stone was transitory,
that the lion's strength was as fragile, his courage as perfect—
you could probably say this all better than I can."

"No. I think I understand," he said. It was her he couldn't
fathom. She was the one process he couldn't analyze, had given
up trying to, which is why perhaps he never grew bored with
her.

He thought he had dismissed the mountain after the first
day, and yet as he paced through the apartment muttering
hypothetical conversations, at the end of his pace he was always on the balcony looking at Big Dog.

"It's never the same twice," he said.

"Have you just noticed that?" she said.

Now he also noticed what she was doing. She had taken out a large sheet of watercolor paper and with a pencil and a straight-edge was lightly platting it out in 2½-inch squares. He sat and watched her. She fumbled hestitatingly through her life, but when she worked she was almost grimly efficient. Now she took an ordinary sheet of paper and cut a 2½-inch square out of the middle of it and held it at arm's length before her, and looked at the mountain through it. With her other hand she did drawings of the mountain, and when she had one that pleased her, she traced it on her tracing paper. Then she turned her tracing paper over and blacked the backside with a soft pencil. She turned the paper face up again and placed it over the first of the squares on her big sheet of watercolor paper, and with a hard pencil went over the lines of her original drawing, so that the carbon underneath transferred the line to the watercolor paper. Slowly and carefully she repeated this over each square.

He began taking an interest in the process. "You know there is such a thing as carbon paper, that would do the job a lot quicker and easier."

She ignored him.

"What you're going to do now is paint it every time it changes, right?"

"Mm-hmm."

"Now's the time to start," he said, beginning to take over. "There's a neat lenticular cloud forming over the peak. Here, I'll set up a chair and table for you."

"I have to fix your lunch right at the moment."

"That can wait. This is more important. It's already shifting."

But she went in and began preparing lunch. Partly, she was resisting having him take over. She could be as stubborn as he was. More so. In her soft but persistent way she could wear him down as water does stone. He knew this and felt helpless now, wishing he had not said anything. He had not meant to take over her idea, it's just that it had seemed like such a good idea to him, and he was already anticipating the pleasure he would have in seeing the mountain captured in each new view. He told himself not to say another word, otherwise she would not do it at all. Even as he looked, the lens cloud was lifting and losing its shape, and before he sat down to lunch it was gone forever.

In the morning when he opened his eyes, it immediately came to mind, and though he would like to have lain there holding her small intensely warm body, he got up and rushed to the balcony. After a night of high winds—the stormy season was fast approaching—the air was absolutely clear. The mountain seemed much closer, and the slant light gouged a deep black shadow across part of the front. The hard rock glowed in the sun.

"You should see it now," he said eagerly, going back to the bed. "It's the absolutely primal rock right now, no atmospheric effects, simply what is there, the bare bones." He said it as temptingly as possible, barely restraining himself from saying, "This is the time to start." She was not buying, however. She wanted something else for the moment and reached her arms up to him.

When he got up the second time a bank of cloud as solid as whipped cream was pushing up against one side of the mountain, and puffy clouds were appearing in a line above the horizon. He stopped himself from remarking on it, but she read his eyes perhaps. She went into the kitchen and began preparing their breakfast.

While they ate breakfast, the space between Big Dog and two smaller closer mountains filled in with solid cloud or fog, and a high overcast crept over the sky subduing the light, except for a point of sun still illuminating the peak, as if at the end of a gloomy tunnel. Then the overcast thickened, and the light on the mountain failed, and it was only a dull gray outline. The cloud system moved rapidly, clearing from behind them, and soon the sky was clear overhead, and sun covered the land, leaving only the mountain in a swirling gloom. He was in agony watching the changes, each ideally illustrative of a new facet of the mountain's personality, and each quickly lost. In the meantime she had gone out to do the shopping.

In the evening it went through all the same or similar changes in reverse, only this time everything bathed in fire, until at last the mountain, clear again, was stark and black against a sky like a thin sheet of molten steel slowly cooling and darkening. They sat long over their after-dinner coffees watching until the last spark was extinguished.

In the middle of the night he got up and came to look at it. The clouds had built up again and all outside was intensely purple black, except where reddish lightning flickered about the peak as if around the head of some monster about to be brought to life. He went back to the bed, aching to tell her, to get her to see it, but she was breathing easily, fast asleep.

The next day, she packed him lunch and a thermos, which he put in his backpack, and he took off on his bike heading for a town twenty-five miles down the coast, on the other side of the mountain, where he would have a different view of it. The wind had shifted direction and was coming from the mountain, and thunderheads were building behind it. He didn't bother to take a raincoat. He only had on a T-shirt, shorts, and sneakers, so it didn't matter if he got wet. He headed down the coast road, his huge legs pumping into the wind, his eyes squinted against the dust. When he reached the other town, it was windy, but clear and warm, tourists heading for the beaches. He could see the tremendous clouds over the mountain and what looked like a dense curtain of rain heading toward the apartment. The whole storm system seemed to be generated directly out of the mountain itself. He thought of her alone in the apartment with the storm approaching. She would be worrying about him, not realizing he was clear out of it, sitting against a tree and having a cup of coffee. He looked at the apartment in his mind room by room and thought what ought to be done. They had had strong winds before, so she knew to latch the shutters and not leave a door or window open in such a way that the wind could slam it shut and shatter the glass. But they had not up to now had rain. He remembered a stupid design flaw. The flat roof of the apartment complex drained down a large pipe which idiotically emptied onto their black-walled balcony and thence out a small hole in the floor of the balcony.

In a real torrential downpour, he estimated, that hole might be just fast enough to empty the balcony and keep it from backing up and flooding the kitchen. But, and here was a problem, there was a complicated grate fitted into the hole, which he should have removed as soon as he saw it, but had not. It created enough of an obstruction that it would stop the balcony from draining fast enough. He had not bothered to tell her to remove it in case of a storm, imagining that he would be there himself to do it. He thought of her coping with the flood, putting up towels against the door to dam the flood, bailing into the sink, and then he saw clearly the refrigerator with its electric motor on the bottom. Two inches of water in the kitchen—which she would be standing in—would reach the motor and short it out, electrocuting her.

Now he rode the bike with the wind and like the wind, his half-full thermos lying beside the road where he dropped it. Ahead of him the clouds thickened. Then he was over wet ground and deep puddles where the storm had passed, plowing through six inches of flood water in low parts of the road. The black wall of rain beyond which all was obscured was still ahead of him. Then he heard and felt the first big splats of water and in moments the rain was so thick he could barely see. To make things worse, as he crossed the edge of the cyclone, the wind shifted around until it was driving straight against him again, blinding him and now stinging him with hail, like shrapnel from the lightning bursting all around him. His broad body worked like a negative sail, an air anchor, holding him back as in a dream of running underwater. His massive thighs were nonetheless equal to any temporal wind and he pumped grimly, and, if such a word could be appropriate here, remorselessly. Then he had reached the edge of town, the rain coming with new fury, and turned up the side street off the front, leaped off the bike, feeling with surprise the sudden weakness in his legs, sprinted up the flight of stairs, threw open the front door, and punched the off button on the circuit breaker box. She was in the kitchen, towels against the door, bailing frantically into the sink. The water had just reached two inches deep. He pushed past her onto the back balcony, reached down into the deep swirling water for the grate, pulled it out and threw it as far as he could. The sky was already clearing.

Time was passing, and if in her patient and dreamy way she might someday get around to painting the mountain, she still had already missed thousands of changes never again to be repeated. He couldn't stand it anymore, and rented a car and drove across the island to the one city and bought an expensive camera and a heavy surveyor's tripod. He was too busy to spend years studying art and training his hand to reproduce what his eyes saw. So why not get a machine, a piece of apparatus, that will do it at once, and more accurately than the hand could ever do? He felt in his pride of the machine the faintest contempt for the patient art of his wife. That was a bit mean, so he altered that to feel instead guilty that he was trespassing on her turf, or sorry that he would so easily and quickly accomplish what she was still only contemplating. The dreamers and the doers. Of course it was her idea. He wouldn't have thought of it. But that's always the way, the reason we need the dreamers on this planet.

Yet it was not guilt or sympathy he felt setting his camera up on its tripod and aiming it at the mountain. It was self-consciousness, because though she said nothing, and seemed outwardly to show only the most generous interest, he felt she would be judging him, judging his results by criteria he was not altogether sure of. He looked through the viewfinder, aware that he was repeating the process of holding the paper with the hole cut out at arm's distance in front of him. His was only a more sophisticated version. And though when she was doing it, it was all he could do to restrain himself from taking it out of her hands and looking himself and telling her just where to do it from, it seemed so obvious to him, here now that he was actually doing it from this spot rather than that, he felt the whole weight of her competency bearing down on him. He actually felt himself sweating with this new kind of labor. He began to understand her exasperation with him at times, and wanted to turn and say Let me do this my way!—when he noticed she was in the bathroom running a bath and singing to herself.

One angle of the mountain did seem to show it the way he most often thought of it, and he locked the tripod into place. He realized he had already learned something. What he wanted was not *the* mountain, but rather, the mountain as *he* thought of it. At any rate he thought that *the* mountain, and the mountain the way *he* thought of it, were pretty close. He took the light reading carefully—it was altering as he took it, clouds crossing, then leaving the sun—and pressed the cable release to take his first picture. Click. He had caught it. This time it hadn't got away.

Throughout the day, as he did other things, he watched the mountain out of the corner of his eye, and as it altered, he snapped it. She was at the table painting a tiny white autumn flower. The last picture on the roll was a several-second-long exposure of the sunset, which this evening was like a gorgeous swirling bruise. He felt it would definitely be the most spectacular. He had made a few notes with each exposure, describing the state of the mountain in a few concise words. He had a feeling after all that if he approached it systematically he would find that the seemingly endless changes would reduce themselves to a manageable few that repeated themselves. Perhaps a relatively small number of pictures, say a hundred, would tell the whole story of the mountain. In the morning he took the film to a shop that promised twenty-four-hour service.

In the end it was three full days before he got them back. He had been in the shop a dozen times, his temper beginning to fray. But he smiled openly like a child when the shop-keeper, equally relieved, held up the packet as he entered. One satisfaction was that in all this time his wife had only managed to paint two petals on her flower. He ripped open the package as he was leaving the shop and could hardly believe what he saw. The giant mountain that had dominated his imagination for nearly two months came out in his pictures like a tiny pimple. Not only that, the colors were all wrong, much too blue at times, much too red at others, and everything he had seen as sharp and crisp was pale and washed out. The sunset was particularly flat and uninteresting. There was going to be more to this than he thought, and he set his jaw grimly, and went back into the shop and bought a big book on photography.

He read it straight through, and returned to the pertinent pages several times. He rented the car again and went back to the city and this time bought some filters to cut out haze and to correct color, and a longer focal length lens to bring the mountain forward to give it the magnitude he saw with his eye.

In the meantime she had completed her small perfect painting. The flower itself was blown and dry and unrecognizable, having faded in two days.

If things won't give in to your first rush, then you must be persistent and systematic. With an uneasy feeling that he was backing off slightly from his first resolve to record Big Dog in all its moods, he decided, for an initial objective, he would record it perfectly in *one* of its moods. He was so eager to begin he was up before dawn setting up the tripod. The sun, rising behind his back, illuminated the mountain before anything else, in a delicate faded pink, almost white, and it seemed like a fragile cone of infolded petals, until the sun was fully disengaged from the earth, when it took on the harsh black shadows and the glaring rocky face of its true substance. That's what he was waiting for, and he photographed it with his long lens to bring it up tall in the sky, crowding over the tops of the closer mountains, and he tried it with each filter, with every combination of aperture and duration, carefully noting down in his notebook which combinations he had used. It took the pictures a week this time to come back from the twenty-four-hour place, but they were terrific. There was the overbearing face, the metallic sky, the strong relief shadows. He showed them to her, and she said Yes, that's it, that's really good, and the childlike smile was on his face. She had found a tiny winter flower in bloom, and brought a blossom and a bit of leaf back, and set it in a jar to paint. But the old couple across the way needed her. She had been doing their shopping for them—the old man's pension check was so meager, and food was so expensive, she had been secretly augmenting it when she bought their food—and doing a few other chores. She had started out with gestures, but had word by word picked up the local dialect from them until now they conversed quite well. But the man was ill, growing worse. His wife needed all her time to care for him, so she had been doing everything else, cooking, washing. After she and the wife got the old man through a particularly bad spell, she found her winter flower had dried out past the point of her being able to recreate it in paints.

For a few days he was complacent, but then he went back and looked at his pictures more critically. With the blush of newness off them, they seemed less good, compared less favorably with the actual mountain. Further, he could see now how sloppily they had been developed, stains, dust spots, small patches where the color was the wrong tone. He rented the car, and went back to the city and this time returned with an enlarger and darkroom equipment. He took more pictures, then blacked out the bathroom and went in and developed his first roll. He liked the instant service. The waiting had killed him. And he was absolutely careful about dust, and keeping the temperature right, and of course had made sure all his chemicals were fresh. He started with a roll of black and white, figuring after he got the hang of it, he would return to color. But when he showed her the results she said, "Do you know what? It's better in black and white than it was in color." "How can that be?" he said, but he was only arguing from logic, because now that she had said it, he could see it too.

He caught the mountain in a few more moods, and was at least moderately pleased with the results. He thought he was learning better to make the camera record what he saw. But there were calls on his time as well. He was becoming quite proficient with the language, and was now helping the budding language school—it had been started by talented and ambitious young students with not much money or expertise. Rather than using textbooks based on some professor's notion of the most used words and grammatical constructions, they had adopted his technique of taping actual speech in the shops and on the streets, and using that—the language really used every day—as the basis of each lesson. The school, as the tourists began returning in the spring, began operating profitably and gained a reputation, and they got a publisher interested in the textbook they were putting together based on their new method. He showed them how to set up records and keep books, drafted the English parts of the textbook, and even went with them to take their petition to the provincial government to be licensed as a corporation. So that very often the camera sat pointing at the mountain through its various moods, but no one was there to press the cable release. And when he did complete a roll of film, it sat for weeks before he had a chance to develop it.

He had not lost any of his sixty extra pounds, but nevertheless bought some running shoes and started running. "I don't know why you bother to get advice from people if you're not going to follow it," she said. "I probably know my strengths and weaknesses better than a doctor who's only seen me a couple of times," he said. "You don't have any sense at all of your weaknesses. That's why you worked too hard and had to see the doctor in the first place." "It was just nerves, nothing physical." "He said that your heart—" "My heart's okay." "Your problem is you don't respect anyone or anything except yourself. You'd think after you got that head injury in college you would have realized you're not immortal." "You'll notice it's my head I've gone on to make my living with. Your problem is you respect everything and everybody *except* yourself. You have no concept of how strong you are in your own way. And how good. You're like an angel come back to earth sometimes. People think *I'm* good, just because I'm connected to you."

There was certainly no way she could respond to that, and he took off downstairs running.

Spring was progressing, the weather clearing. The mountain, which had often been obscured behind clouds and mist, was not visible again, but the camera and tripod, in the way of everything she wanted to do in the front room, was seldom used, though he often paused meditatively to look through the viewfinder. They were still trying to get the school officially licensed but the red tape was incredible. She noticed he was beginning to eat more, a bad sign. He kept up with his running faithfully, each day running as far up the mountain as the road went and back. Most days now this sweaty shaggy bear of a man, looking even more ludicrous, brought back in his big hand a tiny new spring flower for her to paint. She was

deluged by the bounty. Twenty flowers withered and died
while she struggled to paint one. It might take her all day to
paint one petal—and that was when she had all day to work on
it. The old man was better, but the wife was ill, and this was
worse than the other way around, because she had to nurse his
wife as well as shop and clean, plus trying to keep the old man
from sinking into depression. Then the woman was well, and
both of them had come through another winter, the time
when old people die if they are going to, and they were fiercely
proud to have survived again. She had part of the day to herself
again, and sat down to her paints and a tiny flower. He had
taken a day off too, and set off running right after breakfast.
She finished doing the breakfast dishes and came out to look at
the mountain. The morning had started clear and warm without a leaf moving. But as she looked she saw a huge thunder-
head rising up directly out of the summit of the mountain. She
looked with her binoculars and saw it seething and pumping.
There was not a sound. She tried to go to her painting, but in a
few minutes was back looking at the mountain. The cloud rose
ten thousand feet straight above it in the still air, solid as an
iceberg. While she looked she saw a flicker of light through it.
Trees only grew to about the three-thousand-foot line, so for
the last few miles he would be above them, and would himself
be the highest point on the exposed road. She wrung her hands
helplessly. Two thick bolts of lightning struck the mountain in
quick succession, jarring into it like fists. She set her jaw
grimly, and went down to the garage two blocks from them,
the one he always went to, and rented a car. "I know I'm just
being stupid," she said to herself, but she drove like the wind.
She came out above the trees and saw the lone runner near the
end of the road several switchbacks ahead of her. The sky was
black but there was complete stillness in the air. She downshifted and spun around the switchbacks, sending up a skein of
gravel against the safety railings. From one hundred yards'
distance she could see the hair was standing straight up around
his head like an eerie aurora. He ran on, totally absorbed in
what he was doing.

*   *   *

He reached the top of the road, the turn-around point, shrugging the stopwatch out of his pocket and raising it up to look at his elapsed time. With the other hand he was trying abstractedly to smooth down his hair. *Heart-attack, goodbye*

She didn't hear the stupendous crack of thunder either, she was too intent on getting the car stopped and getting out beside him, which she did in seconds, smoke still rising from the charred pieces remaining of his sneakers, a black afterimage dividing her vision. She rolled him onto his back and put the side of her head to his vast sinewed ribcage. He was not breathing, nor could she detect a heartbeat. This was one process she did know something about. Because of the time she spent with old people, she had made herself take an advanced first aid course. She thumped at the huge chest, the defunct bellows, with her tiny fists, but knew that was not enough, and stood up on his chest and bounced her whole weight on it at one-second intervals, and the heart, like a well-tuned engine, caught at the first try. Then she jutted out the sandpapery lower jaw, to open the wind pipe, and covered his mouth with hers, and blew in her child's breath as hard as she could, and again he took the spark of life from her, and was breathing. She has no idea how she got him into the car, only knows that the next day all the muscles down her side were pulled and were never quite right again.

In the hospital they told her she had plainly saved his life by being there at that second and knowing just what to do. It was a miracle, they kept saying. She began to find that a bit insulting. They found he had lost sixty pounds at the moment he was struck, body fluids simply vaporized, and every muscle in his body was shredded, and his calves and feet severely burned. He was already fully conscious and discussing with the doctor what steps he would need to take in his recovery, and how soon he could think about starting up his running again. He looked up at her, grinning. "You've got your nerve, following me around and thinking you know better than I do."

Everyone except him was amazed at the speed of his recovery. In less time than can be imagined he was back at the apartment, getting around a little bit on crutches. She gave him all her time, but he was very undemanding, a surprisingly good, obedient patient. Also he was obsessed again. This time, of all things, with photographing a plain drinking glass not quite full of water. Oh, he continued to photograph the whole mountain, and he continued, by telephone, doing some of the business of the language school, but maybe he had been just a bit chastened, and wanted to cover his bets by also trying to come at the whole by looking closely at one of its parts.

"You can't believe how challenging this is," he told her. "I must have taken fifty pictures of this thing and I still am just learning what to see in it."

She for her part continued her exacting painting of the single leaf, the single flower, but at moments during the day she let her point of focus come out a bit. She picked up her sheet of platted-out outlines of the mountain. None of the paintings took her more than two or three minutes to do. She filled sheet after sheet, her confidence and speed growing. She had been to that mountain, and felt she knew something about it. He had arrived at one position, one angle of light, that he thought was perfect, and he thought he was beginning to learn exactly how he wanted to develop the negative. By then however their time was up and they left the island.

PAUL LESLIE

EXITS

FROM SEVENTEEN

ᔓ

I CONCENTRATE ON DETAILS. The sun is hot through the wind-
shield. Will I really not get a sunburn? Though I don't feel it,
the highway slides by, the white lines charge me. The sun,
huge, and now on my left, seems to pulse. Its vague fringe
circles the center like rings around an atom.

This is futile. Other thoughts keep gnawing like insects.
Block them.

Details: patches of shade race parallel to the small clouds
above them, cut across the highway, and are gone into the
trees. The man at the Shell station had thinning hair. My back
is sticking to the vinyl seat. I feel the sweat near my hairline,
and I know that if I don't get a breeze soon, it will begin to roll
down my face. I am fighting that, too. Car, red, going other
way, girl driving. Lee. Not Lee, not Lee, notlee.

I cannot block it. She has crashed back, and the rest will
follow soon. A drop of sweat is slipping down my neck.

So where am I? I am nowhere, I am driving.

The thing is, I'm not sure what Trent would do. He might, on the one hand, continue. Finish the trip. Go to her door. If something was bothering him so much, Trent wouldn't, he just wouldn't, let it keep bothering him. At least not without confronting it, right?

Then again, I'm not sure *any* of my friends would let a girl like Lee bother them in the first place.

So I continue driving. I have counted the exits; there have been twenty-four. At the beginning, each one passed with such an enveloping strain, I was certain that at the next one I would turn back. Get the car back home. You still have time. Say you ran out of gas, stopped at Mark's or Trent's, *had an accident.* It's not as if she'll overlook the fender and headlight, anyway.

But I continue driving. Hypnotized, I guess, by the way the sun has wrapped and stretched the cool, broad morning highway into a tight, ever-narrowing strip. The exits, once clear and compelling, now pass almost unnoticed. I am hot. I once said to Mark that for some reason, it always seems hotter on the highway. He concurred: "It must be something in the concrete."

I could, after all, tell Mom I stopped at the grave site. Tell her the carnations were still blooming, or had faded, or were no longer there—some detail to assure her that I actually did stop.

I shouldn't lie. But the thing is, I shouldn't have taken her car without asking. I shouldn't have driven it over a hundred miles, and I certainly shouldn't have hit anything.

It wasn't my fault. My mom's brakes are so slow. If I had *my* car—but that's no excuse. I should have had it fixed months ago. It will be ready, I told Trent and Mark, by the time summer vacation starts. It wasn't my fault about the deer. Still, my hands are vibrating on the wheel. And I can just imagine what my grandmother would say if she knew. Wasted life, she would say, so careless! So irresponsible! If your father knew about this, well, he'd turn over in his grave. Just turn right on over.

*   *   *

Lee, thank you so much for all the letters and phone calls.

I knew that in a stressful time like this, I would be able to count on you for emotional support.

Hey, wait.

I know, I know. If I'm going to be fair about this, there is a good chance, since she went back to her cottage three weeks ago, that she may not have heard about Dad. Still, that doesn't make up for her not writing. I'll know, I once told her, that something is wrong if I ever say I love you and you don't say I love you, too.

Maybe I am more like Grandma than I'd like to admit. Maybe everyone's like her in that, to some extent, we put our greatest faith in little rituals.

It is somewhat coincidental that Trent and I just had a conversation about dead animals by the road. We were driving back from his parents' cottage on Lake Geneva five days after the funeral. I saw at least three rabbits, a skunk, two or three sparrows, and a dog. All of them on the shoulder and out of the way. I asked, When an animal gets hit, how does it get to the side of the road? I mean, you rarely see one right in the middle.

Maybe it had something to do with the touchiness of death at the time. Whatever the reason, Trent didn't deliver his usual logical solution. Well, you figure, he said. You figure most of the animals will get hit sometime before they get to the center. But there have to be some that get hit in the middle.

I said, Do they get blown over to the side by passing cars and trucks? Or do the people who hit them carry them off?

I don't know, he said.

The sign says Art's Mobil. A fat man is mowing the lawn outside the station—probably Art. His blue T-shirt is puddled with sweat and shows every bulge of his stomach. He is straining to push the lawn mower through the grass. It looks futile. I am angry and want to shout at him.

There is something annoying and frustrating about him. He seems to reflect the discomfort of this whole day: the way the sun has become an adhesive, the way it's settled in the dry dust by the road, the way it seems to be choking everything. It will always be like this: dry, lifeless, and without direction.

I do not stop.

Thank you, Lee, *so* much for all the letters.

We were all sitting—mother, grandmother, brother, sister, and I—in the small, white room at the funeral parlor. It was the same funeral home, and the same room, I am certain, in which my friend John Paulson and his family sat for *his* father's wake.

It seemed to be taking forever, and, despite the air conditioning, I was hot. We were all hot. I kept shifting in that stiff, wooden chair. There were so many friends of Dad's: friends of Dad's from the office, friends of Dad's from college, friends of Dad's from his favorite restaurant. Most of them I had either never seen or, at most, met once.

My brother, who is two years younger than I, noticed my politeness had worn thin. Jamie, he told me quietly, I wish you'd quit acting like such a jerk. I was looking for something, *anything*, that would give me an excuse to get out of there, if only for a minute.

Come here, I said and angrily led him outside.

I stood there on the hill behind the funeral parlor, and I stared at my brother, who I must say looked pretty sharp in a suit and tie. And I noticed that at some point in the past year, he had grown to be about two inches taller than me.

I said, and I knew even at the time that it was completely irrational, Look here, Danny, I don't have to take that from you or anyone else.

I wanted him to get mad. I wanted him to lash out at me with an irrational remark of his own. It was humid. I wanted him to tempt me, to say, Get serious, to give me even the trace of a reason to wind up and punch him in the stomach. He just looked at me. He didn't smile. His eyes didn't waver. I remember thinking, He pities me, damn it, he pities me.

He didn't say anything. He moved the dirt a little with his shoe. I said, So you just keep your mouth shut. All right?

All right, he said.

*   *   *

I can tell Trent, the next time I see him, exactly what I think happens when an animal gets hit. It gets hit, the car drives off, and it lies there in the middle of the road. And maybe the person who hit it, after driving a few miles, begins to think that perhaps it isn't dead, and it is lying in the road suffering.

And either that person continues on or pulls off at the next wayside or exit, returns to that hill or flat stretch or curve, and drags the very dead animal off to the side of the road.

It's like this, Lee. You are there, and I am here, and I'm driving. And I keep hearing songs on the radio that remind me of that weekend Mark, Kera, you, and I spent at your cottage. And I realize that as much as anything else, that weekend is the reason I am here, on my way to your cottage. There is still some faith in that scene I replay where you and I are walking on that path in those woods behind your cottage. *Are these woods yours? Yes, right up to that shed . . . my dad likes to sort of scout around in here and look for garbage.* And there is still some hope that you will again turn to me suddenly, kiss me lightly on the cheek, laugh as you always do, and say, I love you.

They were all so deathly serious and grim. Everyone looked tired. Some were crying in the pews. What is this? I whispered, a funeral? Trent didn't laugh; he just half-smiled to assure me he understood.

I love you, I said, the night before she went back to her cottage.

Good-bye, she said.

It was probably nothing. After all, she said she had a lot of packing to do. Maybe her father, who won't shake my hand, was in the room, and she would have felt awkward saying it. Still, I can't help feeling that if it was I who wanted to start slowly breaking the news that it was time to split up, move on, start anew, I might use, as my first subtle hint, the destruction of a trusted ritual.

* * *

I stood next to it, there on the highway, and I kicked it. I was crying. Damn you, I yelled, damn you! As if it had known it would be whipping into my bumper at sixty-five.

So I dragged it off, pulling it by its two bottom legs. A bone protruded from its side, and the blood around it looked almost black.

The two of us were all alone. Bonded, I guess, in a sense. But definitely alone. There was no one, *nothing*, I was certain, for a hundred miles.

But, Grandma, I said, as she drove my brother, sister, mother, and me out the cemetery gate. My grandma's 1974 Cadillac Seville, which has, at the most, ten thousand miles on it, always smells like air-conditioned baby powder.

But, Grandma, I said. My grandma, who has been living with us for several weeks now, is old. She is also rich. She is also religious. None of these things, by itself, do I consider bad in any way. But combined, they give my grandma the quality of being always a little too judgmental, a little too self-righteous, and a little too inconsistent. She buys dresses and earrings for hundreds of dollars, but I know, because I have seen her, that there are few things that get her as excited, that give her spine as special a twinge, as pulling into a parking space and finding she will be spared the quarter for the meter. She talks about God and starvation a lot, but what really gets her upset is when I have left my bed unmade or my little sister hasn't hung up her towel.

But, Grandma, I said. How can you believe there is someone up there watching out for our every move, someone who listens to everything we say, when people like Dad die so early?

Because, she said, I have faith in the Lord.

I scoffed. But there was something in her voice, and for a moment, I believe, I was jealous.

Thank you so much, Lee, for all the letters and phone calls.

There are no clouds anywhere. I watch the double yellow line as I drive, and it seems to pull me through the turns. The sun swings right to left, left to right, depending on the curve. On the night we got back from Lake Geneva, Trent and I sat in my bedroom listening to Elvis Costello. Above the stereo, I have a corkboard on which I've pinned pictures, drawings, ticket stubs, and other things. We weren't talking. I looked at a picture of Mom and Dad taken last year, on my seventeenth birthday. It's strange, I know, but he looked different. Fake. I don't know. I've glanced at the photo hundreds of times, but that night, he didn't look real. Trent noticed it, too. He said, You know, when someone dies, I think their picture goes with them.

The attendant at the Shell station said dint instead of didn't. He was a friendly old guy, but every sentence or two, he would say, quite clearly, dint. He was talking about the man in the blue Torino who had been in such a hurry to get gas.

You dint have to let him go ahead of you, you know. You dint have any trouble with the self-serve, did you? I dint think it would be so hot today.

He kept talking, though I hardly said anything, for nearly ten minutes. Not that I minded. He probably doesn't get too many customers out here. And it is nice, sometimes, when you are driving alone, to stop and talk for a while. That way, when you pull off the gravel, there are someone else's words on your lips for a few miles.

But it seemed odd, as I started down the highway, that it had never really occurred to me, or at least never bothered me, that there are lots of people that you meet once and never see again.

This is the way things are: Animals always get hit by cars, little brothers never really fight back, people cry at funerals, songs become personal. Lee.

I love you. Good-bye, she said. Maybe it was nothing.

The deer saw the car coming. Of that I am certain. And yet it stood there, staring, as the brakes squealed and the horn honked. If you had moved, for God's sake, we wouldn't be in this mess: you in the tall grass, me facing the point-blank command to face up.

*   *   *

The deer is dead, I checked it out. Not that there was a great deal of doubt in my mind before I turned around. But it is dead, and now it is lying in the tall grass by the side of the road. No one can see it, I made certain, when they drive by. There is a persistent uneasiness as I continue driving. My hands continue to perspire and slide on the wheel. It's as though I've forgotten something, as though I should have stayed there in the grass and just sat with the deer for a couple of hours.

Let's go, he was shouting, standing half in, half out of the Torino. Let's move it. He was smiling, but I could tell from his eyebrows that he was serious. His thin hair lay limply on top of his head.

Let's go, he repeated, forcing a smile. I don't have all day— I'm balding here. He laughed nervously.

My car will never get done, Art will never lose weight or leave the gas station. There will never be a letter. That man will continue to go bald. I will never see Dad again.

So you are there, and I am here. And I am wondering what you will say when I arrive, unannounced, at your cottage. It's like all the past talks, kisses, gestures—indeed, all the things in which I had absolute faith—are now in question.

So you are, and I am. There. Here. Should I, after all this, turn back? The count is now twenty-seven.

So where am I? I am nowhere, I am driving. And the sparrows, like pigeons, don't move until I pass over them. I hope they fly off. I don't look back.

There was that day during the halftime of the football game when we played catch, and I dropped, what was it? thirteen in a row? Dad kept saying, that's all right, Chief. Whenever you're ready. That's all right. I should have been there. He was dying, and I knew it. I should have been right there by his bed.

If you continue, you know, and she is distant or coy, well, that will be it. There are such things as gradations of acceptance. Are there? Why not? There are certainly gradations of despair and anger.

And doubt.

Do you ever notice the silence, the complete, steel-gray silence, when the radio is suddenly turned off? Things seem to stand up and give notice. That exit sign for instance. Doesn't it seem strong?

JAMES McCULLA

HOW ESCO MIZE GOT RELIGION

FROM PLOUGHSHARES

ᔐ

"I DON'T BELIEVE IT, not a bit of it," Esco Mize said. "I've heard about them kind of preachers all my life and I ain't seen one yet that wasn't holding a snake with one hand and reaching in your pocket with the other. Lord, he must think we're just a bunch of hicks here."

"Well, we'll all find out tomorrow night," I said.

The revival at the Bob Mountain Church of the Savior had ended with the traveling preacher promising a sign of the power of the Spirit the next night. He would allow a rattlesnake to bite him all over his body. "The serpent is evil," Preacher Stiles shouted, his arms stretched wide, like he wanted to bear hug the whole congregation. "But the blood of the Savior is all good. I'm washed in the blood, so what can harm me?"

Now we were heading home. The shoulder-wide footpath winding to the top of the ridge was black except for the yellow-green flash of lightning bugs and the soft glow of fox

157

fire. Tree branches overhead blocked the moonlight. Esco led the way; I followed the white of his T-shirt. He kept throwing questions over his shoulder.

"Roy, you mean you're actually going back there? You believe all that?"

"I guess so," I said. "Mom and Dad always have. I guess I do too."

"How much did they give tonight?" Esco asked.

"I saw Dad put a twenty in the plate."

"How bout you?"

"All I had was a dollar."

Esco's laugh rang through the woods. "Well, that slick preacher may have put something over on you all, but not me. You know why?"

"Cause you just plain hate preachers since . . ."

"That ain't it at all." He stopped climbing the footpath and faced me. "It's because they think they can come up here and put one over on us poor ignorant hillbillies. And you prove them right, forking over your last dollar. Well, my dad set me straight on these here fly-by-night preachers. They love to come around telling folks no rattlesnake or copperhead can hurt them. They can do it cause they bring their own snakes with them. And you can bet before these preachers do one revival someone's worked them snakes over good with a pair of pliers. Dad and me traveled all over this state and down into Kentucky and Tennessee besides when he was looking for work. We saw plenty of revivals. This here preacher ain't no different."

"I don't believe that," I said. "Preacher Stiles is a good man. You're making all this up."

Esco didn't say anything for a minute. I listened to his quiet breath.

"You calling me a liar, Roy Eller? Me and my dad?"

He took ahold of my arm and squeezed. It hurt. I'd forgotten never to cross Esco Mize.

"Well?" he asked, and his grip tightened some more.

"No," I said. "Let go."

He did. "I was telling you out of friendship, Roy. We're friends, ain't we?"

"Sure." I shook the pain out of my arm.

"I know your daddy ain't got no twenties to spare. Is it right for him to give money to a fake? I'm just trying to help out and set you all straight. I been around a lot more'n you. I seen things you ain't. You ever been out of these hills, Roy? Ever been to Charleston, or Huntington, or up to Wheeling?"

"No, but my mom and dad have always believed and that's the way I was raised up and it's good enough for me. They ain't ignorant."

Esco started up the steep footpath again, me following. We topped the hill, out of breath and sweaty, and stood in a clearing along the backbone. Light from the full moon made the broom sedge look silver. Esco stood looking at the sky, and I watched an evil smile split his face. I felt uneasy. Folks said Esco Mize had the devil in him. After his mom died Esco and his dad went drifting while his dad looked for work. He didn't find anything steady. They came back just long enough for the old man to leave Esco and take off again. He never came back and Esco stayed put, living on his own. I don't know how he got by, but he did, and he seemed to like it.

Most of the other kids thought Esco was something, though they didn't say it too loud around their folks. I guess I thought he was something too. Esco was older than me and bigger. He could shave everyday if he wanted to but he didn't. He knew the black whiskers made him look even older and meaner. Nobody wanted to mess with him. Esco was tough. He licked me in arm wrestling and Indian wrestling every time, and once when we really mixed it up it was all over in two punches, one to my nose and one to my mouth. He could swallow a mouthful of whiskey without a coughing fit.

Esco Mize had had no use for religion or preachers of any kind since he got churched. That happened after his dad hit the road and Esco started running wild. Mister Hershel Keener was a church deacon, the salt of the earth, but that didn't stop Esco from taking his daughter Mary up in the woods above the Bob Mountain Church one night. They were sprawled under a laylock when Esco saw the lanterns come bobbing through the woods, heard Deacon Keener hollering, "Esco Mize, when I catch you I'm gonna nail your hide to the barn door." Esco did up his pants and ran. He ran to my house and Dad let me hide him in the cellar till folks cooled down. Esco kept his hide but they did call him up in front of the church board. "Will you marry her?" "Hell, no." So they churched him. Before, some folks had felt kind of sorry for Esco, him not having either a mom or dad, but after that they wouldn't speak to him.

Now, standing in the hip-deep brush, Esco took a pack of cigarettes from his shirt pocket and lit one.

"Roy, if it's proof you want, we'll get it. We'll get this religion thing settled. Tomorrow's the last night of the revival and folks from all over these hills will be there to see what happens. We'll straighten it out for all of them. Come morning you meet me here. Bring a poke and your knife with you."

"What's your plan?" I asked.

"I aim to go up to that old Darnell place. Last time I was there, me and Lizzie DuBose, I found a ball of rattlesnakes in the fireplace, snakes as big around as my arm. When I stirred them up with a stick it sounded like a buzz saw in there. I'll need your help, Roy. We'll bag us a real fighter and switch snakes on Preacher Stiles. You wanna help? Or are you chickenshit?"

"I ain't scared. I was just thinking he might notice the difference."

"Oh, he will." Esco grinned and the smoke sifted out. "When he feels them fangs go in his arm he'll notice the difference right away. Once a long time ago my daddy got bit while he was chopping wood at the woodpile. He rolled a log and there one was. Bit him on the hand. It wasn't no more'n half a minute before his arm was swelling up. Swelled up twice as big and Daddy was flat on his back for two months. The preacher will notice the difference. But why should that bother you? You believe. You believe this preacher's a man of God. You believe I'm telling you a lie. If no snake can hurt him cause he's got the Spirit, what difference will it make if we switch snakes? We'll find out the truth. I'm wrong, or you're wrong."

He had me there. I couldn't think of a way out and he knew I couldn't. That grin of his. He was so sure and it made me mad. I wanted to prove him wrong. He finished his smoke, threw the butt away, toed it out in the dirt.

"I think you are chickenshit," he said. "About catching snakes and about putting this here preacher to the test. Chickenshit about everything."

"No, I ain't."

"Then see you here tomorrow. Early. And Roy—" he stepped closer— "don't tell nobody about this or it'll be bad for you." He turned away. I watched him go across the clearing and into the woods, moving quiet as a deer.

I went on my way. Going down the other side of the ridge I saw in the valley below the lights on at my house, the pickup in the driveway, so I knew my folks were home from the revival.

"Hey," Dad said when I came in. He was stretched out on the couch reading the paper, his bifocals down to the tip of his nose.

"Where's Mom?" I asked, and sat down.

"Making coffee. I looked for you after the service. I figured you'd want a ride home. Where'd you run off to so quick?"

"I felt like walking. I walked part of the way with Esco."

Mom came out of the kitchen, her hands dripping suds. I heard the coffeepot begin to perk.

"Roy, I wish you wouldn't spend so much time with that boy. He's a bad influence."

"He's just another guy, Mom. He don't tell me what to do."

"You smell like cigarettes."

"Esco was smoking, Mom, not me," I said.

Dad pulled in his feet so Mom could sit at the end of the couch. "I swear," she said, "I never thought that boy would dare show his face in a church again."

Dad grunted behind his paper. "Well, the roof didn't fall in. If he's as bad as you think church is the best place for him."

"You don't think he's wild?" Mom asked.

"Every boy goes through a spell where he's fighting against everything. Esco's got it worse than most. You just raise them right and hope they'll come back to the right path sooner or later."

"You think Esco Mize is coming back?" Mom was doubtful.

"It's possible," Dad said.

"I suppose," Mom said. "Well, if he is he couldn't have picked a better night. That Preacher Stiles can speak the Word. I never heard anyone like him."

"He's a good one." Dad turned a page of the paper, slapped it flat. "Been a long time since we had a revival like this one around here."

"Are you all going tomorrow night?" I asked.

"I wouldn't miss it," Mom said. "Why do you ask?"

"I just thought maybe tonight would be enough for you all," I said.

"You never want to pass up a chance to hear a preacher like this one," Mom said. "You're going, aren't you, Roy?"

"I guess."

"Well, I'm happy to hear that."

"Where is that verse, Mom? The one the preacher was talking about."

"It's in Mark." Mom went upstairs and came back with her *King James Family Bible*, a heavy book with gold lettering on the white leather covers and Jesus' words in red. The Bible had a special section in the front where she kept a record of the Eller family births, deaths, marriages, and baptisms. The most recent entry was my baptism three years before, when I was thirteen.

"You all listen," Mom said, and she read the verses.

And these signs shall follow them that believe; in my name shall they cast out devils; they shall take up serpents; and if they drink any deadly thing, it shall not hurt them. They shall lay hands on the sick, and they shall recover.

"Dad, you ever seen this kind of preacher before?" I asked.

He put down the paper. "Not that I can remember. I listened to a lot of preachers in my time."

"I have," Mom said. "When I was just eighteen."

"What did he do?" I asked.

"He was a true prophet, Roy. He could pass his hand over fire and not be burned. He drank poison. He allowed himself to be bit by rattlesnakes and copperheads. He had the gift of healing hands. I remember I was sitting on the back bench when I saw the flames of the Holy Spirit on his head. I went up the aisle and he took my hand and I received the Spirit that very night."

"You never saw a preacher get bit and then get sick or die?"

"No," Mom said.

"Now I remember one," Dad said. "I was just a boy. I can't remember his name, but he got bit while he was preaching and he did get mighty sick. Never died, though. He said, 'I just got my mind off the Lord.' He was a good man. Got well and went right back to preaching. Never happened again."

"The Lord protects his servants, Roy," Mom told me. "You remember that." She closed up the Bible and offered it to me. "Do you want to do some more reading?"

"Not tonight. I'm pretty tired. That was a long walk."

"You want something to eat? Have a cup of hot coffee with us."

"I think I'll just go on to bed. I want to get up early tomorrow."

"Good night," Mom and Dad said.

"Night." I went up the steps, wondering if Preacher Stiles was a real servant of God.

The next morning I climbed to the top of the ridge and found Esco waiting for me. When he saw me coming he pulled a flat bottle of whiskey from his back pocket and took a swig. Swallowed it right down with no trouble.

"Drinking and snake hunting don't go together," I said.

He grinned, showing broken gray teeth. "Let me see the poke."

I gave him the old feed sack. It was burlap and plenty big. He yanked my knife from the sheath dangling from my belt and tested the edge across his thumb. A thread of blood oozed out. He showed me.

"Don't feel a thing," he said. "No snake's gonna hurt me."
He took another drink and pushed the bottle at me. "You
take some."

"No, I don't want any."

"Damn, Roy, ain't you ever been drunk before?"

"Sure."

"So take one. Be a man."

I took a sip on my tongue, swallowed, and felt it burn
in my nose and turn my stomach, but I didn't show it. Esco
watched me carefully. I gave him back the bottle and sheathed
my knife.

"I bet you never even laid a girl before," he said.

"Are we going or not?"

"Sure. We're doing the Lord's work, Roy. Exposing the
false preachers. Just keep remembering that when you start
to chickenshit out."

He led the way down the ridge and into the hollow. We
splashed across the swampy bottom and hiked up the next
hill. Out of breath, we rested. That was one; we had two more
ridges to cross.

An hour and a half after we started we saw the Darnell
place, a three-story farmhouse now crumbling to rot. Rasp-
berry bushes, long since gone to seed, curled through the high
brush liked barbed wire.

"The doors and windows are all boarded up," I said.

"Not on the other side they ain't."

We waded through the hacking to the back. One sheet of
plywood had been ripped off a window and was propped
against the ledge like a loading ramp. We climbed right in.

"Back this-a-way," Esco said, and I followed him down
a long hallway to another room, dark as night since all the
windows were boarded. Just slivers of light sneaked in around
the edges. Esco pounded the plywood with his fist.

"Give me a hand here, Roy."

I kicked at the plywood, the nails cried out, and sunlight
filled the room when the sheet fell away.

"There they be," Esco breathed.

It was just like he'd said. Timber rattlers in the fireplace.
They coiled and slithered and bunched up against the creekstones,

and when Esco finished his last drink and smashed the empty whiskey bottle against the fireboard, spraying them with glass, the rattle sounded like an angry beehive.

"How many?" I asked.

Esco went closer. "Three. I see three heads. Damnation, look at the size of that one, Roy. He's the granddaddy of them all. He's the one we want. I never seen such a rattlesnake. Okay, you go cut us two long forked poles. Hurry up."

I went outside and broke off two young saplings and trimmed them with my knife like he said. When I got back he was hunkered down near the snakes, stirring them up by tossing chunks of plaster.

"Gotta draw Granddaddy out of there, Roy. Give me one of them poles. Keep that poke handy."

"Okay."

He looked up, saw where I was standing, and said impatiently, "Well, come on. Get up here and bring him out. I ain't doing this all alone. Come on, this is the easy part."

Sweat burned my eyes. The air in the room smelled like rot, and the sunlight was cloudy with dust. I wanted to back away. But Esco was squatted down on his haunches, the snake-catching pole in his hand, and he was watching me. His grin said *You can't do it.*

I stretched out my pole and raked at the rattlers. The big one struck at the pole, coiled to attack again. The other two snakes pushed back in the corner of the fireplace. I couldn't believe how far that monster rattler could strike, how fast it was.

It was coming out again, coming out to fight that long sharp thing poking at it. When it struck again I slapped the pole across its back, pinned it down. Esco jumped forward and squashed his boot right behind the triangle head. The snake's mouth opened, the forked tongue flicked, and I saw two white fangs.

"I think you killed it," I said.

"Hell, I've cut off their heads before and seen them still try to bite. Besides, a snake won't die till sundown no matter what you do to it." He eased up his boot a second. "He's far from dead. Look at that tail whip. Get the poke."

I dropped my pole and got the sack. "This is the hard part," Esco said. "Once you get ahold you can't let go." He carefully reached under his boot till he had a good grip on the snake's neck. "Got him now." He lifted his boot and held the snake above his head. The tail hung pert-near to the floor, slapped around Esco's thighs and waist. "Hell, look at him," Esco said. "Six foot if he's an inch. Look at him try to bite." I held open the poke, Esco shoved the head in and rammed the long, thick body in after it. He tied off the sack with a length of cord.

"That's it," I said.

"Not quite." Esco got his snake stick and returned to the fireplace. The two smaller snakes were still bunched up in the corner. Using the sharp-pointed pole like a sword, he stabbed and chopped at the snakes till they were still. The dusty hearth stone was smeared with blood. He took my knife, knelt down, sliced off the buttons, and shoved them in his pocket.

"Protection," he said. "Now we're done." He left the pole on the floor and picked up the snake sack. "I'll carry it. Ain't nothing to worry about. Granddaddy won't strike at what he can't see. But he'll be able to see tonight."

I thought of that big snake, how fast and far he could strike. I thought of the story my Dad told.

"I don't think I like this idea anymore."

Esco looked at me. "Yeah, I was wondering when Chickenshit would back out."

"I ain't a chickenshit."

Esco slapped the poke. He didn't say anything for a while.

"All right, Roy. It ain't necessary to have that preacher get bit and maybe die to prove I'm right. I'll tell you what we'll do. We'll show some Christian mercy. That should make you feel good. You and me, we'll sit right up front on the mourner's bench. We'll be able to see everything. When Preacher Stiles goes to open the box, I'll just lean forward and say, 'Preacher, the eye of God is on you tonight. That ain't your snake, that's mine. And he's got teeth.' That'll end the revival mighty quick. How bout that, Roy?"

"You swear you'll tell? Cause if you don't, I will."

"I swear. Let's go to the church now and hide Granddaddy in the woods. We'll switch snakes tonight right before the revival starts."

Esco was late. I saw on the front steps of the Bob Mountain Church of the Savior waiting for his grinning face to come out of the woods. Around the little clearing by the church lanterns hung from tree branches, a cloud of moths and gnats around each lamp. Folks were talking, laughing. Every once in a while a family would break away from their neighbors and come toward the door. When they went by me into the church their smiles went slack. The revival was serious business, a solemn occasion. Silently, Mom and Dad went in, and I was just about to join them when Esco appeared at the edge of the clearing, nodded at me, and went around to the back of the church.

I followed. He stopped under the locust tree where he'd hid the snake sack and felt around in the darkness.

"Got it," he said, and held the sack up, gave it a shake and listened. "Granddad don't like to be disturbed. Ready?"

"I guess. Just remember what you promised."

"I remember. Let's get on with it." He dropped the snake sack. "The box should be right in back of the pulpit."

We went in the church back door into the little room where folks change their clothes after being baptized. We opened another door that led onto the altar. No one was there, but we could hear the voices of the people already seated. We crawled along the wall to the pulpit. The congregation couldn't see us; the pulpit blocked their view.

The snake box was wood with a hinged lid and drill-bit-sized holes in the top. Esco grabbed it and we backed out. We carried it to the edge of the woods.

"I need a light," Esco said. "I want to take a look."

"Use a match."

He felt his pockets. "I ain't got a match. I'm all out. You didn't bring a light?"

"You didn't say to."

"Damn, do I got to tell you everything?"

"What do you want a light for? Just heave whatever's in there down in the gully."

"I want to show you his snakes ain't got no fangs."

There was nothing he could do. It was too dark under the trees away from the light of the church. Most everybody had gone in and Preacher Stiles would be arriving any minute. "Damn it to hell," Esco said, and turned the box over into the gully. Something fell; we heard it sliding through the dry brush.

"Untie the sack," Esco said.

I yanked the cord from the poke, but I couldn't dump that big snake into the box. I couldn't.

"Come on," Esco said.

"No."

"Chickenshit!" He grabbed the sack and dumped the rattler in the box. I heard an angry buzzing before he slammed the lid.

"Now you take the box back in," Esco said, and pushed it at me. "You're in this as much as me."

"I ain't doing that either."

I didn't even see the punch coming. Suddenly I was laying on my back in the grass, staring up at the night sky. My nose felt like it was stuffed with cotton and there was a warm trickle underneath. I wiped it away, sat up, and watched Esco go in the back door, the box under his arm.

I hurried around to the front of the church and followed the last groups of people in. Everyone was seated, women on the left, men on the right. I saw Dad at the end of one aisle; he'd saved a place for me. Mom waved at me from the other side, then looked mighty surprised when I went to the front to sit on the mourner's bench. I kept glancing back to see if Esco was at the door. I figured he'd left when I saw him come in and strut up the aisle like he was the preacher himself. Ignoring all the whispering, he sat by me and jabbed his hand hard into my kidney.

"I changed my mind," he said. "You tell that preacher one word and you'll really get a licking tonight. You'll be picking your teeth out of the dirt." And he jammed his fist into my side again.

The congregation fell silent when Preacher Stiles appeared. A little man, he had pepper-colored hair and looked to be in his fifties. He wore black, his suit coat hung loose on him, and when he took it off to roll up his shirt sleeves he showed arms no bigger'n sticks of kindling. He didn't speak from the pulpit, but paced back and forth across the altar, and the way he looked at the congregation with his black eyes made you feel he was staring directly in everyone's eyes at the same time.

"One bite and he'll keel right over," Esco sneered.

"Let's have some singing," Preacher Stiles said in a loud voice.

Three men with guitar, banjo, and mandolin rose and stood in a corner. Tuning up, one said, "You all join in now, you know the words."

> *You can't be a beacon if your light don't shine.*
> *You can't be a beacon if your light don't shine.*
> *There's a little light in all of us by God's design,*
> *And you can't be a beacon if your light don't shine.*

"Let the Lord hear you!" Preacher Stiles shouted. Everyone sang louder.

> *How can you ask for truth when you do not truthful live?*
> *How can you ask forgiveness when you don't forgive?*
> *I don't mean to bring you down or speak to you unkind,*
> *But you can't be a beacon if your light don't shine.*

"What're you singing for?" Esco asked. I stopped.

> *You can be a beacon if you let it shine.*
> *You can be a beacon if you let it shine.*
> *There's a little light in all of us by God's design,*
> *And you can be a beacon if you just let it shine.*

"Praise the Lord," Preacher Stiles said when the singers sat down. "Who here believes in the Savior?"

The congregation murmured, but a few hollered right back, "I do! I do!"

"Who has the Spirit?"

"I do!" More voices this time. "I do!"

Two men came out of that little room behind the pulpit and picked up the snake box. They put it at Preacher Stiles's feet. He didn't even look at it.

"Friends," Preacher Stiles spread his arms wide, "have you heard the Good News? Through the blood of the Redeemer you can be saved. I've been washed in the blood, I'm free of sin, and I'm wearing the armor of the Savior. What can do me harm?"

There was a commotion in the back, someone shouting. It was Evie Carpenter, standing in the aisle, swaying, her hands reaching for the rafters while she talked to angels, using words I couldn't understand. Other ladies, my Mom included, gathered around her, hugging her, trying to receive the Spirit too.

"The Spirit is working tonight," Preacher Stiles said. "He's here. He's touched our sister. Who else has heard Him speaking to the heart?"

An old wrinkled man I didn't know hobbled to the foot of the altar steps. His face and neck were sunburn red, and he wiped tears from his cheeks with a dirt-brown hand.

"That's Curley Pennington," Esco whispered. "I've bought booze from him. What's he doing?"

Curley said, "Oh Lord, I'm a man lost. I've lost my way to Glory. Help me, Preacher."

"I can't save you," Preacher Stiles answered, "only Jesus."

"The Lord has picked me up and shook me over the fires of Hell. He's showed me I'm walking in the devil's footprints. Help me, Lord!" Curley fell face down on the altar steps.

'He's gone loco," Esco said.

"You, son!"

Esco gave me another good shot in the ribs. "Not a word," he whispered. I looked up to see the preacher staring at me.

"Why are you here tonight sitting in the mourner's bench?" Preacher Stiles asked. "Is Jesus speaking to your heart?"

Before I could speak a word, Esco said, "He doesn't believe. Not a word of it. He wants to see a sign of God, not some preacher talking."

"Here's a soul who was lost and now has found his way back." Preacher Stiles pointed to Curley, who was still moaning on the steps. "There are ladies blessed with the gift of tongues."

"No," Esco said. "Another sign." He pointed to the box. "Then he'll believe."

"Is that what you want, son?" Right at me now.

All I had to say was no. All I had to do was warn him. But I didn't. It wasn't because of Esco; he'd whipped me before. I don't know why I didn't say no, didn't speak up.

"Yes," I said. "I do. I want to see it."

Esco grinned.

"The Spirit is strong armor," Preacher Stiles said. "Stronger than the poison of serpents, stronger than Satan."

He flipped the box lid up and reached in. If he noticed the snake was a different one he didn't let on. He stood up, the long granddaddy rattler in his hand. He held it in the middle, not tight behind the head like Esco had done. The warning buzz quieted the church. I heard a woman say, "Oh my, that snake." The long tail wrapped around Preacher Stiles's skinny arm like a thick brown vine.

"Bite me," Preacher Stiles said, "and show poison can't hurt me. Bite me, rattlesnake. Show how evil can't touch them who believe."

He held the rattler close to his body and it struck. The snake bit him on the arm, then on the shoulder, and every time Preacher Stiles got bit the congregation went "Oh!" like they were hit in the stomach. Preacher Stiles swung the rattlesnake around his scrawny neck and the snake struck his cheek. I watched for the swelling, but there wasn't any. I waited for the poison to reach his heart and him fall, but he didn't. Then I noticed the preacher's eyes weren't on me anymore. He was watching Esco.

"Here's God's sign, son." Preacher Stiles dropped the snake to the floor, where it coiled around his shoes. He pulled up his pant leg and the rattler bit into his calf.

"What did you do to my snake?" Esco demanded, and his face was fiery red. "You fake, you pulled his fangs too."

"It's the Lord, son."

"It's a damn pair of pliers is what it is." Esco jumped off the mourner's bench. "And I aim to show everybody."

He got one foot on the altar steps. Then quick as only an angry snake can be the rattler struck. The long body stretched down the steps and bit Esco on the knee. The congregation went "Oh!" and Esco fell backward, sprawling in the aisle by the bench, taking the rattler with him.

"Get it away! Get it away!" Esco screamed, the color gone from his face. The snake coiled between his legs and Esco kicked at it, missed, and the rattler bit him on the inside of the thigh. "Roy, help me!"

I reached down, grabbed the shaking tail, heaved the snake up on the altar. Preacher Stiles calmly picked it up and put it back in the box.

"I'm on fire. It burns," Esco groaned. "I'm dying."

The congregation was all around him, whispering.

"Look at it swell up."

"Two . . . was it two bites?"

"I think it was three."

"Lose the leg at least."

"I need a doctor," Esco cried. He rocked on the floor, holding his leg. "Take me to a doctor!"

"Somebody go find some rattlesnake weed. That'll do it."

"Naw, whiskey. He's gotta drink a whole bottle right quick."

"Esco, he'd probably like that for a cure."

"Cut across them bites and make a paste outa fat meat and salt and turpentine and rub it on good."

"Comes in here blaspheming, what do you expect?"

"Roy?" Esco asked. "Roy?"

The congregation parted to let Preacher Stiles through. He knelt down beside Esco and took his hand.

"Ain't no doctor here, son. Even if there was, he couldn't do you no good. Two bites, and that last one was right near a big vein. You'll never make it to a doctor."

"Try! I'm dying!"

"Look at me, son." Preacher Stiles pointed to the bite on his cheek, on his arm. "Do you see me dying? Look how I'm bit. Only the Lord can save you."

"Amen," someone said.

"The blood of Jesus will rid your blood of the serpent's poison. Do you believe it will? Believe and you'll live."

Esco looked wild-eyed at the quiet crowd, gasping like that day he'd come to my house, running from Deacon Keener. He looked at me, then touched the swelling in his leg.

"Jesus save me! I believe, Jesus!"

"Lay the healing hands on, friends," Preacher Stiles said. "Kneel down everyone, close your eyes and let's pray. Another lost soul has found the path home."

I watched the congregation kneel one by one, bow their heads. There was Mom kneeling, and Dad. There was Evie Carpenter, still muttering strange words, and Curley Pennington, looking mighty confused. Hands covered Esco's body, so many hands I couldn't see him. I could only hear him sobbing.

"Our Father, who art in heaven . . ." Preacher Stiles stopped, looked at me standing there. "Kneel down, son, and lay on your hands to help your friend. Only by believing can you help him."

"I was in on it too," I said.

"I know. Kneel down now."

And I did.

BOB SHACOCHIS

EASY IN THE ISLANDS

FROM PLAYBOY

✍

THE DAYS WERE SMALL, pointless epics, long windups to punches that always drifted by cartoon fashion, as if each simple task were meaningless unless immersed in more theater and threat than bad opera.

It was only Monday noon and already Tillman had been through the wringer. He had greased the trade commissioner to allow a pallet of Campbell's consommé to come ashore, fired one steel band for their hooliganism and hired another, found a carpenter he was willing to trust to repair the back veranda that was so spongy in spots that Tillman knew it was only a matter of days before a guest's foot burst through the surface into whatever terrors lived below in the tepid darkness, restocked on vitamins from the pharmacy, argued with the crayfish regulatory bureau about quotas. And argued with the inscrutable cook, a fat country woman who wore a wool watch cap and smoked hand-rolled cigars; argued with both maids, muscle-

174

bound Lemonille and the other one, who wouldn't reveal her name; argued with the gardener, who liked to chop everything up; argued with the customs house; argued with the bartender, Jevanee. And although he had not forthrightly won any of these encounters, he had won them enough to forestall the doom that would one day descend on Rosehill Plantation.

But now the daily defeats and victories were overshadowed by a first-class doozy, a default too personal to implicate the local population. The problem was to decide what to do about his mother—Mother, who had thought life wonderful in the islands. Now she rested stiffly in the food locker, dead and coated with frost, as blue as the shallow water on the reefs, protected from the fierceness of the sun she had once loved without question or fear, a sun that was never really her enemy, no matter how it textured her skin, no matter what it revealed of her age.

In her room on Saturday, Mother had died mysteriously. As Lemonille had said when the two of them carried her out after the doctor had been there, "Mistah Tillmahn, it look so you muddah shake out she heart fah no good reason. Like she tricked by some false light, ya know."

His mother's body had been strong and brassy, her spirit itself unusually athletic for a woman only weeks away from sixty. In her quick laugh was as much vitality as a girl's, and yet she had died. In bed, early in the evening, disdainful of the bars and clubs, reading a book—Colette, rediscovered on her latest Continental visit—her finger ready to turn the page. Tillman was astonished. Only after Dr. Bradley had told him that he suspected his mother had been poisoned did Tillman begin to calm down, his imperturbable self returning by degrees. Such a conclusion made no sense. The terms of life in the islands were that nothing ever made sense, unless you were a mystic or a politician or studied both with ambition. Then every stupidness seemed an act of inspiration, every cruelty part of a divine scheme. There was no dialectic here, only the obverting of all possibilities until caprice made its selection.

Bradley couldn't be sure, though. Neither he nor any of the three other sanctioned doctors on the island knew how to perform an autopsy with sufficient accuracy to assure one another or anybody else of the exact nature of death when the cause was less than obvious. Still, Bradley earned moments of miraculous credibility, as when the former minister of trade was brought into the hospital dead of a gunshot wound in his chest. To the government's relief, Bradley determined the cause of death as "heart failure," an organic demise and unembarrassing.

"I will take your permission, mahn, to cut de body open ahnd look in she stomach," Dr. B. had said to Tillman as they stood over his mother's corpse in the sunny hotel room on Sunday morning, a breeze off the ocean dancing the curtains open, billowing sunlight throughout the room and then sucking it back outside. A spray of creamy rosebuds tapped against the louvered window, an eerie beckoning in the air silenced by death.

"For God's sake, why?" Tillman had said. It sounded like the ultimate obscenity to have this fool, with his meatcutter's stubby hands, groping in his mother's abdomen.

"To determine what she eat aht de time of succumption."

"I told you what she was eating," Tillman said, exasperated. "She was eating a can of peaches with a spoon. Look here; there are still some left in the can." He shook the can angrily and syrup slopped onto his wrist. In disgust, Tillman wiped the sticky wetness on his pants, half-nauseated, associating the liquid with some oozy by-product of dissolution. "Take the peaches if you need something to cut into, but you're not taking Mother. This isn't one of your Bottom Town cadavers."

Bradley had reacted with a shrug and a patronizing twist to his smile. "Dis racial complexity—what a pity, mahn."

How often Tillman had heard this lie, so facile, from the lips of bad men. "One world," he said, biting down on the the syllables as if they were a condemnation or a final sorrow.

Tillman refused to let him remove the body from Rosehill. He wrapped his mother in the mauve-chenille bedspread she had been lying on, restacked several crates of frozen chicken parts, and arranged her in the walk-in freezer until he could figure out just what to do. It was easy to accept the fact that you couldn't trust a doctor in such circumstances. What was most unacceptable was that Bradley had told the police that there was a possibility the old lady had been murdered. The

police, of course, were excited by this news. They had sent
Inspector Cuffy over to Rosehill to inform Tillman that he was
under suspicion. "You're kidding," Tillman had said.

He suggested the inspector should walk down to the beach
bar the hotel maintained on the waterfront and have a drink,
courtesy of the house, while he took care of two new guests
who had just arrived in a taxi from the airport. "I don't believe
it," the new man said in an aside to Tillman as he checked them
in. "The skycaps at the airport whistled at my wife and called
her a whore." His wife stood demurely by his side, looking a
bit overwhelmed. Tillman could see the dark coronas of nipples
under her white-muslin sun dress.

"Hey, people here are more conservative than you might
think," he told the couple, and to the woman he added, "Unless you want little boys rubbing up against your leg, you
shouldn't wear shorts or a bathing suit into town."

"But this is the tropics," the woman protested in an ado-
lescent voice, looking at Tillman as if he were just being silly.

"Right," Tillman conceded, handing over the key. He
escorted the couple to their room, helping with the luggage,
and wished them well. Wished himself a dollar for every time
their notion of paradise would be fouled by some rudeness,
aggression or irrelevant accusation.

He crossed back over the veranda out onto the cobbled
drive, past the derelict stone tower of the windmill, where
every other Saturday the hotel sponsored a goat roast that was
well attended by civil servants, Peace Corps volunteers, and
whatever tourists were around, down the glorious green lawn
crazy with blossom, down, hot and sweaty, to the palm grove,
the bamboo beach bar on its fringe, the lagoon dipping into the
land like a blue pasture, Tillman walking with his hands in the
pockets of his loose cotton pants, reciting a calypso and feeling,
despite his troubles, elected, an aristocrat of the sensual lati-
tudes, anointed to all the earthly privileges ordinary people
dreamed about on their commuter trains fifty weeks a year.
No matter that in a second-class Eden, nothing was as unprof-
itable as the housing of its guests. Even loss seemed less dis-
couraging in the daily flood of sun.

Jevanee was glaring at him from behind the bar. And the

inspector sat grandly on his stool, satisfied with being the big shot, bearing a smile that welcomed Tillman as if they were to be partners in future prosperity, as if the venture they were to embark on could only end profitably. He gave a little wink before he tipped his green bottle of imported beer and sank the neck between his lips.

"Dis a sad affair, mahn," he said, wagging his round head. Jevanee uncapped a second bottle and set it before the inspector, paying no attention to Tillman's presence. Tillman drew a stool up beside Cuffy and perched on it, requesting Jevanee to bring another beer, and watched with practiced patience as the bartender kicked about and finally delivered the bottle as if it were his life's savings.

"What is it with you, Jevanee? What am I doing wrong?" The bartender had come with Rosehill when he had inherited the hotel eight months ago. Somebody had trained him to be a terror.

"Mistah Trick!" Jevanee whooped. He was often too self-conscious to confront his employer head on. Nevertheless, he would not accept even the mildest reproach without an extravagant line of defense or, worse, smoldering until his tongue ignited and his hands flew threateningly, shouting in a tantrum that would go on forever with or without an audience, a man who would never be employed to his satisfaction. He turned his back on Tillman and began muttering at the whiskey bottles arrayed on the work island in the center of the oval bar.

"Mistah Trick, he say what him doin' wrong, de Devil. He say daht, he mean, 'Jevanee, why you is a chupid boy ahs blahck ahs me boot cahnt count change ahnd show yah teef nice aht de white lady?' He say daht, he mean, 'Javanee, why you cahnt work fah free like you grahnpoppy? Why you cahnt bring you sistah here ta please me?' " Without ceasing his analysis of what the white man had meant, he marched out from the bar and into the bushes to take a leak. Tillman forced himself not to react any further to Jevanee's rage, which appeared to be taking on a decidedly historical sweep.

The inspector, who had not shown any interest in Jevanee's complaints, began to tap the long nail of his index finger on the surface of the bar. He made a show of becoming serious without wanting to deprive Tillman of his informality, his compassion, his essential sympathy, etc.—all the qualities he believed he possessed and controlled to his benefit.

"Who else, Tillmahn, but you?" he finally concluded as if it hurt him to say this. "Undah-stahnd, is only speculation."

"Who else but me?" Tillman sputtered. "Are you crazy?" The inspector frowned and Tillman immediately regretted his choice of words. Cuffy was as willfully unpredictable as almost everybody else on the island, but in a madhouse, an outsider soon learned, truth was always a prelude to disaster, the match dropped thoughtlessly onto tinder. He should have said, "Look, how can you think that?" or "Man, what will it take to end this unfortunate business?" But too late. The inspector was pinching at his rubbery nose, no longer even considering Tillman, looking out across the harbor, the anchored sailboats bobbing like a display of various possibilities, playing the image of artful calculation for his suspect.

Tillman sighed. "Why do you think I would kill my own mother? She was my *mother*. What son could harm the woman who carried him into the world?"

The inspector pursed his lips and then relaxed them. "Well, Tillmahn, perhahps you do it to have title to dis property, true?"

The absurdity was too great even for Tillman, a connoisseur of island nonsense. "To inherit this property!" Now Tillman had to laugh, regardless of the inspector's feelings. "Cuffy, nobody wants this place. In his will, my father was excessively sorry for burdening me with Rosehill Plantation and advised I sell it at the first opportunity. My mother had absolutely no claim to Rosehill. He divorced her long ago."

Tillman paused. As far as he could tell, he was the only one in the world, besides the government, who wanted Rosehill Plantation. It had been on the market for years, not once receiving an honest offer. Its profits were marginal, its overhead crushing. But the hotel was his, so why not be there. What he had found through it was unexpected—the inexplicable sense that life on the island had a certain fullness, that it was, far beyond what he had ever experienced back home, authentic in the most elemental ways.

Cuffy had become petulant, studying him as if he were spoiled, an unappreciative child. Tillman was not intimidated. "Why should I tell you this, anyway? It has absolutely no relevance to my mother's death."

"Um-hmm, um-hmm, I see," the inspector said. "So per-hahps you muddah take a lovah, a dark mahn, ahnd you become vexed wit' she fah behavin' so. You warn she to stop but she refuse. So . . ." He threw out his hands as if the rest of the scene he conceived were there before him. "Is only speculation."

Tillman was tiring fast. Inspector Cuffy had no use for what was and what wasn't; his only concern was his own role in the exercise of authority. It killed boredom, boredom amid the splendor. It created heroes and villains, wealthy and pov-erty. No other existence offered him so much.

He discovered that he was grinding his teeth, and the muscles in his jaw ached. Jevanee had slipped back behind the bar, and every time Tillman glanced over there, Jevanee, now bold, tried to stare him down.

"My mother was an old lady," he told the inspector. "She was beyond love. She liked books and beaches, fruit, seafood, and rare wines. Traveling. There was no man in her life. There never was. She was even a stranger to my father."

"You just a boy," Cuffy noted in a way that made Tillman think it was a line the inspector must use frequently. "Nobody beyond love, ya know."

"So?"

"So, nobody beyond pahssion, ahnd nobody beyond crime."

Tillman blinked. Damn, he thought, Cuffy's starting to make sense.

"Even ahn old womahn need a good roll to keep she happy," the inspector concluded.

"Oh, for Christ's sake," Tillman said, standing up. "I have to get back."

He couldn't get away before Jevanee butted in. Ignore Jevanee and life might go on. The bartender used his mouth like a gun, the words popping spitefully while he focused on whatever spirit he had summoned to witness his oppression.

"Daht ol' bony bag he call his muddah grabbin' aht every blahck boy on de beach. I see it wit' me own eyes."

"Jevanee, shut up."

"Oh, yes, massa, suh. Yes, massa." He feigned excessive servitude, wiping the bar counter, the cashbox, the bamboo supports with his shirt sleeve. The time would come when Tillman would have to face up to Jevanee's vindictiveness. He had been steaming ever since Tillman had told him not to hand out free drinks to his friends from the village. Jevanee insisted that no one but Rosehill's tourists, which were not regular, would ever patronize the beach bar if it weren't for him. Maybe he was right. Nobody was coming around anymore, except on Friday nights, when the band played. More and more, Jevanee wanted Tillman to understand that he was a dangerous man, his every move a challenge to his employer. Tillman was still trying to figure out how to fire the guy without a lot of unpleasantness.

"Don't listen to Jevanee," Tillman told the inspector. "He's pissed at me these days because of a disagreement we had over a charitable instinct of his."

"I give me bruddah a drink," Jevanee said in a self-deprecating way, as though he were the victim and Cuffy would understand. Jevanee's mood would only escalate if Tillman explained that the bartender's "bruddah" was consuming a case of Scotch on his drier visits, so he refused to debate Jevanee's claim. The inspector turned on his stool with the cold expression of a man whose duty it is to make it known that he must hurt you severely, that he may cripple you or make you weep, if you disobey him.

"Look now, you," he said, taking moral pleasure in this chastisement. "Doan you make trouble fah Mistah Tillmahn. You is lucky he give you work."

"Dis white bitch doan give me a damn t'ing," Jevanee snarled, shaking an empty beer bottle at Tillman. "I work in dis same spot a long time when he show up. Ahnd what you doin' kissin' he ahss?"

"Doan talk aht me daht way, boy, or I fuck you up. Hell goin' have a new bahtendah soon if you cahn't behave."

Jevanee tried to smile, a taut earnestness that never quite made it to his mouth. Tillman arranged chairs around the

warped café tables, backing away. "OK, then, Cuffy. I'm glad
we had this opportunity to straighten everything out. Stay and
have another beer if you want."

Cuffy looked at his gold wristwatch. "You will be around
in de aftahnoon?"

"Why?"

"I wish to view de deceased."

"Uh, can't it wait till tomorrow?" Tillman asked. "I have
errands to run in town. A shipment of beef is coming in from
Miami."

From his shirt pocket, Cuffy had taken a note pad and was
scribbling in it. He talked without raising his head. "Okay,
dere's no hurry. De old womahn takin' she time goin' nowheres."

Tillman nodded, now in stride with the process, the havoc
of it. "Cuffy, you're a thorough man. If anybody's going to
get to the bottom of this mess, it's you."

The inspector accepted this flattery as his due, too certain
of its validity to bother about the subtle mocking edge to
Tillman's voice. His eyes relaxed, hooded and moist. Tillman
started up the footpath through the palms, kicking a coconut
ahead of him, a leaden soccer ball, turning once to check what
fared in his absence and—yes—Cuffy and Jevanee had their
heads together, the bartender animated, swinging his hands, the
inspector with his arms crossed on his wide chest. Jevanee had
too much energy today. Maybe his attitude would defuse if he
were somewhere other than the bar for a while. He seemed to
live there. Tillman shouted back down to them. "Jevanee, after
the inspector leaves, lock everything up and take the rest of the
day off."

The bartender ignored him.

Tillman jogged up the perfect lawn along an avenue of
floral celebration—tree-sized poinsettias, arrow ginger, bougainvillea, oleander—a perfumer's tray of fragrance. On the knoll,
graced with a millionaire's view of the channel, was the old
plantation house, a stubborn remnant of colonial elegance, its
whitewashed brick flaking in a way that benefited the charm of
its archaic construction, the faded red of the gabled tin roof a

human comfort against the green, monotonous sheets of the mountains that were its background. Farther south, the cone shell of the windmill stood like a guard tower or a last refuge. Tillman had huddled there with his guests last summer during a hurricane, the lot of them drunk and playing roundhouse bridge, the cards fluttering from the storm outside.

When he was a teenager, Tillman had flown down to the island during a summer off from Exeter to help his father build the two modern wings that flanked the manor, one-level box rooms side by side, as uninspired as any lodging on any Florida roadside. Tillman's father was a decent man, completely involved in his scheming, though his interest invariably flagged once a puzzle was solved, a challenge dispatched. The old man had worked for J. D. Root, one of the big ad agencies in New York, handling the Detroit accounts. His final act was an irony unappreciated—he perished in one of the cars he promoted, losing control on the Northway one rainy evening, going fishing up on the St. Lawrence, convinced that this time, he would hook a muskellunge. Rosehill Plantation was his most daring breakaway, but he never really had time for the place. Throughout his ownership, Rosehill lost money, and after his death the checks from the estate in New York flowed like aid from the mother country. When a lawyer's telegram reached Tillman, asking if he wanted to pursue more aggressively the sale of the plantation, he decided to dump his Lower East Side loft, where he had been mulling for two years since graduate school, sweating out the draft, and make his claim on Rosehill. Besides, Nixon had just been reelected. The States no longer seemed like the right place to be.

Awash in perspiration, Tillman turned the corner around the east wing, his blood pressure a little jumpy, the skin on his face at the point of combustion, wondering if all the friction of a fast life could suddenly cause a person to burst into flame. Sometimes he felt as if it were happening. It wasn't very easy to find peace on the island unless you hiked up into the mountains. Whereas it was very easy to catch hell.

In the exterior courtyard behind the estate house, the new arrivals, husband and wife from Wilmington, Delaware, were

inspecting one of Tillman's few unequivocal successes, the gazebo that housed his parrot aviary, in it seven of the last
rainbow parrots on earth. The project was really that of the
veterinarian at the ministry of agriculture, a man who hated
goats and cows but spent all his spare time bird-watching or
digging up pre-Columbian artifacts, storing them in his living
room until the far-off day a museum would be built. Together,
he and Tillman had waged a public campaign on the island, the
parrots' sole habitat, to prevent their extinction. A law was
passed for appearances, its advantage being that it clearly de-
fined for the bird smugglers just who needed to be paid off and
who could be bypassed with impunity.

After the crusade, Tillman had decided to contact some
poachers himself. They were kids, tough miniature bandits, the
nest robbers. One was nine, the other eleven—Basil and Jacob,
tree climbers *extraordinaire*, both as skinny as vanilla beans.
They lived in a mountain village, a clump of wattle huts, one of
the outposts before the vast roadless center of the island, all
sharp peaks, palisades, and jungle. When the hatching season
had ended, Tillman and the boys trekked into the lush interior,
camping overnight, Tillman's neck strained from looking up
into the canopy, his ears confused by the wraithish shrieks and
skraws—skra-aaa-aw!—unable to pinpoint where the sound had
come from in the infinite cathedral of growth. But the kids
knew their business. They were fearless, scaling to the top of
the highest mahogany, indifferent to the slashing beaks of the
females that refused to abandon the nest, shinnying down the
trunks with the chicks held gently in their mouths, polycolored
cotton balls, the fierce tiny heads lolling helplessly out from
between the embrace of boyish lips.

Tillman thought he would tell his guests from Delaware
the story. The woman was scrutinizing the birds rather sternly.
She would cluck and whistle at them, tap the chicken-wire wall
of the cage, but she did so without affection. When he finished
talking, she turned to look at him, her eyes obscured behind
oversize sunglasses, her mouth in a pout. Tillman guessed she
was a bank teller, something that had made her very sure of
herself without placing any demand on her intelligence.

"It's cruel," she said.

"It is not cruel. It's heroic. These islands have a way of forcing everything but the lowest common denominator into oblivion."

"Hero," she said sardonically. The husband looked skeptical. Light reflected off her glasses and sliced back at Tillman. He shrugged his shoulders. Perhaps he should bar Americans from Rosehill. Canadians made the better tourists. They allowed for a world outside themselves.

The Land-Rover started painfully, a victim of mechanical arthritis. Soon it would take no more to the prosthetic miracle of wire, tin, and hardware junk. Spare parts appeared from across the ocean as often as Halley's Comet.

Onto the narrow blacktop road that circumnavigated the island, Tillman drove with reckless courage and whipping flair, showing inner strength when he refused to give way to two flatbed lorries painted up like Easter eggs, one named Sweetfish, the other Dr. Lick, passengers clinging to everything but the wheel hubs, racing down the coastal hill side by side straight at him, Dr. Lick overtaking Sweetfish just as Tillman downshifted reluctantly to third and toed the brake pedal. Someday the lorries will spread carnage across this highway, Tillman thought. It will be a national event, the island equivalent of a 747's going down.

In the capital, a pastel city breathtaking from the heights above it but garbage-strewn and ramshackle once you were on its streets, Tillman honked his way through the crowds down along Front Street, inching his way to the docks. On the quay, three pallets of frozen steaks destined for Rosehill were sweating pink juice onto the dirty concrete. Beef from the island was as tough and stringy as rug; if a hotel wanted to serve food worthy of the name, it had to import almost everything but fish. He located the purser in one of the rum-and-Coke sheds that filled every unclaimed inch of the wharves like derelict carnival booths. There was no use complaining about the shipment's being off-loaded without anybody's being there to receive it. That was Tillman's fault—he had been too preoccupied.

He signed the shipping order and then scrambled to hire a driver and boys to break down the pallets and truck the cartons out to Rosehill's freezer before the meat thawed completely.

There were other errands, less urgent—to the marketing board in search of the rare tomato, to the post office, to the stationer for a ballpoint pen, to the pharmacist, who was disappointed when Tillman bought only aspirin. Most of his regular white customers spent small fortunes on amphetamines or Quaaludes. When Tillman had finished there, he drove over to the national hospital on the edge of town. Without a death certificate from Bradley, Mother was destined to be the morbid champion of cryogenics, the queen of ice in a land where water never froze in nature.

The old colonial hospital was a structure and a system bypassed by any notion of modernity. Someone yelled at him as he entered the shadowed foyer, but it wasn't apparent who or why. The rough wooden floor boards creaked under his feet. The maze of hallways seemed to be a repository for loiterers—attendants, nurses, nuns, clerks, superfluous guards, mangled patients, talking, weeping, spending the day in rigid silence. One naked little boy asleep on the floor, hugging the wall.

He found Bradley's office and went through the door without knocking. Bradley, chief surgeon, head physician of Saint George's National People's Hospital, an agnostic operation if Tillman had ever seen one, was reading in his chair, a paperback romance, a man hovering over a fallen woman on its cover. The room smelled of sweet putrefaction and Lysol. The scent of jasmine wafted in through open, screenless windows. Tillman sat down on a wooden bench against one bare wall. Flies buzzed along the ceiling. Bradley slowly broke off from his reading, dropping his feet one by one from where they were propped on the broad windowsill. His lab coat, smudged with yellow stains and laundered blood, sagged away from his middle. He recognized Tillman and smiled grudgingly.

"Mahn, I been callin' you, ya know. I examine dem peaches you muddah eat. Dey was no good. I think we solve dis big mystery."

Tillman knew this was his chance to end the affair, but he could not forgive Bradley his smugness, his careless manner, the suffering he had sown.

"You're sure? What'd you do, feed them to a chicken and the chicken died?"

"Mahn, Tillmahn, you doan have enough troubles, you must come make some wit' me? Why is daht?"

"You're telling me she died of botulism?"

"It seem so, seem so."

Tillman was incited to fury. "Botulism, doctor, causes vomiting and extreme pain. How can you not know that? My mother died a peaceful death."

Bradley turned with eyes murderous. "If it's so, de autopsy prove so. I cahnt know oddahwise."

"You're not touching her. Somebody else can do it, but not you."

"Mahn, daht's irrational."

Tillman jumped up from the bench and stood in front of the doctor's cluttered desk. "You'd be the last person on earth to touch her."

"Get out, Tillmahn."

Tillman was in no hurry to leave. "Remember Freddy Allen?" he asked.

"Who?" Then Bradley remembered and his face lost its arrogance.

"He was a friend of mine, a good one. He helped me out at Rosehill whenever I needed it."

"Tillmahn, consider I am only human."

"Yes, you are. So was Freddy until he came to you. You gave him bromides for acute appendicitis. The damn vet can diagnose better than you."

Bradley stood so fast, his eyes full of menace, that Tillman tensed to defend himself. "Get out!" he shouted, pointing his finger at Tillman. "You muddah now a permahnent guest aht Rosehill till you come to you senses. Get out!"

The doctor came around from his desk to open the office door and then kicked it shut behind him.

* * *

Tillman, island hotelier, master of the business arts, student of impossibility, fond of weather that rarely oppressed, a man of contingencies and recently motherless—Tillman knew what to do. Whatever it took.

Whatever it took, Tillman told himself, back out on the streets, heedless in the late-afternoon traffic. Sometimes that meant nothing at all; sometimes the gods spared you muckery, blessed you with style, and everything was easy.

At the airport, he parked next to a single taxi out front, no one around to note this familiar island tune, the prolonged pitch of tires violently braked. Through the dark, empty airport that always reminded him of an abandoned warehouse, Tillman searched for his friend Roland, the free-lance bush pilot from Australia, maverick and proven ace. Roland leaped around the warm world in his Stearman, spraying mountainsides of bananas with chemicals that prevented leaf spot and other blights. Tillman suspected that the pilot was also part of the interisland ring sponsored by the most influential businessmen to smuggle drugs, whiskey, cigarettes, stereos—whatever contraband could be crammed surreptitiously into the fuselage of a small plane. He seemed to be able to come and go as he pleased.

Roland's plane wasn't on the tarmac, nor in the hangar. Sunset wasn't far away. Wherever Roland was, waltzing his plane through green, radical valleys, he would have to return before dark if he was coming in tonight. Tillman left a message with a mechanic in the machine shed for Roland to come find him at Rosehill.

Twilight had begun to radiate through the vegetation as he arrived back at the hotel, lifting the mélange of colors to a higher level of brilliance, as if each plant, each surface, were responding to the passage of the sun with its own interior luminosity. Inspector Cuffy was on the veranda of the west wing, laughing with Lemonille, her eyes flirtatious. They clammed up when Tillman appeared beside them.

"You haven't been waiting for me, have you?"

"Well, doan trouble yourself, mahn. I been interviewin' dis pretty young lady."

Tillman looked at Lemonille, who averted her eyes shyly.

"Perhahps we cahn view de body of you muddah now." Cuffy said this without the slightest conviction. Tillman understood that for the time being, the inspector was only interested in chasing Lemonille.

"I've had a hell of a day. Can I ask you to wait until tomorrow?"

"Daht strike me ahs reasonable," Cuffy said, allowing Tillman to experience his generosity.

"Besides, case solved, Cuffy," Tillman said, remembering the doctor, the hospital. "Bradley says something was wrong with the can of peaches my mother was eating when she died." ("If you want to believe such crap," Tillman added under his breath.)

"I will study daht report," the inspector said. From the way he spoke, Tillman knew the investigation would drag on for days, weeks—especially if Lemonille played hard to get.

"Mistah Till-mahn?" Lemonille buried her chin, afraid to speak now that she had drawn attention to herself. More woe, thought Tillman. More hue and cry.

"What's wrong?"

"De cook say she 'fraid wit' you dead muddah in de freezah. She say she not cookin' wit' a duppy so close by."

"All right, I'll go talk to her."

"She gone home."

"All right, I'll take care of it." He began to walk away.

"Mistah Till-mahn?" The big woman's soft and guarded voice made him stop and turn around.

"What, Lemonille?"

"De men come wit' de meat, but dey won't stock it."

Tillman inhaled nervously. "My mother again, right?"

Lemonille nodded. "Damn!" Tillman said and scuffed the dirt in frustration.

Lemonille had one last piece of news. "Jevanee in a fuss 'cause you fire him."

"I didn't fire him. I told him to take the day off."

"Oh."

"Cuffy was there. He heard me." Cuffy looked into the trees and would not support or deny this allegation.

"Oh. But Jevanee tellin' every bug in de sky you fire him. Daht mahn be fulla dread you goin' put him out since de day you poppy die."

"Well, it's not true. Tell him that when you see him."

Tillman took these developments in stride, closing the restaurant for the evening by posting a scrawled note of apology at the entrance to the modest dining hall in the manor. For an hour, he shuffled the cartons of dripping steaks from the kitchen to the freezer, stacking them around the corpse of his mother as if these walls of spoiling meat were meant to be her tomb.

Event upon event—any day in the islands could keep accumulating such events until it was overrich, festering or glorious, never to be reproduced so wonderfully. This day was really no different except that his mother had triggered some extraordinary complications that were taking him to the limit.

After showering in cold water, Tillman climbed the stairs in the main house to the sanctitude of his office, his heart feeling too dry for blood to run through it, another fire hazard. What's to be done with Mother? On a hot plate, he heated water for tea, sat with the steaming mug before the phone on his desk. Ministry offices would be closed at this hour and besides, the minister of health was no friend of his, so there was no use ringing him up.

Finally, he decided to call Dr. Layland. If Layland still were running the island's medical services, the day would have been much simpler; but Layland, a surgeon who had earned international respect for his papers on brain dysfunction in the tropics, had lost his job and his license to practice last winter when he refused to allow politics to interfere with the removal of a bullet from an opposition member's neck. Although the case was before the federation, there was little hope of reinstatement before next year's elections.

"Frankly," Layland told him, his accent bearing the vestige of an Oxford education, "your position is most unenviable, my friend. A burial certificate, likewise permission to transfer the corpse back to its native soil, must be issued by both the national police and the chief medical officer. The police, pending their own investigation of the cause of death, will not act without clearance from the CMO. In cases where the cause is unclear, it is unlikely that the CMO will agree to such clearance, especially for an expatriate Caucasian, until an autopsy is performed."

"But Bradley said it was the peaches, a bad can of peaches." Tillman jerked his head away from the telephone. How absurd and false those words sounded.

"Unlikely, but I see what you're getting at. Any cause is better than none, in light of your problem. But you know what sort of humbug that foolish man is. And you shan't have him on your side, since you refused to have him do the autopsy."

Layland further explained that there was no alternative to removing the corpse from the walk-in freezer unless he had another to put it in or unless he committed it to the island's only morgue, in the basement of the prison at Fort Albert— again, Bradley's domain. The final solution would be to bury her at Rosehill, but even this could not be accomplished without official permits. The police would come to dig her up. Tillman asked if it were a mistake not to allow Bradley to cut open his mother.

"I'm afraid, Tillman, you must decide that for yourself," Layland answered. "But I think you must know that I am as disgusted by my erstwhile colleague as you are. Well, good luck."

Tillman pushed the phone away, rubbed his sore eyes, massaged the knots in his temples. He tilted back in his chair and almost went over backward, caught unaware by a flood of panic. Unclean paradise, he thought suddenly. What about Mother? Damn, she was dead and needed taking care of. Hard to believe. Lord, why did she come here, anyway? She probably knew she was dying, and figured the only dignified place to accomplish the fact was under the roof of her only child. A mother's final strategy.

Outside on the grounds, one of the stray dogs that were always about began a rabid barking. Tillman listened more closely, the sounds of squawking audible between the gaps in the dog's racket. The protest grew louder, unmistakable. Tillman was down the stairs and out on the lawn in no time at all, running toward the aviary.

There was some light from the few bulbs strung gaily through the branches of frangipani that overhung the parking area, enough for Tillman to see what was going on, the wickedness being enacted in blue-satin shadows. In the gazebo, an angry silhouette swung a cutlass back and forth, lashing at the amorphous flutter of wings that seemed everywhere in the tall cage.

"Jevanee?" Tillman called, uncertain. The silhouette reeled violently, froze in its step, and then burst through the door of the cage, yelling.

"Mahn, you cy-ahnt fire me, *I quit.*"

Tillman cringed at the vulgarity of such a dissembled non sequitur. All the bad television in the world, the stupid lyrics of false heroes, the latent rage of kung-fu and cowboy fantasies had entered into this man's head, and here was the result, some new breed of imperial slave and his feeble, fatuous uprising.

"I didn't fire you. I said take the day off, cool down."

"Cy-ahnt fire *me*, you bitch."

The parrots were dead. Hatred exploded through Tillman. He wanted to kill the bartender. Fuck it. He wanted to shoot him down. He sprinted back across the lawn, up on the veranda toward the main house for the gun kept locked in the supply closet behind the check-in desk. Jevanee charged after him. A guest, the woman recently arrived from Wilmington, stepped out in front of Tillman from her room that fronted the veranda. Tillman shoulder-blocked her back through the door. She sprawled on her ass and, for a second, Tillman saw on her face an expression that welcomed violence as if it were an exotic game she had paid for.

"Stay in your goddamn room and bolt the door."

Tillman felt the bad TV engulfing them, the harried scriptwriter unbalanced with drugs and spite. Jevanee's foot plunged through the rotten boards in the veranda and lodged there. An exodus of pestilence swarmed from the splintery hole into the dim light, palmetto bugs flying blindly up through an increasing cloud of smaller winged insects.

At the same time, stepping out from the darkness of a hedge of bougainvillea that ran in bushy clumps along the veranda was Inspector Cuffy, pistol in hand. Tillman gawked at him. What was he doing around Rosehill so late? Lemonille had been encouraging him or the investigation had broadened to round-the-clock foolishness. Or, Tillman surmised, knowing it was true, Cuffy apparently knew Jevanee was going after him and had lurked on the premises until the pot boiled over. A shot whistled by Tillman's head. Jevanee had a gun, too. Tillman pitched back off the deck and flattened out in the shrubbery.

"Stop!" Cuffy shouted.

What the hell? thought Tillman. Where's Jevanee going, anyway? He was near enough to smell the heavily Scotched breath of the bartender, see his eyes, as dumb and frightened as the eyes of a wild horse. Another shot was fired off; then a flurry of them as the two men emptied their pistols at each other with no effect. Silence and awkwardness as Cuffy and Jevanee confronted each other, the action gone out of them, praying thanks for the lives they still owned. Tillman crawled away toward the main house. He couldn't care less how they finished the drama, whether they killed each other with their bare hands or retired to a rumshop together, blaming Tillman for the sour fate of the island. There was no point in getting upset about it now, once the hate had subsided, outdone by the comics.

He sat in the kitchen on the cutting table, facing the vaultlike aluminum door of the refrigerated walk-in where his mother lay, preserved in ice among more ordinary meats and perishables.

He wanted to talk to her, but even in death she seemed only another guest at the hotel, one with special requirements, nevertheless expecting courtesy and service, the proper distance kept safely between their lives. She had never kissed him on the lips, not once, but had only brushed his cheek when an occasion required some tangible sign of motherly devotion. He had never been closer to her heart than when they cried together

when he was in high school and lost his first girl, less than a
year before his parents divorced. She had entered his room late
at night and tuned the radio loud to a big-band station and
held him, the two of them together shivering on his bed. She
had not written that she was coming to visit but had showed up
unannounced with only hand luggage, a leather grip of novels,
a variety of bathing suits, caftans and creams. Behind her she
had left Paris, where the weather had begun its decline toward
winter. Whatever else she had left behind in her life was as obscure
and sovereign as a foreign language. He wanted to talk to her,
but nothing translated.

The pilot found him there sometime in the middle of the
night, Tillman forlorn, more tired than he could ever remember
feeling. Roland looked worn out, too, as if he had been stuck
in an engine for hours, his cutoff shorts and colorless T-shirt
smudged with grease, his hiking boots unlaced; and yet, despite
this general dishevelment, his self-confidence was as apparent
as the gleam of his teeth. Tillman remembered him at the beach
bar late one night, yelling into the face of a man dressed in a
seersucker suit, "I get things done, damn you, not like *these*
bloody fools," and the sweep of his arm had seemed to include
the entire planet.

Tillman smiled mournfully back at him. "Roland, I need
your help."

The pilot removed the mirrored sunglasses he wore at all
times. "You've had a full day of it, I hear. What's on your
mind, mate?"

Like an unwieldy piece of lumber, his mother's frozen
corpse banged to and fro in the short bed of the Land-Rover,
her wrapped feet pointing up over the tail gate. With a little
effort and jockeying, they fit her into the tubular chemical
tank in the fuselage of the Stearman after Roland, Tillman
standing by with a flashlight, unbolted two plates of sheet
metal from the underbelly of the craft that concealed bay
doors. "You can't smuggle bales of grass with only a nozzle
and a funnel," Roland explained.

Tillman was worried that an unscheduled flight would foul

up Roland's good grace with the authorities. "Man," Roland said, "I've got more connections than the friggin' PM. And I mean of the UK, not this bloody cow pie." He thought for a second and was less flamboyant. "I've been in trouble before, of course. Nobody, Tillman, can touch this boy from down under as long as I have me bird, you see. Let us now lift upward into the splendid atmosphere and its many bright stars."

The chemical tank smelled cloyingly of poison. With his head poked into it, Tillman gagged, maneuvering the rigid body of his mother, the limbs clunking dully against the shiny metal, until she was positioned. Roland geared the bay doors back into place. The sound of them clicking into their locks brought relief to Tillman. They tucked themselves into the tiny cockpit, Tillman behind the pilot's seat, his legs flat against the floor board, straddled as if he were riding a bobsled.

The airport shut down at dusk, the funding for runway lights never more than deadpan rhetoric during the height of the political season. Roland rested his sunglasses on the crown of his blond head as they taxied to the landward end of the strip, the mountains a cracked ridge behind them, the sea ahead down the length of pale concrete. Out there somewhere in the water, an incompatibly situated cay stuck up like a catcher's mitt for small planes whose pilots were down on their agility and nerve.

Roland switched off the lights on the instrumentation to cut all reflection in the cockpit. Transparent blackness, the gray run of concrete stretching into nearby infinity.

Roland shouted over the roar, "She's a dumpy old bird, but with no real cargo, we should have some spirited moments."

Even as Roland spoke, they were already jostling down the airstrip like an old hot rod on a rutted road, Tillman anticipating lift-off long before it actually happened. The slow climb against gravity seemed almost futile, the opaque hand of the cay suddenly materializing directly in front of them. Roland dropped a wing and slammed the rudder pedal. The Stearman veered sharply away from the hazard, then leveled off and continued mounting upward. Tillman could hear his mother thump in the fuselage.

"Bit of a thrill," Roland shouted. Tillman closed his eyes and endured the languid speed and the hard, grinding vibrations of the plane.

Roland put on his headset and talked to any ghost he could rouse. When Tillman opened his eyes again, the clouds out the windscreen had a tender pink sheen to their tops. The atmosphere tingled with blueness. The ocean was black below them, and Barbados, ten degrees off starboard, was blacker still, a solid puddle sprinkled with electricity. Along the horizon, the new day was a thin red thread unraveling westward. The beauty of it all made Tillman melancholy.

Roland floated the plane down to earth like a fat old goose that couldn't be hurried. The airport on Barbados was modern and received plenty of international traffic, so they found it awake and active at this hour. Taxiing to the small-plane tarmac, Tillman experienced a moment of claustrophobia, smelling only the acrid human sweat that cut through the mechanical fumes. He hadn't noticed it airborne, but on the ground it was unbearable.

They parked and had the Stearman serviced. In the wet, warm morning air, Tillman's spirits revived. Roland walked through customs, headed for the bar to wait for him to do his business. Two hours later, Tillman threw himself down in a chair next to the pilot and cradled his head on the sticky table, the surge of weariness through his back and neck almost making him pass out. He listened to Roland patiently suck his beer and commanded himself up to communicate the failure of the expedition.

"Bastards. They won't let me transfer her to a stateside flight without the right paper."

"There was that chance," Roland admitted.

All along, Tillman had believed that Barbados was the answer, that people were reasonable there, that he had only to bring over the corpse of his mother, coffin her, place her on an Eastern flight to Miami connecting with Boston, have a funeral home intercept her, bury her next to her husband in the family plot on Beacon Hill. Send out death announcements to the few relatives scattered across the country, and then it would be over, back to normal. No mother, no obligations of blood. That was how she had lived, anyway.

"Just how well connected are you, Roland?"

"Barbados is a bit iffy. The people are too damn sophisticated." He left to make some phone calls but returned with his hands out, the luckless palms upturned.

"Tillman, what next?"

Tillman exhaled and fought the urge to laugh, knowing it would mount to a hysterical outpouring of wretchedness. "I just don't know. Back to the island, I guess. If you can see any other option, speak out. Please."

The pilot was unreadable behind the mirrors of his glasses. His young face had become loose and puffy since he had located Tillman at Rosehill. They settled their bar bill and left.

In the air again, the sound of the Stearman rattled Tillman so thoroughly that he felt as though the plane's engine were in his own skull. He tried to close his sleepless eyes against the killing brightness of the sun but could not stop the hypnotic flash that kept him staring below at the ocean. Halfway through the flight, Roland removed his headset and turned in his seat, letting the plane fly itself while he talked.

"Tillman," he shouted, "I didn't bolt the plates back on the fuselage."

Tillman nodded absently and make no reply.

Roland jabbed his finger, pointing at the floor. "That hand gear there by your foot opens the bay doors."

He resumed flying the plane, allowing Tillman his own thoughts. Tillman had none. He expected some inspiration or voice to break through his dizziness, but it didn't happen. After several more minutes, he tapped Roland on the shoulder. Roland turned again, lifting his glasses so Tillman could see his full face, his strained but resolute eyes, Tillman understanding this gesture as a stripping of fear, tacit confirmation that they were two men capable of making such a decision without ruining themselves with ambiguity.

"Okay, Roland, the hell with it. She never liked being in one place too long, anyway."

"Right you are, then," Roland said solemnly. "Any special spot?"

"No."

"Better this way," Roland yelled as he dropped the air speed and sank the Stearman to one thousand feet. "The thing that bothers me about burial, you see, is caseation. Your frigging body turns to cheese after a month in the dirt. How unspeakably nasty. I don't know if you've noticed, but I never eat cheese myself. Odd, isn't it?"

Tillman poked him on the shoulder again. "Knock it off."

"Sorry."

Tillman palmed the gear open. It was as easy as turning the faucet of a hose. When they felt her body dislodge and the tail bob inconsequentially, Roland banked the plane into a steep dive so they could view the interment. Tillman braced his hands against the windscreen and looked out, saw her cartwheel for a moment and then stabilize as the mauve-chenille shroud came apart like a party streamer, a sky diver's Mae West. The Stearman circled slowly around the invisible line of her descent through space.

"Too bad about your mother, mate," Roland called out finally. "My own, I don't remember much."

"I'm still young," Tillman confessed, surprising himself, the words blurting forth from his mouth unsolicited. Tears of gratitude slipped down his face from this unexpected report of the heart.

He looked down at the endless water, waves struggling and receding, the small carnation of foam marking his mother's entrance into the sea, saw her, through the medium of refraction, unwrapped from her shroud, naked and washed, crawling with pure, unlabored motion down the shafts of light and beyond their farthest reach, thawed into suppleness, small glass bubbles, the cold air of her last breath, expelled past her white lips, nuzzled by unnamed fish, a perfect swimmer, free of the air and the boundaries of the living, darkness passing through darkness, down, down, to kiss the silt of the ocean floor, to touch the bottom of the world with dead fingers.

They had watched her plummet with a sense of awe and wonderment, as boys do who have thrown an object from off a high bridge. The pilot regained altitude and they continued westward. The realization came into Tillman, a palpable weight in his chest. "I don't belong here," he said to himself, and immediately resisted the feeling, because that must have been the way she felt all her life.

Then, with the rich peaks of the island in sight, the heaviness dissipated. "It's beautiful here," he heard himself saying.

"What's that?" Roland shouted back.

"Beautiful," he repeated, and throughout Roland's clumsy landing, the jolt and thunder of the runway, "Mother, be at peace."

RICHARD SPILMAN

THE OLD MAN TELLS HIS STORY AND GETS IT WRONG

FROM TRIQUARTERLY

৶

THEY SAT IN THE SHADOW of the house. Bright sunlight hurt the old man's eyes—even from the shade he could not look into the yard without squinting. They sat in redwood chairs on a lawn speckled with daisies and dandelions, and as Carl talked, he rocked his chair back and forth on two legs. Three empty beer bottles stood on a small bench between them. His daughter had gone, saying she would be back soon. He tried to remember where but gave it up, afraid that he would lose track of what the boy was saying. His grandson had just returned from a summer ROTC camp and was full of wonders—rifles that found their targets in the dark and tiny round grenades with a range so wide they'd kill the man who threw them carelessly—which fascinated him and brought back memories of the War. He rubbed his hands, which were cold despite the nearly smothering late spring heat, and his eyes wandered from the bed of withered daffodils to the line of button bush along the fence, wrapped in flowering honeysuckle, into the oak above them, whose branches spread over the entire house. He heard explosions and rifle fire, and from the tree, the cries of hundreds of birds.

With a sound like the creaking of canvas, the chair rocked up and down, pushed by a bare foot in a torn sneaker, while the boy's pale voice described blast holes and shivered targets. Still no meat on him, his grandfather thought.

The old man hated to be alone with strangers, and over the last whatever number of months it was almost everyone but the daughter he lived with had become a stranger, even Carl. Sooner or later he would lose track of the conversation. There would be silence, the two of them smiling the way people do when they can't understand each other's languages, and even though the boy knew, he would have to say, "Grandpa ain't what he used to be." As if he knew what he used to be.

"The last night was a real trip," the boy enthused. "E and E—Escape and Evasion. They take you out at night and drop you in the middle of nowhere and leave you to find your way back. The seniors play the enemy. If they catch you, you're dead."

All your life, his grandfather thought. Escape and Evasion. His father, his wife, the banks, the lawyers, the Germans— he'd fought them when he could, and when he couldn't, he'd run away. Most of the time it was useless and some of the time it was wrong, but even when he had hated himself, it had felt good to fight. Imprisoned now in a body that would not obey, he envied the boy's ability to do things he might regret.

A breeze rippled across the grass, through the swaying shadow of the oak. He barely felt it.

He had expected that senility, if it appeared, would come gradually, an enemy he could recognize and confront. But it hadn't. After a weekend of storms, he had gone out on the river in his boat. A flood had washed out one end of the little dam across Sumner Creek, and bass had swum up the river to feed on the shad that came through the breach. Where the rough water smoothed into a current, there were underwater stumps. Casting among them, he began to feel strange, as if the water were glass, a thick murky glass that his lure just skidded across, and the men fishing from the bank and the clouds moving above them were slowly hardening into glass. Dark shapes moved beneath the surface, and he was afraid any second they might break through. The fear took such a hold that he had to stop. But when he turned the boat, the brush along the creek seemed to merge into a solid mass. In a panic he tried to force his way through and grounded the boat on a bar. Someone had to wade out from shore to help.

High blood pressure, the doctors agreed, and something to do with valves. They gave him pills, but the confusion did not go away. It lay in the shadows of his mind like a whisper at the bottom of a gravel pit. If he listened even for a second, he forgot where he was.

"No compass, no map, no nothing. And it was cold at night. I was the only one in my unit who had the sense to bring his jacket. The guys called me a pussy, but they call anybody a pussy who doesn't pretend he's got iron balls. I told them, if there's war it'll be the guys who don't pretend that make it through."

The old man harrumphed, remembered the bodies lying like busted grain sacks in a field of new wheat and later, in occupied Germany, pictures of the dust and gravel that had once been Hiroshima. Go ahead, he thought, wear your jacket.

From this he fell to mourning how quickly a man disappeared in his children. In his prime people had told him he looked like Humphrey Bogart, and though his back had stiffened he could still carry an eighty-pound sack of cement from the truck to the garage. Yet across from him sat a thin, blond, gangling creature, who had to use both hands to lift his chair, and this was his grandson. Two generations and what was left? Blue eyes, a crooked smile, and long-fingered hands—the rest swallowed up in others. He studied his own hands, which were swollen at the knuckles, the age-spotted skin so papery he could flake it off with a fingernail like the scales of a fish, and glowered at the boy as if he'd stolen something.

Once they'd almost got killed, the boy was saying, because a couple of smart-asses had taken a shortcut across a moonlit slash of open ground. For an hour they'd had to lie in stinking mud at the edge of a slough and listen to the under-brush crackling around them.

The smell of ripe silage rose in his grandfather's memory from the marsh he had slogged through, the day his regiment had parachuted into France. He was tempted to tell the boy, but it would turn into a story and that was too much trouble. His daughter would raise hell. You don't talk to people, she complained, you just tell them stories. Next thing I know, you'll be peeing your pants.

What could he say? There was no way to explain how it felt, to live with nerves that would spin him into nightmare at the backfire of a truck, in a world where a flash of light could make him anxious for hours and where often he could not walk around the block without losing his way. So how could he describe the joy of telling a story through from beginning to end, feeling it draw him on and the pieces fall into place as they had seemed to do when his mind was whole. All his daughter heard was an old man repeating himself.

Anyway, it was a story to tell among men, that one. A woman wouldn't listen to killing, but if you said to a man, "I was scared, I was mad, I wanted to kill them, and when I did, it felt good," he'd hear you out. He knew what you were talking about.

Carl's chair thumped down, startling him, and he found himself face to face with his own crooked smile.

"I'm going to get another beer. You want one?"

The old man shook his head, thinking that if he followed the boy into the house, he could turn on the TV and they'd have an excuse not to talk. But it was afternoon—the soap operas were on. He couldn't watch soap operas, they jumped around too much. Through the glass of the patio door, he watched the boy's vague form moving around in the kitchen. The heat felt as solid as a gag in his mouth.

He tried to imagine guns that saw in the dark, but couldn't. It seemed to be in the nature of things nowadays that he could not understand them. In the old world, his world, things acted the way everybody but a damned fool supposed they would. You could depend on them. Which was not to say accidents didn't happen, but even the accidents were solid—the bank went under, the girl got pregnant, the crop failed—and you grew around them the way a tree roots around a rock. Now the girls had pills and the farmers had insurance, and there were atoms and the insides of atoms and the insides of the insides (niceties the boy had once tried to explain to him). He felt a kind of pity for the boy, and for himself. Because he was an old man, gone frail in infuriating ways, and because the world that was worth a damn had gone feeble too. And because the boy probably liked it that way.

His grandson stepped through the sliding door and pranced across the patio singing,

> *You've got yoga, honey*
> *I've got beer*
> *You got overpriced*
> *And I got weird*
> *But it's all right. . . .*

He plucked his empty off the bench. "You sure you don't want another? I won't tell." And flipped it high, end-over-end, toward the trash barrels behind the garage. It landed with a "whang" that rolled through the old man like a sudden scream. "Goddamn you!" The glare leaped from the garden and burned all around him.

"Missed." Carl plopped into the chair. "What's wrong?"

He waited, trembling. The light slowly retreated. A cloud of images settled around him like sparks from a disturbed fire, dying before he could tell what they were. His stomach hurt.

"Did I scare you?"

"I've been scared since I was born," he said, wearily. Then realizing this was a confession of sorts, added, "Army gave me a medal for it."

"For being scared?"

"For running." Stuck in a hedge, a muddy parachute strained one way and another in the wind.

Carl ran a hand through his mare's nest of yellow hair. "You okay?"

The question was so transparent, he laughed out loud.

"Hell, no, I'm not okay. But there's nothing you can do about it!"

"Mom says you're better."

"Your ma don't know her ass from a hole in the ground." Carl sipped his beer and gazed down the line of hedges and fences where the backyards joined. "I wonder what I'd do if the bullets were real."

"The last thing you'd expect to do, probably." The jigsaw of fields lay below him, beautiful and strange, and he could feel himself falling. "They say you get used to the fear, but you don't. You stumble along, shooting at people you can't see and wondering where the hell the war is. And about the time you think you're not scared anymore, some poor bastard steps on a lump of loose dirt, and there it is. Like a wall."

"What *did* they give you the medal for?"

"Machine-gun nest. I must have told you that story—the woods and the machine guns and all?"

"Unh-unh. I think you tried to once, but Mom wouldn't let you."

"That don't surprise me. It's the killing. She says I ought to be ashamed of myself." His apprehension disappeared as the familiar flow of the story began to carry him along. "They don't mind you saying you were glad to win the war, but God help you if you say you were glad to kill a German."

The boy grinned, and once again, briefly, he saw himself mirrored. "Well, you know, I was old to be a paratrooper, but if you were in good shape and wanted it bad enough, they wouldn't stand in your way. And I wanted it. I was tired of farming for my father, and your grandma and I weren't getting along too well, and anyway, the times got into my blood. If it had been hippie time, I'd probably have been a hippie; but it was wartime, so I went to war.

"We shipped to England in the wintertime and trained near Scotland. Dropped into the moors around dawn, with the frost on the heather bushes to light the way. Getting the timing down, you know, because a minute late and you're a mile from nowhere. Then we'd attack a mock-up town and the sheep pasture behind it.

"Then we came south and sat. Nothing to do, not much

news—just air raids and drills. We played poker and drank infirmary alcohol mixed with a chocolate drink we'd stole from the Navy, but after a while it got so that even when we were sober we didn't know what day it was. Then one night the drill turned out to be real, and we were airborne before dawn. They had us packed in rows facing the back of the plane, my platoon right up next to the fuselage." He saw it ribbed and riveted like the inside of a boxcar, the skin of the plane swelling in and out in the dusky light, and heard the drone of the engines. "The lieutenant repeated what we'd heard in the hangar: form fast, take the highway, take the town, if we could, or go around it, take the hill behind the town, and hold on. It was cold as a witch's tit and the air stank like a gas station and nobody said much. The kid next to me kept mumbling 'Combien baiser, Mademoiselle?' in hillbilly French. You understand French?"

The boy nodded.

"Your grandpa, he just fiddled with his harness."

"Were you scared?"

"I don't know. All I remember was wishing I could blast a hole in the side of that plane, so we could get some air. Finally we passed over some antiaircraft fire. You wouldn't believe what a relief it was to hear those guns. Hallelujah! Somebody's out there, and they're trying to kill us!"

Carl burst out laughing. It surprised him that from such a thin voice the laughter should be so deep.

"Not long after, they lined us up and shot the doors open, and the hillbilly got sick on my boots. It was like everybody had been sleeping. We just stood there looking at that door as if we expected somebody to climb in. Some they had to push, and by God, one of them fought back. I just kept my eyes on the helmet in front of me until I saw the wingtip in that little square of gray sky. The sergeant shouted 'Go!' and I went.

"The air gave me a jolt, and the parachute, when it opened, gave me another one. But I tell you, after the inside of that plane, the biggest shock was all that green down below. The reconnaissance photos had been black and white, you know? They made it look like a place you'd shoot somebody. Looking down, I kept thinking, there can't be a war here. It's too pretty."

The hills clothed in forest, the hedged black fields, the town with its four-spired Gothic church still untouched, the sun on the horizon shining through the morning haze like a lamp through a gauze curtain. And everywhere the sky was crisscrossed by double strands of falling soldiers. They were west of their target, at the edge of the woods, and he'd had to pull back hard on the straps to keep the tow from carrying him in. Even while he fought to stay clear of the trees, even while the man next to him dropped his arms and swung like a bob, he felt the beauty of the land below—still felt it after forty years. An uneven line of collapsed parachutes spattered the fields. The line came closer, the ground seemed to leap, and he rolled down in a spray of mud.

"The Army don't teach you to think."

"Don't think—react!" the boy agreed.

"They know the man who thinks is going to end up dead, so they put that little switch in your brain—see the enemy/hit the dirt. You'll find that's a sound bit of advice. Any time you see trouble—bill collectors, preachers, salesmen—hit the dirt!" the old man whooped. "They'll get you in the end, but by God you can take a few of them with you.

"Anyway, there I am trying to wad up the chute, the field spinning around me like a circus horse, when all of a sudden a machine-gun burst rips through the canvas and makes a hole right through my cloud of breath. So what do I do?"

The boy grinned. "Hit the dirt!"

"Shit no. I ran like a bat out of hell towards the woods. Didn't run for cover, didn't look back, just ran. Even when I got to the trees I kept going, till I got so far in that I began to be scareder of what might be ahead than what I was running from. So much for training. I sat on a log to catch my breath and clean the mud from my rifle. It must have rained the day before; the woods stank of wet leaves, and there were puddles. It wasn't till I was sitting there that I saw, for the first time, one of those stone huts with the sod roof and a cockeyed window near the door, and the gun flashes out of the window. That's the strange thing about running scared—you don't notice much at the time, but later on, when you stop, it comes to you.

"I went back almost to the edge of the woods. There was a strip of rough pasture with the stone house at one end, a dirt road near it, and on the other side of the road were fields ankle-high in wheat. The Germans were searching bodies. My friends, some of them. They looked like pieces of something big that had fallen out of the sky and gone bust. But I didn't think 'my friends'—you don't at the time. I worried about being cut off. And while I watched, three truckloads of German troops come tearing down the road, heading east, and a soldier ran out from the house to wave them down. I went back, figuring maybe I could get around them through the woods—the fighting sounded light. I thought, in maybe fifteen or twenty minutes I could work my way out. But that was no Illinois woods."

The pines were tall and bunched together as if on purpose to block out the light; where the light shone through, there were alders, and the ground was tangled with brush. He picked his way slowly, using his rifle like a hand to push back branches in his way. Every few yards he would slip on a buried limb or lurch into a hole, making his stealth ridiculous. With the Germans out of sight, he began to populate his surroundings with imaginary enemies. In every thicket, rifles glinted. Shadows waited for him to come within range. And more than once he spun around quickly, only to discover that the footsteps he'd heard were the forest's pale echo of his own.

"Took me about five minutes to get lost—and that only because I was walking slow. It's amazing how you can know exactly where you're going, and get there and not know where the hell you are. So I wandered for a while, till I stumbled across a path, which I followed because it was a path and I was lost. But then I started to go light-headed and had to hide myself behind a rock so as not to faint in the open. God's truth, the minute my butt touched the ground I curled up and shook like a dog in a thunderstorm. I thought I was going to die. I saw myself out in that wheat field with the rest, watching those bastards coming towards me and nothing I could do. After the shaking quieted I sat up and listened—not for anything in particular. My mind was as blank as if I'd just woke from a nap. Then I went on."

The forest of glints and shadows had disappeared. In its place the smell of pine needles, the rustling of the trees beneath the distanceless crackle of rifle fire, the roughness of the bark as he leaned on a hemlock, smoky-white shafts of sunlight angling through the trees to spotlight a circle of brush, a small tree.

"The path was a lot of paths. Every half mile or so it forked, and hell, I didn't know one direction from another, I just followed the angle of the light. Later on, it dawned on me that the angles should be pointing east and the town was east, but at the time I was on automatic. I walked maybe two miles, looking for a way out. A ridge rose up on the left and seemed to get steeper the farther I went. And on the right there was a pretty easy slope the path kept climbing toward but never quite reached. The mortars were pounding away now, but it was hard to tell whose was whose—the sound came from everywhere at once."

Though he tried to keep his eyes peeled for some flicker of gray ahead, what he saw were GIs running in a crouch from stone doorway to stone doorway through a town he'd never seen but seemed more real to him than the woods because it was where he ought to be.

He paused for a moment. So much talking had brought a flush to his face. He touched his cheek and discovered that his fingers were icy.

"Where was I?"

"Where the projection of the town was more compelling than the reality of the forest."

He snorted, partly because of his grandson's language and partly to hide his embarrassment—so he'd spoken those private thoughts. Next thing, he *would* be pissing his pants.

"Interesting idea," Carl added.

"I don't need no psychoanalysis."

The boy set his bottle on the bench and curled his legs under him like an Indian.

"After a mile, maybe, the path began to switch back up the ridge. About halfway up, it came to a kind of plateau with huge gray rocks scattered over it. For the first time in a long while I could see the sky—light blue and not a cloud anywhere. You would have sworn it was glass. In the middle of the plateau was a tall pine absolutely loaded with starlings the battle had chased from the fields. I got rid of my pack and helmet and climbed a tree to have a look. But the hill on the right wouldn't give me a view of the fighting. All I could see was where I'd been, which didn't look like much—a nice, gentle slide downhill. Like nobody but an idiot could have got lost there.

"Then I saw little flashes of light, like a fish makes when he swims near the surface, and they were coming towards me. They stopped and started again, and I just hung there and watched. I'd seen so much trouble that wasn't there, I'd got like doubting Thomas—I didn't believe my eyes. But when they started up the third time, near the bottom of that hill, I slid down the tree like a fireman—scraped half the skin off my hands.

"The suddenness must have scared the birds because that big pine exploded—oh, you should have seen it!" They rose with a single shriek, keeping some of the shape of the tree in their flight, and the sunlight flickered on their wings. Even in their terror, they did not break away, but slued back and forth together, giving the flock the appearance of a man trying to fight his way out of a sack. Then slowly they returned, and the tree became what it had been.

Again, he ran, but this time he ran easily, the rifle swinging from one hand, the other flung out for balance. The enemy! The old man felt exhilarated. On the far side of the plateau, the path split, one branch climbing farther up the ridge while the other dipped down to follow a stream. "I figured sooner or later that stream ought to let out on the farmland below the town, so I took the low road. It was prettier that way too. The slope was rocky, but there were yellow flowers everywhere. The stream and the path went, nice and easy like a double set of stairsteps down into the pine forest."

The sun fell behind the ridge as he descended. Once into the shade of the pines, he could see his breath again—and the trail of the bullet. The creek bank had grown steeper. Small trees, half-uprooted, leaned over it, and in places it had cut into the path. This side of the plateau, the rain from the night before had not seeped into the ground. In some low spots the path had disintegrated, and dozens of boot tracks cut their own trails across the mud.

He stopped talking and felt for his helmet and pack. Where were they? He couldn't have left them behind. In forty years of telling this story, he'd never left them behind. But his memory was playing tricks on him. There he was, clear as day, a squat, black-haired young man without a pack, pounding the butt of his rifle on a tree that had fallen near the path and cussing himself for forgetting them. He looked toward his grandson but saw only himself without a helmet. It was as if the part where he'd picked up his gear again had been washed away, and the story had continued without it. Bewildered, he went on, but listening now to his own words the way the soldier listened to the forest.

Because there were no shafts of sunlight, he could not tell direction, but soon the stream curved around an incline and he knew he had reached the hill that had blocked his view. A humped wooden bridge crossed the stream, but the path it led to, after skirting a couple of soggy glades, returned to parallel his on the opposite side. Then a crease appeared in the hill. The creek veered toward it, drew in its banks, gathered speed, and plunged straight down into a narrow ravine. Leaning cautiously over a steel railing bolted to the rock shelf at his feet, he peered over the edge. The water spread like a fan as it fell and broke into spray on a heap of boulders maybe forty feet below. But instead of gathering itself back together, it remained spread shallowly in a kind of rocky marsh. A mist hung around its trees like smoke, and there was a sharp, ripe smell that reminded him of silage.

Running his fingers over the pitted bar, he tried to picture what this spot would be like for the people of the town. He could hear them puffing as they clambered up the trail, the last ten feet or so holding onto a rope threaded through metal loops nailed into the rock. He saw them leaning over the edge to watch the falls and then carrying their baskets across the humpbacked bridge to one of the glades, where German soldiers searched the bodies of the dead. He saw them spreading picnic cloths to the sound of mortars and rifle fire. He thought, strange . . . His mind stuck on the word and would not go on.

Strange. Overhead, the flight of starlings rushed by like a black river, with a sound not very different from that of the falls.

The path at the bottom lay more or less underwater, but there were blazes on tree trunks and strips of cloth tied to bushes. No way he could tell footing. Rocks went swimming under his weight; boggy spots turned out to be hard underneath. Several times he lurched into water above his knees. His feet went numb, and the rest of him ached. Yet he sloshed forward from blaze to blaze, happy as a hog because he was getting through. Somewhere on the other side of this foolishness, he would come out into the open. There would be a town or a highway or fields; there would be real soldiers fighting a real battle and dying real deaths. And once he could see where he was, he would find them. Feeling the young man's eagerness, and knowing how it would end, he trembled as if he were really running along the edge of the meadow through a dapple of sunlight and shade.

Mist hung everywhere over the water, thin as a whore's nightie and drifting with winds too light for him to feel. Hiding nothing, but playing tricks on the eyes. He would halt, casting about for the next blaze, and find it on a tree he'd looked at twice before; a strip of white cloth tied to a bush not far away would be gone when he got there or transformed into a bit of soggy gray newspaper in German. Even then, this obscuring and revealing had seemed magical, as though there were someone just ahead laying down the path—and if he hurried, he might catch up.

Soon the ravine began to widen, islands of solid ground appeared, and the pine woods crept down into the basin. The young man worried about what would happen when he returned to his own lines, to men who were not his friends and would wonder where he'd been. What could he say? That a machine gun had chased him into the forest and a couple of hours later he'd wandered out? Lost, they would repeat. There were plenty of ways to desert. If he could tell them, "I heard a runner coming toward me. I waited in ambush, and here is the message he carried." But he had nothing to show.

The walls of rock grew green, relaxed, and sprawled back into the trees, the marsh shrank to a creek with banks, and once more he walked a path torn by bootprints. The mist still drifted above the water—thicker, it seemed, for being penned in—and the path weaved in and out of it. The ravine slipped behind a nub of the hill. It was the old man who noticed. The soldier glanced over his shoulder, saw nothing, and was satisfied. But something had changed. His eyes probed the bushes along the path. He listened but heard only the intermittent rifle fire and the thump of his own footsteps. Gradually it dawned on him that he was listening to an absence. The mortars had stopped.

But knowing the cause only added to his unease. The forest had paused to wait. He could feel himself drawn forward.

Then, in the mist ahead a wavering shadow (he would say, "a runner broke from the mist"), as if someone were answering his fear ("and I waited for him to come within range"). The shadow resolved vaguely into the figure of a man. But the figure was not running—it appeared to be turning small circles, like a man tamping down the earth around a mine. Close to the water. He approached slowly, ready to jump for cover, but the figure kept to its task. Something was wrong. Pinning his gun against the trunk of a tree, he shouted. No response. He shouted again, and again no answer. So he pulled the trigger.

"First time in my life I ever shot at a man."

The sound echoed back from the ravine, and somewhere up ahead a machine gun caught the echo and sent it back. The mist leaped aside like a startled deer. The old man lowered his rifle and spat into the stream. "Shit."

One of his own—one of the bunch who played basketball on the courts next to the commissary. The boy circled like a pendulum in his straps, his feet inches above the water, his parachute tangled in the trees he'd fallen through. Arms and legs bent and rigid, head lolling against the top of the pack, he seemed to have been frozen in midstep as he'd thrown his head back to laugh. And the old man saw himself falling, saw the town with its four-spired cathedral, saw the swath of green below and realized this time he would not be able to pull back—he blinked away the vision. Watching the dead man revolve to the creaking of his canvas straps, he thought, I must be close to the edge of the forest. His head throbbed. All around him he saw dead men matting the wheat; it would be easy to lie down like them. The hand he leaned on the trunk of an alder began to shake. He snatched it away.

He'd missed, apparently, because there were no wounds—he looked the body over again to be sure. Not a one. A little purple welt on the neck, and a man had become a coat hanger.

Eyeing the bindings of the dead soldier's pack, the old man felt a queasy "No!" in the pit of his stomach. But he needed a blanket and rations—it would be cold tonight, and God only knew whether they'd have a field kitchen. The corpse swung by not far from the edge of the bank. With luck he could slip the pack off. Grabbing hold of a nearby bush, he leaned out over the water. But the first time, at the touch of that rigid arm, he flinched away, and the corpse turned in its harness as if it were trying to shrug him off. The second time, he caught the harness and drew the body towards him. The young man's head, which had been nodding in time with the revolutions, paused, then suddenly slid to the edge of the pack and stared, white-eyed, straight at him.

He let out a yelp, lost his balance and fell backwards into the stream, which dragged him a couple of yards and nearly took his feet from under him. The water was freezing cold. As he scrambled out onto the muddy bank, a stiff foot brushed his backside.

Still on his hands and knees, trembling, he let out a pure gut-scream of frustration and pain that was answered somewhere in the trees above him by the shriek of a bird. Then he laughed. The laughter caught in the old man's lungs and turned into a coughing fit that shook him from head to heel. When he'd swallowed his phlegm and had begun to breathe evenly again, the young man on the bank took his hands from his knees, and picked up his rifle and went on. His whole body felt numb. Out of plain stubbornness he did not once look around. But he could feel the dead man's eyes burning into his back like tiny disks of ice.

The path angled away from the stream, as it always had. He would follow it till the stream was out of sight. Then at the top of a knoll the forest would open upon a sunlit meadow. Over a crescent of trees on his right he would see the tops of the spires. Yes, and as he walked out from the cover of the trees, the Germans would begin to shell the town from the hill above. He would be running towards the explosions, looking ahead, and he would not see the soldiers with their machine gun until he was almost on top of them. One who had been lighting a cigarette would drop it, grab his rifle by the stock and lunge wildly. The bayonet would pass under the old man's arm. He'd club that man to the ground and shoot the other two before they could turn the gun; then he'd swing back to the first, kneeling beside him, open-mouthed and blinking, and would empty the rest of the clip into him.

The old man grunted, relieved that he could see ahead to the end. Yes, he had been scared, he had been lost, he had taken to shooting at shadows, but finally, almost by accident, he had killed his Germans—and from there he was able to find his way back.

The man in the forest had continued some distance along the path. Gun drooping, he limped slowly ahead, favoring his left leg despite the fact that there was no feeling in it, and wearing his shame and anger as resignedly as he wore his wet and muddy clothes. The more pain he felt, the more vivid the woods around him became. The thinning stand of pines, the ground beneath strewn with leaves, brush, fallen branches—he saw them now as distinctly as he had seen the flashes of gunfire from the window of the hut. Under a patch of sunlight a dark thicket spread, covered with new growth like a coat of light-green fur, overrun everywhere by a tall, spiny weed with purple-rimmed leaves. In the middle of it, three small pines grew out of and around the remains of a fallen log. He thought, strange. And remembered the sun nosing up between the hills as he descended, checkering the town with light and shadow. He understood now that it was the strangeness that made them beautiful. The strangeness that—what was the boy's word. Compelled. Because it was wrong. Like a whore's whisper that you couldn't help going back to.

As the path began to climb a shelf of white rock, he smelled nitrate. The path was sprinkled with wood chips and dirt. At the top he had to use his rifle as a cane to step around a shell crater and a small shivered birch. Trees nearby were freckled with flame-shaped wounds, each with a fragment of blackened metal burrowed into its meat. The path continued up a low knoll. Beyond its rim the outlines of the trees were blurred with sunlight. And he knew where he was. He walked more easily, feeling the breeze on his face, and watched the sky rise above the rim of the knoll. There was the meadow glazed with white and yellow wildflowers, and on the other side of it a macadam road and a gray frame farmhouse, and there were the spires of the cathedral. As they should be. He approached haltingly through a dapple of sunlight and shade, and on cue the shelling began.

Awkwardly, but without pain, he ran along the edge of the woods towards the road, across uneven ground whose every dip and roll he knew. The Germans behind their hillock of grass cried out. Startled, as he had always been, the old man tried to stop, but his feet had turned to air. One of the Germans reached for his rifle slowly, and when he lifted his face the old man saw with horror that the eyes were blank. As the German lunged, it was as it had been at the door of the plane, where he could not tell if he had been drawn forward by the air or pushed from behind. Either way he could not stop himself.

"No!"

But the bayonet was already a cramp in his guts, and he had fallen backwards to the ground. He tried to get up and felt it higher, thrusting him down again. He screamed at the pain, as though his anger could hurl it back, but his head dropped back onto the grass. The line of trees above him solidified into a black ring, as sharp as a barrel's rim, and there were waves in the sky. Then there was no sky at all.

Where it had been he heard the boy crying, "God! Oh, God!" And wished he could tell him it didn't matter. The pain had disappeared, and the warmth flowing out of him gave him a fugitive pleasure. The voice that had shouted "No!" told him he was dying, but he didn't believe it. Because the voice came from too far away and because all the while his body was telling him it felt good.

Suddenly, fiercely, the wounds began to hurt and their pain brought back his sight. He lay among the white and yellow flowers looking up to the treetops which seemed to be on fire. The soldiers were arguing in accents he remembered from his childhood, pointing to him and to the town. One was wiping his bayonet with a fistful of grass. An officer stepped out from the trees and snapped an order. And the soldiers, muttering to themselves, quickly broke down the gun and hurried away in the direction the officer had come.

"Esel!"

The officer descended to where he lay. The German was thin and young, and his yellow hair stuck out at odd angles where his helmet had been. One of his hands swung uselessly at his side—a big hand with long fingers. He knelt to look at the wound but immediately stood up again.

"*Nutzlos, mein Bekannter.*" Unsnapping his holster.

He tried not to struggle, but he could not even lift his head. Sharp-nosed pistol in his good hand, the German knelt beside him. He could only whisper, "No!"

The young officer's grimed face cracked into a weary half-smile, and he answered in English. "Haven't you killed enough of us?"

The old man looked away and contemplated the fire in the trees. The rippled sky glittered like glass and he could not breathe for the thickness in his mouth. It was wrong, but that did not matter. Once again he was falling through the freezing dawn air—the hedged fields below, to the east the rolling forest and the cathedral town—and the earth was rising up to meet him.

MARIAN THURM

ICE

FROM MS.

ᔕ

DAISY HAS KNOWN for a long time that Vivian has flipped; is losing her marbles one by one. It's been a painful thing to witness and sometimes Daisy cries over it, but discreetly, so that Vivian won't notice and say, "*Now* what are you crying about?" Vivian is her live-in companion, and her salary is paid by Daisy's sister, who had the good sense to marry a rich man and hang onto him forever. Daisy's husband sold apples on street corners during the Depression and was never quite the same after that, never quite able to recover from the loss of dignity. He lived uneasily for another twenty-five years and then he fell sick and died, without giving much advance warning. "Cancerous," Daisy says out loud, but Vivian ignores her, just goes on with what she is doing, which is hurling handfuls of ice cubes from a five-pound plastic bag to the living-room floor, then smashing the ice with the bottoms of her thick-soled walking shoes. This is to exorcise the smell of evil that

Vivian claims has permeated the apartment. According to Vivian, the ice cubes are the only thing that will do the trick. That and the ammonia that she pours all over the lovely parquet flooring. Watching her, Daisy says, "The landlord's going to have our heads, yours and mine both, I guarantee it."

"The evil," says Vivian, "is everywhere in this apartment."

"Do you know what all that ammonia does to you?" Daisy says. "It destroys lung tissue, that's what." She picks herself up from the couch and wanders into the kitchen, where she fixes two bowls of Frosted Mini-Wheats and milk, and adds some sliced banana. She is a small woman with surprisingly long, beautiful legs. Her hair is thick and white, cut short with bangs, like a young girl. ("A pixie cut," Daisy calls it.) She spent her life as a bookkeeper and was furious when, long ago, she reached seventy and was forced to give up her job. ("A clear case of anti-Semitism," she insists.)

"This is the Lord's work I'm doing here," Vivian hollers. "So don't give me any lectures about lung tissue."

"Are you too busy doing the Lord's work to have some dinner?" Daisy asks. No response. She flicks on the radio next to her cereal bowl and listens to a call-in show that is hosted by a psychologist. She loves listening to the show, which makes her feel that she is right out there in the middle of the world, missing nothing. The caller speaking now is a woman with three grown children, two sons and a daughter. Her sons, the woman says in a trembly voice, are homosexuals, her daughter, a lesbian. "It's a pitiful thing," Daisy says. The woman begins to weep as she talks about her children. The psychologist, also a woman, advises the caller that tears are sometimes productive. "Go ahead and cry," the psychologist urges. The woman weeps on the radio for a moment or two longer, and soon there is a click, and she has hung up. Daisy is crying too. She thinks of calling the psychologist and saying, "My friend is losing her marbles." Of course, she'd make an effort to put it a little more delicately than that: "My friend is so busy doing the Lord's work that she forgets all about eating and sleeping and doing the grocery shopping. Not to mention the laundry." Daisy looks down at her housecoat. It is paisley-patterned against a dark background and doesn't show much dirt. She brings a sleeve up close to her face and sniffs the fabric. "Vivian," she yells. "If cleanliness is next to godliness, I'd advise you to hop to it and get a laundry together."

Vivian appears in the kitchen, tracking slivers of ice onto the linoleum. She is dressed in a short white uniform, white stockings with runs leading straight up from her knees, and white oxfords. Above her breast pocket is a plastic name badge that says "Vivienne." For years she worked at New York Hospital as a nurse's aide, until one day she felt too old and cranky for the job and decided to quit. (Or else it was the patients who were too old and cranky; Daisy can never remember which.) Vivian has four children, all boys, all of whom send her flowers on Mother's Day—hearts and horseshoes covered with carnations, and once, a single white lily that Vivian dumped immediately into the trash. ("The flower of death," she hissed, as Daisy went right into the garbage and retrieved the lily, saying, "Even the flower of death has got to be better than no flowers at all on Mother's Day.") The rest of the year, Vivian hears not a peep from any of her children. "Once they're grown, you can forget it," she tells Daisy. "They need you like a hole in the head and that's okay. Because what are you going to do with four big tall men getting tangled up in your furniture and messing up your house with no regard for how much effort it takes to keep things in order." Daisy understands. Her daughter, Elizabeth, has lived in Los Angeles for several years now. She complains on the phone every week that it's a city full of shallow people but at least the weather is good. "Catch a plane and come visit," Elizabeth always says. "My treat. And of course bring Vivian with you." Daisy and Vivian find this hilarious. Neither of them has ever been on a plane and they wouldn't dream of risking their necks for a little good weather. Whenever she thinks about it, Daisy has to admit that she enjoyed Elizabeth more as a child: all that kissing and hugging and those open declarations of love. Still, she wishes she weren't afraid to travel across the sky like the rest of the world. On bad days, she misses Elizabeth with an ache that settles under her skin and will not budge, like Vivian when she mopes in the Barcalounger, contemplating the evil she's sure is thriving right under their noses. ("Why here?"

Daisy wants to know. "What's so special about this broken-down rat trap, anyway?" But Vivian's not giving out any answers.)

Vivian sinks down into a seat at the table now and takes Daisy's face into her hands. "Oh, Jesus," she says, squinting at her. "Jeepers."

"Eat your cereal," says Daisy. "Notice there's banana in there, plenty of potassium for you." Vivian is smaller than Daisy and thin, growing thinner all the time, it seems. Daisy worries that one day she will slip right out of her uniform and just disappear, leaving behind only a puddle of white.

"You've got whiskers growing out of your chin," Vivian announces. "Just like a man." Her fingers against Daisy's face smell strongly of ammonia; Daisy pushes her away.

"Hormones," says Daisy. "Too little of one kind, too much of the other." She tries to make light of it, but brushing her fingertips over her chin, she feels herself blushing.

"Don't you move from that table, miss," Vivian says. Soon Daisy hears her in the bathroom, fooling around in the medicine cabinet. Bottles of pills tumble into the sink; something made of metal clatters to the tiled floor.

"Easy," Daisy yells. "One of these days you're going to destroy this place altogether. Raze it right to the ground."

Then Vivian is standing over her with a pair of manicure scissors and a small bottle of Mercurochrome. Daisy shoves the back of her chair against the wall, covers her face with one arm. "Not today, thanks," she says.

Smiling, Vivian says, "We've been together for what, three, four years now, and all of a sudden you're backing away from me?"

"Seven," says Daisy.

"Imagine that," says Vivian. "I must have lost track of the time somehow." Slowly she lowers Daisy's arm from her face, squeezes her hand in a friendly way.

"Somehow," says Daisy, shutting her eyes as Vivian comes toward her with the manicure scissors. Then she tells Vivian, "You remind me of my mother-in-law. She didn't care much for me and I didn't care much for her and one day she sneaks up on me and cuts a piece of my hair off just for spite."

"A deranged woman," says Vivian. She snips cautiously at Daisy's chin. "My poor baby doll," she says. She dots Daisy's chin with Mercurochrome, to prevent infection, she says.

"How about a mirror?" says Daisy, and immediately changes her mind. "Not a pretty picture, I'm sure," she says.

"Don't be so hard on yourself. You're cute as a button," says Vivian. "For an old lady."

"Old old old," Daisy says, tapping a spoon on the edge of her glass cereal bowl. "What's the point?" Rising and walking to the kitchen window, she rests against the blistered ledge and stares two stories down to the street corner. Lights have just been turned on in the dusk below. It is nearly April now, nearly spring. She watches as some teenagers strip a long black car parked in front of the apartment house: first the hubcaps, front and rear, then the antenna. A radio and two small speaker boxes are next. The thieves are thin boys in their shirt sleeves. Daisy raises the window. "Why do you work so hard to make your parents ashamed of you?" she hollers to them. "How about a Blaupunkt radio, cheap?" one of the boys yells back. Daisy goes to the phone, dials 911, and is put on hold. Eventually, a woman comes on and takes down the information. She is bored with the details, bored with Daisy. At the end of the conversation she says, "Have a nice day."

"This neighborhood," Daisy says, rubbing her chin with two fingers. When she takes her hand away, the fingers are bright orange with Mercurochrome.

Vivian lights a cigarette and tosses the match into one of the cereal bowls, where it sizzles for an instant, then floats between two slices of banana. She smokes without speaking, leaning one elbow on the table, her head propped against her palm. "There's nothing wrong with this neighborhood," she says finally, "that a few bombs wouldn't cure."

Nodding, Daisy says, "I'm going to watch my boyfriends, Mr. MacNeil and Mr. Lehrer, on the television."

"Boyfriends!" Vivian hoots. "Any minute there's going to be a knock on the door, right, and the delivery boy will be saying, 'Flowers from MacNeil and Lehrer,' right?" She laughs in that choked way that Daisy doesn't like, soundlessly, her feet stamping hard under the table.

"Well, at this point, they're the only boyfriends I've got," Daisy says, but she has to laugh at the thought of those flowers arriving and the miniature card tucked inside the miniature envelope that says, "To our sweetie pie."

"Got any money?" Vivian says when at last she stops laughing.

"You finally decided to do the grocery shopping?"

"Just going out for some ice," says Vivian, and Daisy is amazed at how ordinary and innocent the words sound, as if she had said, "Just going out for a pack of cigarettes." It's the ordinary sound of it that gives Daisy a chill, and also Vivian's eyes, round eyes wide open with alarm.

"What do you see?" Daisy asks for the hundredth time. Not that she expects an answer. On the subject of "the evil" (as Daisy thinks of it), Vivian is resolutely inarticulate.

Now she shrugs her shoulders and says, "Can I have two dollars?"

Daisy breathes through her teeth. The shrug makes her feel desolate, as if Vivian were already far away, striding down the block toward the supermarket, a tiny dark madwoman with the moon shining on the shoulders of her hooded corduroy coat.

Vivian is holding out her hand, palm upward. "Ten dollars, please," she says patiently.

"Beggar," says Daisy, but not loud enough for Vivian to hear. She tears off the month of February from a small calendar perched on top of a low glass-and-wood cabinet. On the back she makes a list: 99% fat free (1 qt.), cottage cheese (California style), Hydrox cookies, toothpaste (anything but Crest). "This is an act of faith, Vivian," she says, handing her the list and a ten-dollar bill.

"That February was something else," Vivian says. "I bet I had to use about thirty pounds of ice, maybe more." Out into the dark hallway she goes, hood up around her face, a large pair of men's canvas work gloves covering her hands.

In the living room, Daisy turns on the TV set, but the tenant in the apartment directly overhead has decided to vacuum. Daisy gets a broom and bangs bravely on the ceiling; all she gets is more static. She shuts off the set and calls her sister Elsie on Sutton Place.

"Oh," says Elsie, "hello and good-bye. You caught me in the middle of a Great Books night. A few of my lady friends are over, and we're doing Dante's *Inferno*."

"The *Inferno*?" says Daisy, and laughs. "You ought to invite Vivian to join your group. That's right up her alley these days."

"Vivian?"

"I'm worried sick, to tell you the truth."

"Is it money?" Elsie whispers into the phone. "I can write you a check in the morning."

"She's ruining my living-room floor," says Daisy, "but that's the least of it."

"How about wall-to-wall carpeting in there?" says Elsie. "I'll send somebody over from Macy's and you'll be all set."

"It isn't that," Daisy tells her. "It's something unearthly, I think."

"I have to hang up now," her sister says. "You can let me know about the wall-to-wall whenever you want."

Sitting in the Barcalounger, her feet tilted toward the ceiling, hands folded into fists in her lap, Daisy says, "Damn." Her life was spent at an adding machine, getting things right, making sense of things. Tiresome work, though she has to admit she was good at it. But what does she know of unearthly things? At the end of her life, she doesn't have much patience left. Ice storms in her living room, shards of melting ice everywhere, the sharp, unpleasant scent of ammonia lingering on her skin, her clothes. But in all the world there is only Vivian calling her baby doll, cupping her face in her hands, painting her delicately with Mercurochrome. At the end of your life, you're no fool; you take what is offered.

Later, past midnight, Daisy dreams of a carpet of shattered glass spread shimmering over the floor. In her warm bed she shivers, and slides deep under the covers.

ELLEN WILBUR

SAFE

FROM REDBOOK

§

WHEN HE WAS SEVEN he daydreamed about his mother. He sat at
his desk in school wondering what she was doing at just that
moment: whether she was changing beds, dusting, ironing,
vacuuming, or polishing the silver. He saw the Groveniers'
white house, where she went to work three days a week. She
had described it to him hundreds of times. He saw her climbing
the circular staircase with the beautiful red carpet leading up to
the second floor. He watched her pass down the white hall,
under the crystal chandelier, and turn left into Mrs. Grovenier's
blue bedroom. He knew every room in the house though he
had never once been there. Nights when his mother lay down
with him just before he went to sleep, he asked her to describe
the house.

"Tell me about the kitchen," he would say, though he
could already see the long, bright room with the black-and-
white checked floor, the smooth white counters, and the round

glass table by the door. Over the sink was a large window with a view of the back lawn and Mrs. Grovenier's garden.

At school he often saw his mother's tired face take shape in the air outside the window, until she was more real than anything in the busy yellow classroom and he was alone with her in a place where there was no sound or motion and nothing to separate them.

Miss Arnold sometimes startled him. "Are you listening, Jerry? Try to pay attention, please." One time she came up the aisle and stooped down so her face was right in front of him. "What is it, Jerry? Is something bothering you? Why can't you pay attention?" He gazed at her silver earrings, her pink sweater and her wide red mouth. She was smiling at him. She smiled often. She also laughed, at least once every day, a high light laugh, and she ran her fingers through her yellow hair.

"How old are you, Miss Arnold?" he asked her. She seemed surprised.

"I'm twenty-four," she said. "Why, Jerry?"

"My mother is thirty-six," he told her.

He was small for his age, the smallest in his class, a red-haired boy with serious eyes. His mother said he was too small to play out on the street unless she was at home to watch him. After school he stayed with Mrs. Kelso, who lived on the sixth floor in the apartment across the hall from them. She was in her sixties, a graying, heavy woman with a florid face who only left the building once a week to do her shopping. Her husband was dead and her only son, her boy named Tom, had been killed in Vietnam. "I'm only biding my time," he'd heard her tell his mother. "I've nothing to live for. Absolutely nothing."

"Is that you, Jerry?" Mrs. Kelso asked when he rang the bell at four. She had three locks to open on her door. "Come in, dear. I've been waiting for you. Look, I've baked some cookies." In winter Mrs. Kelso's apartment was too warm. She said she suffered from the cold. Her little kitchen was compressed with heat. She sat across from him while he ate his snack.

"Now tell me what happened in school," she said, and

while he did, she sometimes stopped him. "It's so good to talk to someone. You can't imagine how lonely I get," she said.

Her crowded living room was full of photographs, and often she took down albums of pictures to show him.

"This was our house," she said. "It wasn't large, but it was just right for three of us. We were way out in the country. You've got to get to the country, Jerry. Do you see the apple trees? You can't imagine how delicious those fresh apples were. I must have made a thousand pies. Tom always loved a pie. We had a garden too. You've never tasted a tomato like the ones we grew, so large and juicy. You just can't get them in the city." From time to time she talked about her husband, John, but mostly she liked to tell him about Tom. Jerry had seen so many pictures of the dark-eyed, lanky boy, he felt as if he'd heard his voice and spoken with him.

Three days a week his mother cleaned house for the Groveniers. The other two, Tuesdays and Thursdays, she waitressed at the Scottish Inn. She hardly ever talked about the restaurant and she didn't like her job there. The owner, Mr. Revere, was a hard man who shouted at the help and seemed to have no feeling for them. But the tips were good, his mother said, and for the work she made good money.

She worked from nine to four at both her jobs and she got home each night at six o'clock. She had to take three buses to get home. Then she had to walk the last three blocks, which frightened her in the winter because the streets were dark and the neighborhood was rough. People sold drugs, drunks and bums slept in the alleyways or on the door stoops, and there were hard-faced teenage kids who ran in groups and looked for trouble. There had been a murder on their street. He'd heard Mrs. Kelso telling his mother about the girl who was stabbed and robbed at eight o'clock one night.

"And all he got was ten dollars," Mrs. Kelso had said in a shrill, excited voice. "Can you imagine killing a person for ten dollars?"

At five-thirty each afternoon he pushed Mrs. Kelso's rocking chair up to the living room window. He pressed his face close to the glass. A tiny draft of cold air came from the corner of the window, cooling his overheated face, and he sat with his elbows on the sill looking down at the street below and the lighted corner where his mother would turn and come into view. Sometimes he imagined her stepping off the bus at Ryder Circle, and he plotted every step of her walk home. He imagined her crossing the streets one by one as the neighborhood got rougher, and if he felt dark forces threaten her, he concentrated all his energy on her like a hard wall of protection that no violence or evil could cut through. It was his secret thought that if he kept his daily vigil by the window, she would arrive home safely.

Some evenings while he waited there'd be people on the street. He'd look them over carefully and watch them with suspicion. When his mother came into view, most often she'd be wearing a scarf on her head and carrying a grocery bag of food for supper. He'd watch her come up the dark street, past the steps of all the dingy brownstone buildings, her head bent forward, hurrying as if she were being chased. She carried a can of mace in her purse. She'd told him never to touch it.

One night his mother was very late. "I wonder what's keeping her," Mrs. Kelso kept saying. She came and stood behind him, looking out the window. "She's never been so late," she said.

It was seven-thirty when he saw his mother coming up the street. The elevator wasn't working, and by the time she got to Mrs. Kelso's door she was out of breath from the stairs.

"I'm sorry, Grace," she said. As she came in, she brought the freshness of the cold night air into the overheated room.

"The buses weren't running right today," she said, still out of breath. "I had to wait almost an hour at McKinley Station."

"Sit down a minute," Mrs. Kelso urged her. "I made Jerry's supper. I had it ready an hour ago, but he wouldn't eat it till you got here. He's been watching for you all this time."

The women's eyes turned softly on him. The boy sat at the table, his food before him. He began to eat. "I don't know what I'd do without you," his mother said to Mrs. Kelso. She pulled her scarf off and shook out her short brown hair. Her nose was prominent and sharp in her thin face, and there were shadows like dark stains under her eyes. She sat down without taking off her coat. "It's been a terrible day," she said. She bit her lip, then looked at Mrs. Kelso. "One of the waitresses quit last night. She just walked out. Now Mr. Revere wants me to work two nights a week. I told him about Jerry, that I've got to be here nights, but he said if I want to keep my job I have to work Fridays and Saturdays for the next month, at least, till he can train somebody else. I don't know what to do," his mother said. Tears started in her eyes. "I wish I had the luxury of walking out like some of these girls, but I've got no one to help me. No family. No one," she said.

"Don't worry about it, Ruth," Mrs. Kelso said. "I'll be here. Where am I going? Jerry can stay with me."

"I can't ask you to do that," his mother said, shaking her head. "You already do so much for me." Her face was wet and she kept wiping the tears away with her hand. The boy watched her.

"Sometimes it's good to cry," Mrs. Kelso said, looking at him. She handed his mother a tissue. "We all need to cry sometimes. It clears the system. Isn't that right, Ruth?"

"Yes," his mother replied. She dried her eyes and blew her nose.

"We'll work everything out," Mrs. Kelso said. "You need to go home now and put your feet up. You look done in."

His mother cooked herself a hamburger. She sat eating with one elbow on the table and her head bowed forward resting on her hand. He played on the kitchen floor, humming to himself, making a row of all his cars, lining them up according to size.

When she finished eating, she looked up at him. "It's late. Get ready for bed and I'll come in."

He put on his pajamas. His mother's voice came down the hall. She was talking on the phone. He brushed his teeth, watching himself in the mirror. He took one thin strand of his hair, yanked it, and held it up before the light. It was red, the color of his father's hair. He'd never seen his father, Jim Dwyer, who was a carpenter. His mother didn't like to talk about him. "When I told him I was pregnant, he skipped town. He didn't want to marry me," she'd said.

In his room he lined his cars up on the shelf beside his bed according to their colors. He put the blue cars first in all their shades of blue. When he'd finished, he pulled back the covers, climbed into the bed and lay waiting for his mother.

Some nights his mother sang to him when she came in. Once she started singing, she sang song after song until he fell asleep. Most nights she did not sing. They talked for half an hour or more. She'd switch the light off by his bed. She'd kick her shoes off. "My aching feet," she'd say, rubbing her toes. Then she'd lie down with her head beside him on the pillow. The light from the hall showed up her face and he could look at her. "Ah, this is nice," she'd sigh, turning to him. Then he could say anything to her and she would listen. At times he told her about school. She listened carefully and her eyes looked softly at him, full of love. "My Jer," she said, and touched his cheek. Some nights her mood was sad. "How I wish we could move. This is no place for a child to grow up. It's a terrible place. Terrible," she repeated, shaking her head. When she sounded like this, he asked about the Groveniers. "What does the garden look like?" he might ask. Once she got started talking about the Groveniers, the worry went right out of her eyes and there was happiness in her voice and face. "You know," she'd say, "when I walk into that house I feel so peaceful. The moment I walk in. It's the funniest thing. I feel safe, as if nothing bad could ever happen there. You'll see it when you go there," she'd said more than once. "Some Saturday I'm going to take you for a visit." But they had never gone.

His mother had stopped talking on the phone. She was washing dishes. "Are you coming?" he called.

"I'll be right there," she said. She slammed shut the cabinet where she kept the pans. Then she came down the hall into his room. She was frowning. She switched off the light by his head and sat down on the bed. "I was talking to Grace a minute ago," she said. "I have to work this Friday night and Saturday too. Grace says you can stay with her and sleep there. I know you don't want to." She reached across and smoothed his hair back from his face. "But I can't think what else to do."

"What time will you get home?"

"It'll be after midnight. You couldn't stay here by yourself. It will only be for a few weeks. Then I won't have to do it anymore."

He pulled her arm. "Lie down," he said.

"I can't tonight." She leaned over him, still smoothing his hair. "I'm too tired. Tomorrow I will." He put his arms around her neck.

"Go to sleep now," she said. She kissed his forehead, then stood up and left the room. He heard her sigh as she walked down the hall.

All week his mother was unlike herself. She said little, and when he spoke to her she hardly seemed to hear him. On Thursday at five-thirty he pulled Mrs. Kelso's rocking chair up to the window. He pressed his face close to the glass and breathed the draft of chilly air. It was completely dark outside and snow was falling heavily. There were no lights in the blackened building across the way. There'd been a fire there years ago, Mrs. Kelso had told him. Now all the windows were boarded up and everyone had moved away. Down below he saw a bum on the front stoop of the empty building. The man was slumped to one side with his face hunched forward, buried in his coat. He wore no hat, and the snow was thick on his head and shoulders. The boy watched the man, who never moved, and looked like something dead, a shape covered with snow. He turned to check the clock on top of Mrs. Kelso's TV set.

When he looked back out the window, there were two teenage boys walking up the middle of the street. They were big boys. Both wore leather jackets, and their hands were shoved in their pockets. One of them had on a wide-brimmed hat and the other wore nothing on his head. The hatless boy paused for a moment under the light and brushed the snow out of his spiky blond hair. They walked until they saw the bum, and then they stopped in front of him. The blond boy shoved him with his foot. Then he kicked him viciously three times. Looking down, his nose pressed to the glass, the boy's heart started pounding.

"Stop it," he said in a sharp whisper, and the blond boy did stop immediately, almost as if he'd heard him. The two teenagers turned and sauntered away without looking back. The bum stood up slowly. Snow fell off his back. He rubbed his face. Then he raised his fist in the air and started yelling. He was yelling so loudly that the boy could hear him. The man stamped back and forth before the building, punching the air. He seemed to get more angry by the minute. The boy swung around and saw that it was exactly six o'clock. He watched the corner for his mother, and he watched the bum who now was kicking at the steps, still shouting. When his mother rounded the corner, the boy stood and put both hands up to the window. "Go away," he said out loud to the bum, and the man, as if he'd heard him, stopped kicking the steps. His anger seemed to disappear. He hunched his shoulders and shambled down the street away from the approaching woman.

His mother hadn't even seen the bum. She hurried toward the entrance of the building with her head bent low. The boy stayed standing with his hands against the window until she was inside.

Later, when he was eating supper with his mother, he tried to tell her about the bum and the teenage boys, and how they'd seemed to obey him.

"Isn't that something," she said, but she wasn't really listening.

After supper, when he'd gotten into bed, she came and lay down beside him.

"You're going to the Groveniers' tomorrow," he said, looking at her.

"Yes, then I'll go straight from there over to the inn. I won't see you till Saturday morning. You'll be good for Grace, won't you?"

"Yes," he said.

"I know you will."

"Will Mrs. Grovenier ask about me?"

"I wouldn't be surprised," his mother said. "She always asks me how you are. It's a shame they don't have children. I think it makes her very sad," she said, looking at him. "I know she wants to have them. When you think of all they could give a child, it seems there isn't any fairness in the world."

He tried to imagine Mrs. Grovenier looking sad. He saw her in her new fur coat, the one that Mr. Grovenier had given her for her birthday. His mother had described the coat, and many times she'd said that Mrs. Grovenier was the most stylish woman she had ever seen, with perfect skin, lovely blue eyes, and copper-colored hair. She had three closets full of clothes. "She must have fifty pairs of shoes," his mother had told him.

"Will you sing one song?" He watched his mother's face in the pale light from the hall. She was looking at the ceiling, thinking.

"Just one," his mother said. Then she began to sing.

On Friday night he watched television with Mrs. Kelso after supper. At ten o'clock she brought out a pillow and two blankets and made a bed for him on her couch. "I think you'll be comfortable," she said, and when he'd put on his pajamas, she tucked the blankets around him.

"There," she said. She turned off the lights in the room. "Will you be all right now?" He could see her bulky shape and feel her looking at him through the dark.

"Yes," he said.

"Then sleep well," Mrs. Kelso said, and she left the room. The moment she was gone he threw off the blankets. He was sweating and the whole room was so hot that it seemed hard to breathe. He listened as Mrs. Kelso shuffled between the bathroom and her room. After a while everything was quiet. The clock on the TV shone in the dark. It read ten-thirty. He lay on his side for a while, but then he sat up. He dangled his legs over the edge of the couch and watched the clock. After a while he could hear Mrs. Kelso snoring. He stood up, padded slowly around the room and sat down again. His mother had never told him much about the Scottish Inn, but he imagined her carrying large trays of dishes out to the kitchen, cleaning the tables and preparing to leave the restaurant. At eleven o'clock he crossed the room and inched the rocking chair around and over to the window with hardly a sound. He sat down. The night was cold. He pressed his forehead to the frigid glass.

Everything he saw along the street was frozen still. There was no motion anywhere and no one was in sight. It seemed to him the street had never looked so bleak. The chair rocked slightly when he moved, and he sat watching the lighted corner for an hour. Then he stood up, drummed his fingers lightly on the sill, and sat down again.

At last, at twelve-thirty, his mother appeared. He half-smiled at the sight of her and watched her with intensity as she approached the building. Once she was safely inside, he inched the rocking chair across the floor, returning it to its proper position. Then he went quietly to the couch. He lay on his back, listening as the elevator stopped. The metal door swung open, and he heard the click of his mother's shoes along the hall, the jangle of her keys across the way, and finally, the door to their apartment closing behind her. Then he was asleep.

On Saturday the wind was high. He walked with his mother to the grocery store, feeling the gusty blasts of cold cut through his coat as if he wore nothing. They passed the playground where the empty swings shuddered and stirred in the wind. His mother wouldn't stop to let him play. She said it was too cold. The sun struck on the silver metal of the slide, and he imagined the feel of the icy metal against his back. He yanked his woolen cap down over his ears, and by the time they reached the store their faces were stiff with cold.

"My God, it's bitter," his mother exclaimed, and she shuddered as they went in. He followed her up and down the aisles. When at the checkout counter, she let him pick the package of red licorice he wanted. He watched her toss the candy into the grocery bag. Before they left the store, she took off his woolen neck scarf, wrapped it around his face over his nose, and tied it tightly behind his neck.

"There," she said. They went outside and hurried up the street. The wind was behind them now and the cold did not seem so severe, but his mother rushed along, and once they were inside the apartment building, she gasped. "Oh, did you ever feel such cold? And it will be worse tonight," she said, more to herself than to him. "I'll freeze when I come home."

After lunch his mother took a nap. While she slept, he took out his crayons and drew pictures at the kitchen table. He could hear the wind outside blowing around the building, but the kitchen felt quite snug. He drew cars at first—long, curving, two-lane highways with lines of cars and trucks speeding in opposite directions. Then, to please his mother, he began a picture of the Groveniers' house, a kind of floor plan of the rooms. He'd never tried to draw the house before, but he found it was easy. He started with the wide front hall. Then he put in the dining room and kitchen. There were two bathrooms on the first floor, one just off the hall and one beside the kitchen. He made the circular staircase up to the second floor, put in the master bedroom with its own bathroom, then Mrs. Grovenier's book-lined study, the little sewing room beside it, the two large guest rooms at the end of the hall, and the small bathroom between them. When he'd finished sketching all the rooms, he went back over them and began to draw in the furniture, thinking how surprised his mother would be to see how well he knew where everything was. At different times he'd questioned her about each room in the house, asking the colors of the couches and the chairs, where they were, the sizes of the tables, the placement of the lamps. He'd asked her what was hanging on the walls. If there was something he could not clearly see, he'd asked her to describe it carefully. His mother never minded. In fact she delighted in his questions and never seemed so happy as when she was talking about the house. He found it a surprising pleasure to draw the picture. He put in all the windows and colored in the carpeting, starting with the dark red rug that filled the hall and went up the stairs. He was sketching in the back garden, drawing in the small rock fountain in the center of it, when his mother came into the kitchen.

"Look," he said, and his face was flushed as he handed her the picture. "It's the Groveniers' house." She sat down at the table, looking at it. "This is the chest in the front hall and that's the closet where they keep their coats," he said, and, standing beside her, he pointed out where he'd put everything. He didn't stop until he'd shown her all the rooms. His mother seemed dumbfounded.

"How did you ever do this, Jerry?" She looked at him, amazed. "It's exactly the way it is," she said, shaking her head. "As if you'd been there."

*   *   *

After supper that night he played cards with Mrs. Kelso. "Tom liked to play cards. When he was young I used to play with him just like this," she said. "He hated to lose a game, and sometimes I let him win just to keep him happy." She smiled sadly.

At ten o'clock she put him to bed on the couch. He lay in the dark waiting for her to go to sleep. The wind outside was blowing harder than ever. It rattled the window and made a low and moaning sound around the building. Sometimes the sound of the wind was high and shrill, like someone screaming. The noise was eerie, and he kept the blankets over him a while even though the room was close and he was sweating.

It was eleven o'clock before he heard Mrs. Kelso snoring. He tossed the blankets back, hopped up lightly, and crossed the room, turning the rocking chair and inching it across the floor up to the window. He sat with his elbows on the sill, watching the street. His head was aching slightly. There were points of pain throbbing above his eyes, and he rubbed his forehead with his hand. Across the street below him was a tree. He watched the wind blow it. The wind would die away to nothing for a while, and then it would come back in a fierce blast that bent and shook the little tree until it looked as if it might be torn up from the ground or snapped in two. When the wind came up it lashed the window, and the draft of cold air came in a surprising gust across his face and neck and shoulders, making him shiver. The clock read eleven-fifteen, and he imagined his mother standing on the sidewalk huddled in her coat against the wind, waiting for the bus. Down on the street a sheet of newspaper was lifted on the wind and hurled against a little tree. The paper seemed to struggle, blown and tangled in the branches. Then it freed itself and began to rise above the tree, changing shape and spreading open like something menacing and living. The sight of it was disconcerting to him. The wind came in a blast that wouldn't stop and the newspaper kept rising, flapping through the air up toward him, its huge shape wrenched and changing. His heart beat faster and he closed his eyes against the sight of it. Then the wind died away and he watched the newspaper sail down from side to side through all the layers of the air until it lay crumpled on the ground. He was tired and he leaned back from the drafty window, drawing his knees up to his chin. He closed his eyes, feeling the points of pain in his forehead, letting the chair rock gently back and forth.

When he woke up, he was dismayed to see that it was two A.M. and that he'd missed his mother. By now she would be sleeping in her bed. He wanted to cross the hall to see that she was safely there, but he knew she would be angry with him if he woke up Mrs. Kelso. His head heavy with sleep, he wandered over to the couch. He lay down listening for the wind, but it was gone. Mrs. Kelso had stopped snoring and there was nothing but stillness around him, an enormous stillness, heavy and unbroken. He pulled the blankets over himself and for a long time lay staring into the dark. He was thinking of his mother, imagining her alone, crossing the empty streets, her body blown and buffeted by fierce gusts of wind. He could see her face, clenched and anxious, twisted up against the wind and cold. The more he thought of her, the more alert and wide awake he grew with a nagging sense of fear that would not go away. He turned onto his side, bunching the blankets tight against him, watching the crawling movement of the clock. At last he closed his eyes, and his mind swam with images and brilliant scenes, like a great vortex that had been waiting to engulf him.

He dreamed it was morning. In his dream Mrs. Kelso came into the room, both hands up to her face. "Your mother is dead. She was robbed last night," she said, and he could see the horror in her eyes. "They hit her on the head!" she cried, running forward, throwing her arms around him and pressing him hard against her skirt. Then she stepped back and looked at him, her eyes whirling. "Your poor mother!" she wailed. "And what's to become of you, Jerry? What's to become of you now?"

In his dream he stood rigid and stony in front of her. "It's my fault," he said and, pulling away from Mrs. Kelso, he turned and threw himself down on the couch.

Mrs. Grovenier appeared. She was wearing the fur coat,

and he recognized her the moment he saw her. Her face was pale. She crossed the room and sat beside him on the couch.

"I'm so sad about your mother. So terribly sad," she said. He gazed at the perfect skin, the blue eyes, and the copper-colored hair.

"I'd like to take you home with me," she said.

In his dream there was a car waiting downstairs with a man sitting behind the wheel. Mrs. Grovenier opened the door and they sat together in the back seat. Her hands were folded in her lap. She was wearing brown gloves that matched the color of the fur coat. He looked up at her face. Then the car pulled off, and as they drove away he began to cry. Once he'd started crying, he couldn't stop.

"It's good for you to cry," Mrs. Grovenier said. She put her arm around him and he felt the fur against his face. "You need to cry," she said, and she handed him a tissue from her purse.

All the way across town he kept crying, wrenched and sick with longing for his mother, and beneath it all he saw the house they were approaching. He imagined all the rooms that were now rushing toward him, ready to take him in, surround and wrap him with their beauty like his mother's own embrace.

JOY WILLIAMS
HEALTH

FROM TENDRIL

∾

PAMMY IS IN AN UNPLEASANT TEXAS CITY, the city where she
was born, in the month of her twelfth birthday. It is cold and
cloudy. Soon it will rain. The rain will wash the film of ash off
the car she is traveling in, volcanic ash that has drifted across
the Gulf of Mexico, all the way from the Yucatán. Pammy is a
stocky gray-eyed blonde, a daughter, traveling in her father's
car, being taken to her tanning lesson.

This is her father's joke. She is being taken to a tanning
session, twenty-five minutes long. She had requested this for
her birthday, ten tanning sessions in a health spa. She had also
asked for, and received, new wheels for her skates. They are
purple Rannalli's. She had dyed her stoppers to match although the match was not perfect. The stoppers were a duller,
cruder purple. Pammy wants to be a speed skater but she
worries that she doesn't have the personality for it. "You've
gotta have gravel in your gut to be in speed," her coach said.

239

Pammy has mastered the duck walk but still doesn't have a good, smooth crossover, and sometimes she fears that she never will.

Pammy and her father, Morris, are following a truck which is carrying a jumble of television sets. There is a twenty-four-inch console facing them on the open tailgate, restrained by rope, with a bullet hole in the exact center of the screen.

Morris drinks coffee from a plastic-lidded cup that fits into a bracket mounted just beneath the car's radio. Pammy has a friend, Wanda, whose step-father has the same kind of plastic cup in his car, but he drinks bourbon and water from his. Wanda had been adopted when she was two months old. Pammy is relieved that neither her father nor Marge, her mother, drinks. Sometimes they have wine. On her birthday, even Pammy had wine with dinner. Marge and Morris seldom quarrel and she is grateful for this. This morning, however, she had seen them quarrel. Once again, her mother had borrowed her father's hairbrush and left long, brown hairs in it. Her father had taken the brush and cleaned it with a comb over the clean kitchen sink. Her father had left a nest of brown hair in the white sink.

In the car, the radio is playing a song called "Tainted Love," a song Morris likes to refer to as "Rancid Love." The radio plays constantly when Pammy and her father drive anywhere. Morris is a good driver. He is fast and doesn't bear grudges. He enjoys driving still, after years and years of it. Pammy looks forward to learning how to drive now, but after a few years, who knows? She can't imagine it being that enjoyable after awhile. Her father is skillful here, on the freeways and streets, and on the terrifying, wide two-lane highways and narrow mountain roads in Mexico, and even on the rutted, soiled beaches of the Gulf coast. One weekend, earlier that spring, Morris had rented a Jeep in Corpus Christi and he and Pammy and Marge had driven the length of Padre Island. They sped across the sand, the only people for miles and miles. There was plastic everywhere.

"You will see a lot of plastic," the man who rented them the Jeep said, "but it is plastic from all over the world."

Morris had given Pammy a lesson in driving the Jeep. He

taught her how to shift smoothly, how to synchronize accelera-
tion with the depression and release of the clutch. "There's a
way to do things right," Morris told her and when he said this
she was filled with a sort of fear. They were just words, she
knew, words that anybody could use, but behind words were
always things, sometimes things you could never tell anyone,
certainly no one you loved, frightening things that weren't even
true.

"I'm sick of being behind this truck," Morris says. The
screen of the injured television looks like dirty water. Morris
pulls to the curb beside an oriental market. Pammy stares into
the market where shoppers wait in line at a cash register. Many
of the women wear scarves on their heads. Pammy is deeply
disturbed by Orientals who kill penguins to make gloves and
murder whales to make nail polish. In school, in social studies
class, she is reading eyewitness accounts of the aftermath of the
atomic bombing of Hiroshima. She reads about young girls
running from their melting city, their hair burned off, their
burned skin in loose folds, crying, "Stupid Americans." Morris
sips his coffee, then turns the car back onto the street, a street
now free from fatally wounded television sets.

Pammy gazes at the backs of her hands which are tan, but,
she feels, not tan enough. They are a dusky peach color. This
will be her fifth tanning lesson. In the health spa, there are ten
colored photographs on the wall showing a woman in a bikini,
a pale woman being transformed into a tanned woman. In the
last photograph she has plucked the bikini slightly away from
her hipbone to expose a sliver of white skin and she is smiling
down at the sliver.

Pammy tans well. Without a tan, her face seems grainy
and uneven for she has freckles and rather large pores. Tanning
draws her together, completes her. She has had all kinds of
tans—golden tans, pool tans, even a Florida tan which seemed
yellow back in Texas. She had brought all her friends the same
present from Florida—small plywood crates filled with tiny
oranges which were actually chewing gum. The finest tan Pammy
has ever had, however, was in Mexico six months ago. She had
gone there with her parents for two weeks, and she had gotten
a truly remarkable tan and she had gotten tuberculosis. This

has caused some tension between Morris and Marge as it had been Morris's idea to swim at the spas in the mountains rather than in the pools at the more established hotels. It was believed that Pammy had become infected at one particular public spa just outside the small dusty town where they had gone to buy tiles, tiles of a dusky orange with blue rays flowing from the center, tiles which are now in the kitchen of their home where each morning Pammy drinks her juice and takes three hundred milligrams of isoniazid.

"Here we are," Morris says. The health spa is in a small, concrete block building with white columns, salvaged from the wrecking of a mansion, adorning the front. There are gift shops, palmists, and all-night restaurants along the street, as well as an exterminating company that has a huge fiberglass bug with X's for eyes on the roof. This was not the company that had tented Wanda's house for termites. That had been another company. When Pammy was in Mexico getting tuberculosis, Wanda and her parents had gone to San Antonio for a week while their house was being tented. When they returned, they'd found a dead robber in the living room, the things he was stealing piled neatly nearby. He had died from inhaling the deadly gas used by the exterminators.

"Mommy will pick you up," Morris says. "She has a class this afternoon so she might be a little late. Just stay inside until she comes."

Morris kisses her on the cheek. He treats her like a child. He treats Marge like a mother, her mother.

Marge is thirty-five but she is still a student. She takes courses in art history and film at one of the city's universities, the same university where Morris teaches petroleum science. Years ago when Marge had first been a student, before she had met Morris and Pammy had been born, she had been in Spain, in a museum studying a Goya and a piece of the painting had fallen at her feet. She had quickly placed it in her pocket and now has it on her bureau in a small glass box. It is a wedge of greenish-violet paint, as large as a thumbnail. It is from one of Goya's nudes.

Pammy gets out of the car and goes into the health spa. There is no equipment here except for the tanning beds, twelve tanning beds in eight small rooms. Pammy has never had to share a room with anyone. If asked to, she would probably say no, hoping that she would not hurt the other person's feelings. The receptionist is an old, vigorous woman behind a scratched metal desk, wearing a black jumpsuit and feather earrings. Behind her are shelves of powders and pills in squat brown bottles with names like DYNAMIC STAMINA BUILDER and DYNAMIC SUPER STRESS-END and LIVER CON-CENTRATE ENERGIZER.

The receptionist's name is Aurora. Pammy thinks that the name is magnificent and is surprised that it belongs to such an old woman. Aurora leads her to one of the rooms at the rear of the building. The room has a mirror, a sink, a small stool, a white rotating fan and the bed, a long bronze coffinlike apparatus with a lid. Pammy is always startled when she sees the bed with its frosted ultraviolet tubes, its black vinyl headrest. In the next room, someone coughs. Pammy imagines people lying in all the rooms, wrapped in white light, lying quietly as though they were being rested for a long, long journey. Aurora takes a spray bottle of disinfectant and a scrap of toweling from the counter above the sink and cleans the surface of the bed. She twists the timer and the light leaps out, like an animal in a dream, like a murderer in a movie.

"There you are, honey," Auroa says. She pats Pammy on the shoulder and leaves.

Pammy pushes off her sandals and undresses quickly. She leaves her clothes in a heap, her sweatshirt on top of the pile. Her sweatshirt is white with a transfer of a skater on the back. The skater is a man wearing a helmet and kneepads, side-surfing goofy-footed. She lies down and with her left hand pulls the lid to within a foot of the bed's cool surface. She can see the closed door and the heap of clothing and her feet. Pammy considers her feet to be her ugliest feature. They are skinny and the toes are too far apart. She and Wanda had painted their toes the same color, but Wanda's feet were pretty and hers were not. Pammy thought her feet looked like they belonged to a dead person and there wasn't anything she could do about them. She closed her eyes.

Wanda, who read a lot, told Pammy that tuberculosis was

a very romantic disease, the disease of artists and poets and "highly sensitive individuals."

"Oh yeah," her stepfather had said. "Tuberculosis has mucho cachet."

Wanda's stepfather speaks loudly and his eyes glitter. He is always joking, Pammy thinks. Pammy feels that Wanda's parents are pleasant but she is always a little uncomfortable around them. They had a puppy for a while, a purebred Doberman which they gave to the SPCA after they discovered it had a slightly overshot jaw. Wanda's stepfather always called the puppy a sissy. "You sissy," he'd say to the puppy. "Hanging around with girls all the time." He was referring to his wife and to Wanda and Pammy. "Oh, you sissy, you sissy," he'd say to the puppy.

There was also the circumstance of Wanda's adoption. There had been another baby adopted, but it was learned that the baby's background had been misrepresented. Or perhaps it had been a boring baby. In any case the baby had been returned and they got Wanda.

Pammy doesn't think Wanda's parents are very steadfast. She is surprised that they don't make Wanda nervous, for Wanda is certainly not perfect. She's a shoplifter and gets C's in Computer Language.

The tanning bed is warm but not uncomfortably so. Pammy lies with her arms straight by her sides, palms down. She hears voices in the hall and footsteps. When she first began coming to the health spa, she was afraid that someone would open the door to the room she was in by mistake. She imagined exactly what it would be like. She would see the door open abruptly out of the corner of her eye, then someone would say, "Sorry," and the door would close again. But this had not happened. The voices pass by.

Pammy thinks of Snow White lying in her glass coffin. The Queen had deceived her how many times? Three? She had been in disguise, but still. And then Snow White had choked on an apple. In the restaurants she sometimes goes to with her parents there are posters on the walls which show a person choking and another person trying to save him. The posters take away Pammy's appetite.

Snow White lay in a glass coffin, not naked of course but in a gown, watched over by dwarfs. But surely they had not been real dwarfs. That had just been a word that had been given to them.

When Pammy had told Morris that tuberculosis was a romantic disease, he had said, "There's nothing romantic about it. Besides, you don't have it."

It seems to be a fact that she both has and doesn't have tuberculosis. Pammy had been given the tuberculin skin test along with her classmates when she began school in the fall and within forty-eight hours had a large swelling on her arm.

"Now that you've come in contact with it, you don't have to worry about getting it," the pediatrician had said in his office, smiling.

"You mean the infection constitutes immunity," Marge said.

"Not exactly," the pediatrician said, shaking his head, still smiling.

Her lungs are clear. She is not ill but has an illness. The germs are in her body, but in a resting state, still alive but rendered powerless, successfully overcome by her healthy body's strong defenses. Outwardly, she is the same, but within, a great drama had taken place and Pammy feels herself in possession of a bright, secret, and unspeakable knowledge.

She knows other things too, things that would break her parents' hearts, common, ugly, easy things. She knows a girl in school who stole her mother's green stamps and bought a personal massager with the books. She knows another girl whose brother likes to wear her clothes. She knows a boy who threw a can of motor oil at his father and knocked him unconscious.

Pammy stretches. Her head tingles. Her body is about a foot and a half off the floor and appears almost gray in the glare from the tubes. She has heard of pills one could take to acquire a tan. One just took two pills a day and after twenty days one had a wonderful tan which could be maintained just by taking two pills a day thereafter. You ordered them from Canada. It was some kind of food-coloring substance. How gross, Pammy thinks. When she had been little she had bought a quarter of an acre of land in Canada by mail for fifty cents. That had been two years ago.

Pammy hears voices from the room next to hers, coming through the thin wall. A woman talking rapidly says,

"Pete went up to Detroit two days ago to visit his brother who's dying up there in the hospital. Cancer. The brother's always been a nasty type, I mean very unpleasant. Younger than Pete and always mean. Tried to commit suicide twice. Then he learns he has cancer and decides he doesn't want to die. Carries on and on. Is miserable to everyone. Puts the whole family through hell, but nothing can be done about it, he's dying of cancer. So Pete goes up to see him his last days in the hospital and you know what happens? Pete's wallet gets stolen. Right out of a dying man's room. Five hundred dollars in cash and all our credit cards. That was yesterday. What a day."

Another woman says, "If it's not one thing, it's something else."

Pammy coughs. She doesn't want to hear other people's voices. It is as though they are throwing away junk, the way some people use words, as though one word were as good as another.

"Things happen so abruptly anymore," the woman says. "You know what I mean?"

Pammy does not listen and she does not open her eyes for if she did she would see this odd bright room with her clothes in a heap and herself lying motionless and naked. She does not open her eyes because she prefers imagining that she is a magician's accomplice, levitating on a stage in a coil of pure energy. If one thought purely enough, one could create one's own truth. That's how people accomplished astral travel, walked over burning coals, cured warts. There was a girl in Pammy's class at school, Bonnie Black, a small owlish-looking girl who was a Christian Scientist. She raised rabbits and showed them at fairs, and was always wearing the ribbons they had won to school, pinned to her blouse. She had warts all over her hands, but one day Pammy noticed that the warts were gone and Bonnie Black had told her that the warts disappeared after she had clearly realized that in her true being as God's reflection, she couldn't have warts.

It seemed that people were better off when they could concentrate on something, hold something in their mind for a long time and really believe it. Pammy had once seen a radical skater putting on a show at the opening of a shopping mall. He leaped over cars and pumped up the sides of buildings. He did flips and spins. A disc jockey who was set up for the day in the parking lot interviewed him. "I'm really impressed with your performance," the disc jockey said, "and I'm impressed that you never fall. Why don't you fall?" The skater was a thin boy in baggy cut-off jeans. "I don't fall," the boy said, looking hard at the microphone, "because I've got a deep respect for the concrete surface and because when I make a miscalculation, instead of falling, I turn it into a new trick."

Pammy thinks it is wonderful that the boy was able to say something which would keep him from thinking he might fall.

The door to the room opened. Pammy had heard the turning of the knob. At first she lies without opening her eyes, willing the sound of the door shutting, but she hears nothing, only the ticking of the bed's timer. She swings her head quickly to the side and looks at the door. There is a man standing there, staring at her. She presses her right hand into a fist and lays it between her legs. She puts her left arm across her breasts.

"What?" she says to the figure, frightened. In an instant she is almost panting with fear. She feels the repetition of something painful and known, but she has not known this, not ever. The figure says nothing and pulls the door shut. With a flurry of rapid ticking, the timer stops. The harsh lights of the bed go out.

Pammy pushes the lid back and hurriedly gets up. She dresses hastily and smooths her hair with her fingers. She looks at herself in the mirror, her lips parted. Her teeth are white behind her pale lips. She stares at herself. She can be looked at and not discovered. She can speak and not be known. She opens the door and enters the hall. There is no one there. The hall is so narrow that by spreading her arms she can touch the walls with her fingertips. In the reception area by Aurora's desk, there are three people, a stoop-shouldered young woman and two men. The woman was signing up for a month of unlimited tanning which meant that after the basic monthly fee she only had to pay a dollar a visit. She takes her checkbook out of a soiled handbag, which is made out of some

silvery material, and writes a check. The men look comfortable
lounging in the chairs, their legs stretched out. They know one
another, Pammy guesses, but they do not know the woman.
One of them has dark spiky hair like a wet animal's. The other
wears a red tight T-shirt. Neither is the man she had seen in the
doorway.

"What time do you want to come back tomorrow, honey?"
Aurora asks Pammy. "You certainly are coming along nicely.
Isn't she coming along nicely?"

"I'd like to come back the same time tomorrow," Pammy
says. She raises her hand to her mouth and coughs slightly.

"Not the same time, honey. Can't give you the same time.
How about an hour later?"

"All right," Pammy says. The stoop-shouldered woman
sits down in a chair. There are no more chairs in the room.
Pammy opens the door to the street and steps outside. It has
rained and the street is dark and shining. The air smells fresh
and feels thick. She stands in it, a little stunned, looking. Her
father will teach her how to drive, and she will drive around.
Her mother will continue to take classes at the university.
Whenever she meets someone new, she will mention the Goya.
"I have a small Goya," she will say, and laugh.

Pammy walks slowly down the street. She smells barbe-
cued meat and the rain lingering in the trees. By a store called
IMAGINE, there's a clump of bamboo with some beer cans
glittering in its ragged, grassy center. *IMAGINE* sells neon
palm trees and silk clouds and stars. It sells greeting cards and
chocolate in shapes children aren't allowed to see and it sells
children stickers and shoelaces. Pammy looks in the window at
a huge satin pillow in the shape of a heart with a heavy zipper
running down the center of it. Pammy turns and walks back to
the building that houses the tanning beds. Her mother pulls up
in the car. "Pammy!" she calls. She is leaning toward the
window on the passenger side which she has rolled down. She
unlocks the car's door. Pammy gets in and the door locks
again.

Pammy wishes she could tell her mother something, but
what can she say? She never wants to see that figure looking at
her again, so coldly staring and silent, but she knows she will,

for already its features are becoming more indistinct, more general. It could be anything. She coughs, but it is not the cough of a sick person because Pammy is a healthy girl. It is the kind of cough a person might make if they were at a party and there was no one there but strangers.

Marge, driving, says, "You look very nice. That's a very pretty tan, but what will happen when you stop going there? It won't last. You'll lose it right away, won't you?"

She will. And she will grow older, but the world will remain as young as she was once, infinite in its possibilities and uncaring.

TOBIAS WOLFF

SOLDIER'S JOY

FROM ESQUIRE

᧡

ON FRIDAY Hooper was named driver of the guard for the third night that week. He had recently been broken in rank again, this time from corporal to Pfc., and the first sergeant had decided to keep Hooper's evenings busy so that he would not have leisure to brood. That was what the first sergeant told Hooper when Hooper came to the orderly room to complain.

"It's for your own good," the first sergeant said. "Not that I expect you to thank me." He moved the book he'd been reading to one side of his desk and leaned back. "Hooper, I have a theory about you," he said. "Want to hear it?"

"I'm all ears, Top," Hooper said.

The first sergeant put his boots up on the desk and stared out the window to his left. It was getting on toward five o'clock. Work details had begun to return from the rifle range and the post laundry and the brigade commander's house, where Hooper and several other men were excavating a swimming pool without aid of machinery. As the trucks let them out they gathered on the barracks steps and under the live oak beside the mess hall, their voices a steady murmur in the orderly room where Hooper stood waiting for the first sergeant to speak.

"You resent me," the first sergeant said. "You think you should be sitting here. You don't know that's what you think because you've totally sublimated your resentment, but that's what it is all right, and that's why you and me are developing a definite conflict profile. It's like you have to keep fucking up to prove to yourself that you don't really care. That's my theory. You follow me?"

"Top, I'm way ahead of you," Hooper said. "That's night school talking."

The first sergeant continued to look out the window. "I don't know," he said. "I don't know what you're doing in my army. You've put your twenty years in. You could retire to Mexico and buy a peso factory. Live like a dictator. So what are you doing in my army, Hooper?"

Hooper looked down at the desk. He cleared his throat but said nothing.

"Give it some thought," the first sergeant said. He stood and walked Hooper to the door. "I'm not hostile," he said. "I'm prepared to be supportive. Just think nice thoughts about Mexico, okay? Okay, Hooper?"

Hooper called Mickey and told her he wouldn't be coming by that night after all. She reminded him that this was the third time in one week, and said that she wasn't getting any younger.

"What am I supposed to do?" Hooper asked. "Go AWOL?"

"I cried three times today," Mickey said. "I just broke down and cried, and you know what? I don't even know why. I just feel bad all the time anymore."

"What did you do last night?" Hooper asked. When Mickey didn't answer, he said, "Did Briggs come over?"

"I've been inside all day," Mickey said, "Just sitting here. I'm going out of my tree." Then, in the same weary voice, she said, "Touch it, Hoop."

"I have to get going," Hooper said.

"Not yet. Wait. I'm going into the bedroom. I'm going to pick up the phone in there. Hang on, Hoop. Think of the bedroom. Think of me lying on the bed. Wait, baby."

There were men passing by the phone booth. Hooper watched them and tried not to think of Mickey's bedroom, but now he could think of nothing else. Mickey's husband was a supply sergeant with a taste for quality. The walls of the bedroom were knotty pine he'd derailed en route to some colonel's office. The brass lamps beside the bed were made from howitzer casings. The sheets were parachute silk. Sometimes, lying on those sheets, Hooper thought of the men who had drifted to earth below them. He was no greater lover, as the women he went with usually got around to telling him, but in Mickey's bedroom Hooper had turned in his saddest performances, and always when he was most aware that everything around him was stolen. He wasn't exactly sure why he kept going back. It was just something he did, again and again.

"Okay," Mickey said. "I'm here."

"There's a guy waiting to use the phone," Hooper told her.

"Hoop, I'm on the bed. I'm taking off my shoes."

Hooper could see her perfectly. He lit a cigarette and opened the door of the booth to let the smoke out.

"Hoop?" she said.

"I told you, there's a guy waiting."

"Turn around, then."

"You don't need me," Hooper said. "All you need is the telephone. Why don't you call Briggs? That's what you're going to do after I hang up."

"I probably will," she said. "Listen, Hoop, I'm not really on the bed. I was just pulling your chain. I thought it would make me feel better but it didn't."

"I knew it," Hooper said. "You're watching the tube, right?"

"Somebody just won a saw," Mickey said.

"A saw?"

"Yeah, they drove up to this man's house and dumped a truckload of logs in his yard and gave him a chain saw. This was his fantasy. You should see how happy he is, Hoop. I'd give anything to be that happy."

"Maybe I can swing by later tonight," Hooper said. "Just for a minute."

"I don't know," Mickey said. "Better give me a ring first."

After Mickey hung up Hooper tried to call his wife, but there was no answer. He stood there and listened to the phone ringing. Finally he put the receiver down and stepped outside the booth, just as they began to sound retreat over the company loudspeaker. With the men around him Hooper came to attention and saluted. The record was scratchy, but, as always, the music caused Hooper's mind to go abruptly and perfectly still. The stillness spread down through his body. He held his salute until the last note died away, then broke off smartly and walked down the street toward the mess hall.

The officer of the day was Captain King from Headquarters Company. Captain King had also been officer of the day on Monday and Tuesday nights, and Hooper was glad to see him again because Captain King was too lazy to do his own job or to make sure the guards were doing theirs. He stayed in the guardhouse and left everything up to Hooper.

Captain King had gray hair and a long grayish face. He was a West Point graduate with twenty-eight years of service behind him, just trying to make it through another two years so he could retire at three-quarters pay. All his classmates were generals or at least bird colonels, but he himself had been held back for good reasons, many of which he admitted to Hooper their first night together. It puzzled Hooper at first, this officer telling him about his failures to perform, his nervous breakdowns and Valium habit, but finally Hooper understood: Captain King regarded him, a Pfc. with twenty-one years' service, as a comrade in dereliction, a disaster like himself with no room left for judgment against anyone.

The evening was hot and muggy. Little black bats swooped overhead as Captain King made his way along the rank of men drawn up before the guardhouse steps. He objected to the alignment of someone's belt buckle. He asked questions about the chain of command but gave no sign whether the answers he received were right or wrong. He inspected a couple of rifles and pretended to find something amiss with each of them, though it was clear that he hardly knew one end from the other, and when he reached the end of the line he began to deliver a speech. He said that he had never seen such sorry troops in his life. He asked how they expected to stand up to a determined enemy. On and on he went. Captain King had delivered the same speech on Monday and Tuesday, and when Hooper recognized it he lit another cigarette and sat down on the running board of the truck he'd been leaning against.

The sky was gray. It had a damp, heavy look and it felt heavy too, hanging close overhead, nervous with rumblings and small flashes in the distance. Just sitting there made Hooper sweat. Beyond the guardhouse a stream of cars rushed along the road to town. From the officers' club farther up the road came the muffled beat of rock music, which was almost lost, like every other sound of the evening, in the purr of crickets that rose up everywhere and thickened the air like heat.

When Captain King had finished talking he turned the men over to Hooper for transportation to their posts. Two of them, both privates, were from Hooper's company, and these he allowed to ride with him in the cab of the truck while everybody else slid around in back. One was a cook named Porchoff, known as Porkchop. The other was a radio operator named Trac, who had managed to airlift himself out of Saigon during the fall of the city by hanging from the skids of a helicopter. That was the story Hooper had heard, anyway, and he had no reason to doubt it; he'd seen the slopes pull that trick plenty of times, though few of them were as young as Trac must have been then—nine or ten at the most. When Hooper tried to picture his son Wesley at the same age doing that, hanging over a burning city by his fingertips, he had to smile.

But Trac didn't talk about it. There was nothing about him to suggest his past except perhaps the deep, sickle-shaped scar above his right eye. To Hooper there was something familiar about this scar. One night, watching Trac play the video game in the company rec room, he was overcome with the certainty that he had seen Trac before somewhere—astride a water buf-

falo in some reeking paddy or running alongside Hooper's
APC with a bunch of other kids all begging money, holding up
melons or a bag full of weed or a starving monkey on a stick.

Though Hooper had the windows open, the cab of the
truck smelled strongly of after-shave. Hooper noticed that Trac
was wearing orange Walkman earphones under his helmet liner.
They were against regulation, but Hooper said nothing. As
long as Trac had his ears plugged, he wouldn't be listening for
trespassers and end up blowing his rifle off at some squirrel
cracking open an acorn. Of all the guards, only Porchoff and
Trac would be carrying ammunition, because they had been
assigned to the battalion communications center, where there
was a tie-in terminal to the division mainframe computer. The
theory was that an intruder who knew his stuff could get his
hands on highly classified material. That was how it had been
explained to Hooper. Hooper thought it was a load of crap.
The Russians knew everything anyway.

Hooper let out the first two men at the PX and the next
two at the parking lot outside the main officers' club, where
lately several cars had been vandalized. As they pulled away,
Porchoff leaned over Trac and grabbed Hooper's sleeve. "You
used to be a corporal," he said.

Hooper shook Porchoff's hand loose. He said, "I'm driving a truck, in case you didn't notice."

"How come you got busted?"

"None of your business."

"I'm just asking," Porchoff said. "So what happened,
anyway?"

"Cool it, Porkchop," said Trac. "The man doesn't want to
talk about it, okay?"

"Cool it yourself, fuckface," Porchoff said. He looked at
Trac. "Was I addressing you?"

Trac said, "Man, you must've been eating some of your
own food."

"I don't believe I was addressing you," Porchoff said. "In
fact, I don't believe that you and me have been properly
introduced. That's another thing I don't like about the Army,
the way people you haven't been introduced to feel perfectly
free to get right into your face and unload whatever shit they've

got in their brains. It happens all the time. But I never heard anyone say 'Cool it' before. You're a real phrasemaker, fuckface."

"That's enough," Hooper said.

Porchoff leaned back and said, "That's enough," in a falsetto voice. A few moments later he started humming to himself.

Hooper dropped off the rest of the guards and turned up the hill toward the communications center. There were oleander bushes along the gravel drive, with white blossoms going gray in the dusky light. Gravel sprayed up under the tires and rattled against the floorboards of the truck. Porchoff stopped humming. "I've got a cramp," he said.

Hooper pulled up next to the gate and turned off the engine. He looked over at Porchoff. "Now what's your problem?" he said.

"I've got a cramp," Porchoff repeated.

"For Christ's sake," Hooper said. "Why didn't you say something before?"

"I did. I went on sick call, but the doctor couldn't find it. It keeps moving around. It's here now." Porchoff touched his neck. "I swear to God."

"Keep track of it," Hooper told him. "You can go on sick call again in the morning."

"You don't believe me," Porchoff said.

The three of them got out of the truck. Hooper counted out the ammunition to Porchoff and Trac and watched as they loaded their clips. "That ammo's strictly for show," he said. "Forget I even gave it to you. If you run into a problem, which you won't, use the phone in the guard shack. You can work out your own shifts." Hooper opened the gate and locked the two men inside. They stood watching him, faces in shadow, black rifle barrels poking over their shoulders. "Listen," Hooper said, "nobody's going to break in here, understand?"

Trac nodded. Porchoff just looked at him.

"Okay," Hooper said. "I'll drop by later. Me and the captain." Hooper knew that Captain King wasn't about to go anywhere, but Trac and Porchoff didn't know that. Hooper behaved better when he thought he was being watched and he supposed that the same was true of other people.

Hooper climbed back inside the truck and started the engine. He gave the V sign to the men at the gate. Trac gave the sign back and turned away. Porchoff didn't move. He stayed where he was, fingers laced through the wire. He looked about ready to cry. "Damn," Hooper said, and he hit the gas. Gravel clattered in the wheel wells. When Hooper reached the main road a light rain began to fall, but it stopped before he'd even turned the wipers on.

Hooper and Captain King sat on adjacent bunks in the guardhouse, which was empty except for them and a bat that was flitting back and forth among the dim rafters. As on Monday and Tuesday nights, Captain King had brought along an ice chest filled with little bottles of Perrier water. From time to time he tried pressing one on Hooper, but Hooper declined. His refusals made Captain King apologetic. "It's not a class thing," Captain King said, looking at the bottle in his hand. "I don't drink this stuff because I went to the Point or anything like that." He leaned down and put the bottle between his bare feet. "I'm allergic to alcohol," he said. "Otherwise I'd probably be an alcoholic. Why not? I'm everything else." He smiled at Hooper.

Hooper lay back and clasped his hands behind his head and stared up at the mattress above him. "I'm not much of a drinker myself," he said. He knew that Captain King wanted him to explain why he refused the Perrier water, but there was really no reason in particular. Hooper just didn't like the idea.

"I drank eggnog one Christmas when I was a kid, and it almost killed me," Captain King said. "My arms and legs swelled up to twice their normal size. The doctors couldn't get my glasses off because my skin was all puffed up around them. You know the way a tree will grow around a rock. It was like that. A few months later I tried beer at some kid's graduation party and the same thing happened. Pretty strange, eh?"

"Yes, sir," Hooper said.

"I used to think it was all for the best. I have an addictive personality, and you can bet your bottom dollar I would have been a problem drinker. No question about it. But now I wonder. If I'd had one big weakness like that, maybe I wouldn't have had all these little pissant weaknesses I ended up with. I know that sounds like bull-pucky, but look at Alexander the Great. Alexander the Great was a boozer. Did you know that?"

"No, sir," Hooper said.

"Well he was. Read your history. So was Churchill. Churchill drank a bottle of Cognac a day. And of course Grant. You know what Lincoln said when someone complained about Grant's drinking?"

"Yes, sir. I've heard the story."

"He said, 'Find out what brand he uses so I can ship a case to the rest of my generals.' Is that the way you heard it?"

"Yes, sir."

Captain King nodded. "I'm all in," he said. He stretched out and assumed exactly the position Hooper was in. It made Hooper uncomfortable. He sat up and put his feet on the floor.

"Married?" Captain King asked.

"Yes, sir."

"Kids?"

"Yes, sir. One. Wesley."

"Oh my God, a boy," Captain King said. "They're nothing but trouble, take my word for it. They're programmed to hate you. It has to be like that, otherwise they'd spend their whole lives moping around the house, but just the same it's no fun when it starts. I have two, and neither of them can stand me. Haven't been home in years. Breaks my heart. Of course, I was a worse father than most. How old is your boy?"

"Sixteen or seventeen," Hooper said. He put his hands on his knees and looked at the floor. "Seventeen. He lives with my wife's sister in San Diego."

Captain King turned his head and looked at Hooper. "Sounds like you're not much of a dad yourself."

Hooper began to lace his boots up.

"I'm not criticizing," Captain King said. "At least you were smart enough to get someone else to do the job." He yawned. "I'm whipped," he said. "You need me for anything? You want me to make the rounds with you?"

"I'll take care of things, sir," Hooper said.

"Fair enough." Captain King closed his eyes. "If you need me, just shout."

Hooper went outside and lit a cigarette. It was almost midnight, well past the time appointed for inspecting the guards. As he walked toward the truck mosquitoes droned around his head. A breeze was rustling the treetops, but on the ground the air was hot and still.

Hooper took his time making the rounds. He visited all the guards except Porchoff and Trac and found everything in order. There were no problems. Finally he started down the road toward the communications center, but when he reached the turnoff he kept his eyes dead ahead and drove past. Warm, fragrant air rushed into his face from the open window. The road ahead was empty. Hooper leaned back and mashed the accelerator. The engine roared. He was moving now, really moving, past darkened barracks and bare flagpoles and bushes whose flowers blazed up in the glare of the headlights. Hooper grinned. He felt no pleasure, but he grinned and pushed the truck as hard as it would go.

Hooper slowed down when he left the post. He was AWOL now. Even if he couldn't find it in him to care much about that, he saw no point in calling attention to himself.

Drunk drivers were jerking their cars back and forth between lanes. Every half mile or so a police car with flashing lights had someone stopped by the roadside. Other police cars sat idling behind billboards. Hooper stayed in the right lane and drove slowly until he reached his turn, then he gunned the engine again and raced down the pitted street that led to Mickey's house. He passed a bunch of kids sitting on the hood of a car with cans of beer in their hands. The car door was open, and Hooper had to swerve to miss it. As he went by he heard a blast of music.

When he reached Mickey's block Hooper turned off the engine. The truck coasted silently down the street, and again Hooper became aware of the sound of crickets. He stopped on the shoulder across from Mickey's house and sat listening. The thick pulsing sound seemed to grow louder every moment.

Hooper drifted into memory, his cigarette dangling unsmoked, burning its way toward his fingers. At the same instant that he felt the heat of the ember against his skin Hooper was startled by another pain, the pain of finding himself where he was. It left him breathless for a moment. Then he roused himself and got out of the truck.

The windows were dark. Mickey's Buick was parked in the driveway beside another car that Hooper didn't recognize. It didn't belong to her husband and it didn't belong to Briggs. Hooper glanced around at the other houses, then walked across the street and ducked under the hanging leaves of the willow tree in Mickey's front yard. He knelt there, holding his breath to hear better, but there was no sound but the sound of the crickets and the rushing of the big air conditioner Mickey's husband had taken from a helicopter hangar. Hooper saw no purpose in staying under the tree, so he got up and walked over to the house. He looked around again, then went into a crouch and began to work his way along the wall. He rounded the corner of the house and was starting up the side toward Mickey's bedroom when a circle of light burst around his head and a woman's voice said, "Thou shalt not commit adultery."

Hooper closed his eyes. There was a long silence. Then the woman said, "Come here."

She was standing in the driveway of the house next door. When Hooper came up to her she stuck a pistol in his face and told him to raise his hands. "A soldier," she said, moving the beam of light up and down his uniform. "All right, put your hands down." She snapped the light off and stood watching Hooper in the flickering blue glow that came from the open door behind her. Hooper heard a dog bark twice and a man say, "Remember—nothing is too good for your dog. It's 'Ruff ruff' at the sign of the double R." The dog barked twice again.

"I want to know what you think you're doing," the woman said.

Hooper said, "I'm not exactly sure." He saw her more clearly now. She was thin and tall. She wore glasses with harlequin frames, and she had on a white dress of the kind girls called formals when Hooper was in high school—tight around the waist and flaring stiffly at the hip, breasts held in hard-looking cups. Shadows darkened the hollows of her cheeks. Under the flounces of the dress her feet were big and bare.

"I know what you're doing," she said. She pointed the pistol, an Army .45, at Mickey's house. "You're sniffing around that whore over there."

Someone came to the door behind the woman. A deep voice called out, "Is it him?"

"Stay inside, Dads," the woman answered. "It's nobody."

"It's him!" the man shouted. "Don't let him talk you out of it again! Do it while you've got the chance, sweetie pie."

"What do you want with that whore?" the woman asked Hooper. Before he could answer, she said, "I could shoot you and nobody would say boo. I'm within my rights."

Hooper nodded.

"I don't see the attraction," she said. "But then, I'm not a man." She made a laughing sound. "You know something? I almost did it. I almost shot you. I was that close, but then I saw the uniform." She shook her head. "Shame on you. Where is your pride?"

"Don't let him talk," said the man in the doorway. He came down the steps, a tall white-haired man in striped pajamas. "There you are, you sonofabitch," he said. "I'll dance on your grave."

"It isn't him, Dads," the woman said sadly. "It's someone else."

"So he says," the man snapped. He started down the driveway, hopping from foot to foot over the gravel. The woman handed him the flashlight and he turned it on in Hooper's face, then moved the beam slowly down to his boots. "Sweetie pie, it's a soldier," he said.

"I told you it wasn't him," the woman said.

"But this is a terrible mistake," the man said. "Sir, I'm at a loss for words."

"Forget it," Hooper told him. "No hard feelings."

"You are too kind," the man said. He reached out and shook Hooper's hand. "You're alive," he said. "That's what counts." He nodded toward the house. "Come have a drink."

"He has to go," the woman said. "He was looking for something and he found it."

"That's right," Hooper told him. "I was just on my way back to base."

The man gave a slight bow with his head. "To base with you, then. Goodnight, sir."

Hooper and the woman watched him make his way back to the house. When he was inside, the woman turned to Hooper and said, "If I told him what you were doing over there it would break his heart. But I won't tell him. There've been disappointments enough in his life already, and God only knows what's next. He's got to have something left." She drew herself up and gave Hooper a hard look. "Why are you still here?" she asked angrily. "Go back to your post."

Captain King was still asleep when Hooper returned to the guardhouse. His thumb was in his mouth and he made little noises as he sucked it. Hooper lay in the next bunk with his eyes open. He was still awake at four in the morning when the telephone began to ring.

It was Trac calling from the communications center. He said that Porchoff was threatening to shoot himself, and threatening to shoot Trac if Trac tried to stop him. "This dude is mental," Trac said. "You get me out of here, and I mean now."

"We'll be right there," Hooper said. "Just give him lots of room. Don't try to grab his rifle or anything."

"Fat fucking chance," Trac said. "Man, you know what he called me? He called me a gook. I hope he wastes himself. I don't need no assholes with loaded guns declaring war on me, man."

"Just hold tight," Hooper told him. He hung up and went to wake Captain King, because this was a mess and he wanted it to be Captain King's mess and Captain King's balls that got busted if anything went wrong. He walked over to Captain King and stood looking down at him. Captain King's thumb had slipped out of his mouth, but he was still making sucking noises and pursing his lips. Hooper decided not to wake him after all. Captain King would probably refuse to come anyway, but if he did come he would screw things up for sure. Just the sight of him was enough to make somebody start shooting.

A light rain had begun to fall. The road was empty except for one jeep going the other way. Hooper waved at the two men in front as they went past, and they both waved back. Hooper felt a surge of friendliness toward them. He followed their lights in his mirror until they vanished behind him.

Hooper parked the truck halfway up the drive and walked the rest of the distance. The rain was falling harder now, tapping steadily on the shoulders of his poncho. Sweet, almost unbreathable smells rose from the earth. He walked slowly, gravel crunching under his boots. When he reached the gate a voice to his left said, "Shit, man, you took your time." Trac stepped out of the shadows and waited as Hooper tried to get the key into the lock. "Come on, man," Trac said. He knelt with his back to the fence and swung the barrel of his rifle from side to side.

"Got it," Hooper said. He took the lock off and Trac pushed open the gate. "The truck's down there," Hooper told him. "Just around the turn."

Trac stood close to Hooper, breathing quick, shallow breaths and shifting from foot to foot. His face was dark under the hood of his glistening poncho. "You want this?" he asked. He held out his rifle.

Hooper looked at it. He shook his head. "Where's Porchoff?"

"Around back," Trac said. "There's some picnic benches out there."

"All right," Hooper said. "I'll take care of it. Wait in the truck."

"Shit, man, I feel like shit," Trac said. "I'll back you up, man."

"It's okay," Hooper told him. "I can handle it."

"I never cut out on anybody before," Trac said. He shifted back and forth.

"You aren't cutting out," Hooper said. "Nothing's going to happen."

Trac started down the drive. When he disappeared around the turn, Hooper kept watching to make sure he didn't double back. A stiff breeze began to blow, shaking the trees, sending raindrops rattling down through the leaves. Thunder rumbled far away.

Hooper turned and walked through the gate into the compound. The forms of shrubs and pines were dark and indefinite in the slanting rain. Hooper followed the fence to the right, squinting into the shadows. When he saw Porchoff, hunched over the picnic table, he stopped and called out to him, "Hey, Porchoff! It's me—Hooper."

Porchoff raised his head.

"It's just me," Hooper said, following his own voice toward Porchoff, showing his empty hands. He saw the rifle lying on the table in front of Porchoff. "It's just me," he repeated, monotonously as he could. He stopped beside another picnic table ten feet or so from the one where Porchoff sat, and lowered himself onto the bench. He looked over at Porchoff. Neither of them spoke for a while. Then Hooper said, "Okay, Porchoff, let's talk about it. Trac tells me you've got some kind of attitude problem."

Porchoff didn't answer. Raindrops streamed down his helmet onto his shoulders and dripped steadily past his face. His uniform was soggy and dark, plastered to his skin. He stared at Hooper and said nothing. Now and then his shoulders jerked.

"Are you gay?" Hooper asked.

Porchoff shook his head.

"Well then, what? You on acid or something? You can tell me, Porchoff. It doesn't matter."

"I don't do drugs," Porchoff said. It was the first time he'd spoken. His voice was calm.

"Good," Hooper said. "I mean, at least I know I'm talking to you, and not to some fucking chemical. Now, listen up, Porchoff—I don't want you turning that rifle on me. Understand?"

Porchoff looked down at the rifle, then back at Hooper. He said, "You leave me alone and I'll leave you alone."

"I've already had someone throw down on me once tonight," Hooper said. "I'd just as soon leave it at that." He reached under his poncho and took out his cigarette case. He held it up for Porchoff to see.

"I don't use tobacco," Porchoff said.

"Well, I do," Hooper said. He shook out a cigarette and bent to light it. "Hey," he said. "All right. One match." He put the case back in his pocket and cupped the cigarette under the picnic table to keep it dry. The rain was falling lightly now in fine fitful gusts like spray. The clouds had gone the color of ash. Misty gray light was spreading through the sky. Hooper saw that Porchoff's shoulders twitched constantly now, and that his lips were blue and trembling. "Put your poncho on," Hooper told him.

Porchoff shook his head.

"You trying to catch pneumonia?" Hooper asked. He smiled at Porchoff. "Go ahead, boy. Put your poncho on."

Porchoff bent over and covered his face with his hands. Hooper realized that he was crying. He smoked his cigarette and waited for Porchoff to stop, but Porchoff kept crying and finally Hooper grew impatient. He said, "What's all this crap about you shooting yourself?"

Porchoff rubbed at his eyes with the heels of his hands. "Why shouldn't I?" he asked.

"Why shouldn't you? What do you mean, why shouldn't you?"

"Why shouldn't I shoot myself? Give me a reason."

"This is baloney," Hooper said. "You don't run around asking why shouldn't I shoot myself. That's decadent, Porchoff. Now, do me a favor and put your poncho on."

Porchoff sat shivering for a moment. Then he took his poncho off his belt, unrolled it, and began to pull it over his head. Hooper considered making a grab for the rifle but held back. There was no need, he was home free now. People who were going to blow themselves away didn't come in out of the rain.

"You know what they call me?" Porchoff said.

"Who's 'they,' Porchoff?"

"Everyone."

"No. What does everyone call you?"

"Porkchop. *Porkchop.*"

"Come on," Hooper said. "What's the harm in that? Everyone gets called something."

"But that's my *name*," Porchoff said. "That's *me*. It's got so even when people use my real name I hear 'Porkchop.' All I can think of is this big piece of meat. And that's what they're seeing too. You can say they aren't, but I know they are."

Hooper recognized some truth in this, a lot of truth in fact, because when he himself said, "Porkchop," that was what he saw: a pork chop.

"I hurt all the time," Porchoff said, "but no one believes me. Not even the doctors. You don't believe me, either."

"I believe you," Hooper said.

Porchoff blinked. "Sure," he said.

"I believe you," Hooper repeated. He kept his eyes on the rifle. Porchoff wasn't going to waste himself, but the rifle still made Hooper uncomfortable. He was about to ask Porchoff to give it to him, but decided to wait a little while. The moment was wrong somehow. Hooper pushed back the hood of his poncho and took off his fatigue cap. He glanced up at the pale clouds.

"I don't have any buddies," Porchoff said.

"No wonder," Hooper said. "Calling people gooks, making threats. Let's face it, Porchoff, your personality needs some upgrading."

"But they won't give me a chance," Porchoff said. "All I ever do is cook food. I put it on their plates and they make some crack and walk on by. It's like I'm not even there. So what am I supposed to act like?"

Hooper was still gazing up at the clouds, feeling the soft rain on his face. Birds were starting to sing in the woods beyond the fence. He said, "I don't know, Porchoff. It's just part of this rut we're all in." Hooper lowered his head and looked over at Porchoff, who sat hunched inside his poncho, shaking as little tremors passed through him. "Any day now," Hooper said, "everything's going to change."

"My dad was in the National Guard back in Ohio," Porchoff said. "He's always talking about the great experiences he and his buddies used to have, camping out and so on. Nothing like that ever happens to me." Porchoff looked down at the table, then looked up and said, "How about you? What was your best time?"

"My best time," Hooper said. The question made him feel tired. He thought of telling Porchoff some sort of lie, but the effort of making things up was beyond him and the memory Porchoff wanted was close at hand. For Hooper, it was closer than the memory of home. In truth it was a kind of home. It was where he went to be back with his friends again, and his old self. It was where Hooper drifted when he was too low to care how much lower he'd be when he drifted back, and lost it all again. He felt for his cigarettes. "Vietnam," he said.

Porchoff just looked at him.

"We didn't know it then," Hooper said. "We used to talk about how when we got back in the world we were going to do this and we were going to do that. Back in the world we were going to have it made. But ever since then it's been nothing but confusion." Hooper took the cigarette case from his pocket but didn't open it. He leaned forward on the table.

"Everything was clear," he said. "You learned what you had to know and you forgot the rest. All this chickenshit. This clutter. You didn't spend every living minute of the day thinking about your own sorry-ass little self. Am I getting laid enough. What's wrong with my kid. Should I insulate the fucking house. That's what does it to you, Porchoff. Thinking about yourself. That's what kills you in the end."

Porchoff had not moved. In the gray light Hooper could see Porchoff's fingers spread before him on the tabletop, white and still as if they had been drawn there in chalk. His face was the same color.

"You think you've got problems, Porchoff, but they wouldn't last five minutes in the field. There's nothing wrong with you that a little search-and-destroy wouldn't cure." Hooper paused, smiling to himself, already deep in the memory. He tried to bring it back for Porchoff, tried to put it into words so that Porchoff could see it, too, the beauty of that life, the faith so deep that in time you were not different men anymore but one man.

But the words came hard. Hooper saw that Porchoff did not understand, and then he realized that what he was trying to describe was not only faith but love, and that it couldn't be done. Still smiling, he said, "You'll see, Porchoff. You'll get your chance."

Porchoff stared at Hooper. "You're crazy," he said.

"We're all going to get another chance," Hooper said. "I can feel it coming. Otherwise I'd take my walking papers and hat up. You'll see, Porchoff. All you need is a little contact. The rest of us, too. Get us out of this rut."

Porchoff shook his head and murmured, "You're really crazy."

"Let's call it a day," Hooper said. He stood and held out his hand. "Give me the rifle."

"No," Porchoff said. He pulled the rifle closer. "Not to you."

"There's no one here but me," Hooper said.

"Go get Captain King."

"Captain King is asleep."

"Then wake him up."

"No," Hooper said. "I'm not going to tell you again, Porchoff, give me the rifle." Hooper walked toward him but stopped when Porchoff picked up the weapon and pointed it at his chest. "Leave me alone," Porchoff said.

"Relax," Hooper told him. "I'm not going to hurt you." He held out his hand again.

Porchoff licked his lips. "No," he said. "Not you."

Behind Hooper a voice called out, "Hey! Porkchop! Drop it!"

Porchoff sat bolt upright. "Jesus," he said.

"It's Trac," Hooper said. "Put the rifle down, Porchoff—now!"

"Drop it!" Trac shouted.

"Oh Jesus," Porchoff said and stumbled to his feet with the rifle still in his hands. Then his head flapped and his helmet flew off and he toppled backward over the bench. Hooper's heart leaped as the shock of the blast hit him. Then the sound went through him and beyond him into the trees and the sky, echoing on in the distance like thunder. Afterward there was silence. Hooper took a step forward, then sank to his knees and lowered his forehead to the wet grass. He spread his fingers through the grass beside his head. The rain fell around him with a soft whispering sound. A blue jay squawked. Another bird called out, and then the trees grew loud with song.

Hooper heard the swish of boots through the grass behind him. He pushed himself up and sat back on his heels and drew a deep breath.

"You okay?" Trac said.

Hooper nodded.

Trac walked on to where Porchoff lay. He said something in Vietnamese, then looked back at Hooper and shook his head.

Hooper tried to stand but went to his knees again.

"You need a hand?" Trac asked.

"I guess so," Hooper said.

Trac came over to Hooper. He slung his rifle and bent down and the two men gripped each other's wrists. Trac's skin was dry and smooth, his bones as small as a child's. This close, he looked more familiar than ever. "Go for it," Trac said. He tensed as Hooper pulled himself to his feet and for a moment afterward they stood facing each other, swaying slightly, hands still locked on one another's wrists. "All right," Hooper said. Each of them slowly loosened his grip.

In a soft voice, almost a whisper, Trac said, "They gonna put me away?"

"No," Hooper said. He walked over to Porchoff and looked down at him. He immediately turned away and saw that Trac was still swaying, and that his eyes were glassy. "Better get off those legs," Hooper said. Trac looked at him dreamily, then unslung his rifle and leaned it against the picnic table farthest from Porchoff. He sat down and took his helmet off and rested his head on his crossed forearms.

The clouds had darkened. The wind was picking up again, carrying with it the whine of distant engines. Hooper fumbled a cigarette out of his case and smoked it down, staring toward the woods, feeling the rain stream down his face and neck. When the cigarette went out Hooper dropped it, then picked it up again and fieldstripped it, crumbling the tobacco around his feet so that no trace of it remained. He put his cap back on and raised the hood of his poncho. "How's it going?" he said to Trac.

Trac looked up. He began to rub his forehead, pushing his fingers in little circles above his eyes.

Hooper sat down across from him. "We don't have a whole lot of time," he said.

Trac nodded. He put his helmet on and looked over at Hooper, the scar on his brow livid where he had rubbed it.

"All right, son," Hooper said. "Let's get our story together."

ABOUT THE AUTHORS

Lee K. Abbott's first collection of stories, *The Heart Never Fits Its Wanting*, won the St. Lawrence Award for fiction; a second, *Love Is the Crooked Thing*, was published in 1986; a third, *Stranger in Paradise* (Putnam's) has just been released. His work has appeared in *The Atlantic, The North American Review*, and *The Georgia Review*, among others, and his stories have been included in both the *Prize Stories: The O. Henry Awards* and *The Best American Short Stories.*

Linsey Abrams is the author of two novels, *Charting by the Stars* and *Double Vision*. Her stories have appeared in *Redbook, Mademoiselle*, and other periodicals. Born in Boston, she now lives in New York City and teaches in the writing program at Sarah Lawrence College.

Madison Smartt Bell is the author of three novels: *The Washington Square Ensemble, Waiting for the End of the World*, and *Straight Cut*. Originally from Tennessee, he now lives in Baltimore, teaching at Goucher College and at the Poetry Center of the 92nd Street Y in New York.

T. Coraghessan Boyle is the author of two collections, *Descent of Man and Other Stories* and *Greasy Lake and Other Stories*, as well as two novels, *Water Music* and *Budding Prospects*. His forthcoming novel is *World's End*.

Ron Carlson is the author of two novels, *Betrayed by F. Scott Fitzgerald* and *Truants*. His third book, *The News of the World*, a collection of stories, will be published early in 1987 by W. W. Norton. In 1986 he was awarded an NEA fellowship in fiction and was Writer-in-Residence at Arizona State University.

Deborah Eisenberg was born in Winnetka, Illinois. She is the author of a play, *Pastorale*, produced by the Second Stage in New York in 1982, and a book of short stories, *Transaction in a Foreign Currency*, published by Knopf in 1986.

Tess Gallagher's collection of stories, *The Lover of Horses*, was published in 1986 by Harper & Row. Her stories have been selected for *The Best American Short Stories* and *Short Story*

Masterpieces. She has also published three volumes of poetry, the most recent of which is *Willingly* (Greywolf Press). She lives most of the year in Port Angeles, Washington, and teaches at Syracuse University each fall.

Ellen Gilchrist, who lives in New Orleans and Jackson, Mississippi, is the author of *In the Land of Dreamy Dreams*, *The Annunciation*, and *Victory Over Japan: A Book of Stories*, which won the National Book Award.

Ernst Havemann was born in 1918 in Zululand, South Africa. He served in the Middle East with the South African contingent of the Allied Armies in World War II, was involved in local government in Durban, South Africa, then worked for Shell Petroleum on three continents. He took up fiction in retirement on Lake Kootenay, British Columbia.

Norman Lavers teaches creative writing at Arkansas State University. His fiction and criticism have appeared in such magazines as *APR, KANSAS QUARTERLY, MISSOURI REVIEW, NORTH AMERICAN REVIEW, NORTHEAST, OHIO REVIEW, PEQUOD, TRIQUARTERLY*. His most recent books are *JERZY KOSINSKI* (Twayne, 1982) and the novel *THE NORTHWEST PASSAGE* (Fiction Collective, 1984).

Paul Leslie recently graduated from the University of Wisconsin, where he edited *The Madison Review*. He is currently enrolled in the creative writing program at Stanford University. "Exits" was the winning story in *Seventeen* Magazine's short story contest.

James McCulla was born and raised in West Virginia. He is a graduate of West Virginia University and the Iowa Writers' Workshop.

Bob Shacochis's collection of stories, *Easy in the Islands*, won the American Book Award for First Fiction in 1985. He is currently at work on a novel.

Richard Spilman teaches at Marshall University in West Virginia and is currently working on a novel.

Marian Thurm's stories have appeared in *The New Yorker*, *The Atlantic*, *Mademoiselle*, and in *The Best American Short Stories: 1983*. She is the author of a short story collection, *Floating* (Viking, 1984), and of a novel that will be published this spring by Random House.

Ellen Wilbur's first book of short stories, *Wind and Birds and Human Voices*, was published in 1984 by Stuart Wright and brought out in paperback by New American Library in 1985. She lives in Cambridge, Massachusetts, with her husband and son.

Joy Williams has published two novels, *State of Grace* and *The Changeling*, and a collections of stories, *Taking Care*. She lives in Florida.

Tobias Wolff received the 1985 PEN/Faulkner Award for *The Barracks Thief*. He is also the author of two collections of short stories, the most recent being *Back in the World* (Houghton Mifflin, 1985). He teaches at Syracuse University.

ABOUT THE EDITOR

George E. Murphy, Jr. is the editor of *Tendril* Magazine, an independent literary journal, and is the editorial director of Wampeter Press, Inc. He is the author of a book of poems, *Rounding Ballast Key* (Ampersand Press, 1985), and a children's book, *Teddy: A Christmas Story*. He is also the editor of two anthologies, *The Poets' Choice: 100 American Poets' Favorite Poems*, and (with poet/biographer Paul Mariani) *Poetics: Essays on the Art of Poetry*. In 1983, he won the New York Contemporary Press Poetry Prize. In 1985, he was awarded the Joseph P. Shaw Award from Boston College for distinguished contributions to contemporary literature. He currently lives in Key West and is working on a novel and compiling *The Key West Reader: An Historical Literary Anthology*.